True Story

RANDOM HOUSE 🏠 **NEW YORK**

True Story

A COMEDY NOVEL

Bill Maher

All rights reserved under International and Pan-American
Copyright Conventions. Published in the United States by
Random House, Inc., New York, and simultaneously in Canada
by Random House of Canada Limited, Toronto.

Library of Congress Cataloging-in-Publication Data
Maher, Bill.
True story : a comedy novel / Bill Maher.
p. cm.
ISBN 0-679-75337-0
1. Comedians—United States—Fiction. I. Title.
PS3563.A356T78 1994
813'.54—dc20   94-554

Manufactured in the United States of America
2 4 6 8 9 7 5 3

First Edition

To my friends in comedy.
The good parts are all you.

They loved each other because they shared a dream . . . but they hated each other because there wasn't enough of it to go around.

Contents

True Story

The Act You're Not
Good Enough to See

Five comedians sat on a train. They were Dick, Shit, Fat, Chink, and Buick, so pseudonymed for their specialties de fare: Dick, who did dick jokes; Shit, who did shit jokes; Fat, who did fat jokes; Chink, who made fun of the way Oriental people spoke; and Buick, the observationalist, whom everyone called Buck, and so he came to be called Buck.

"Hey, get down off there!" ejaculated the conductor, and the giggling colleagues dismounted and took their rightful places inside the gleaming trispangled Amtrak Bullet, bound for Trenton, Philadelphia, Wilmington, Baltimore, and Washington, D.C., towns where comedy was king and the audience peasants.

Near the back of the train, the comedians found a suitable enclave where three could face two and sprawled inside it. Fat took up two seats alongside his mentor, Dick, while the Damon and Pythias of comedy, Shit and Buck, sandwiched their protégé, Chink, on the opposing bench. The boys were dressed in the casual attire of the day: sneakers, Sasson jeans, sweatshirts, button-downs, and almost-leather jackets or blue hooded parkas. Except for Buck, who enjoyed the distinction of always dressing in a sports jacket and tie. They could have passed for any other five young white men who were completely out of their minds.

After the train pulled out of Penn Station, Shit got up to use the bathroom and then returned to his seat completely naked. The other boys laughed at the sight of him, although certainly not as hard as they would have laughed if it was the first time they'd seen him do such a thing. It *was* the first time for the other passengers, however—but since they were New Yorkers, they probably had seen naked people in public before, probably that day. What they didn't know was that Shit and his friends were not actually dangerous, just comedians—young comedians at that—and playing was simply their day job.

Amtrak conductors dreaded groups of young comedians. Sometimes comedians could cohabit for a while in an enclosed area, but more often than not, play-fighting would get out of hand or one of them would attempt to pick something off another's fur and cause a yelp, or drop a rock on his head, and pretty soon the conductor would have to come by and distract them with bananas. This quintet counted itself more mature than most young comics, which is a little like saying absolutely nothing at all.

It was difficult, in fact, even to measure maturity among comedians by any of the usual societal yardsticks; certainly, age was not a factor. Shit and Dick—who, in fairness, had outgrown their nicknames, earned during those first few panicky months of stand-up, when mention of those subjects was the only way they knew to ensure the steady oxygen of laughter—were the eldest, at twenty-nine and thirty-five. But Shit, as worldly as he was—and he was—just liked to get naked. He was especially fond of walking into the men's room of a nightclub when one of his friends was onstage, then emerging sans attire for a casual stroll back to the bar. Of course, the comic onstage would have to stop Shit to ask if he hadn't forgotten something, at which point Shit would feign embarrassment and hasten back to the loo, only to reemerge with a drink in his hand and a thanks for the reminder. Not that trains and nightclubs were the only places where Shit liked to get naked: bachelor parties, double dates, hotel rooms, Yankee Stadium—any place where other comedians were around to appreciate it, and the chance for arrest minimal, would do.

The chance for arrest on the train was getting a little stronger as Shit remained nude in his seat, but Dick was in the middle of a story, so Shit's arrest, if it came, would have to wait. Especially since the story was about Shit and Dick and another comedian getting naked the week before at an all-girl Catholic school in upstate New York, where the trio had been hired to perform.

"You didn't tell me about that," Buck whined.

"Do I have to tell you every time it happens?" Shit joshed. Still, Buck was a little hurt.

"So we walk in," Dick continued, "and there's two nuns and another woman—not a nun but, you know, nunlike—and they were all real nervous that we were gonna say something improper or do something like, Christ, I don't know, get naked or something."

"Why did they book you in the first place?" Fat asked.

"Who knows, shut up," Dick said quickly, but then smiled at his idolator. "Anyway, they didn't want us anywhere near the girls, so right away they hustle us down into this underground rec room with a lot of pictures of Jesus on the walls and a Ping-Pong table."

"Jesus loved Ping-Pong. He invented that Chinese grip," Buck offered.

"Although for some reason he's better known for other things," Shit added.

"They had Ping-Pong leagues back then—the National and the Aramaic," Chink topped, with—to no one's surprise—the better joke.

"Anyway," Dick tracked, "they put us down there and tell us to stay put until it's time to do the show."

The boys were laughing already, because they knew the punchline.

"I had to." Shit smiled, and everyone nodded sympathetically, as one might for a more normal addiction, like gambling or defecating on glass coffee tables.

"But *I* didn't have to!" Dick shouted with a big laugh. "Except now I'm the only one with my clothes on, so—"

"Peer pressure," Buck said.

"Exactly—I mean, hey, what am I, not gonna get naked? No. So then the two nuns and the other chick come back, and these boneheads are playing Ping-Pong—"

"Naked?" Fat asked.

"Have you been listening to the story?" Shit asked him.

"Yeah, naked," Dick scolded Fat. "Naked, okay? We were naked, this is a naked story. We're naked. And then the nuns come in—the nuns were not naked, did I make that clear?—and they see two guys playing Ping-Pong, and their dicks are flopping around, and I'm standing on a chair over the net like I'm judging!"

Everybody howled at that. Then Fat asked: "Who won?"

More howling. More big passenger-alarming howling, which made the conductor come by, and he was howling mad. But Shit had talked his way out of nakeder spots than this, and he toddled off to the bathroom to get dressed. When he returned, though, Shit was in a decidedly fouler mood than when he'd left, which may have been due to the restrictiveness of clothing or just because he liked descending into fouler moods.

"Mind if I eat while you smoke?" he snarled at Dick and Buck, who had lit up just as Shit removed the foil on his Amtrak-microwaved lunch.

"Easy, pal," said Buck. "God, you're as ornery as . . ."

"As a man stuck for a metaphor?" Shit countered.

"Boy, you're in a mood," the normally apolitical Chink interposed. "What's eatin' ya?"

"Comedy, boys. Comedy is eating me alive."

With that the others sang out in ridicule of Shit, condemning him for the negative attitude he was now imposing upon their jolly sojourn. They all liked to perpetuate the myth amongst themselves, and especially among civilians, that they were special members of society by virtue of their exemption from all accouterments of the rat race—i.e., alarm clocks, regular hours, long days, bosses, offices, or the need to concentrate on anything for more than a few seconds. They wore the deadly sin of sloth like a badge of honor, and they relished the chance run-in with childhood friends who'd listen, mouth agape, to the description of a life comprised of recess.

But Shit wasn't buying it today. He bullishly pressed on with a discussion of reality.

"We're being exploited," he said. "They're filling that

room every night of the week, getting a five-dollar cover and a two-drink minimum, and we're getting cab fare.''

Shit was referring to The Club, the premier Manhattan showcase club on the Upper East Side, where the boys were among forty or so young comedians and comediennes presently getting their acts together. On this particular Friday afternoon, however, they were taking those acts on the road, and on the road—well, the wages sucked there, too: $250 a weekend for the headliner, $150 for the middle act, $75 for the MC.

But at least now, in 1979, there *was* a road. Veterans like Dick and Shit, who'd already been at this game for four years, remembered when the only places for a young comic to get onstage were the handful of showcase clubs in New York and L.A. These hot spots, of which The Club was currently the hottest, presented a score of comedians every night, offering them exposure in the country's media capitals and a place to "work out" in exchange for their services, gratis. But as the decade drew to a close, a major new trend in the comedy boom was catching fire: the local comedy club. In cities all across the country, a new vaudeville was slouching to be born. Restaurant basements, hotel lounges, old coffeehouses—even storefronts—were being converted into clubs where two or three of these young comedians from New York or L.A. could be brought in each weekend to perform stand-up comedy. It was a trend that fed on itself: Encouraged by the expanding number of young comics available, clubs opened up by the score, and encouraged by all the places to work, hundreds of young men and women began to quit their day jobs.

So what wasn't to like?

To Buck, the recent comedy boom was the ultimate in bad luck. Because *he* was not part of a trend! He was one of the ones who was born to do it! He would have been a comedian in any era, and curse the luck that he came of age just as every asshole in America who had ever gotten a laugh at a fraternity party was now crowding the field. For decades, to be a comedian had meant you were literally one in a million, as there were certainly no more than two hundred professional comedians in the whole country. But now, just as he was ready to fulfill his lifelong dream, comedians were positively pullulating, breeding like mosquitoes after a wet spring in these stagnant pools they called comedy clubs. Buck laughed every time Johnny Carson brought a new comedian on *The Tonight Show* with the standard comedy-is-the-hardest-commodity-in-our-business-to-find introduction.

Hardest commodity to find? You could barely swing a dead cat nowadays without hitting some dickhead who called himself a comedian!

And the more comedians there were, the more the bargaining power of each descended.

"How many seats in the Washington club?" Shit continued, still on his high horse, "Three hundred? Same with Philly. And they're collecting five or six at the door, plus drinks, times four shows. You figure it out."

"You're just pissed because you're middling for me," Buck kidded, with a mischievous glint in his eye.

"Blow me," Shit responded, with absolutely no glint.

Shit, Buck, and Dick, you see, were on a mission of mercy this weekend, helping the novice members of the group, Chink and Fat, secure their very first out-of-town gigs, as MCs in Baltimore and Wilmington, respectively. Unlike at The Club, the MC job in an out-of-town club was the least important, consisting mainly of warming up the crowd for fifteen minutes, then introducing the middle act and the headliner, who performed the bulk of the real comedy for the evening. Thus the task of local MC was normally handled by someone local— even, at times, by a noncomedian, like the owner of the club or a hostess or Gallagher. But Buck and Shit had persuaded the owner of Shennanagins, the Baltimore club, to let Chink get his feet wet on the road in this manner, and in return for this favor, they had agreed to co-headline, thereby ensuring that the show would at least have two veteran acts should Chink prove to be a disaster. Dick, being perhaps the strongest and most in-demand performer currently working in the New York comedy pool, was not asked to make a similar concession—not that Buck and Shit should have been asked to, either. But if the owner of Shennanagins, Harvey Karrakarrass, had given a comedian something for nothing, he would have faced possible disciplinary action from the Schmucks' Association, to which all club owners belonged.

And, in truth, Buck and Shit were happy to do it: They loved Chink and believed in him. Moreover, they enjoyed doing good, almost as much as they enjoyed the idea that they were doing good. Children of the sixties, Shit and Buck held forth on the train about the new humanity alive at The Club—how different it was from the bad old days there! Why, in days gone by, the senior acts barely spoke to the rookies, and certainly never gave them a helping hand. But then a revolution of kindness swept over the comic landscape behind its charismatic leader, Shit. Upon gaining his own stature at The Club, Shit reached out to the tyros who came along after him. One of them was Buck, who'd arrived on the scene only a year and a half ago—not that you'd know it by the way he carried himself. Buck was the kind of guy who could have headlined only twice before in his life and make it sound for all the world as if he was a grizzled veteran. And since he *had* only headlined twice before, this talent came in handy.

Now, if he only had an act.

An act would have really been helpful a few months earlier, when Buck did his second headlining gig, in Montreal. The owner there wanted an hour from the headliner, and Buck assured him an hour would be no problem. But in truth, an hour was quite a problem, because Buck did not have an hour of material. He did not have a half hour of material, but with a liberal sprinkling of "Where you from?"'s with an uncommonly receptive audience, he had been able to clock in close enough to the usual forty-five-minute headliner finish line to pass muster on his first headlining gig, at Shennanagins.

So Buck went to Montreal feeling pretty cocky—quite a feat for a comedian who was 90 percent attitude and 10 percent act. Of course, a formula like that was right at home in the Big Apple: One colleague had already suggested that Buck bill himself as "the act you're not good enough to see." Buck enjoyed that. He liked having a reputation, even if it was a bad one.

And he didn't want to lose it. So when he got back to New York and everyone asked how things had gone up in Canada, he said they had gone well—referring, apparently, to timely air service, pleasant hotel accommodations, and delightful sightseeing in the day.

As for the shows, he had suffered only a bit less horribly than the crowds who had had to watch him that weekend—watch him die four slow, painful deaths. Nothing in his past experience as a comedian—and almost all of it to that point had been pretty tough—had prepared him for that. At The Club, yes, the first year had been a nightmare onstage, but every comedian's first year is a nightmare: going on for three drunks at two in the morning, desperately trying to find a distinctive voice, and being rudely awakened to the fact that having been a funny guy all your life is a world apart from being a professional comedian. But at least at The Club you were just one comic in a nightly parade, and the worst beating never lasted more than twenty minutes. But in Montreal, there he was, fifteen minutes into an hour show, and pretty much wad-shot of material.

And no closing bit! The Jordache jeans commercial—which he "parodied" by sticking his ass out—did not run in Canada. The biggest laugh Buck got in Montreal that weekend came from his unintentionally mispronouncing the name of the rene-gade Quebecian prime minister, René Levesque.

Onstage those nights, Buck thought about stealing from his friends—who would know, it's Canada—but he had too much pride for that. He even had too much pride to get off at forty-five or fifty or fifty-five, for crying out loud! How much more merciful that would have been for all concerned, not least the audience. Sitting through Buck was like watching an insect that suffers the misfortune of being only half stomped under someone's heel. He writhed and stammered and got hostile atop a little wooden platform in a small basement that had a liquor license while people despised him in two languages.

Buck was not a comedian who bombed gracefully. It was just so hard for him to say nothing when a good joke died. That was all he ever had to do—say nothing and go on to the next one; the crowd wouldn't even have realized a joke had been told, and they would have still liked him. What could be easier than to just shut up?

Except for one thing: It *hurt*. To Buck, an unrequited joke was like offering someone a gift and having it thrown back in your face.

That, and one other tiny, little thing: They were wrong! *They*, sitting there, staring at him as if it were *his* fault! To say nothing would be acceding to that misconception—and what kind of weenie takes upon himself the sins of others?

Jesus Christ?

Oh, *Him*.

At night in the hotel room, Buck cried and thought about something from Greek History 201, some character named Silenus, who told somebody in some play or book or something: "You ask what is best for you? Nothingness. To never have been born. To not be."

Well, hey—who needs to listen to a gloomy gus like that? Especially since, other than Montreal, things had finally started going well for Buck. Just the fact that he was working out of town proved that he was finally "on the raft": that was the image that kept going through Buck's mind all through that first year at The Club, when he wanted so badly to pull himself out of the intolerable nobody-newcomer sea and get on board with the dozen or so regulars, like Shit and Dick. Their support sustained him in those trying times—it meant so much to have their respect, to know they thought of him as a contender and not a pretender—but it still wasn't being one of them. It wasn't being part of the elite cadre, who went on at a decent hour any night they came in and who treated each other like peers and who did real paying gigs around the city, for fifty bucks here, seventy-five there, and sometimes, on weekends out of town, for even more, enough to finally start earning their living from comedy.

From comedy! What a rush that was, to actually be making your living from this! Maybe even to be despised by the waiters at the Blue Spoon diner: that was the ultimate sign of arrival, because the actors who waited tables at the Blue Spoon hated

the comedians who ate there—you could see it in their eyes
and by the way they threw the food at them—because actors
had to work a real job until they hit pay dirt, whereas comedians
were finaglers who knew how to survive without busing tables
for Greeks. The more the actor-waiters hated the comics, the
more the comedians loved it. Oh, how wonderful that would
be, Buck thought—to be someone waiters hated and threw
food at!

But to move up at The Club was an ordeal even for so
ambitious a comer as Buck. There was something of an old-
boy network in place, and the dozen or so spots in prime time
(after ten and before one, or between the time the crowd warmed
up and burned out) went to the same comics every night, the
ones who'd been there for three or five or even seven years. At
The Club, seniority counted.

Seniority really pissed Buck off. This was show business,
he thought—not the Ford motor plant. How could they keep
putting up the same people, the same people who obviously
weren't going anywhere or else they'd have been there by now?

Buck had a point about that. Some of the guys on the raft
really weren't that talented. Buck wanted to whisper that opin-
ion to Dick or to another supportive colleague, Norma, because
they were the reigning MCs at The Club and as such had the
power to choose who went on—but he hesitated. That is, he
paused for half a second before saying it.

"He rambles on so much before the punchline," Buck might
say with a cringing disdain about some poor act who couldn't
hear him because he was busy onstage.

"Yeah," Dick would giggle. "And after."

Damn, you just couldn't denigrate another comedian behind
his back enough for it to have any impact. Everybody bitched
about everybody, so nobody really listened.

Eventually, though, perseverance paid off for Buck one Friday night. The other off-the-raft comics didn't even come in
on the weekends because, unlike the weeknights, the Friday-
Saturday lineups were prescheduled, so there wasn't even a
chance for a rookie to get on—unless somebody didn't show
up. For months this was what Buck had been hoping for—that
some comic with a scheduled spot would be unable to find a

cab or would oversleep or, if it had to be, would get bludgeoned to death on the subway.

When it finally happened (the comedian, thank God, survived the bludgeoning), Buck at long last got his chance in prime time. He was nervous and he was raw and he still had a lot of bad habits. But Buck was right about one thing: He was born to do it, and that night he proved it.

After the show, Buck went home to his shithole studio apartment on West 49th Street and exulted, just sat up all night and exulted. He was on the raft. He'd broken through, and it was a feeling that compared to only two other moments in his life— the day he came in to the Little League championship game as a relief pitcher and saved it for his team before the whole town, and the night during sophomore year in high school after his first successful date, when he walked home in such a stupor that he overshot his own house by half a mile.

Buck smiled and thought about those two moments and now this third one.

Then he stopped exulting: Twenty-four years old, and I can count only three great moments in my life?

Jesus, this show business shit *better* pay off.

"I see Ted Kennedy's going to announce today."

Shit leaned back against the Amtrak-brown upholstery and spread *The New York Times* before him.

"Throwing his hat into the river, is he?" Dick asked.

"Illegal spritz," Buck announced, using the term that meant a comic was committing the faux pas of deploying stage material in a social setting.

"Get outta here," Dick answered. "I don't do political stuff."

"Nobody does anymore," Shit lamented.

"I do," Buck protested, perhaps referring to his insightful routine about the choice in the last election being akin to someone asking, "If you had to, what would you rather eat, shit or puke?"

"I mean nobody does it exclusively, like Mort Sahl," Shit explained.

"Who?" Fat wanted to know.

"Kids today," said Shit, shaking his head. "It's gonna be him and Reagan."

Oh, thought Fat: Mort Sahl would be running against Reagan.

"You think Kennedy'll beat Carter for the nomination?" Buck asked Shit.

"Oh yeah. The Democrats can't resist nominating a Kennedy. Will Rogers said, 'I don't belong to an organized party, I'm a Democrat.' "

"I hope he didn't open with it," Dick snickered.

"Why do you hate the Kennedys so much?" Buck asked Shit. "I never understand that—you're Irish, Catholic, charming, witty, arrogant. You grew up in Boston. Is it just that you think you should have *been* a Kennedy?"

"They're just horrible people. Snot-nosed rich kids on an ego trip."

Buck bridled: "So? You can't do good for people if you're on an ego trip? Isn't there such a thing as an ego trip for good? A fucking snotty-ass Park Avenue surgeon, okay—but he's brilliant, his ego trip is saving lives: 'Saved another one today, honey. They didn't think it could be done, but luckily I was around.' I mean, he's a dick, but he saves lives."

"So why does he have to be a dick about it?" Shit objected.

"Why? Who the fuck knows. Maybe because he wouldn't have the confidence to cut open your chest if he wasn't. You take away all the people who do important things because they're dicks, who'd be left to run things?"

"So this is your we-need-the-dicks-to-run-things theory," Shit mocked with a gentle smile.

"Are you familiar with the no-room-at-the-inn syndrome?" Buck shot back.

"No, but I am familiar with the no-room-*service*-at-the-inn syndrome. That's where you have to go down to the coffee shop for incense and myrrh, which is just as well, because room-service myrrh is usually wildly overpriced," Shit joked.

"No, it means the world does not want a powerful birth. When they know a Jesus is coming into the world, there's never any room at the inn."

"Maybe they were remodeling that week," Dick kidded.

"And you're saying that's why they killed the Kennedys?" Shit asked.

"No, I wasn't, but now that you mention it, that's exactly right. It's always the people that give hope who get shot—Lincoln, King, the Kennedys."

"McKinley," Fat said, surprising everyone.

"Ah yes, McKinley," Shit said. "Gave every kid in America hope, 'cause they figured if he could grow up to be president, everybody had a shot."

"Ted Kennedy," Chink piped up. "His brother was a hero because he smashed his boat during the war, this guy drives a car into a river. Close, Ted, real close, but it's gotta be a boat. There's gotta be some kinda war goin' on."

"That's so funny," Buck pronounced. "You gotta do that."

"He speaks in material," Shit added.

"Do we have to talk about politics?" Fat asked, pissed that once again Chink had scored with the big boys.

"Everything's politics," Shit said. "Talking about us getting paid what we deserve, that's politics."

"So stop talking about it." Dick laughed.

"You know, the reason we don't get paid at The Club," Buck rejoined, unable to forgo the argument he and Shit had already rehearsed a dozen times, "is because The Club is a place to work out, not to work. It's a trade-off. They use us, and we use them to get our act together. If they paid us real money, we'd be obligated to do our best set every time. We couldn't experiment."

"Oh, come on," Shit returned. "How much experimenting is really going on in there? Everybody's so afraid they'll lose their place at the trough, they do their best set every time anyway."

"I don't," Buck said.

"You don't have a best set," Dick teased.

"No, you need a guitar for that," Buck came back, implying that Dick's use of a musical instrument adulterated the purity of straight monologuy.

But Dick was genuinely ungored. Most comics were thin-skinned and easily goreable, but not Dick. He was hard to gore, no matter how many brightly colored sharp sticks one stuck into his back.

"That place is our studio," Buck continued. "Stand-up comedy is an art form. You don't pay the artist to go to class and learn shading and perspective."

"We need a union," Shit stated flatly, and then launched into his speech about how the club owners were scum and how the comedians could break their exploitative lock if only they would band together.

But the comedians did not want to talk politics on this afternoon, so Shit's jeremiad was quickly hushed. Dick especially was bored by the subject because he was—and would be the first to admit that he was—still a little boy. Not that this wasn't true of most comedians, but with Dick it was more literal. He was a little boy who continued to enjoy all the pleasures of little boydom—pinball, video games, comic books, cartoons—although none of those pleasures came close to supplying the fun that kept on coming from the best new toy any towheaded lad could ever hope to receive on his thirteenth birthday: an erection. And being a comedian was just the best job in the world for a boy who wanted to play with that toy all the time.

Dick's reputation as a hound was so notorious in the comedy world that on the signature wall of one club's green room, below where Dick had signed his name, someone had added the words *fucked this* and then punched a small hole in the wall.

Dick did not mind. He remained so permanently pleased at his accomplishment of avoiding work and getting a lot of women that he was not even bothered by the slightly embarrassing predicament of being a thirty-five-year-old young comedian. It may not have been the perfect situation, but, like for Russians who once defended communism because they remembered the czar, it beat the old life—which for Dick was his twenties, when he had worked as an engineer and hated every minute of it. Dick never tired of explaining why being a comedian had it all over anything else a man might do to make his living.

"If you work in an office, you see the same chicks every day. Okay, four of them are married, one's a dyke, two of them are ugly—so after you fucked the pretty one, you're done. But us—say you do five shows a week, average a hundred people a show, half of them are women, that's two hundred and fifty new women you could meet every week.''

Of course, Dick's ceaseless philandering did have its downside, such as it sometimes bothered his wife—but since she'd already divorced him, there wasn't much she could do about it except move out, which she so far hadn't done. This arrangement baffled everybody: a couple divorced for three years yet still living as man and wife with their eleven-year-old son, Joel, in a nice apartment in the Riverdale section of the Bronx. (Dick also maintained a small pied-à-pussy on the East Side of Manhattan.) People who didn't know the couple well surmised that it was a marriage of convenience, devoid of passion, but that was not the case. It was, in fact, a marriage of constant *inconvenience*, with plenty of passion. Dick loved having sex with Janet, because wooing her out of the constant state of resentment and hatred she felt for him was just a different form of the song and dance he had to perform for strange women to get *them* into bed. It was the song and dance, more than the sex, that motivated Dick—and the fact that the one form of it always made the other more exciting was the beauty of his system. Dick often told his cronies how much he loved to come home to his marital bed after a weekend away cruising bimbos—although even Janet drew the line the time she found a blond hair while removing her husband's underpants. Janet didn't like the arrangement; she wasn't a happy woman. But for some reason, she let Dick have his cake and fuck it, too. She knew he wouldn't change, but she was tragically unable to extricate herself from a man who believed that ''finding a blond hair in your underwear is what show business is all about.''

Perhaps, then, they stayed together for the child. Janet could not deny that Dick and Joel had a special relationship. Certainly, no son could have asked for a more constant playmate, even if it did come in the person of his father. Dick often took Joel on gigs near home, especially if it was a club where they could play pinball or video games together before he went onstage. Then, after the show, Joel would watch his father try to score in a different way. Dick never betrayed the slightest embarrassment while chatting up a girl closer to his son's age than his own, although on the way home he always told the boy, "Don't tell your mother about this."

As for Joel, he seemed to take it all in stride. He was a bit of a brat, but only because Dick simply had not an iota of will to discipline his boy. Discipline was not a part of their relationship, or of Dick's character or in his vocabulary. To hear Dick and his son talk to each other was a riot, because it sounded more like two young brothers—arguing over trivial matters, calling each other names, leading each other into childish conversational traps. And Dick loved it. He didn't want to be his kid's father, not in the way his father was to him, remote and strict and fatherlike. Dick preferred being the older brother—although, in truth, it was Joel who more often took on that role, routinely shepherding Dick toward the more responsible course of action when Dick wanted to delay a show so he could finish a Pac-Man tournament or have sex in the bathroom.

Of such behavior Shit took a dim view. Dick had once explained to Shit that his ease in bedding so many women had, in fact, hurt his career, reasoning that men only entered show business to garner the fame and wealth for which women were the natural reward—but if he was getting the reward already, whither the motivation to succeed?

What really made Shit furious, though, was when he caught Dick flirting with women from the stage, because the idea that stand-up comedy, a legitimate art form, should be used as a means to troll—that was too much. Even more disturbing were the recent, albeit pathetic, attempts by Fat to emulate this tawdry behavior, so much had the impressionable youngster come to idolize Dick. The friendship of Fat and Dick was a natural, Dick feeling most comfortable around fellow little boys, and Fat, thrilled for once in his life, to have a powerful friend—or any friend.

On the train, the talk among the comedians turned, as usual, to show business, a profession the boys were under the illusion they were in. Dick was advising Fat on the advantage of having a manager, as if the eighteen-year-old kid who made calls on

Dick's behalf during his lunch break (at his father's tuxedo store) could, under even the loosest of show business standards, be considered a "manager."

But at the level the boys were on, this eighteen-year-old kid actually aroused envy among the other comedians. Because if you had a manager—any manager, even one who really sold tuxedos—well, then you could . . . you could say you had a manager! You could always say, "You'll have to talk to my manager," and then you'd really feel like you were in show business.

Which was, of course, what the boys wanted more than anything.

Especially Dick, Shit, and Buck, because they were still on a high from having reached that first rung of the ladder: they were, technically, *professionals*. They did not have day jobs; they did not live at home with their parents. And they were big fish in their own little pond, even if it was almost too little to be called a pond. But even if it was just a puddle, it was a puddle called show business, or so they thought. Of course, it bore very little resemblance to actual show business, where performers got paid by check, retained legitimate representation, and had strangers halt their progress in the street.

Dick, Shit, and Buck were not in that.

But at least they were not in it together, because it is equality of stature that on all levels of show business forges the key element of bonding. Frank and Dean and Sammy were always comfortable walking into a casino three abreast, because no one of them felt bad that the other two were stars and he wasn't; nor did any of them feel like he was wasting his time with inferiors—and that psychology goes all the way down the line. And when it gets far enough down, you have Dick, Shit, and Buck—the bottom of the barrel—but, at least for them, the same barrel. Of course, if you lifted up the barrel there would be Fat and Chink, the greenest of the green, en route to their very first paying gig out of New York, scared and excited and looking at Buck, Shit, and Dick as if they were Frank, Dean, and Sammy.

And the way Buck, Shit, and Dick talked, you'd have thought they *were* Frank, Dean, and Sammy. Because in the absence of any hard evidence linking them to the show business fraternity, the boys *talked* about show business a lot. They told stories involving big stars, but in a way that made it seem as if they could easily have been in the story themselves, instead of at that fifty-dollar gig in Passaic, New Jersey, and they discussed the latest trends in the movie industry with such intimacy that one would have thought it had some effect on them beyond the price they paid for a ticket at their neighborhood theater. And they constantly professed their love of show business. Over and over they told themselves that show business was their life, even though there was every chance that their future might include employment in a completely different industry.

That was the one thing they could never admit. As in war, the comedians clung to the belief that it would be the other guy who didn't make it.

In the meantime, surviving, waiting for stardom to strike—and for some it had been on strike for quite some time—the comics shared a camaraderie. And although they did not know it, they were presently living the purest part of their careers, because this was the time when *being funny* was still the hardest currency. All of them wanted to be, and tried to be, the funniest one, wherever and whenever they were. Like cats who constantly need to keep their claws sharp, the boys were forever verbally clawing, using anything, including each other, as scratching posts. And when somebody tried to be funny but wasn't? Only the manner in which the Israeli government deals with terrorists was harsher than the reprisals visited upon a bum ad-lib.

Knowing this, Fat and Chink kept relatively quiet on the train. Neither of them needed a trauma before his first real gig, or, for that matter, ever again in his life. Life had not been easy for either of them, and for that reason, it seemed to Buck and Dick and Shit that Chink and Fat should be better friends, sympathetic to each other for their common plight—kind of like the way it was with blacks and Jews, at least in the minds of people who had never seen blacks and Jews together.

But Fat, for his part, was too competitive, too insecure, and too ambitious to allow around him any lean and hungry men,

especially lean. And now he and Chink were fighting again,
and if the kids were going to fight, well then, the train would
just have to pull off the road. And what were they fighting
about? Nothing was more typical of the newcomer's insecurity
than the custody battles waged over a joke. A rudimentary
knowledge of astronomy would have been helpful here, especially as regards the sun, under which there was nothing new—
but being as green as the tyros were, they believed each of their
jokes had just crossed its first mind.

But Fat accusing Chink of stealing from him? That was like
a plagiarism suit brought against Homer by Harold Robbins.
Nevertheless, Fat and Chink repeated the argument already
rehearsed a thousand times by a hundred other young comedians:

"You know that McDonald's bit you did? That's my bit."

"I never saw you do it."

"I didn't say you did, I'm just telling you I already do it."

"How long have you been doing it?"

"I've been doing it a long time."

"So have I."

"How long?"

"Long."

"But you've only been doing comedy six months."

"I know, but it's in my notebook from before I started. I
can show you."

"You could have just written it in."

"No, I can prove I didn't."

"How?"

"It's on papyrus."

It was always a silly argument, but at least it settled nothing.
And after a while comedians did get tired of having it. That's
when they adopted the ''mature'' viewpoint:

"They can steal jokes, but they can't steal *you*."

Shit had given Buck this advice when Buck was just a tad-
pole, and then added: "Material is nothing. Especially yours."

Buck was not insulted. It was a generic joke, driven by
rhythm and opportunity, so he stopped right before the fork
reached Shit's neck.

But Chink and Fat were not yet this mature, and as their battle escalated, Dick noticed Shit and Buck stirring to the sound of the debate—Shit and Buck, who fancied themselves mentors, guidance counselors, solvers of other people's problems, despite the fact that they did not seem able to solve their own obvious problems, or even agree with each other most of the time. But an exchange between the two novices would surely drag them into the conflict on opposite sides, much the way the skirmishes among the tiny Balkan nations had suckered in the major combatants of World War I. Since Dick did not want to see the lights go out all over the train, he turned the focus to the one topic he knew would rivet everyone's attention like flies to a dog's mess.

"Pussy? Her name is Pussy?" a wide-eyed Fat asked upon hearing the swear-to-God moniker of a waitress who worked in the Baltimore club.

Buck shot up in his seat. He had also made the acquaintance of this waitress, on his previous visit to Baltimore—but he was stunned to discover that she had shared with someone else so intimate a revelation: Pussy, of course, was not her real name but rather a pet name given to her by some either very naïve or very disturbed parents, based on her childhood fondness for the pussy willow tree. Pussy had shared that part of her past with Buck during a night in which she revealed a great catalog of personal secrets, secrets that, up till now, Buck had thought were . . . secret.

Was it possible Dick knew *two* girls who were nicknamed Pussy because they liked a tree?

No, that did not seem possible, even for Dick.

"She told you that?" Buck asked Dick.

"Yeah. I think if you fuck her she'll tell you anything." Dick chuckled.

Buck was crushed. Then he was angry at his own naïveté. Wouldn't it have been more odd if there was a waitress on the road who Dick *hadn't* fucked? And yet, this girl, she seemed different. Buck was sure he had started something special with her. After all, wasn't that why he *didn't* fuck her?

Well, not exactly. It actually had more to do with the fact

that at the time, Buck didn't know how to fuck. Darn the luck, because it was not long after that when said skill finally revealed itself to him, epiphanylike, with another waitress, whilst middling on another road gig. Like everything Buck learned, he learned it late, but once learned, he locked it in solidly. For that reason, Buck had been looking forward to this trip to Baltimore to show Pussy what he'd learned.

Shit looked up from his newspaper in time to catch the hurt Buck was hiding. Shit loved Buck too much, and was too secure in his own standing with women, to reveal that Dick was not the only comedian to have bedded Pussy. Ironically, or perhaps prophetically, Pussy had somewhat grown into her nickname, but Shit knew that her immense popularity with stand-ups sprang not so much from easy sex as from easy understanding, the empathy that comedians crave more than, and confuse with, sex. Pussy was a great audience, and nothing got to a comic's heart more than that. If a comic had the plans to our NORAD system, an adversary would only have to cackle shamelessly at him for an hour to steal them.

Buck meanwhile reflected on the night he had spent at Pussy's apartment. He had stayed up with her until dawn, lying fully clothed in a wonderful warm embrace, talking until she fell asleep on his chest. Buck had always dreamed of a girl so simultaneously beautiful and interesting that he'd be forever torn between using his mouth for kissing or for talking.

Pussy, alas, was not that girl. But she did laugh at everything he said, including sometimes when it wasn't a joke. No, she wasn't the ultimate girl, because she didn't really understand his problems; giving someone understanding is not the same thing as actually understanding. But it sure beat having someone rattle on about her own problems! And it certainly was reason enough to have sex with her.

Now Buck was locked in a fierce big head–little head debate. On the one hand, he didn't want to—in the parlance of the profession—follow Dick—and God knows who else—onto Pussy's stage; on the other hand, he was getting turned on by the news that she was such a slut, and hoped the others didn't notice the large pool of foamy drool forming on his chin. He

weighed the arguments of the one hand and then the other hand
and then decided, in the interest of giving his own hand a much
needed rest, that he would, after all, fuck Pussy.

But all that was neither here nor there. What really mattered
was that Fat was loose on the train with a mountain of food.
The theme from *Jaws* began to play, even though the picture
of Fat struggling with a piled-high tray of grub was actually
quite funny, although possibly not to the people on either side
of the aisle, who got sprayed with french fries and soda as the
train lurched to and fro. In units of time too small to be measured by civilian instruments, the boys inhaled their food, then
waited for the movie to begin. Remembering this was not an
airplane, they instead took turns stepping into the rear compart-
ment for a breath of fresh joint.

Massive giggling naturally ensued—mostly from the other
passengers, who couldn't believe these guys thought they were
fooling anybody about not being stoned. Back at their seats,
Fat started to crack up during a conversational lull. The others
wanted to know what was so funny.

"No, it's too stupid," Fat protested, getting no argument
from his colleagues.

"So," Chink asked Fat, "which one of us do you think will
be banned from the city we're going to for the rest of our life?"

"I think I can do good," Fat betrayed.

Fat was a bit insecure. As a nineteen-year-old virgin with a
fat person's squeaky voice and a fat person's wardrobe (he had
vests with sweat stains under the arms), Fat had yet to taste any
of the joys of life. He still lived at home with his parents in
Brooklyn, and there endured their daily scorn for becoming a
comedian instead of going to college. For that, Fat's parents
threatened him with every possible reprisal, including being
thrown out on the street.

Fat never flinched. And sadly, his parents never recognized
how rare it was for a teenager to be as focused as Fat was, as
determined. The only use Fat had for every day of his life was
to get one step closer to this dream—comedy. It was the way
out of the nightmare. And as certain as obesity had brought on

the nightmare, it would also be the means to realizing the dream.

Fat had paid dearly his entire life for being fat, and he was dead set that what had always made him a pariah would now make him a cynosure, not that he knew what either of those things was. He once considered losing weight as a way to acceptance—for about ten seconds—before he said to himself: "Fuck that—fuck everybody who scorns me for being what I am!" Fat wasn't going to give in just because Americans were fatist; there was a better way to stake his claim, and that was comedy.

God bless comedy—that was Fat's view. Was there another profession that held out the potential of turning obesity into an asset? Comedy was made for fat people, because Americans insisted on believing that fat people were jolly, as ridiculous as that was.

Fat knew how ridiculous that was, but if that's what people wanted to believe, Fat had no problem feeding the lie back to them—hell, comedians did that all the time! TV was full of sitcoms where black people acted like stupid niggers, and those stupid niggers laughed about it all the way to the bank. And that's what Fat would do: laugh about it all the way to the bank. And when he got to the bank, he was going to take out a big wad of money and buy all sorts of things for his parents—not because he wanted to bring them joy, but just so there would be all this stuff in the house to remind them, every time they used it or sat on it or turned it on, of how wrong they had been about their son, the assholes.

In one of the ironies of human nature that induces one to fruitless analysis, Chink had endured a childhood remarkably similar to Fat's and yet wound up taking an opposite approach in his comedy. Chink never entertained the idea of compromising with his audience, and for that reason his audience often felt he didn't have very entertaining ideas. At twenty-one, scrawny and beset by bad skin that he tried to cover with a beard that just wouldn't come in, Chink was still fighting his physicality in the same way as Fat. But Chink was cursed with an additional burden in the form of a mumbly, slurry speech that made it difficult for an audience to understand what he was saying—which, given the esoteric nature of his material, sometimes was the key to his getting any laughs at all.

Not that Chink couldn't have scored, and scored big, because his ideas were always just flat-out funny. But Chink had yet to break that mystical barrier that every comedian must break, where one night you recite a certain set of jokes and get no response and the next night the same routines bring down the house. It is the X factor in comedy, the unexplainable connection with a roomful of strangers that cannot be practiced. One can hone material, rehearse delivery, bone up on all the tangibles, but in the end it comes down to something very much like what makes a man and a woman have enduring passion—something that no one can ever know, because such knowledge, like that coveted by Adam and Eve, would itself be the agent of destruction. It is the mystery itself of why two people are drawn together that gives the relationship its power, and a similar chemistry must obtain between a comedian and his audience. This was what Chink was still looking for.

Unfortunately, the stage at The Club, circa 2 A.M., was a tough place to look for anything; there was definitely better light over there at ten-thirty. But although the MCs believed in Chink and gave him a good spot whenever they could, there were other considerations, like not having to explain to Bo Reynolds, the owner of The Club, why the audience was leaving. For Chink, it was especially trying that the showcase clubs had ceased for some years to be great venues of experimentation. The Club in 1979 was not the Village Gate in '63; in the audience there were no poetic types in berets hoping to be challenged by a Lenny Bruce. It was a lot of tourists and bachelor parties from Brooklyn and New Jersey hoping to hear dick jokes. The more the non-cognoscenti took over the club scene, the more the comedians tailored their acts along crowd-pleasing lines to survive. And the more the comedians did that, the more the people in berets stayed away.

Or maybe it was just that the cover charges had gone up. At those prices, comedians could experiment on their own time—these audiences wanted product. This was a bottom-line generation, and they didn't want to pay a cover and a minimum *not* to laugh. They wanted laughs guaranteed, neat and easy, every fifteen seconds. They were spoiled, mainly by TV, and they didn't want to do the work. They weren't stupid. They just knew what they wanted.

And Chink wasn't it.

But why should comedy be different? All his young life, Chink was a guy who had loser written all over him. When one night at The Club this literally came to pass—some asshole stuck a sign on his back that actually said LOSER—Chink went home in tears. It was just like school, where Chink had endured the kind of cruelty of which only children are capable. SS shock troops, the ones even other Nazis feared, could find no better venue for a refresher course in sadism than a fourth grade classroom—and like those elite Nazis, Chink's classmates conducted exhaustive medical research on him, day after day testing his limits of endurance by thorping (flicking with a painful fillip from the middle finger) his ears until he cried. Chink served his classmates as the butterfly whose wings were pulled off when no butterfly was available, the frog whose head was sacrificed to a firecracker when no frog was around. School for Chink was a prison, a prison in which he suffered the worst of both worlds: thrown into solitary, yet never left alone from abuse. Chink was that person who brought out in some people what is perhaps the most despicable trait in the human catalog, the inclination to perpetrate cruelty on the very thing that will suffer from it most and that can retaliate least.

And now he had chosen to be a comedian.

So Chink slunk silently, with his head braced against the madly vibrating window as the train rattled south through the blighted landscape that was Amtrak's eastern corridor—a 261-mile stretch of track that never disappointed in its ability to produce images of ugliness: junkyards, swamps, abandoned good and bad ideas, toxic dumps, dirty laundry hanging in tiny backyards, landfills, tire repositories, gutted anything, graveyards—and, always, the end of town that brought to mind the phrase *wrong side of the tracks*.

Chink considered the dwindling number of hours before he would have to go onstage and thought about the prospects for disaster in Baltimore. He wanted to do good, more to justify the faith that Buck and Shit had shown in him than for himself.

But he could not think of any reason why Baltimore should be any different from New York.

Fat still wanted to know how you got a manager.

"Well . . . do you have a Jewish friend who's kind of obnoxious?" Dick asked in absolute sincerity.

The others took this in and snickered at the preposterousness of Dick's remark, then got quiet trying to think of a Jewish friend. The comedians sat quietly for a while, looking out the window or playing with something that could be easily destroyed.

In the eerie quiet of the train, with only the sound of the engine roaring and the conductor calling out stops and seven babies crying and a shouting match among two Puerto Rican families and a bomb going off and the wheels screeching off the track into a ditch, the weary travelers found time to cultivate their own unique thoughts: Fat thought about girls; Shit thought about women; Buck thought about fucking; and Dick thought about pussy.

Chink, ever the iconoclast, thought about love. He was in love—not that she knew it. But he spent a lot of time with her, and he thought about her constantly, and about nobody else. He was always thinking of her, and never telling anyone that he was.

He couldn't, because she was one of them. She was a comedienne.

After Trenton, another trip to the food-and-beverage car was in order for Fat and Dick. Chink decided to join them, so Shit decided to share his thoughts about women with Buck.

"Celibacy?" Buck repeated, way too loudly for a train.

"Yes. I've been thinking about it a lot."

"Why? I mean . . . why would anyone . . ."

Buck could not fathom the notion of celibacy. He was nonplussed, not to mention jealous. He couldn't believe a guy could have had so many women that he was full.

"I don't know," Shit said. "I'd just like to try it. I'm not in love with anyone right now, and I just don't feel like fooling around."

Don't feel like fooling around! Do you have a fever or some-thing? Are you sick, man?

"I think I could really concentrate on my career if I wasn't thinking about women, and that's what I need to do."

Buck just stared at him as if he was announcing plans to cut off his head.

"Hey, it doesn't kill you, you know."

Yes—yes, of course it kills you! That's exactly what it would do, it would kill you!

"They say celibacy is the strangest perversion of all," Buck finally managed.

"Well, you're always saying I'm strange."

"You are strange."

Yes, Shit was strange. Buck sometimes wondered if he should be growing so close to someone so strange—but he couldn't help himself. Shit was everything Buck wanted to be when he grew up: worldly, charming, urban, urbane, a ladies' man—not a hound like Dick, who'd screw any skank that didn't slap him, but a ladies' man. And a man's man, as well.

And best of all, a man about town—what a thing to be, a man about town! Shit knew every single place in New York worth knowing, and every single person in town who also knew the worth-knowing places. Wherever he went, Shit ran into somebody he knew, and the somebody and Shit would then recall one of the great nights in all of Christendom: They had started out here, then they went there, then they met some other fabulous people, who had their own great memories of nights with Shit, and then some amazing women turned up, so they went downtown, uptown, that little place, this terrific joint that's not there anymore, finally winding up at—big surprise— some other great place that Buck also had never heard of, or heard of only because he'd read about it in a magazine and wondered if it was really as fabulous as the article said it was.

It was.

I don't know any great place, Buck thought—they'd have to call a place Great Place and list it in the Yellow Pages under "Schmuck" and give directions on the phone.

And even then, who would I bring?

Shit, no doubt—at least he'd know some people there. Definitely the bartender. Shit absolutely did know every bartender in Manhattan, which was such a cool thing. Peering into this Irish-New York cosmos that Shit inhabited made Buck feel like he was living on the cover of *The New Yorker*: old New York—this marvelous, dynamic circuit of wit and fun and sophistication that had been going on for centuries, and Shit the very point man in carrying on the tradition.

No wonder Shit loved New York. Not the way Buck loved New York—out of obligation, because everybody said it was the greatest city in the world, and, geez, what am I gonna be, an asshole and not love a thing like that? Buck wanted to be like Shit. He wanted to be the kind of person the city was made for, the kind of person who barely noticed all the crap a New Yorker had to put up with, because he was too busy using it for pleasure and enlightenment. But not being that person, Buck latched on to one who was, and hoped it would rub off.

Not that there was anything cynical in Buck's affection for Shit. Buck loved Shit—and could even tell him so. Buck had never had a male friend like that, somebody older and secure in his masculinity and unabashed about discussing feelings, someone who was unafraid to say, "I cried," or, "I love you," or any of that sort of formerly yucky and embarrassing, now adult and enlightened, stuff.

For Buck, having Shit in his life was like having the hippest uncle in the world for a best friend. Shit did things uncles did, but he did them hip: He told stories, but they were great stories, sharp and funny and dirty, and always with that sense of New York history. Shit belonged to a men's club, but when you were there with Shit, it was not a stuffy old Miss Havisham–smelling relic, it was the coolest place in the world. Sitting in those overstuffed leather chairs, with uniformed old men tending to the chore of bringing more Champagne, which sat in a silver bucket stand—geez, a whole piece of furniture just for that—it made a guy feel so cool he wished there were some girls around, until that guy realized what a genius idea it was to have a place where that ubiquitous maybe-I'll-meet-someone-here tension was taken away, so you could really relax.

But Buck didn't know how cool that place was until he asked Shit one day, early in their relationship, a question he'd been asking all the veterans at The Club: "How do you live?!" Buck was living on money he'd saved from cutting lawns as a teenager, plus some he'd saved from selling pot in college and some he was making now from selling pot to comedians. But how did everybody else get by, he wondered. Nobody, at that point, was making enough money to survive from just doing comedy, and yet none of the comedians seemed to have a day job.

"I find money on the street when I need it," one comic told him—and he was serious. This was not a joke. None of the answers were, and one was more vague and unemulatable than the next: "I invented something that I sell through the mail"; "I get paid to bring people down to this place"; "I'm partners in a company, but I never have to show up"; "I do something on the phone."

And those weren't even the schemes; there were some real beauts there. The best was from a comic named Arnie Brillstein, who earned his way for a while by—get this—giving away money. Arnie would set up a table on the sidewalk of a well-to-do neighborhood, and on it he would place a jar labeled FREE MONEY, which was prestuffed with coins and bills. Then, as passersby stopped to inquire, Arnie would tell them: Yes, if you really need money, take it.

But—if, on the other hand, you are one of the lucky ones who can afford to *give* some money for those who really need it . . .

And he got away with it!

What?

Buck couldn't get a straight answer out of anybody. Finally, Shit explained it to him.

"Comics are finaglers," he said. "They just know how to get by without working."

Period, end of explanation.

Then Buck asked Shit how he made *his* daily bread.

"I play poker," Shit said.

And *he* was serious! The man played poker for a living! He went down to that men's club every Wednesday night and played poker—for a living!

Buck couldn't get over the balls, the coolness, of that—how

civilized! It was like what James Bond would do if he were a young comedian.

Shit lived by the Mike Todd dictum: "I've been broke, but I've never been poor." Shit was always living beyond his means, but he never let a little thing like money, or the lack of it, affect his lifestyle. He squired women around New York like he owned the Chrysler Building, and not easy-to-please-looking women, either. Shit was always with interesting women, women who were sophisticated and fun and, undoubtedly, dynamite in the sack. And he always took them to interesting places too, places he really wanted to go, not just time killers till the fucking part of the night came around. Shit never acted like he cared if he got laid, so of course he always did.

And so, Buck thought, how could a guy like that consider celibacy? And if he's serious about it, who's gonna be the one from now on to start talking to the two women I'm afraid to start talking to? Who's gonna tell me whether one of them was giving me the eye or just has something *in* her eye? And who am I going to fight with over which one of us gets the one who must be a little overweight or else she wouldn't be wearing such a loose outfit that who knows what her ass looks like?

Shit's celibacy would be a great loss for Buck. Always a good student, never afraid to admit ignorance, Buck prized the knowledge about women, and everything else, that Shit passed on to him.

But especially about women. Like the time, a Friday afternoon it was, when Buck phoned Shit to see about pursuing the avocation in which they had become expert, the assassination of a day. Shit said he was going to the Guggenheim with a girl, and invited Buck; Buck declined, not wanting to be a third wheel, and not being hungry for German food. Shit explained that the Guggenheim was a museum and that the girl—although a former flame—was now just a friend. He urged Buck to go, dangling the prospect that the girl might be someone Buck would like and then claim for his own.

Buck did like the girl. At the museum, he essayed to be his charmingest, funniest, and especially—since this was a museum—most knowledgeable self. He strained to recall every stray fact he'd once crammed into his head for the Modern Art final, and what he couldn't remember, he made up. He waged a tireless campaign to impress Shit's old flame with his vast knowledge of the subject at hand. And he actually thought it was working. Yeah, she really seems interested, he thought— and quite appreciative that so astute a guide had come along.

Of course, as a *guide* was exactly how she saw Buck: a sexless, verbose, eggheaded, might-as-well-be-wearing-a-silly-uniform factotum. Buck thought he was getting to her, until in a single moment it became crushingly, blindingly plain what a fool he was.

Near the end of the day, the woman of Buck's soon-to-be-dashed dreams turned to Shit and teasingly asked: "Why don't *you* tell us something about one of the paintings?"

Shit paused and looked deeply into her eyes. "I don't know anything about them," he said. "I just know none of them are as beautiful as you."

To say that she melted would be to set an impossible standard for applications of extreme heat the world over. But to say that she wanted Shit so bad at that moment that she would have been happy to use Buck as a cot would be just another ridiculous exaggeration.

As for Buck, he just wanted to crawl inside the windmill of an old Dutch painting.

Days later, after Shit and his rekindled flame had spent some quality time remembering where they used to like to touch each other, Shit summed it all up for Buck: "Women want you to be interested, not interesting."

Yeah, that was Shit, all right—a Renaissance man, something out of a different age, out of a time when wit and class and sophistication were the qualities civilized people admired and to which they aspired.

Boy, was he in the wrong business now!

Unfortunately for Shit, it was no time to be a throwback to that gentler age when humorist wasn't a dirty word in comedy; in 1979, humorist *was* a dirty word, the way *liberal* was becoming a dirty word in politics. Shit worked in the tradition of the Noël Cowards, the Bob Hopes, the Jack Bennys—comedy giants perhaps, but giants who would never have gotten past audition night had they started in 1979. The revolutions that each American generation stages in its choice of popular music are more noticeable but no less real than those in comedy, and Shit's style was essentially the comedic version of the cabaret singers The Club put up from time to time, to break up the comedy—the thirtyish blondes in billowy gowns who sang medleys of songs lionizing New York or inspirational I-can-climb-the-mountain-find-my-lucky-star-reach-the-impossible-dream show tunes of the sort that homosexuals seemed to enjoy so much.

But this was the *eighties*, man. Who was looking for the next Lainie Kazan? For that matter, who was looking for Lainie Kazan? The current vogue in music was punk-rockers, very few of whom included in their evening's menu a charming, pre-scripted minute of chat under a tinkling piano, unless you count "Eat my shit, assholes" as patter.

At The Club, Shit had seniority going for him, and he had the city of New York to play to, where there was still some residual sophisticated bonhomie. But even New York was becoming a town more concerned with subway fare than savoir faire, and in such an age, Noël Coward was just an old English douche bag with no props and no dick jokes. When Shit told the audience that so-and-so was "such a conservative, his idea of a great musical is *Across the World in Eighty Days* . . ."

Well, there just weren't enough of the kind of people around anymore who knew how funny it was.

Thank you, ladies and gentlemen, as your delightful master of ceremonies just told you, it's true, I was on a soap opera—I used to play Dr. Matthew Michaels on Lives of Our World. *And I'll tell you how I got the job. I was only supposed to work one day—one line. I was supposed to go into the hospital room of the star of the show and say, "That eye looks fine. You can go home tomorrow." But this was live TV. Live. I leaned over the bed and said, "My God, that eye looks awful—I'll be in to see you tomorrow." I kept that shit up for two years.*

I recently got my big break when I was cast in the all-WHITE version of Porgy and Bess—*ah, a couple of fans of the musical theater here tonight—with songs like*

"Bess, You ARE *My Woman Now"* and *"It* ISN'T *Necessarily So."*

I snagged the part of Porgy. Next week they cut my legs off at the knees—which is great, 'cause I always wished my dick would touch the ground.

Rex Harrison is doing a car commercial—have you seen that one? Professor Henry Higgins, the greatest linguistic mind in English history, waxing poetic about a Chrysler. But since Rex Harrison is the only celebrity I can imitate—because I can't sing, either—here is Mr. Harrison, as Professor Henry Higgins, performing the song that the commercial really wanted him to do:*

Why can't a woman be more like a car?
One car in a million may stall a bit
Now and then one may test your mettle
Occasionally you'll see one that you'd call a
    piece of shit
But mostly they're a wonderful hunk of metal!

If I forgot to change your oil, would you
    bellow?
If I didn't tune you up, would you fuss?
Would you despise me if your anti-freeze turned
    yellow?
Why can't a woman—be more like a bus!

You folks have been . . . well, an audience. If you want to see me again, on the tenth of September, on the Johnny Carson show—write him.

---

*"Sung" to the tune of "A Hymn to Him" from *My Fair Lady*

2

More Green, Asshole

"Wilmington! Wilmington!"

Dick and Fat dutifully obeyed the announcer's exhortation to "gather all personal belongings from the overhead rack," including some of their own. They departed with all the ebullient good cheer one would expect from humans going to Wilmington, while Buck, Shit, and Chink continued on to their appointed destiny in Baltimore.

"All right, you slugs, do good—and say hello to my close friend Mr. Scuzzhole."

Buck was referring to Dino Scuzzoli, the renowned (to them) owner of the Comedy Cave, the club in Wilmington, and this year's millionth variation on his name elicited approving chortles from the departing pair.

"And, Fat"—Buck halted him with a bark that put thinness back in his face: "Make me proud."

"Bye-bye . . . bye-bye," and as soon as they were out of sight: "Losers!" a label applied to whichever of their friends had just turned a corner.

Finally there was some peace and, not inconsequentially, more room aboard the Minuteman. Shit got up to visit the bathroom, first naming Buck as his beneficiary should he not return. Buck stretched out in the place where Dick and Fat had been and measured the polite young man who, from the first, had had the good taste to idolize him. He could see that Chink was nervous about his imminent debut in Baltimore and so offered what, for Buck, constituted reassurance.

"Baltimore isn't a bad place to start," he began, "because it'll never get worse. Playing Baltimore is like swinging three bats before you step up to that plate. And by the way, if you go out for a sandwich after dark, make sure you *are* swinging three bats, because they'll kill you down there. Very creepy racial tension in that town—you know, blue-collar, everybody thinks everybody else is going to take their fucking job away from them, like it wouldn't be a blessing to have your fucking job taken away from you there.

"But that's neither here nor there to you—you want the lowdown on the comedy landscape, and low-down is certainly the right way to describe it. Actually, they're okay there—you know, people are people, they're the same everywhere. Unfortunately.

"I will tell you something useful about the club, though: There's a big window behind you when you're onstage, and the key thing while you're on is to try not to jump through it. No, seriously, it's very distracting—I mean, you can imagine, you're doing lines, and behind you they're watching a rape or something. So don't let that throw you. Also, the acoustics are terrible, big high ceiling, Tiger Emenee sound system.

"I don't know what to tell you, pal. You're the funniest man in America—you know it, I know it, and someday America will know it. As for the people of Baltimore, tell 'em your jokes and count as lucky the ones who catch on. In ten years the ones who didn't will say they did anyway."

"Ten years?" Chink balked.

"Okay, eight," said Buck.

"Eight?"

"All right, tomorrow, whaddaya want from me? It does take years to build a career, you know. Especially for someone like you, who's laboring under the awesome burden of quality."

"Thank you."

"You know what I mean. Hey, we've all got a few wavelength jokes, but you're broadcasting from a station that's not even on the dial in most markets. But at least your Chinese thing always kills.''

''Oh please. I haven't done that in a while. I hate that bit.''

''I know you do, because the audience has the incredible bad taste to applaud it. But, my little friend, you'll notice they call it show business—not truth business, not show art, show *business*.''

Chink listened, but he didn't swallow. Wasn't Buck pontificating only an hour ago about what artists these comedians be?

Yes, he was, but Buck was much better at rendering advice than heeding it, even from himself—which was actually a lucky thing for him, because Buck very authoritatively did not know what he was talking about. He had all the tools to be a great comedian, including some fabulous jokes and absolutely the best timing of anyone on the circuit; but knowing all that, he was too blinded by pride—some might say arrogance—to see that there was still more, much more, for him to learn. Unfortunately, the fact that comedy was going through a very mass-oriented, culturally fallow period (but then, what wasn't in the seventies: SEE Suits, leisure; Music, disco) fed Buck's weakness for blaming the audience instead of seeking to improve his own ability to communicate his ideas to them. Buck got mad at audiences the way John McEnroe scowled at linesmen, infuriated that people who could not even play the game were passing judgment on his artistry. When a joke bombed, Buck never thought it was because the joke just might not be that funny. He knew it was funny because—well, because it *was*, goddamnit! Who was the comedian around here, anyway? Plus, the other comedians laughed at it, and that was the ultimate proof.

It was also the ultimate trap. Getting mad at the crowd like Buck did was certainly not wise, but it wasn't the worst thing a comedian could do, either. Because just as apathy and not hatred is the opposite of love, so Buck's anger at least reflected his desire for the audience's approval, a desperate desire at that. Chink, on the other hand, was vulnerable to the pitfall of developing an act so highly pitched that only other dogs—the canine colleagues who honored one of their own by coming into the showroom to watch his set—could hear it. Chink was in the situation that Buck had recently been in himself: going on late every night and, in the absence of a viable audience, playing to those hounds in the back of the room who tended to howl loudest at what was rarefied and esoteric.

But if "band laughs" became more important than the laughs from a real audience, that was dangerous. Approval from the masses was akin to making the all-star team in baseball, where fan voting often resulted in ludicrous selections and the other players knew it; they knew it, but they still wished they'd made the team. Buck, who always wanted to make the team more than anything, did not want to become one of those old, bitter has-been comics he'd seen come into The Club from time to time, the ones who justified their failure as artistic martyrdom and survived on strokes from within the fraternity—yes, a comic's comic, a guy the other comics, who were rich and famous now, told stories about: how great he was, and what a shame he never got the recognition he deserved.

In comedy, camaraderie could kill you. Around The Club, it was already comedically correct to agree that Chink was a genius, but Buck's instincts told him that was a dangerous word in his business. Thank God, he thought, that so few of his peers had yet to hang that albatross of a label around his neck— although how anyone couldn't see that he was a genius, too, he'd never know.

"Look, I'm not saying we have to like it," Buck continued. "Sometimes I want to tell those fucking people, 'Hey, if you don't get it, fine, don't laugh—but don't boo like it's my fault, because it isn't.' "

"You *do* tell them that," Chink reminded.

"Yeah, well . . . I shouldn't. And you shouldn't."

"I don't."

"I know. I know you don't, I'm just saying, I know the frustration, because we're trying to be artists, right? But art is something that realizes its greatest potential when it's daring, when it's doing something new. But when experimentation is interpreted as failure . . ."

"We're fucked."

"Bad timing. You know, there used to be a comedy club *called* the Vanguard—that was actually a selling point! Can you imagine how great it must have been back then?"

"No," Chink said. "I can't. In the restaurant of life, someone always orders for me."

"People wanted to be challenged back then," Buck went on. "Oh, by the way, I meant to tell you, I heard that John Connally thing last night, it's great."

"That's new. You like that?"

"Hysterical. Except, of course, they don't know who he is, or they kind of know, but they don't see the essence of him, the Texas-size ego—your thing is that he thought Oswald was shooting at *him*, right?"

"Yeah. Oswald hits Kennedy, and Connally goes, 'Whew, they missed me.' "

"That's great. But I don't think it'll ever work."

Chink sighed internally, then asked: "You think it really used to be different? I mean, everything looks better when . . . you're not alive for it."

"I don't know. But yeah, I think there used to be a stand-up element that was more like jazz—jazz, you know, it's not a mass thing, but a small, loyal audience in a big country, that's plenty. Jazz guys do their thing for their crowd and they make good money, not Barry Manilow money, but good, and everybody's happy. Even musicals, really, same thing—there's stuff for that vast, unreasoning beast, the public, but then there's Sondheim. He's got his crowd, so he doesn't have to change notes so the lowbrows will find it more hummable."

"I didn't know you liked Sondheim."

"I don't. I hate musicals," Buck stated as he swatted a fly away from his penis. "The point is, stand-up lost that crowd. I'm sure they're out there—I'm sure in New York City there's half a million people who would get that joke and love it and love you for telling it. But they're skeptical now. They're afraid a night at the comedy club is gonna be dominated by dickheads, and fuck 'em, they do have a point."

"We should, like, do comedy in a museum. I hear museums get a real egghead crowd."

"Art? Are you kidding? Talk about tunneling into your audience! The my-five-year-old-could-paint-that people just don't go to museums, period. I think maybe art can only really be art when you do it alone, like a painter or a sculptor or a writer— here it is, you don't like it, fine, I'll be in my loft not taking calls.''

Buck's voice began to rise in a combination of righteousness and the giddy sense a comic gets when a bit might be in the making. It certainly sounded like a bit, if the ''punching up'' of key words for comedic effect was any indication:

''I'd like to see what Picasso's stuff would look like if he had three hecklers in his studio going, 'More green, asshole!' ''

''But painters and writers suffer worse than we do.''

''They do?''

''Sure. Look at Van Gogh—never sold a painting while he was alive.''

''Exactly. When you work at the top of the art form, by the time everybody catches on, you're dead.''

The boys shut up for a minute and contemplated the depths of despair they'd talked themselves into. Then, as it always happened at the end of such a comedic complaint session, one of the comedians said:

''But, hey—I wouldn't want to do anything else!''

''Oh no, are you kidding, do something else?'' and they were back to the more pleasant terrain of discussing the great good fortune of having a license—nay, an obligation—to be young and silly forever.

''We have so much fucking fun and good times even when we're suffering,'' Buck concluded. ''It's so great when all your friends are comics and everybody is always funny. I don't know how anybody else can even live at all without that. Can you imagine always being with people who aren't funny? I'd die.''

As Buck wiped a tear from his heart, Shit returned from the bathroom. Chink could rest now, because with Shit's arrival, there was no longer any need for him to participate in the discussion of his own life.

''Why are you telling him to do the Chinese bit if he doesn't want to?'' Shit asked Buck.

''I'm not, I'm just saying I know it'll work.''

''He shouldn't do it if he doesn't believe in it,'' Shit commanded. Then he asked Chink what he planned to use for an opener.

"I was thinking about the Nazi bird-watcher thing," Chink answered.

"Oh brother." Buck sighed.

"What's that one?" Shit wanted to know.

"You know, that thing he does about everything in life tends toward entropy—the Nazi party started out as a bird-watching society."

"Oh, that's funny," Shit said.

"Entropy? In Baltimore? You gotta be kidding," Buck responded.

"Then say, 'Everything gets worse,' " Shit proposed.

"It's still too conceptual," Buck said.

"I'm not gonna change the wording," Chink said softly.

"Have you tried 'big cock'?" Shit asked.

3

It's a Living Hell, but It's a Living

In Wilmington, Dick and Fat were sharing a joint with a cab driver on the way to the Executive Inn, a motel that claimed it was a hotel and would be home to the chums for the next forty-four hours. All comedians relished the thought of staying in a hotel, for even the sleaziest fleabag would almost certainly constitute a jump in living standards from their New York digs. Hotels had clean sheets, air-conditioning, color TV, fresh towels, strong water pressure and, sometimes, cute young maids, whom Dick tried to fuck, and sometimes did.

But hotels were already getting to be a luxury of increasing rarity on the road. The ever frugal club owners attempted to save money by hosteling the comedians almost anywhere else, including their homes, their bartenders' homes, their mothers' homes and, in one instance, their bartender's garage—converted into an "apartment" by placing a velveteen portrait on the oil-stained wall where a tire used to hang and accessed, of course, by raising from floor to ceiling one complete wall of the "apartment."

Mostly, however, club owners found the acquisition of a condominium to be the most economical answer to the problem of housing a different trio of comedians every week. In each city, the owner referred to the condominium as the comedy condo. And although a condominium might sound pleasant enough, the thought of sleeping on a bed used exclusively by other young comedians is—well, it's not so much a thought as an emetic; to say nothing of the rest of the condo, which is precisely what deserves to be said about it. Nothing—and its companion, nothingness—accurately describes the amount and flavor of the furniture and decor in the living quarters, which is just as well, since young comedians would only vaporize whatever wood or metal fibers existed there anyway. Club owners may be cheap and sleazy—and they are—but comedians, when in an environment owned by someone else, wield a destructive power four times that of the Hiroshima blast. After a year of such habitation nothing can live in a comedy condo; salt is sown into the carpet. And the newest waitress at the club, whose extra duty it is to clean the condo on Sunday after the last batch of comics has left, takes one look around upon seeing it for the first time and throws herself out the ten-story window, never wondering if she made the right decision.

But for this two-day gig, Dick and Fat would live in middling luxury, clean and quiet behind the DO NOT DISTURB signs and left to their own devices, which, incidentally, took up half the space in Dick's traveling duffel bag.

Shit, Chink, and Buck—they would get a condo.

"Baltimore!"

Now it was the turn of the Baltimore three to wait for the standard comedy club pick-up-at-the-train-station ride that never materialized. Time after time, the various young comedians were promised rides from the various old club owners, and time after time they believed them, even though no solid evidence of an actual ride had ever been recorded. There were various sightings of rides, and certain comics that everyone suspected of being half crazy insisted they had caught a glimpse of a 1971 Dodge Dart that they say was driven by an employee of a club, but these stories came to be regarded as apocryphal, and no government agency would corroborate the existence of such a ride.

So Buck, Shit, and Chink got into a cab and headed for the comedy condo that would be their home for the next two days. With the impeccable inefficiency they had come to expect from out-of-town clubs, the boys did not find the key to the condo in its assigned hiding place, under the welcome mat—what criminal would think to look there?—and had to call the club and wait for its delivery.

Once inside, the boys flipped a coin to see who would shower first, and the loser, Chink, then donned a gas mask and braved a first look at the bathroom. Outside of a layer of dirt around the sink that had been roped off by paleontologists so they could study the Pleistocene-era fossils embedded therein, and several monsters, the bathroom seemed condo-normal, and Chink emerged to signal the all-clear. Shit took a nap.

In the living room, Buck called Pussy the minute after the minute it looked to Chink like it was the first thing on his mind. To Buck's dismay, Pussy's number was no longer in operation. Buck called information and asked the operator to look under new listings. In another minute, he heard Pussy's voice. With his face, he asked Chink for some privacy.

"I got your letter," Pussy told Buck. "You're so sweet."

Buck smiled. He took satisfaction in the knowledge that his amatory missives could wetten panties from great distances. But there would be no more smiling for Buck.

"I'm not working at the club anymore," Pussy reported. "I'm living with a guy."

Buck was stunned. He had missed his chance, and now there would not be another. He pretended to be happy for her, and was so completely convincing that she believed him. He told her to keep in touch, meaning Keep in touch if your boyfriend is killed in a soccer riot.

Then Buck thought of the letter he had sent to her, and his face got hot. It seemed now a terribly pretentious letter, a letter in which, between smarmy blandishments, he had informed Pussy, via annoyingly clever innuendo and suggestive japes, that he was now ready to consummate their friendship. The time had not been right for them before, he said, but now, like a proud sexual MacArthur, he had decided to return. The nature of the letter was such that if someone had found it lying on the floor of a bus station—and by this time someone may very well have found it lying on the floor of a bus station—he would have guessed upon perusal that Warren Beatty was responding to some infatuated fan who had enclosed a snapshot of her naked self, along with a plea that he write back and arrange an appointment in his busy schedule when he might ravish her.

Buck felt awful. The disappointment, the letter—and now the thought of Pussy getting constantly fucked by yet someone else. It was enough to give a man another large, hard, insistent erection.

At 8 P.M., in the lobby of the Executive Inn, Dick, Fat, and the middle act, Nick Marley, a sad-sack comic from Washington who would be Fat's roommate for the weekend, waited for the arrival of their ride over to the club. It was precisely on club-owner time, which is to say a half hour late or moments from when the show must begin, whichever comes first. And still there was another delay.

The car that was dispatched was a two-seater, and it came with the explanation that a ride to the club was something provided only for the headliner. Dick, being the headliner, smiled and walked out of the lobby with the driver. Fat felt betrayed—until he realized that Dick had gone outside in order to throw a proper tantrum, screaming that he would wait with his friends for a ride they could share or just as happily get back on the train. There were few enough times when a comedian had any leverage over a club owner, so when something like this happened shortly before a weekend show was about to begin, it was too good an opportunity not to act like the prima donna they all wished they could always act like. A phone call quickly produced the owner's lime-green Eldorado, which seemed to have no other use at the time anyway.

The indignity of the episode irked Fat continuously during the ride over to the club, but the magnificence of the room when they arrived must have made him forget his anger as he got right down to the business of kissing Mr. Scuzzoli's ass. Dino immediately, and with genuine pride, pointed out to Dick the improvements that had been made in the club since Dick had been there last—brightly colored balloons festooned nearly several inches of the ceiling behind the bar, and posters of

Groucho Marx, W. C. Fields, and another one of Groucho adorned part of the wall where Dino had run out of bricks and begun to use cement blocks instead.

Truly, Dino had created a party atmosphere.

Soon the show began. Fat trod the stage first, without the benefit of an introduction. As if walking onto a stage cold in a strange city as a total unknown wasn't hard enough, Dino had cued him to begin without remembering to simultaneously cut the recorded music that played before the show, so poor Fat was left to stand helplessly onstage while Dino ambled to the soundboard and leisurely faded out the Frank Sinatra rendition of "New York, New York." It was Dino's favorite record, and as of this night, he had played it one million times.

Thus Fat began the show with people laughing *at* him, a theme he did his best to maintain throughout his self-deprecating performance.

"Hi, I'm a fat guy!" he began, throwing his lot in with connoisseurs of the obvious. Fat was well served by the fact that he both knew where his bread was buttered and in his life had buttered a lot of bread. The audience took a natural liking to Fat as he regaled them with tales of the obese, straying from that subject only long enough to strike the leitmotif of his comic symphony, a discussion of obesity's natural companion, sweat. A visitor from another land not steeped in the culture of American comedy might have wondered how an audience could laugh at someone who was, after all, relating moment after pitiful moment of a life left bereft of joy by this awful affliction.

But unless Dino were to open a club in Tibet, it was not likely the issue would be raised.

> *Sorry I'm late. I was standing around outside and got arrested for unlawful assembly.*
>
> *I know—you're thinking, This guy looks like a turd a giant laid.*
>
> *Hey, any other fat people here tonight? No, don't stand up!*
>
> *People hate us, right? Isn't that true? It is, it's true. People hate fat people, people hate people who are fat.*

People look at me, and I know they're thinking, Hey, stand back, he might belch up a picnic ham!

Okay, I did that a few times—but just around my family.

My family hated me, too. They're all skinny. That's very rare, you know—fat people usually come from other fat people—but my mother's skinny, my father's skinny, my brother's skinny—well, he was, I sat on him.

He made me run away from home, because he was always teasing me. It's true. He was even teasing me as I was going out the window. He said, "Better take the truck route!"

No, it's true. People don't want to look at us, either. That's absolutely true. Either they don't want to look at us, or they STARE! "Wow . . . look at that, Wilma, he's . . . fat. He seems to be carrying a coupla hunderd extra layers around his middle there . . ."

Hey, we're fat—we're not deaf, dumb, and blind!

But you know how fat people always try to tell you that they're fat because of some medical reason or a thyroid or something? It's all bullshit! They're fat because they eat like fucking pigs!

I admit it—I do like to eat. I usually get up for lunch around six-thirty.

You know what my favorite food is? Thirds.

Hey, I gotta go, but remember, you may like me now, but you'll hate me tomorrow if I try to sit next to you on the bus!

Fat bellowed his traditional closing line and then added, "Thank you, you've been a great crowd," to let the assembly know that his portion of the show was over. Sure enough, he was rewarded by a warm round of applause from the near-capacity first show Friday crowd. He beamed with great satisfaction while the applause washed over him, knowing he had acquitted himself admirably on his first out-of-town gig. Then he introduced Nick and ran offstage to find Dick.

Dick was chatting up some of the distaff staff at the club and, to Fat's monumental disappointment, hadn't heard a word he'd uttered onstage. Dick promised to listen at the next show and assuaged Fat's disappointment by telling him: "I don't have to watch, I knew you'd do great."

Fat liked that a lot. He smiled and felt close to Dick. Dick's eyes seemed to say the same thing to Fat, although his mouth said, "Get lost while I'm talking to this waitress, or I'll stab you with a knife."

Okay, okay—I can take a direct threat, Fat thought, and went off to watch the middle act.

The middle act was not doing too well; Fat was elated. What could be better than scoring big *and* seeing a colleague stumble? Then Dick came by, after a small ceremony to mark the one-thousandth time he'd gotten a waitress fired for flirting when she should have been serving drinks. The chums discussed the middle act's problem in the manner in which all young comedians offer instant critiques of their colleagues, unless the colleague is standing nearby, in which case they say, "Good set." Dick asserted that Nick's mistake was in failing to give the audience enough time to switch gears after enjoying Fat. He explained to Fat that it took time and a bit of patience to reorient the crowd to a new performer, especially if they had enjoyed the last one.

"They're a dog, and you're the new mailman," began the barrage of metaphor. "They act like they're gonna bite you, but if you just let 'em sniff you out and bark a little, in about a minute they're on their backs saying, 'Hey, stranger, rub my balls.' "

Fat liked this kind of talk—talk about show business and balls, with comparisons and everything.

"Yeah, right. Like, if you don't bother them, they won't bother you," he offered.

"That's bees," Dick said, hiccupping a laugh at the tyro's lame attempt to join in the fun of connecting two disparate thoughts. Then Dick returned to ground that was always fertile for analogy-reaping.

"An audience is like a woman," he declared. "They want to get fucked, but you gotta put up with a little bullshit first. Girls don't go, 'Great, we both like Chinese food, let's fuck,' and audiences don't laugh at the first joke. Which is why the first bit you do—you know, don't waste something really good. It's a sacrifice bunt.''

"Yeah, right," Fat ad-libbed as he chewed on this valuable new information. Then he added: "Huh?"

"Well," Dick expanded, "an audience and a woman—they both want you to succeed. They know they'll have a better time if they get conquered, but you still have to earn it.''

"Ah-hah." Fat nodded knowingly. He now had enough little learning to be a dangerous thing.

Dick recognized his obligation to elucidate further. "Women want you to call their bluff. A good-looking girl gets hit on about a thousand times a minute, right? So she acts like a cunt to find out who's man enough to take her shit. It's a test for us. Kinda like we do when you suspect a crowd might be stupid, so you put in a little test joke up front, something that requires a little intelligence to get.''

No, Fat did not know about this . . . this test joke of which the learned tribal chieftain spoke.

"Yeah, so then if they don't get it," Dick continued, "you say, okay, this is Jersey-gig time, better stick with real basic shit.''

Here was yet another valuable tip for a novice comedian, one that could spare him grief and succor his progress.

"How do you pass the woman test?" Fat asked, anxious to get back to more important matters.

"By completely ignoring everything she says," replied N.O.W.'s man of the year for 1979.

"Perfect example: Philadelphia," Dick continued. "Hey, you taking notes?" he kidded.

But it was no joke to Fat, who'd already ripped open the back-to-school supply pack he'd been toting in readiness for this very event: a babe-procurement seminar from Dick! Gosh, was there any more renowned professor of pussy than he, or one whose emeritus had seen more action?

"So it's the second show Saturday," Dick went on. "I'm killing, did like an hour—"

"Get to the part about the girl. I wanna hear about the girl!" Fat demanded, as he stuck a big toe through the hole in his

feety pajamas and pulled the covers tight up to his chin and
didn't feel a bit tired anymore now that he was going to hear a
story.

"She's in the front row. Perfect everything. The kind of hard
little tits I love, total knockout, did not belong in Philadelphia
at all. The bad news is she knew it. Comes on at first like she's
thrilled to meet me, then puts me through her private little hell
for—I don't know, it seemed like days. But I knew I was gonna
fuck her because, okay, one, she wanted to get fucked and she
didn't have a boyfriend—not that having a boyfriend would
have stopped her from fucking somebody if she wanted to—
but for a girl like this not to have a date on Saturday night
was like, I don't know, like when all the planets line up or
something—the next occurrence would be in 2049."

"But—"

"And two, she had real long hair. Down to her ass. That's
a sure sign you'll get in her pants."

Fat was so impressed by this Holmesian display of chick-
deducing that he could barely formulate his queries into a coherent sentence.

"Uhajlskjdfl? Whalsglgfslskfdjlskfdj?" he asked.

"Because keeping your hair that long has got to be a huge
pain, right?"

"Flsjnfdmne. Bslslknlelll?"

"Because that's exactly why she does it. The main difference
between men and women is, women don't communicate in
actual words like we do. That would be too easy, and we're
already doing it, so they have to do something different to make
things as difficult as possible, so they communicate in signals."

"Nlskdkjlkgjls?"

"Both. They want us to ignore what they say, but also to
pick up on whatever they're really transmitting over Radio
Chick."

"Hjlasf thasdf sfdppoo?!"

"Okay, I'm getting to that. It's the same as wearing high
heels. Every man should wear high heels for one night. It'd
make you remember that women are really full of shit and just
want to get laid, because you wouldn't do that to your feet
unless the most important thing in your whole fucking life was

making men want to fuck you. And the same goes for wasting three hours every day drying your fucking hair.''

''—''

''Which is proven by the opposite—the married babe who gets that unbelievably short haircut after about the first two years, when she's tried everything she can think of to get her husband to start screwing her again but he still won't, so she gets a crewcut except no butchwax just to say, 'Fuck you. If you don't want to fuck anymore, I might as well look like this.' It's all signals with women. Just think of them like the coast guard.''

''But what happened in Philadelphia?!'' Fat asked the story-teller, as the campfire cast a reddish hue on his fleshy face, which was already quite red on its own without any help from campfires.

''So I say, 'Let's go somewhere and have a drink.' She says no. Okay, so I make up some more conversation until it's time to ask again. She says no again. Okay, fine, she wants more bullshit. I know the game, see if I have more bullshit in me than she has no's in her—and I can tell she has a lot. Most women do, 'cause that's their job, that's the basic command in the Woman Program, to say no, no, no. But I know she also wants to get laid, because women always want to get laid, even more than we do, which is why the control they have that we don't even try to have is so amazing.''

''Golly, Dr. Love!'' said the wide-eyed youth as he listened in rapture while Mr. Rockwell—the artist, not the Nazi—commenced sketching the scene for *The Saturday Evening Post*. ''If women really crave a hard dick pumping pistonlike inside them until tears of joy stain their cheeks—well, gee whiz, where do they get the strength to say no?''

''From a unique priority system, which they absorb, osmosislike, from early childhood, on their planet. To a woman, the most important thing is to not feel like a slut.''

''Wow!'' goshed Fat, too much in awe to notice the other boys around the campfire being sodomized by savage mountain men. The hoary but wise holy man continued his lesson to the portly pilgrim, now made even more humble by the guru's words than when he had started his journey up the mountain.

"The key to success is virtue—the virtue of patience. Man waits for woman. He is practiced in bullshit. He feigns great interest during insufferable detailing of matters that could only interest another chick. He does not count the no's, even though they may be one hundred, for ultimately the woman will say to herself, 'Okay, I tried. I said one hundred no's. Surely no one will now say, 'She is a slut who too easily jumped into bed,' so can we please get it on, because if you don't stick it into me soon I'm gonna do it to myself with a pointy shoe.' "

"I will remember patience, master. It sounds *too* easy, though, if you want to know the truth."

"Well, you know, sometimes patience means buying dinner or something," the shaman intoned, concluding his sermon. "But that's the great thing about being a comedian. You can always say you never eat before a show."

Fat practically flew onto the stage for his introduction of Dick, he had so much to be happy about: He had outdone the middle act, he had found out how to get laid, and he had learned what a metaphor was. All in all, quite a night.

Dick took the stage to a typically tepid, road club so-who-the-fuck-are-you? round of applause. Then, in a perfect illustration of the lecture he had just given Fat, Dick charmed his way through ten minutes of people returning from the bathrooms, talking loudly, and trying to figure out who ordered "tax" on the check.

But Dick let them be rude to him, and when the audience again found their focus for comedy, they discovered onstage a genial, amusing young man who seemed happy and grateful to be before them. And when Dick finally picked up the guitar that had been leaning against the wall behind him, he set in motion a closing ten-minute segment that had this disgusting little rathskeller on a sidestreet in Wilmington, Delaware, rocking with laughter.

A strange and inscrutable phenomenon, laughter: When everyone in the room is doing it, everyone seems to enjoy it immeasurably more than when the verdict is less than unanimous. Laughing alone can be kind of sad; but a unanimous laugh produces not only the good feeling from the laugh itself but an unconscious joy from the audience that they are all agreeing on something—that two hundred people who undoubtedly could never agree on anything else have all found a common bond in something that *that* guy just said. And that is a good feeling—to say nothing of the feeling that guy gets from having caused it.

Which is mostly why he stands up there in the first place.

A lot of people think teenagers today are having sex too early. There's a couple in my building, they start at 9 A.M.—that's too early.

The woman is not ready at 9 A.M. The MAN is ready at 9 A.M. This is an amazing fact of life for a man—that our penises—or is it peni?—get happy at the worst times. The morning is not a good time for sex. She's sleeping, and all of a sudden—hello! "Did I just roll over onto a meat thermometer?"

So now you've got to get her excited in her sleep, and who wants to do that? You have breath like Yogi Berra's jockstrap, shit in your eyes, you gotta take a piss now— which is a big decision, do you get up and take the piss, or do you fuck with that nice piss hard-on and then watch your bladder explode after you come?

Men have no penis control. It's a tragedy, because we get blamed for stuff we can't help. I bet every guy here has had that experience where you're consoling a woman, and she's crying, so you're consoling her, and you're hugging her, and you get like a . . . grief-on? And this, of course, pisses her off . . .

And we're like, "Honey, I'm sorry. I couldn't help it. In my head, I feel really bad . . . down here, I feel a little better . . . no, really, I think it's horrible your mother died—here, lemme help you off with your bra."

We're always struggling against each other. You're doing it here tonight. The men are trying to get the women drunk so they'll get looser and hornier . . . and the women are watching the men drink, 'cause they know alcohol

*takes the starch out of your woody . . . so at the end of
the night, she's so drunk she wants it, and he's so drunk
he can't give it to her . . .*

Yeah, 2 A.M. in a bar—love at last sight . . .

*I miss the sixties. Anybody remember the sixties? Well,
then you didn't have a good enough time.*

*The first girl I ever slept with was a hippie. I'll never
forget the first time we were in bed, and she said—in that
real hippie voice—"When we make love, there's no you
and no me—it's like our bodies are one continuous being."*

*I said, "Okay, but how about paying some attention to
OUR dick?"*

In Maryland, things were not so unanimous. Although the
first show had gone reasonably well, second shows on Friday
were universally dreaded by comedians, and for good reason:
The late Friday audience was legendary for unruly behavior,
being both drunk and cranky from having already put in a full
day of work and a full night of drinking. Now they were up
past their bedtime and this, combined with the peculiar psychology of Friday—the end of the week, the time you get rowdy
and go a little nuts—produced a rabble particularly unenter-
tainable for a monologuist. If Ernest Hemingway had chosen
to limn the world of stand-up comedy instead of bullfighting,
he could have described any Friday second show at any comedy
club in the United States and not lost any of the mano-a-mano
flavor that signs his work.

Onstage for only five minutes, Chink was already being eaten
alive. There was a vicious heckler to his right, a redneck wiseass
in the back, and a drunken, amiable middle-aged woman up
front who had no idea she was carrying on a distracting, continuous private conversation with the performer. Fortunately, she
was mostly drowned out by the unabated, deafening chatter of
the bachelorette party, sixteen strong, to the left. It was the
grassy knoll, the book depository, the motel balcony, and the
box at the Ford Theater all rolled into one. It was a comedian's

nightmare, assuaged only by the fact that no one would ever be expected to produce anything resembling stand-up comedy in such a pandemonium.

Which is why Buck couldn't believe it when he saw Shit getting out *The New York Times*. Shit had never been a practitioner of political material, but then again he had never been a lot of things that he suddenly became as a result of being the one thing he always was: a searcher. And lately his search had led him to the practice of reading from the newspaper onstage, then commenting on it. It was a noble experiment, in the grandest tradition of humorists like Mort Sahl and Will Rogers, who maintained that nothing a comedian could say was funnier than what was actually in the newspaper.

Unfortunately for Shit, the crowd in Baltimore agreed with that: Nothing he said was funnier than what was in the newspaper. Even if Shit had been a crackerjack jokesmith who could zip off a dozen funny lines from the front page—and he definitely was not—this exercise would have been doomed to failure. It was the exact wrong bit for the exact wrong show in the exact wrong city in the exact wrong era *to be even thinking about doing!* Great suffering Christ, man, it's 1979! People don't read the newspaper anymore, they don't care what's going on in the world, and they certainly don't think, 'Oh good—entertainment!' when they see a guy onstage pull out the fucking *newspaper!*

And even Will Rogers knew enough to close with rope tricks.

Buck was his usual sensitive self in imparting this viewpoint to Shit: "Jesus, you're not gonna do that newspaper shit, are you?"

"Why not?"

"You gotta be kidding. You are kidding with that, right?"

"I'm not kidding. You don't think it can work?"

"The newspaper? Yeah, it could work—if you make a hat out of it or cut it up in little strips for a magic trick."

"Well, I think they'll come up to the level of comedy you give them."

"Come up to the level of comedy? Are you getting this out of a manual? Pally, this room is not easy under the best conditions."

"Meaning I have no chance whatsoever," Shit said, hurt.

"No, it's not that." Buck softened. "I know you can make the paper thing work, but maybe at a more appropriate time. I mean, did you see the room? It's . . . Vietnam."

"Well, then lock and load."

And off he went. There was no talking Shit out of doing anything he had a mind to do; Shit was, after all, Irish. He had Irish charm up the ass, but up there with it was a large building or a refrigerator or whatever it is that Irish people have up their asses that makes them so prickly. Shit never took any shit—real or imagined—and whether the shit in question was, in fact, real shit or imagined shit, was very often the provenance of arguments he had with Buck.

That, and Buck's legendary sensitivity. Poor Buck. No matter how nice a guy he really was, he'd always have plenty of detractors, owing to a congenital tragedy: He was born without a mechanism to tell him when he was being an asshole. Although this condition had come to be more accepted in modern America, what with its large attorney, salesman, and now co-median population, from Buck it still engendered enmity. He never meant to hurt, but if a group as abrasive as young comedians found him insensitive, he knew he must be doing something wrong. He just never knew when he was doing it.

Like his crack to Shit on the train: "You're just mad because you're middling for me." It never dawned on Buck that co-headlining with someone who until recently was more a mentor than a peer indicated a transition in the relationship requiring a little tact. At twenty-four, Buck was no more sensitive to Shit's ego in this matter than he had been at twelve, when he beat his father at golf for the first time: He gloated, he reveled in his victory, and he never gave a thought to the fact that a dad might feel bad after losing to his own kid.

As Shit began his opening remarks to the disinterested audience, Buck paced in the back like a fight manager who knows his boy is in for a beating. Not that a boxing ring would have been much more inappropriate a place to read from *The New York Times*.

Christ, at least use the local paper!

But then Buck quickly realized that he was worrying about

nothing. Shit was not going to bring out the newspaper after all.

He was going to walk off!

Buck had seen that look in his eye before. The Irish take-no-shit look. Shit was always gracious if people didn't laugh, but rudeness was something else.

A bulldog face came over him. He looked like Churchill. And the behavior of this crowd was something up with which he would not put.

Now, to walk offstage from an impossible crowd was not an uncommon practice at The Club, where there were a dozen other comics on hand to fill the gap, and what are they gonna do, dock you the three bucks cab fare? But on the road . . .

Oh, don't do it, man. Just stay up there, just stand there if you have to!

Which is what Shit was now doing. Standing there, arms folded, like a schoolmarm waiting for the class to notice the presence of a teacher and quickly come to order. Shit waited for quiet, apparently unaware that on this night quiet had made a reservation under the name Godot, party of one. Finally, he deigned to speak.

"Look, folks, I can't do my show for you like this. I can't hear myself, and if I can't hear myself, I have no timing, and without timing, all I have is . . ."

"Brilliant material!"

Well, that was a friend. Shit couldn't help cracking a smile at Buck's show of support from the back of the room. But his mood was not leavened, certainly not enough for him to begin doing his job. Shit asked the audience why they had paid a cover charge only to talk to each other, then gave the Virgin Mary another thirty seconds to work a miracle.

Buck ran over to the bartender, the only official of the club he could find. Where was Harvey? He wasn't around. Weren't there any bouncers? No. Can't you do something? No, too busy exacerbating the problem by getting people drunker.

Now Shit was sitting on the stool, arms still folded. A few people in the room yelled, "Shut up!" which had a calming effect on other members of the audience, the ones who broke off from potentially violent marital squabbles to yell, "Why don't *you* shut up?!"

Shit looked at his watch one last time. He rose from his seat, waved to the crowd, and walked to the back of the room. There were some boos, some applause, and a lot of people who never knew he was up there to begin with.

Buck immediately began tightening his sphincter muscles in a vain effort to forestall shitting in his pants. Because now he would have to do a very long show—an hour at least—and he remembered how well the last hour-long show had gone. And those people in Montreal weren't out of hand like this crowd. Johnny Cash had never played to a crowd like this.

How could he do this to me, Buck thought—especially when he knows how hard Montreal was! Oh, that's right, he doesn't know. I lied about that. Gee, sometimes lying *is* bad.

Buck quickly grabbed Chink and ordered him, in no uncertain terms, to do the Chinese-talking bit. All that talk about theory and artistic purity on the train just seemed like so much hot air now. Chink didn't argue.

And Shit didn't apologize, which enraged Buck all the more.

"Thanks a lot. I've got to do the whole show now," Buck snarled as Shit passed him on the way out.

"No you don't," Shit countered. "I'll take responsibility for my actions. You don't have to do any more than you normally would."

"Oh yeah, and wind up with a total show of fifty minutes?"

"Hey, look, that's not our fault. If they can't police the room here, that's their problem."

"Tell that to Harvey—you know, sometime when he's not wearing the gun."

"I'll tell it to him anytime. Where is he?"

"He's not here."

"Exactly. He's the one who's not doing his job, not us."

"What do you mean *us*? I'm the one who has to do an hour now!"

"Do what you want, but don't blame it on me. I'll see you back at the condo."

And with that he was gone. There was just no talking to Shit when he thought he was right, which was anytime he spoke about something. With Shit and Buck, it seemed there was just never enough "right" to go around.

Buck looked up to see Chink actually getting a decent laugh with the bit he so hated, and then even milk it a little. That was encouraging, to see that Chink could behave like a cornered dog and fight. So much for art, Buck thought—you want art, buy a painting. This is war.

Boy, was it ever. After the Nazi bird-watcher bit, complete with entropy—like it mattered—the room looked like gym class on a rainy day. Buck had no doubts that this show would be pure "playing the dozens."

Which, truth be told, was not the worst thing that could happen to Buck. The shotgun approach he usually took to his sets at The Club, letting banter with the crowd lead him into set routines, was actually better suited to this kind of a crowd—although not to such an extreme degree—than a quiet, model audience. Buck professed great displeasure at having to get nasty with a nasty group, but when it came to combat comedy, Buck liked having a reputation: the Sundance Kid running out into the village square with both six-shooters blazing.

Buck stood at the back of the room, out of view, and studied a well-worn three-by-five card that he always kept with him for just such occasions. On the card in tiny print were dozens of insults, ripostes, put-downs, comebacks, and other comedy ammunition that would make a good ad-libber seem like a great ad-libber. As Chink slinked off, Buck squinted hard in one last burst of concentration to commit his roster of odium to memory. As he did, he thought of the peculiar circumstance of being in a profession where he was called upon to do his best to remember every unkind thing he'd ever thought of.

It was an ugly job, but somebody had to do it.

And do it and do it and do it!

When your IQ hits fifty, sell . . . I wish we had a prize for you, but the wizard already gave the brain to the scarecrow . . . are you retarded or just auditioning for

the dinner-theater company of Deliverance*? . . . What,*
*did you douche with Mace tonight? (*females only*) . . .*
you turn a lot of heads—and a lot of stomachs . . . do
you have to take a shit or are they paging queers? . . .
that's what I say when I'm as fucked up as you . . . you
must really crack up your bowling team . . . you think
this guy ever heard the words license and registration*?*
. . . it must be tough going through martini with-
drawal. . . . Do you unplug the phone to watch cartoons?
. . . Do you yell at the screen at the movies, too? . . . I
won't dignify that by being able to think of an answer to
*it (*self-deprecation, to keep them honest*) . . . sorry, I*
*couldn't hear you, your dick was in your mouth (*vulgarity,
to keep them honest*). . . . You've got an open mind—I*
can feel the draft from here . . . insulting you is about as
tough as beating an amputee at hopscotch . . . it's okay,
you lost your head—but don't worry, you won't miss
*it. . . . Drinking for two? (*pregnant women only*) . . . if*
I want any more shit out of you, I'll squeeze your head . . .
you don't have a speaking part in this production . . . my
foot just fell asleep, and if you keep talking the rest of me
is likely to follow suit . . . I hold you in contempt, as I
assume everyone here does . . . you're a pain in the neck
and probably a lot lower . . . I've met a lot of people in
my day, and you're not one of them . . . you have a ready
wit, tell us when it's ready . . . if I've insulted you, please,
believe me . . . when this guy goes through lion-country
safari, the animals roll up their windows . . . if I wanted
to talk to a turd, I'd install a pay phone in my toilet . . .
why don't you talk to yourself in the bathroom—it's the
door marked GENTLEMEN*, but don't let that deter you . . .*
you could walk into an empty room and blend right in . . .
why don't you let that cut under your nose heal? . . . Will
Rogers would hate this man . . . look, I know your mouth
isn't the biggest cavity in your head, but right now it's
making the most noise . . . did your mother take a lot of
acid during pregnancy? . . . nice to see people of your
heritage sitting up . . . ad-libbing's not for everyone,
sir . . . look, do I come down to your job and knock the

guy's dick out of your ass? (cleaner version: knock the paper trainee hat off your head?) . . . *I've got an hour up here to make a jerk of myself, and you've got the rest of your life . . . there's a show somewhere in this room, see if you can find it . . .*

Whether it had been a *show* was debatable. But the audience did find something in Buck's battle cry that brought diversion to the end of their work week. As he got off to a loud, whistling ovation, it was as if they were saying to him, " 'Tis cold, and we are sick at heart. For this relief, much thanks."

Yeah, right. Anyway, they liked him, presumably for upholding the great American virtues of working hard, winning, and giving the people what they want.

What Buck and Chink wanted now was food, so they repaired to the bar area to devour the cold cheeseburgers that owner Harvey Karrakarrass insisted, after such a difficult night, would be on the house.

"Talk about perks!" Buck bellowed as he bit into the week-old meat. "Harvey, you're a prince."

Buck was still on as he watched Chink, who had loyally held off from eating until Buck finished onstage, inhale half the patty on the first try.

"Hey, pal, we're not on death row here. There'll be more ground chuck in your career."

Just then Harvey Karrakarrass himself ambled by, all swarthy behemoth of him, his massive belly hanging over his belt, his massive gun visible beneath his massive jacket. Harvey envisioned himself as one of those tough-guy semigangster club-owner types, so there were always plenty of guns and cocaine around him—and in the case of the cocaine, especially around his nose. He sat down for a moment to lend his congratulations to the boys for toughing it out, and Buck launched into the argument that Shit would have launched into had Harvey been around earlier, an argument that comedians never won.

"Harvey, I'm glad you enjoy watching me literally fight for my life, but why don't you police the crowd a little and give us some help? You have a bouncer—let him bounce! What is it that has to happen in that room before you'll speak to someone? I get the feeling if someone emptied a forty-five in my direction, you'd just tap him on the shoulder and say, 'Excuse me, but we have to ask that you not fire directly at the comedians onstage, thank you.' ''

Harvey laughed and said nothing in his Baltimore accent. Not that Buck expected him to; Harvey was not Sergei Diaghilev. He had never claimed to be a patron of the arts, just a seller of drinks. And like so many other bar owners across the country now, he had discovered in the comedy boom a gimmick that drew drinking people to his pub in record numbers. That the gimmick was stand-up comedy was absolutely incidental, and if tarot readings or mud wrestling or John Dillinger's dick were found to better induce the locals into paying a cover and accepting a minimum, then comedy would quickly be a gone gimmick. It had not, in most of these joints, been the first gimmick tried, and after its inevitable run into the ground, it would not be the last.

"You boys want another burger?" Harvey offered, and the chums quickly accepted, only to discover that the kitchen had already closed. Thus all Buck and Chink were left with was another big-fish story about a club owner who had offered a second free burger. Harvey exited with a slap on the back for his hired guns and a wad of five thousand dollars, cash, in his pocket, a sum that would be garnered again tomorrow night, when a full twentieth of the weekend's take would be peeled off and divided among Buck, Shit, and Chink. At the door, Harvey said good night again, then spat on the floor of his own club.

As the bleary-eyed crowd now filed past where the two comedians were sitting, Buck knew he would have to make an effort to be nice. As draining as the performance had been, and as bored as Buck made himself look, inside he was basking in his semivictory, and he looked upon this single file of humanity like a Roman general reviewing a column of shackled Carthaginians brought back to Rome and paraded in tribute to a great conquest. As these new slaves trooped past Buck Baltimorus, each of them had something to say.

Invariably, it was the wrong thing.

"You were great," a couple in identical designer jeans

chorused to Buck upon their exit and then, upon spotting Chink inches away, added, "You were good, too."

Buck and Chink exchanged the look two cops meeting in the middle of the night give each other, a look that says, I know you know, and there's nothing to say. Then Buck broke into a laugh and affectionately tousled his young friend's hair.

"Don't you love that afterthought compliment? 'You were great—oh, and you existed too . . . loved your act—oh, and may I acknowledge that you'd fog up a mirror if given the opportunity.' People, huh?"

"The problem that won't go away," Chink chimed in, knowing that was where Buck was headed, since he never tired of saying it.

"I mean, are they trying to piss us off, or are they just glad to see me, because . . . but, no, they're . . . actually, they're trying to be nice, aren't they? Yeah, they are, they just don't have a clue what to say to a comedian," Buck continued.

"I like it when they tell you a joke that we can 'use,' " Chink said. "Yeah, I'm gonna use the one about ten niggers blowing the pope on a pile of dead babies when I audition for *The Tonight Show*."

"It's what girls say to you that really breaks your heart," Buck furthermored. "Or worse, when they don't say anything—you know, like when you bring a girl in to watch your set and then you get off and she doesn't say anything? I mean, you sit them down, you get them a drink, they watch nothing but you, spewing out opinions on everything from relationships to the Middle East, and then when you retrieve them, it's like you just . . . went away for twenty minutes. What, was I just in the bathroom for twenty minutes? Was I making a phone call? God, if a woman ever came up to me after a show and said, 'Hey, I just wanted to tell you you made me think differently about a few things,' I'd probably marry her right on the spot."

Just then a tall, anorexic blonde giggled and shot a water pistol at Buck and Chink on her way out of the club. Buck gave Chink his best Jack Benny take.

A man on his way out told Buck, "You were pretty good."

Buck said, "Thanks a lot, that's what I aim for."

Another man said to Buck, "I saw you before, and you told some of the same jokes."

Buck thought about explaining that it takes months for even a diligent comedian to come up with five new minutes of presentable material, and how sitting in a room and transforming a piece of blank paper into a piece of paper with a good joke on it was akin to turning a lump of coal into a diamond.

But he was tired, and just said, "Sorry."

The man nodded and asked, "Do you guys write your own material?"

No, a fairy brings it to my doorstep each morning! Buck didn't say.

A man said to Chink, "You had a bad crowd," which was not intended to be an insult but always sounded like one.

"Did you come here to watch the crowd or the comedian?" Buck always wanted to say.

Buck wanted to say a lot of things, but then again, he knew that he didn't have to be there to listen to all this. He wanted to be there, because he wanted more adulation, more praise, more stroking, and he especially hoped that the stroking would come from a pretty girl who had fallen in love with him and wanted to fuck him because he was funny.

Instead, a middle-aged woman told Buck and Chink she thought they were geniuses and that she had never laughed so hard in her life. Then her husband said, "You guys was funnier than shit," and she got hysterical and said she thought her husband should be a comedian, too.

And so left another satisfied customer, illustrating the paradox of anything done well: When you make it look easy, they think it is. Of course, the people in an audience have no obligation to know, any more than comedians would care to learn the nuts and bolts of smelting or insurance, what goes into forming the final, slick presentation they see. And so few of them read the *World Book Encyclopedia* entry on:

COMEDY, STAND-UP—

Step 1. Raw humor is mined by the comedian in two ways: the "hard way," i.e., by deliberately setting time aside to write jokes upon a daunting blank page; and the "easy way," i.e., by spontaneous and informal socializing, with the hoped-for result that among the outpouring of cocktail-party wit—the knack, and joy, of producing which is what encouraged the jokesmith to try and be a professional in the first place—there will be something said that might actually be conducive for public ingestion. The first method requires diligence, the second, vigilance: the vigilance to capture those butterflylike ideas which fly out of the brain and are forever gone if not immediately mounted upon the nearest napkin.

Step 2. From a shoe box of napkins, the raw humor is next subjected to a rigorous winnowing process, wherein 50 to 90 percent of it is discarded by the laughmeister. Among the sludge and unusable byproducts are notes which are no longer legible, or which were recorded in too short a shorthand and now make no sense; ideas that seemed like gold in the giddy, sometimes drug-hued atmosphere of creation, but now, upon sifting through the sieve of sobriety, are found to contain only a small amount of gold, some pyrite, and about a ton of dirt; and notes that are useless because they are dirty, local, or too "inside."

Step 3. Here the giggleworker takes what is finally left to him as unalloyed fodder for the stage and works on forging it into the proper construction. For example, a joke must be told so that what's funny about it comes out all at once, at the end: a joke is like a balloon that is inflated in the set-up and popped suddenly for the punchline; a slow leaking of the air will destroy the effect. But that is not the only thing that can destroy an otherwise funny idea: as a sculptor should use no excess clay, a composer no extra notes, a writer no superfluous, flabby, verbose, redundant wording, so the witmoil must pare his wording down to only what is essential. Conversely, if the jacka-napes omits a key word or phrase, his efforts can also be undone. As all of us probably know from occasionally attempting to re-create a japesmith's routine for our friends, a joke is so delicate that a single word added or omitted or moved to the wrong place or even accented improperly can spell the difference between laughter and silence. And maybe lose us a friend! For the professional drolldrone, however, even when a joke has been completely outrigged for duty, honed to lucidity, pared to a lean, fighting weight, and timed to detonate at precisely the right moment, there is still the matter of finding the right "home" within the existing fleet of jokes where it will have the maximum effect.

Step 4. Finally, the joke must be tried out before an audience, tossed into the potentially traumatic no-man's-land of untried material. It is always tempting for the laughdoggler to stay with what is safe and proven, but a true mirthmaster knows that his act is built brick by brick, and so he throws in a new brick every chance he gets.

For Further Reading, see **Berle, Milton**.

4

Show Me the Most Beautiful Woman in the World, and Somewhere There's a Guy Who's Tired of Fucking Her

Saturday afternoon on the road. It's the perfect time for the quipwizard—er, comedian—to get some writing done, which is undoubtedly why it never happens. Despite the fact that there is nothing to do but work and all the distractions of home are absent, somehow the temptation to waste time far above even home-dissipation levels is too compelling. To begin with, what qualifies as acceptable activities to pass the time in a strange city rivals what men do when thrown into the hole in third-world prisons. Television programs that would not even be considered for at-home viewing are not only watched but planned for; museums in towns like Baltimore and Wilmington are thick with comedians on the weekends, the same comedians who have never stepped inside the perhaps more renowned museums of New York City; and malls—malls become the mesmerizing cities of Oz for comedians on the road searching for a heart, a brain, courage, or any number of sundries that could much more easily be obtained upon returning to their own neighborhoods.

So it was on this Saturday in Wilmington that Dick and Fat hired a taxi to take them to the local mall in order that they might kill a few hours of Wilmington afternoonness. For Dick, especially, this was a de rigueur road activity since, as he explained: "Girls without a date on Saturday night always go to the mall on Saturday afternoon to ease the pain. They buy a pair of shoes and some lip gloss, and they feel better. Girls are like FDR—they try to spend their way out of a depression.''

Again, Fat was still eager to learn about romance, and he importuned the great man for further pearl-dropping.

Dick obliged: ''If you meet a girl after she's seen your show, she's always a little suspicious, because she's only seen an act. Of course, she doesn't know there's a lot more truth in that act than in the one you're about to do for her in the bar, but it just looks better if you meet her as a person first. That's why malls are good.''

And just as he said it, Dick spotted some theory-corroborating quarry in the form of a salesgirl at the register of the Casual Corner. Without announcing his intentions, Dick cut across to the teen emporium with the resolve of a man on fire moving toward a lake. Fat, like a spray of tin cans tied to a newlywed's car, trailed behind and, near the culottes, picked up Dick's smooth gambit.

''Hi, I'd like to look at some . . . ah . . . dresses,'' Dick began, milking charm from embarrassment.

''*You* want to look at dresses?'' the cute thing queried.

''Yeah. Can't a guy buy something for his girlfriend?''

''Oh yeah, sure.''

''Good. I don't have a girlfriend, but when I get one I wanna be ready. What size are *you*?''

The rest is too nauseating to reproduce, but suffice it to say that in moments the girl was giggling, Dick was smiling, and Fat was trying on culottes. Dick's presentation was the tightest six minutes of his life, a seamlessly segued, masterly structured bunch of bullshit that had a great opening and a big finish and would have easily had him on the talk show of his choice were it comedy instead of come-on. This time, however, it left him with an inconvenient dilemma.

The most binding promise that Dick could extract from the salesgirl—Tammi—was that she would ''try to make it down'' to the club for Dick's show, a perfectly annoying middle ground that left Dick with the Hobson's choice of trying to meet another girl at the mall and make a date with her (thus leaving himself open to a *Love, American Style* scenario of having simultaneous dates if Tammi showed up) or counting on Tammi to come and then having nobody if she didn't. To make matters worse, Tammi would not even commit to the first or second show as the one to which she might or might not come down! Thus Dick would have to wait until after the second show to begin his search for a companion, and that did not leave much time— about thirty minutes before every bar in town closed, the equivalent of a two-minute drill in football. And even though Dick was the Johnny Unitas of casual sex, if time did run out before he found someone to share his Saturday bed, the entire weekend would have passed without conquest, and Dick, true to his code of honor, would have to jam a hara-kiri knife through his viscera and across his beating heart.

Across Chesapeake Bay, Buck also faced a dilemma. Shit had just gotten off the phone with Norma, the blond-bleached, fortyish comedienne who, with Dick, made up the MC tandem that ran the show at The Club. Norma had called on a matter of MC business, which to anyone who worked at The Club was serious business, owing to the plumness of that position. To be an MC at The Club meant you no longer had to fight city hall because you *were* city hall, deciding who went on and when. In addition, the job paid, not just cab fare but fifty dollars a night, enough to live on if you did three or four turns a week. Best of all, though, was the carte blanche stage time, as the MC could do as much or as little time as he or she wanted between acts. At The Club, the MC was king, and it was good to be the king.

For the last two years, Dick and Norma had maintained a lock on this princely throne, splitting the week between them. Others hoped a third MC might be brought in, but Dick and Norma never let it happen as it was too sweet a gig to risk letting someone else look good. Norma, especially, guarded the monopoly, because she had been at The Club from day one, and she knew that MCing there was, for her, not only the golden goose, but quite possibly the only goose. Norma wasn't going anywhere in show business, but MCing at The Club was still a lot better than where she'd been—the bad marriages and the bad jobs. It wasn't that she wasn't funny or clever; it was just that by 1979, America had seen the Jewish–New York attitude and the I'm-single-and-can't-get-laid routine, too. Thus did Norma fear the younger and hipper comics who eyed her position with a lean and hungry look; and thus had she of late been shouldering a heavy MC load while Dick took advantage of the better-paying gigs out of town. Norma wanted some of that road money, too, but not enough to risk one of the lean and hungry ones becoming a fatted pig with his snout beside hers in the trough.

But when, on this particular Saturday, a fish decidedly bigger than she suddenly cancelled a convention gig that paid one *thousand* dollars, the show business food chain was set in motion: Norma moved up to doing conventions, and somebody else would finally get to MC at The Club.

The somebody else who was roundly acknowledged as most appropriately first in line for this opportunity was Shit. He had the seniority, and with his cabaret panache and Irish charm, he had the right persona for the job, too. In addition, Shit had been forever telling everyone that Bo Reynolds, the seldom-seen owner of The Club, had long ago promised him the next MC opening, a position he very much coveted. So Norma called Shit in Baltimore and offered him the opportunity that he, and everyone else, had for so long been dying for.

Naturally, Shit turned it down. Although he had walked off the stage at Shennanagins only twelve hours earlier, he was unflinching in maintaining that his commitment to perform there through the weekend was—well, it was a commitment, and that was that. Buck, who was sitting nearby when Shit took the call, urged him to reconsider, but he wouldn't. Buck told him that he was being an idiot, but Shit didn't want to hear it. The two of them had been up fighting until dawn, and Shit's attitude toward Buck this morning was best summed up by the classic salvo that Buck had fired at his audience only hours before: "If I want any more shit out of you, I'll squeeze your head."

Shit put on his jacket and went out for breakfast.

That's when Buck called Norma back. Buck also felt the moral call of honoring his commitment to Shennanagins, and he brooded about it all the way back on the train to New York, or at least tried to get some brooding in when he wasn't exulting over having talked the desperate Norma into letting him take the MC job that night. When Shit got back from breakfast, Chink told him what Buck had done and Shit nearly suffered a concussion from going through the roof. He left a scathing message on Buck's new phone machine, demanding that Buck call him as soon as he got in.

Buck's train arrived in Penn Station at four o'clock, then followed standard Amtrak procedure by taking twenty minutes, after everyone had stood up, to complete the final eight feet of the journey. In his apartment Buck listened to Shit's message, and one from Harvey, who Chink had also been given the duty of informing. Naturally, Harvey was furious and assured Buck that he'd never work at his club again or, if he could get the word around, at any club.

As he listened to Harvey's threat, Buck happily performed the international mime for jerking off. He knew that if he could get a foothold as MC at *The* Club, the Harveys of the world would suddenly mean a great deal less to him; no one important was ever going to see him at any place Harvey could influence, so it was worth it. It was what the comedians called a career move, a generous term considering that most of them did not as yet have a career. None of them, however, doubted that Buck would have one.

As for commitment—well, hadn't Shit just been saying how much the comics were being exploited? He was always saying it, so he must have been just saying it, and as far as Buck was concerned, exploitation was a two-way train track.

After procrastinating as long as he could, Buck called Shit at the condo in Baltimore. He didn't want to call him; he knew how the conversation would go. But he had no choice. It wasn't business, it was personal. He couldn't just ignore him.

After Buck said, "Hel—" Shit started in. His voice was so loud, Buck was able to put the phone down on the bed, and while Shit diatribed, Buck unpacked from the trip, made a sandwich, watched *Gone With the Wind* on television, prepared his back taxes for the last five years, and painted the apartment, having enough time after the primer dried to apply a smooth second coat.

Finally, Buck spoke. "I have a long beard now," he said.

"I'm not laughing. I could have taken that job."

"Then why didn't you?"

"Because I have an obligation, and you did, too."

"Obligation? What happened to all that stuff about us getting raped in these clubs and what slime the owners are?"

"This is being as slimy as them. This isn't how you fight the battle."

"This is how every battle is fought. They use poison gas, you use poison gas."

"Do you know how cynical that is?"

"One man's cynicism is another man's realism."

"Which is supposed to mean what?"

"Just that the world is a brutal place and the people who don't want to recognize that fact think that those who do are cynical. But to me, it's just reality. And the reality in show business is that there is no honor. The law is, everybody fucks everybody as much as they can get away with while they can get away with it. Harvey could get away with paying me shit and letting savagery loose while I was onstage, so he did. I can get away with making him scramble for an act tonight because I can. Anybody who's shocked or even personally wounded when payback day comes is an idiot and shouldn't even be in the business."

"And you don't think you're just perpetuating that cycle of immoral behavior?"

"Immoral? Please! Somebody fucked somebody by backing out of a gig last night, so Norma got a call, so I got a call and fucked somebody, and now some other comic is getting a call to take my spot and he'll fuck somebody else, and Harvey won't say, 'Oh no, don't fuck somebody else,' he'll say, 'When can you get here?' and maybe he'll have to pay him a fair wage because he's desperate—because he has to. Yeah, maybe he'll pay somebody fairly tonight because he has to, but he'll still come out ahead because I left without getting paid—which is only right. I am fucking him, despite the fact that I saved his ass last night. Anyway, the bottom line is, he's a businessman and I'm a businessman. And if you would wake up and smell the coffee, you'd be one, too."

"Well, I think you said it all for me, pal. You're a businessman. I'd rather starve than go into this life and become a businessman. What's the point of doing comedy for a living if you're gonna be a businessman? Why don't you work on Wall Street?''

"We *do* work on Wall Street. Everybody works on Wall Street.''

"You know, there's other ways to get people to act honorably besides the law of the jungle. If the comics got together—''

"Oh, will you give up on that? That's never going to happen, because there's no honor *among* comics, either! Guys like Harvey will always be able to get somebody to work for them, somebody's who's thrilled to get two hundred and fifty bucks for telling jokes. You know he's already gotten somebody for tonight—you know that, don't you? I guarantee that stage is not going to be empty tonight. Somebody will be thrilled with the opportunity, somebody who called Harvey five million fucking times and couldn't get him to return his calls, but now Harvey's calling him and telling him he never got the five million messages, his secretary has Alzheimer's, but he always loved this guy's act, loved it so much that he just has to see it in *three fucking hours*! Which reminds me, I gotta get ready for tonight. I've committed this heinous crime, I might as well be good.''

"Fine, you do that, have a great fucking show. I hope you bring the house down.''

"Why are you so pissed? What does this have to do with you?''

"You know what this has to do with me, you know I was promised the next—''

"Oh man, I can't believe you're bringing that up! I can't believe you think there was anything in that promise! Bo Reynolds would promise anything to anybody—he says yes to everything! Everybody loves Bo—yeah, 'cause he's a businessman, too, but he's one of those smart businessmen who let the people under him do all the dirty work and then just comes around every two weeks and tells everybody how much he loves them. And if you say, 'Bo, can I be the next MC?' of course he's gonna say yes! He'd say yes if you asked him to make you president. Do you know that—''

But Shit had hung up. That wasn't the way Buck had wanted it to go. But he would have been surprised if it had gone any differently.

Back at the ranch—the Mustang Ranch—Dick had lucked out with Tammi from the Casual Corner. She was in the first row of the first show—but Dick was not out of the woods yet, because Tammi was not alone. Fearing that Dick might be after exactly what he was after, Tammi had, as young girls are wont to do, brought along a friend for protection, in this case, another person named Tammy, but with a *y*. It was, however, Tammi with an *i*'s Y that Dick was interested in, and he knew the difficulty that faced him with, because trying to separate two nineteen-year-old girls was like trying to split the atom with a croquet mallet: Older women carried Mace to discourage mashers; nineteen-year-olds carried each other. Wearing his most successful laid-getting outfit—a three-piece pinstripe suit with no shirt—Dick knew he would have to use all his talents, and all his skills, to get alone with the Tammi he had selected for sexual intercourse.

His first option was obvious: Pair off Tammy with Fat or the middle act or Martin Bormann for that matter—just so long as Tammy was, algebraically speaking, factored out. However, more than math would be needed here, since, on Dick's liquor scale of how much one needed to drink before a certain woman looked good, Tammy was about a case of vodka, the kind the Russians used to run tanks on when they ran out of gasoline in World War II. She had an ass you could serve drinks on, with room for the band.

Fat was in love.

Perfect, Dick thought: Get Fat laid, get me laid, no one gets hurt. Between shows, he worked the Tammae shamelessly, milking the coincidence in their names for giggles, the foreplay of very young adults. In a demonstration of one of his most admirable qualities, however, Dick paid equal attention to both Tammi and Tammy. For even though he was a hound of the worst order, Dick also somehow managed to be a gentleman, at least insofar as never making an unattractive woman feel the way many men make such a woman feel, like she's useless on the earth if they don't want to fuck her.

But with the end of the second show, nice-guy time was over. Back in his hotel room with the girls and Fat, Dick was doing his best to get rid of *les unnecessarios*. Fat knew the moment would come when he would be asked to peel off from the formation and fly alone. When he emerged from his thousandth trip to the bathroom to saturate thick, fluffy hotel towels with palm sweat, Dick used the natural break in the flow to suggest that the party "break down into smaller groups." He ignored Tammi's queries as to why and sternly voiced, "Stay down there" under his breath to Fat as the nonplussed tubster and Tammy were ushered out of the room. Dick then walked back to the end of the bed, where Tammi was sitting upright, and, with his hands clasped behind his back, leaned over with a sly smile and kissed her lightly on the lips. She seemed to like it, but when Dick tried to kiss her a little harder, she stopped him.

"What are you doing?" she squealed.

"I'm kissing you."

"Why?"

"Because I want to get to know you while I'm down here."

"Get to know me—does that mean go to bed with me?"

"No," Dick said, and felt his nose growing slightly longer. He thought about the first time he had lied to a woman in such a way, how it had excited him, and suddenly the metaphor of Pinocchio became clear. There was something so sexy about this game men and women played, the one he had tried to explain to Fat earlier. It just would be no fun without the bullshit, the drama, the chase. Even with his wife, the sex was still good because it always came as the denouement to some outrageous battle brought on by the insanity of their arrangement. And without the idea of a wife back home, the Tammis of the world wouldn't be half the fun, either.

After an hour with this Tammi, however, the fun was starting to peter out. Dick was in a holding pattern: He'd kiss her for a while, but when the kissing became passionate, she'd stop him. After each thwarting, Dick unloaded a barrage of mendacity characterizing himself as a simple, shy prince of a guy who was looking for one special girl, then rejoin his mouth to hers. But he got no farther.

Dick had encountered goal-line stands before, and he was the firmest of believers in the no-means-yes theory of intergender communication—but even the best gamblers get dealt the occasional deuce. When women couldn't even be consistent in their inconsistency, it was time to be a good sport and throw in the cards.

Meanwhile, one floor down, all flesh was breaking loose in the bathroom. With middle act Nick Marley asleep in the room, Fat and Tammy had decided to take a roll in the zinc. They entered the darkened bathroom giggling like—well, like fat, desperate, nervous people who needed to get laid more than their next breath. Fat turned on the shrill, hospital-strength phosphorescent hotel bathroom light, which to people in Fat and Tammy's insecurity bracket seemed like radiation treatment. Both of them were thinking the same thing: It wasn't something about the other person they didn't want to see, it was something about themselves they feared would be seen. Fat certainly didn't mind seeing Tammy in all her glory, because every time he saw another flaw in her, it made him think, Maybe this girl will do it with me—with *me*! Maybe *I* will get laid!

He prayed that he would. It had been a wonderful evening so far, and Tammy seemed to Fat like a gift from God, who apparently shops in a hurry. Tammy must have told Fat a dozen times how funny he was and how much she loved his act and how cool she thought it was to be a comedian. Fat took it all in stride, only once beaming so brightly as to blind another man. Tammy was the girl he had always nightmared about: female. And here he was, away from home, working as a comedian, filled with the *Playboy* Philosophy as told by Dick, and now living it out in glorious living color.

In the bathroom, Fat turned off the light. The darkness fell on the lovers like cold meat to a black eye. For the first time all night, they felt comfortable: They couldn't see each other. For Fat, however, the situation of being locked in a small, dark place with a girl brought back a painful memory—but then, for him most things did. This recollection, however, was among the worst: his first boy-girl party, in eighth grade. He could still see the basement of the girl's house and the other kids standing in little cliques and doing a rotten job of concealing their condescension and disappointment about his presence at the party. And then the game—seven minutes in heaven, a glorified spin the bottle wherein the potluck couple go off together for seven minutes of whatever they could do in seven minutes inside a closet.

It sounded like a fabulous game to Fat, but then the bad news struck: The girls would not play as long as he was in the circle. One of the girls said it would be more like seven minutes in hell with him, and everybody laughed at that. Fat, unlike Chink, always prided himself on not giving anyone the satisfaction of making him cry—but not on this night. This was a night he could not come close to forgetting if he lived to be two hundred, which wasn't likely considering his cholesterol level.

But when Tammy kissed Fat, all thought of pain and past flew out of his head. And now the Executive Inn was home to a wonderful irony, because while Dick the makeout king was hopelessly mired in a Vietnam of postadolescence upstairs, down in Fat's room things were moving at breakneck speed. A decade of denial and pent-up longing on the part of either Fat or Tammy would have been enough to carry the day, but with both in such a state, this was opening up a can of fuck and having the proverbial snake pop out.

Fat couldn't believe it—it was really going to happen! From the time he'd first heard the words *today you are a man*, he desperately wanted those words to come true in the way he figured God had meant them to: by getting pussy at your bar mitzvah instead of a ride on an elephant or some stupid tree made out of paper that had money glued to it.

And now he was almost there. The precipice of actualization was nearly unbearable. As clothes flew off and Tammy hungrily chewed at his face, Fat seriously wondered if he was having a heart attack. But then again he wondered that a lot, especially if stairs were involved.

Silently, the lovers began to rut. Inevitably, their unbridled and untried passions led them to seek a supine position. And it was there, in the bathtub, naked and erect, that Fat, like the great William Howard Taft before him, got stuck.

Dick, of course, had been stuck with his Tammi for some time. He blamed it on her age: Really young girls just weren't horny enough. He kissed her one last time, then hugged her, not groping, but in a way that signaled he was resigning the battlefield. Not since Grant accepted Lee's sword at Appomattox had there been so moving a spectacle of the proud warrior holding his head high in defeat. Dick accepted his personal infamy without rancor, holding Tammi's hand in the elevator as they headed down to Fat's room. Among her other apprehensions, it seems Tammi had grown worried about Tammy, worried in the way teenage girls worry about each other when they're each with a boy—worried that one of them might be having a good time getting laid while the other is still upholding some code whose purpose they know not.

When they got to Fat's room, Dick and Tammi found the door slightly open. They crept in and saw Nick asleep in the bed but no sign of Fat and Tammy. They were about to leave to search elsewhere when they heard a strange sound emanating from the bathroom.

It was Fat, struggling vainly against the ungiving dimensions of the tub while Tammy simultaneously diverted her eyes and looked on in horror.

The starcrossed porkers were having a rough time of it. Fat was really stuck. He tried to lubricate his sides with the hotel bar of soap, which was small to begin with but looked positively lost in the place where it was now being used.

Tammy started to laugh—not at Fat, but just because young girls laugh during embarrassing or impossible situations, in this case both.

When Dick and Tammi, listening outside the bathroom door, heard the laughter, after having already been treated to the sound of Fat grunting, there was only one interpretation that came to mind: Fat and Tammy were doing it. Dick, not wanting to be a listening Tom, suggested that he and Tammi give Fat and Tammy the privacy that they had obviously taken such great pains to procure. Tammi went along, but she was shocked. She could hardly believe her angelic friend was acting like such a slut; it was so uncharacteristic of her; it was so against what they had agreed would be allowed to take place with these comedians.

But shit happens, and she didn't want to be the only one, so she ran upstairs and fucked Dick practically in half.

While Dick's Waterloo was turning into the third republic upstairs, downstairs in the bathroom Tammy came up with an idea: to run the water and try to float Fat out. Fat, to say the least, was open to suggestions. Stuck in a tub, naked under the hotel lighting, his girl laughing at him—I'm looking bad! he thought. The evening, which had seemed to hold such promise, was turning out like all the other promise-holding evenings.

Nor did the new plan accomplish much, except to start a flood in the room as water began to spill out under the bathroom door. It was a good thing Nick was a sound sleeper.

"Is it helping?" Tammy asked.

"Yes. I'm drowning," Fat bawled. "Let me drown."

"We can't stay in here forever," Tammy said.

"Yes we can!" Fat differed.

Fat now asked his maker—a deity who must have been proud of that title after seeing such a scene—to do him one solid—Lord knows, he had it coming—and just get him out of the tub! God suggested the obvious, that Tammy pull him out, and Fat relayed the information to Tammy.

What sounded like an orgasm a few minutes later was actually the sound of Tammy successfully dislodging Fat from the place Fat thought he might be spending the rest of his life. Tammy let out a yelp of glee; Fat resolved to lose weight.

Fat stood up, half dried himself off, and got dressed as fast as he could, so eager was he to get out of that bathroom. He went out into the corridor with Tammy, and they sat down with their backs against the wall and started the process of putting their lives back together.

It didn't take long. Within minutes, they were laughing about the whole silly episode. Fat was making lame jokes about his near-death experience, and Tammy was applauding each one. They held hands and tilted their heads against each other. If anything, getting stuck in a tub and trying many ridiculous plans to escape and flooding the room while never waking the middle act had brought them closer.

It had been a night of ironies, not least of which was Fat, although unknowingly, helping Dick get laid. Fat, however, after coming so maddeningly close, hadn't gotten laid after all. But when Tammy hugged him so tightly that he thought he might actually feel it, she gave him something he also had never had: a moment of sympathy and understanding from a woman. She further rose to the occasion by telling Fat she thought he was very sexy and that she wanted to finish what they started under safer conditions.

It took the lovers fifteen minutes after the elevator arrived to finally break off their kiss-interrupted goodbyes. Clutching Tammy's phone number in his pocket, Fat blew her one more kiss as the elevator door closed. Plunged to his nadir only an hour before, Fat now sensed a great turning point in his life, a *weltwende*. He walked to the window at the end of the corridor to look out upon a new world, a world with a real future for him, a world both exciting and awaiting.

But unfortunately he was in Wilmington, and the only thing he could see was a Dumpster, one floor down.

5

Good Evening, Ladies and Geniuses

On Sunday afternoon, when everybody was back in New York, Dick called up Buck on a matter of urgent business: "You got any pot?"

Buck did. Buck always did. He had sold pot to make his way through college and then assumed his place in the comic-finagler tradition by transferring the business to New York. In New York, however, Buck maintained a decidedly sliding scale of price and payment plan for each customer. Dick and Norma, for example, were definitely on the most favored nations list. After all, they were friends, and awfully nice people to boot, and—oh yes: They had all the power.

"I heard you MCed last night," Dick said. "How'd it go?"

"Great," Buck said. "I still have a lot to learn, you know, but I definitely felt comfortable doing it."

"You wanna do it tonight?" Dick asked. "I want to spend some time with my kid."

"Yeah, love to."

"Yeah? Arright. But I was gonna use the fifty bucks to pay for the pot—"

"Forget it, you'll get me next week."

Buck was ecstatic—not just to be off the phone with Dick, but to be MCing two nights in a row. Nothing could better seal the precedent that he was now the third MC, especially since Sunday was audition night, and audition night was important to

The Club. It was the night The Club found new talent, and new talent found the kind of nightmare one can only experience while being awake and on a stage for the first time. Nevertheless, every week there seemed to be more New Yorkers, as well as hopefuls from all over the country, who lined up as early as 9 A.M. for the privilege of doing five minutes onstage twelve hours later. They were all convinced that after those five minutes, The Club would pay their moving expenses from Ohio.

After he talked with Dick, Buck unplugged the phone and caught up on some sleep, having had only nine hours the night before. At 7 P.M. the alarm went off, two hours after he already felt like Tutankhamen and looked no better, except for his hair, which looked worse. Getting up at night was such a ridiculous way to start the week, he thought, but since it was a week, like all others, there was no alternative. As the TV warmed up and Buck heard, "I'm Mike Wallace . . . I'm Morley Safer," he thought: Fu-u-ck yooooou!

Buck was still a little cranky.

A nice hot shower was just the thing to rouse and refresh him, but unfortunately Buck lived in New York, where the hot water for eight million people was kept in one tank, and after one teasing, tepid drop, it was gone. Buck cursed the city he knew he should love, but then he remembered: It was laundry day in the two eastern boroughs, so of course there was no water.

Buck dried his shivering body with a stolen hotel towel, then opened his closet door. A look of great satisfaction crossed his face. There they were—the four velveteen sports jackets he'd bought for $55 apiece in the outdoor Jewish mart downtown on Orchard Street. They'd been hanging in his closet for a month now, but the joy of finally owning four sports jackets, and such cool ones at that, being velveteen and everything, hadn't worn off yet. There they were, his babies: one black, one gray, one brown, and one teal.

And one more awful than the next. Buck was new to fashion, but he carried off his sartorial lapses with the same supreme confidence he brought to all his worldly faux pas, and sheer attitude from Buck was often enough to make reasonable people doubt their own good taste or sophisticated opinions.

But not these jackets. These jackets were *velveteen.*

At eight-thirty, Buck descended the four flights of stairs to the street on West 49th, then walked over to Eighth Avenue and 50th Street to catch the M30 bus that would take him to the east side. The bus was crowded with New York's middle class, weary white people anxious to quit the insanity of another day in the city and jump into the tub at home. Little did they know that Buck had already used all the hot water.

On the bus, Buck couldn't take his eye off a pretty girl sitting across from him, or rather, a pretty girl across from whom he had camped. It was a moment that occurred a hundred times a day in New York, when you were close enough to talk to one of the four million females who lived in town, but what to say? So many times Buck would see a girl he deemed attractive on a bus or an elevator or in a diner—or, most frustrating of all, leaving a show on which he'd just performed—and he'd think, Life is what you do in a single moment: If I meet this girl now, at this moment, my life could branch off in a completely different direction—and if I don't meet her, then I stay on the road taken, which is okay, but it's kind of like the turnpike, and I'd like to try that other road.

And yet what do you say to such a stranger on a bus: "Hi, will you talk to me for a minute so I can see if you'd be good for changing my life?"

Buck could never figure it out.

And he was dying to get laid. It had been so long. God, New York was a shitty place to try and score with women—not that he had ever known a good place. But there was something about women in this city that was especially discouraging—mainly that they didn't fuck him very much. You'd think, he thought, that a guy his age, in his profession, would be able to meet women all the time, like Dick or Shit, but it just wasn't so. However, as so often happens, a boon in the professional arena was soon to lend him some sort of cosmic impetus in the personal sphere.

When Buck got to The Club, the aura of audition night was definitely in the air. It was the same mentality prevalent in auto racing, where the crowd not so secretly rooted for crack-ups more than for success. There was no stock-car racing in New York yet, but for a five-dollar cover and a two-drink minimum, citizens could come to The Club and enjoy the spinout of other people's heartfelt dreams.

What a strange phenomenon—that this was something people wanted to see. Was it because we all can relate to dashed dreams, and here one could actually see one, written on the auditioner's face, the horror that comes from finding out that what some poor sap obviously thought were the wittiest, wisest, cleverest things that had ever bubbled from his brain couldn't even fill five minutes?

Yes.

As ringmaster of this Caligulan rite of passage, the MC had to be a cross between Colonel Tom Parker and the Joel Grey character in *Cabaret*. Buck had seen Dick and Norma handle it, and he sure could remember his own audition, which he passed on the first try thanks to a drunken woman who mercifully never let him utter a word of the material he had planned to do. He knew the MC's job was to break the awful tension that is the unavoidable result of other people stinking onstage. The MC was the audience's link to reality on this night— laughing along with them or, if he chose, at the auditioners.

Buck chose the latter. After all, it would have been a sinful waste not to avail himself of the bagful of one-liners he'd been salting away since childhood that were perfect for this occasion and which he now sprinkled liberally throughout the festivities:

> *Thank you, that was auditioner number six, Steve Snyder. Steve wants to be in show business in the worst way, and apparently that's just how he's doing it.*
>
> *That was Bob Smith, and you'll be hearing a lot about him, I'm sure—he smokes in bed.*
>
> *That was the song styling of Lorna Jones, and it was her first time here, so please, let's have a warm hand for her opening.*
>
> *Al Danforth, wasn't he great? Al just signed a contract with Paramount—starting Monday, he'll be driving chickens up from Maryland.*

That was the comedy of Mr. Sid, proving once again that five minutes can be a very long time.

Buck tried to explain to each departing auditioner that his jokes at their expense were in good fun, as if they had a choice. And on this, his first MC audition night, Buck was thrilled to be asked advice by several of the newcomers, even the ones who were obviously forcing a question just to kiss his ass.

When *I* did that to the guy who passed me, Buck thought, I did it a lot smoother.

In any case, it felt good to be the man. Other people were asking *him* how to do comedy now: what a kick! Buck reveled in holding court at the bar, dispensing wisdom as if he were the comedian he wanted to be instead of the one he was.

Of course, when some of the more hopeless cases asked for Buck's honest critique, it got pretty sticky; answering them was like writing a thank you note for a horrendous gift. But they looked at him with the saddest basset hound eyes, so he told them, "Your stage presence is good, work on material," or, "Your material is good, work on stage presence," interchangeably—it didn't really matter. On several occasions, he had to tell auditioners who had done five verbatim minutes of George Carlin's act that comedians had to write their own jokes, that you couldn't just do jokes that you heard, to which they argued that singers sing songs that other singers . . .

Oh, gimme a break! They were as benighted as the audience! Well, of course they were—they *were* the audience! In fact, one guy said to Buck something he'd heard audience members say to MCs at The Club before: "You're very funny, you should be one of the comedians."

No, idiot, I'm not just the bartender or the owner or something—I'm the MC now!

When Shit arrived at The Club, he knew right away that the MC was one of the comedians—a dirty, rotten, seditious comedian who'd hijacked the MC job from right under his nose.

"Is this official, are you the third MC now?" Shit wanted to know.

"I don't know if it's official," Buck offhanded. "If they call me to MC, I'll MC."

"Well, congratulations then, I'm sure you're the new man."

"I don't know. I don't make the decisions around here."

"But if they offer it to you, you'll take it."

"Of course I'll take it. Why shouldn't I?"

"You should. I'm not saying you shouldn't."

"Well, it sounds like you are."

"Not at all. You're reading that into it. This is a big success for you. Don't ruin it by not enjoying it."

"Oh right, meaning I shouldn't enjoy it because you think it's tainted because I ditched Baltimore on Saturday."

"Look, I'm trying to congratulate you," Shit said, which made Buck bow his head for a moment of silent shame before Shit added: "I think you may be right—in this business you have to justify your successes."

"Well it's better than justifying your failures," Buck snapped, and then, seeing the hurt in Shit, just as quickly regretted what he'd just said; regretted it, and hated himself for doing it again, for saying something he regretted.

And for still not knowing, no matter how hard he tried, how to stop doing it again.

At eleven-thirty, Buck went into the bar to fetch auditioner number nine but instead found Rita Tanaka, a cute twenty-one-year-old coed with whom he had carried on a semitorrid affair the previous winter. Torrid but brief, because Buck had been chilled in all his attempts to make contact with Rita after she returned to college following the Christmas vacation that had brought her to New York and into his acquaintanceship. Buck thought momentarily about bringing up his hurt regarding that chill, but she looked so good, he opted to think about heat instead, the kind he remembered sharing with Rita and which he now hoped they might share again.

Buck had met Rita on a warm December night, when she had come into The Club with her obnoxious friend Judy. Buck flirted with the girls and brought them into the showroom to watch his set, which went uncharacteristically well that night— certainly well enough to fuel his heightened spirits, and expectations, a little later at the Blue Spoon, where he bought the girls salads and hamburgers. But Buck acted hurt when Rita wouldn't leave Judy to come home with him, although not too hurt to beg her to show up again the next night. When she did, carnal union resulted, and for the rest of Rita's month-long Christmas break, while she was staying at her parents' home in Queens, Buck and Rita carried on a relationship, in the narrowest sense of the word.

About every third night, Rita would come to The Club around eleven, wait for Buck to go on, then go back to his apartment, where Buck, newly skilled in the art of fucking, would fuck her, wait fifteen minutes for his soldier to report again for duty, and then fuck her again. Buck would have been happy to try for three, but since Rita was staying with her parents, she had to get home at a reasonable hour, and Buck understood and always walked her down to wherever she'd parked the family Bonneville.

After a final, tongue-swallowing good night, Buck would ask Rita for her phone number, but she never gave it to him, claiming her parents didn't like boys calling the house. Buck again acted hurt, but he was not entirely upset about not being able to talk to Rita on the phone, because even in person, their verbal communication was, to comic proportions, minimal. In the great tradition of Eastern inscrutability, Rita never said two words in a row, and she never spoke unless Buck asked her a direct question, to which she responded, "Yes," "No," and sometimes, "Sometimes." There were no essay questions with Rita. But since she seemed to know absolutely nothing about anything that was interesting, it wasn't like she didn't have a good reason to shut up. Buck never had a clue what was in Rita's mind, but he knew that she liked him and liked to fuck him, two galaxy-size reasons to keep seeing her. She wouldn't let him call her on the phone, and he was too embarrassed by her social silence to ever introduce her to any of his friends— which would have made for a fine, meaningless relationship if Buck could ever really feel as detached as all that, if he could simply screw a woman and then fold her up like an ironing board and put her in the closet.

But Buck could not do that with any woman, because Buck

wanted every woman to love him. And he was beginning to master the tender, fatherly-affectionate demeanor with young girls that engendered just that effect.

And now he had a second chance to practice it on Rita. At 3 A.M. on this Sunday night, now Monday morning, Buck and Rita were indeed picking up where they'd left off in January, with Buck humping away and luxuriating in Rita's tight body— "an ass strung like a canoe," he told her, in what he felt to be a great compliment, not just to her ass, but to the skills of all woodland Indians. But this night was different from those of their previous couplings, because Rita's parents were away on vacation and she was going to get to fall asleep in Buck's arms for the first time.

That is, if he ever stopped mauling her. Always starved for affection no matter how much he got, and horny beyond endurability from the months of loneliness, Buck fucked and cuddled, fucked and cuddled, the one always leading to the other, all night long. Rita had no objections to either, or anything, ever.

So she didn't mind when Buck told her during the evening's forty-third round of sexual intercourse that he loved her. This, of course, is a declaration that a boy more normally makes to a girl for the first time during one of the cuddling moments— but Buck's recent honeymoon with the art of lovemaking had converted him to the belief that anything important a man has to say to a woman is best expressed during penetration; every second the old codpiece was inside producing pleasure made her like you a little bit more. And looking deeply into her eyes while so engaged was a hundred times more intense than looking deeply into her eyes whilst not so engaged. An erection, Buck believed, was the ultimate form of control, and if there was one thing Buck enjoyed, it was control: Making people laugh was one form of it, and having your hard-on inside a girl was another. As long as you had a good, strong woody going, a woman was at your mercy.

And with Buck, she was sooner or later *crying* mercy, because a guy who keeps holding on to his hard-on is good, but only up to a point.

Buck passed that point a lot, now that he knew how to. He pooh-poohed the orgasm as overrated—ten seconds of bliss, granted, but hardly worth losing all that control. To blow your load was to surrender your sword, and if an actual sword could go limp in battle, well, the warrior who brandished it would make pretty darn sure *that* didn't happen. So it was with sex. To lay down your sword was to lose the instrument of your power, the vicar of your will. And then your genitals would just be moist, limp flesh, like—oh God, like hers!

There was no doubt: To make a point, you need a point.

At 5:30 A.M., the light of day began intruding on the preset sexual lighting that Buck always activated for romantic interludes in his apartment: an ambient glow from the bathroom, achieved by leaving the door open a crack, and a green candle-in-a-cup, a candle that wanted to scream out, "He only uses me when he's fucking," but did not. Sexually sated, as evidenced by several layers of skin left on the sheets, and predictably hungry in a postmarathon way, the couple set out in the crisp Monday morning air for the diner on 46th Street and Ninth Avenue. There they ate huge egglike breakfasts, which appealed to Buck only in a postcoital state. During the meal, Buck borrowed a pen from the waitress to write on a napkin several bits he'd thought of while with, or perhaps in, Rita, and told her she inspired him. They held hands across the table in a loving manner and exchanged shy, charged smiles while grumpy construction workers and stevedores who hadn't had sex with their wives since Watergate trundled in for another day's fuel for the salt mine. When the bill came, Buck reached into his bag of comedy chestnuts and told Rita, "This is ridiculous—if I were you, I wouldn't pay it," knowing there wasn't a Chinaman's chance that she'd know the remark came from Groucho Marx, or even who Groucho Marx was.

The look on Rita's face was the same every time Buck made a joke, a combination of nothing and blankness. But Buck just smiled and continued on to the next joke, unaware that this was exactly the approach he was unable to execute with an audience. He went into a riff about the inexpensiveness of breakfast in New York and how it was the only thing in New York that *was* cheap, as if the city were saying to its put-upon population, "Okay, pal, we'll give you breakfast, now you're on your own the rest of the day—good fucking luck!" As the animation of voice and body built in him for this impromptu comedy routine, he looked across at Rita and watched as each new punchline made her eyes dance—slow-dance, that is, like at a prom when they play "Color My World" and you just stand there and shuffle your feet a little.

When the lovers got back to Buck's apartment about the time the world was going to work and the car horns and bus engines were loudest beneath Buck's window, they showered together under the awful, impotent shower, and then, for a change of pace, fucked.

Then they slept. Buck lay on his back, and as he drifted off, he kept gathering Rita closer and closer to his side, until she could be no closer without sleeping fully on top of him, which is how he finally arranged her.

When the lovers awoke late in the afternoon, Rita said that she had better be getting home, an idea that Buck opposed, and he wasn't kidding or being polite. Buck was not like Dick, anxious for his partner's exit as soon as the initial conquest was over. Buck still wanted to do more conquesting, more intense eye-gazing-whilst-genital-joined, more everything, until she never wanted to leave him, until she vowed to jump on his funeral pyre should God call him that very day.

Buck hugged Rita, and Rita hugged back, resigning her feeble, quarterhearted attempt to leave his arms. She didn't want to go; she was simply listening to that deep-seated female instinct to, somewhere along the line, say no to something. But Rita was too young and ingenuous to be much on her guard about men; no experience had yet triggered the mechanism that says, Pull back, build a wall; you've been burned before. A voice was saying those things to her, but it was a distant, mysterious voice, like the Son of Sam dog or a bad Sprint call. And it was no match for the eighteen-hour dose of attention and uninterrupted physical communion she had just received from Buck. The lovers felt themselves getting lost in something, and now they both wanted to get more lost, so lost that they'd never find their way back. Parched with loneliness, they drank and drank of each other until they could feel the water bouncing in their stomachs—emotionally speaking, that is.

At six o'clock, Buck popped the statement again, but this time not during sex. Buck was becoming quite sentimental.

"I love you," he blurted out. "I can't believe how fast the time goes by with you. I look up at the clock every two minutes and an hour has gone by. Someone who can make that happen, well, I'll tell you this: They oughta be with you at the post office."

Rita didn't really get the joke, but she smiled when Buck smiled, and she knew by the way his eyes twinkled that he had made a joke, the way an animal can sense your mood without understanding language. Buck gave her a biscuit. Then he kissed her, as he did between most of his statements, and looked deeply into her eyes. He was afraid to look into her ears on the chance he might see daylight.

"You're a wonderful woman," he told her after stammering and aw-shucksing his way through several other equally preposterous compliments. It was a vintage Buck performance: humble, fumbly, meek—all the things he was not. He was, however, aware that calling Rita a wonderful woman would thrill her in a way that could only thrill someone who was definitely not yet a woman.

Rita did what she always did with Buck. She agreed with him.

"I love you, too," she finally spoke.

6

Love Is When You Don't Feel
Shitty After You Come

At 7 P.M., Buck finally let Rita out of his apartment as they
both had places to go: he, to The Club, she, to her home in
Queens, to do a little packing before the trip back to college
the next day. Buck was sorry that Rita had to leave New York
once more, but then again it would have been tough to top the
night they'd just spent together, what with the vows of love
and the endless sex. Actually, the vows and the sex were fine—
it was the in-between moments, like when people talk, that
made Buck think it was perhaps for the best that he and Rita
were not everyday lovers. Of course, he told her just the opposite.

Buck felt good as he dressed and dragged himself to The
Club. He saw a pretty girl on the bus again, but meeting her
did not seem nearly as compelling as it had the night before,
when the taste of a woman wasn't fresh on his lips. He had fed
his monster well; it lay inside him, sated and dormant. It slept
and belched inside the mouth of the cave.

At The Club, Buck's new status as MC was paying dividends
as an act, too. Norma put him up nice and early, and he
promptly did a shitty set. He was feeling cocky, from MCing
and from Rita, and the audience did not at all take to his you're-
lucky-to-be-seeing-me attitude. And they were right, because
of course he still did not have an act.

Buck hung around kibitzing with the guys until two-thirty,

when the last two people in the crowd filed out of the showroom. He commiserated with the late-nighters, some of whom had gotten on in the last hour for an invigorating round of rejection at the hands of the defatigable crowd, and some of whom hadn't gotten on at all. These, of course, were the lucky ones. Chink had once again been one of these, and he needed some cheering up. Buck suggested he join the gang at the Blue Spoon diner, which at this hour began to fill with comedians from The Club.

The Blue Spoon was typical of any diner in the city—owned by Greeks and staffed by Greeks, Italians, Puerto Ricans or anyone who was dark, spoke English badly, and would be violently out of place anywhere but in New York, including his own country. Many of the waiters, in fact, did not themselves seem certain about their place of origin, perhaps having lied about it so many times they had actually forgotten.

No one who patronized the Blue Spoon, however, would have had it any other way. Like the beat-up old couch you love to lie on because it's comfortable and you know you don't have to worry about damaging it because you can't, the Blue Spoon served its purpose nobly. The food, served on huge, oblong, not-found-in-your-home-size plates, was more funny than sapid, and mostly what was blue was the meat and anyone who ate it. The flatware, impeccably stained at any hour of the day, was not blue; however, the lettuce wasn't green, either. The tuna was green. The lettuce was white, consisting entirely of the stalky part found at the base of the head or, in the case of the Spoon, the neck. The tomatoes were red, but they carried with them no taste whatsoever of tomato. One would see a red slice on the plate and from the memory of that associate it with the taste of tomato, but in actuality there was no tomato taste to be tasted. The comedians did not come to the Blue Spoon for the food.

They came to fill up because there was nothing to eat at home, and to talk, because there was no one to talk to, or eat, at home. Whereas most workers in America go out for a drink after work, comics drink during their work, then repair to places like the Spoon to layer some extremely heavy diner food on top of the booze at two in the morning, just before retiring, which of course is the best time to eat heavy diner food. And like most workers in America, they wound up talking about the one thing they came to get away from—the J-O-B. The thing they all have in common. The thing they cannot get away from.

The difference, however, between comedians and those other workers in America was this: For the comedians, hanging around with your co-workers after the job could be more of a job than the job itself. Not that they didn't enjoy themselves, but for anyone struggling for the respect of his peers, which was everyone—well, there's funny, and then there's *diner* funny, the kind of funny that makes a fellow comedian hock up a piece of meat from the Blue Spoon, thereby saving his life.

At this moment in the Spoon's history, Buck, Norma, Shit, and Dick were pretty much the Gang of Four who dominated the conversations and passed judgment, by their laughter, on those who came to supper and anted in their egos for a chance to play comic's poker. Any comic who essayed to sit in on this game was capable, on any given night, of raking in the biggest pot, and in a very real sense, he would go home richer for it. Especially if it was a new comic, because making the Round Table laugh created an ineluctable pressure for further opportunities in the showroom, even if the audience in there was still not getting it. That was true of Chink now, as it had been true of Buck not so long ago.

Buck, of course, was the comic other comics both loved to hate and hated to love; the former paradox drove him nuts, but the latter was one in which he actually reveled, and during late-night giggle fests at the Spoon, he served himself well in achieving it. Because what had always been most endearing to other comics about Buck was his well-deserved reputation as a great audience. As much as some may have despised him for other reasons, valid and not, no one could help but love Buck and want him to be the friend he resisted being to so many when he laughed his authoritative, unrestrained laugh. So many of the other comedians, in their insecurity and competitiveness, withheld laughter from their colleagues—but not Buck. When you said something that Buck thought was funny, you knew it really was funny, because you knew this was the one guy who never laughed just to be polite.

On this night at the Spoon, Buck was laughing his head off. But it was laughter that wouldn't do any comic a damn bit of good, because Buck was laughing at a waitress—not a waitress from the Spoon, but Jeannie, a skinny brunette who worked at The Club and sometimes joined the comedians for their unhealthy repasts.

When the check arrived, everyone as usual threw in just enough to cover the cost of their food, assuming money for a tip magically grew on a pile of fives and ones. Jeannie counted it up, then informed the group that waitresses worked hard and deserved a good tip. Everyone threw in a single, which was still a shitty tip, so Jeannie left a five behind after the gang left the table.

Outside, it was chilly and time to find transit. Fat, as usual, hailed the subway, and Norma and Chink split the cab ride they always took together through the park. Others followed custom in the city of pounded pavements and walked.

As he opened the door of a proud old Checker, Buck volunteered to drop Jeannie off. He knew her destination wasn't really on the way, but he was feeling studly after Rita, and horny after some phallic food flirting, and it popped into his head that this might be a good night to try and fuck Jeannie. The thought had crossed his mind before, because he thought Jeannie was cute and funny and he liked her, but he'd always stopped himself for a stupid reason: The other guys didn't seem to think she was that cute. Buck knew this was flawed thinking, but at least it was that rare type of flawed thinking that one could actually peg to a specific incident in his past, as opposed to the usual vague knowledge of the ways you were fucked-up without a clue as to why—and without, especially in Buck's case, any desire to spend ten years in analysis finding out. Buck and Shit had debated the uses of psychiatry a thousand times, Shit taking the pro side, Buck taking the even-if-you-do-find-out-about-getting-locked-in-a-closet-at-the-age-of-three-with-a-spider-what-can-you-do-about-it-now? side.

As the taxi headed downtown, Buck flashed back to the specific incident in tenth grade that was still coloring his thinking a decade later. It was a week after that first date of his, the date that provided one of his three great life-moments, and Buck was so beside himself with joy that he wanted to tell the world—the world, like Germany or the Canary Islands, but definitely not the guys at the lunch table. Because, beside himself with joy or not, the girl of Buck's teen dreams had braces and a Roman nose, and she was not on the lunch table–approved list of fuckable girls, the ones who any boy would gain great respect for having fucked, or for even having gotten himself into a situation where he could credibly claim a fuck. Buck's girl was not on that list, and for that reason he wanted to keep their relationship a secret.

Fat chance. When the guys at the lunch table started mocking him, he didn't say a word, because he knew that not responding was the mature way to handle it. That, and also knowing that if he tried to talk, he'd cry. Buck held a lump in his throat for the full forty-minute lunch period. He looked down, he doodled on the cover of his notebook, and he vowed—just like Fat, with whom Buck would never think to compare himself now— to become a big comedy star when he got out of high school.

As Buck's cab bounced over huge potholes in the streets of New York, he asked Jeannie: "Are you tired?"

"Not really. Why?"

"I don't know. We could do something. I mean, there's no law against co-workers fraternizing. We don't work for IBM."

Okay, okay, Jeannie thought, you don't have to justify it.

"Whaddaya wanna do?" she asked.

"I don't know," Buck lied. "We already ate, it'd be stupid to eat again."

"Very."

"Drinking's no good, you know, after just eating and all."

"Nothing's open now anyway."

"Hey, you like-em pot?"

"What?"

"Pot. You know, maryjane, reefer, grass, mari-gee-wana."

"Yeah, sure. Sometimes."

"Well . . . do you want to?"

"Where?"

"Well, I don't have any with me," Buck said, feeling the pipe inside his trouser pocket.

"I know. It's back at your apartment."

"No, I keep it in a locker at the Port Authority. That's where I like to do my really heavy partying."

Up at Buck's place, Jeannie sat in Buck's big leather chair and Buck sat on the round coffee table in front of it. They took turns sucking on his tan ceramic bong and had a ball being high and laughing for about an hour. Buck kept looking for an opportune moment to initiate romantic activity, but he apparently had learned how to fuck while still not knowing how to *get* fucked.

At four, Jeannie announced it was four. She hoped Buck would understand the meaning of four, which was, Do you wanna fuck, dickhead, or are we waiting to watch the sun rise?

Buck maintained his opacity, however, so Jeannie rose and gathered her coat and purse and told him what fun it had been, to which he readily agreed, and almost let her get away.

With the door open and one foot in the hall, Jeannie said: "Well . . . 'bye."

"Well . . . I guess I shouldn't expect a kiss good night," Buck play-acted avec exaggerated hung head, still resorting to comedy as the only social lubricant with which he was comfortable. "An unattractive person such as myself . . . I'm probably repulsive to you."

"Tsk, you are not," Jeannie said, and kissed him lightly.

For the life of him, Buck had not been able to find a way to kiss her first—but he did know how to kiss back. And by the response of her tongue, he finally caught on that it was something she'd wanted him to do for longer than that minute in the doorway.

Jeannie dropped her purse.

"Hey, why don't you come back in for a second." Buck laughed as he pulled Jeannie inside and lit the green candle that was still on the nightstand, but now nearly melted away from the previous night with Rita.

For the next fifteen minutes, Jeannie and Buck were silent— silent but busy. The next words were Jeannie's:

"Don't you come in me!"

"Don't worry about it."

"I'm not using anything, and I absolutely *cannot* get pregnant."

"Well, if you can't get pregnant, what's all the worry?"

"No, I mean—"

Buck knew what she meant, but you can't take the comedian out of the bedroom—not that the two antebellum couches with a thin mattress on top in the corner of his apartment was really a bedroom; it was hardly even a bed. But Buck didn't care about that now, and he even had a new fondness for the old couch set because he was finally, as his mother might say, "getting some good wear out of it," including pumping Jeannie for the next hour like the piston on an old iron train.

When Buck was finally satisfied that he had at least equaled his own impressive endurance record, he withdrew his angry member at the last possible pregnancy-preventing moment, then groaned in ecstasy as the long-restrained seed of orgasm baptized his new lover, his old bed, and the phone, which never quite worked properly again.

"I almost came that time," he joked.

Jeannie struggled to catch her breath after the marathon session, but could not and died.

Buck got up and walked with his best posture over to the half refrigerator in the kitchen section of his studio apartment. He produced a carton of orange juice and swigged it down like a man who'd just done what he'd just done. A resurrected Jeannie opened her eyes.

"Juice?" he offered, but Jeannie could not yet speak or drink. "Suit yourself," the cocky cocksman said, and then continued in his best mock-pitchman's voice: "But, you know, after a grueling round of sexual intercourse, there's nothing I like better to quench a stubborn thirst than Minute Maid orange juice. No matter how many minutes it takes you to get made . . ."

Jeannie laughed, which was, Buck thought, more than Rita had ever done: Boy, why doesn't God ever put a great ass together with a sense of humor?

Buck sat on the bed and asked Jeannie if she was tired.

"Not anymore." She smiled, with the sigh of the recently well fucked.

"Good. In that case, there'll be a short intermission, and then our second feature will begin."

In another hour, as the first light of day dappled his heavy, indescribably ugly broadcloth curtains, Buck quickly brought the second feature to its predictable crescendo. Like some sexual Dracula, Buck regarded daylight as the signal to put quietus to intimacy, lest that old antiromantic Sol throw his high beams on something previously covered by makeup or long ago licked off in the inky cloak of night or the blind eye of horniness. Jeannie was no kid, after all, and dawn was not something Buck wanted sticking its rosy fingers into his sex life.

But the excited new lovers could not sleep. Jeannie, like Buck, was a talker, and the sated twosome kept babbling and giggling twixt the sheets. Like kids at a pajama party, every new pledge of "Okay, really, let's try to sleep now" lasted only five seconds before they both burst out laughing. Finally, at 6:30 A.M., Buck and Jeannie decided to do what all New Yorkers do when they can't sleep: eat.

The crisp morning air of the newly minted day felt good to the satisfied ones, and on the way to the diner—the same diner where Buck had taken Rita twenty-four hours earlier—Jeannie thought about how quickly she had come to like this guy. She had worked by him night after night for months, sometimes flirting, but with no imperative crush—and now, in the space of a few hours, she felt smitten. It had never dawned on her, even after a year inside the showroom at The Club, that comedians made their living by doing to audiences precisely what Buck had just done to her—i.e., manufacturing affection in a big hurry. At The Club, after all, a comedian had only twenty minutes to make the roomful of strangers love him.

But strangers in an audience, marvel as they might at the rapid takeover of their hearts, didn't expect anything after the twenty minutes. Jeannie did.

Buck, on the other hand, didn't know what to expect. He was too busy thinking how fabulous it was to have gotten laid two nights in a row—and with two different girls no less! Two nights, two girls: that was real ladykiller stuff, just like Shit.

Well, not really like Shit, because Buck's conquests weren't exactly fabulous and sophisticated women.

Okay, like Dick—but a milestone nonetheless.

And so typical of the incomprehensibility of romance: Why, after such a long drought, now this veritable downpour of babes? And why was that so typical? Although this was the first time there'd actually been two distinct, confirmed kills on consecutive days, there'd been plenty of other times, two days here, three days there, when a sudden freshet of romantic possibilities presented themselves—and then nothing again for months. It was like women smelled something on you for those couple of days, flirting with you, looking back when you looked at them on the bus, accepting offers for dates—what was it? And why did it go away as fast as it came? And couldn't the people at Procter & Gamble come up with something that preserved it?

Apparently not. And that's why Buck was not awash in guilt on this particular morning. Of course, he felt bad about Rita—or actually, he felt bad about *not* feeling bad. But if you spent your life feeling bad about not feeling bad, well—that would be bad!

So Buck made his peace with the fact that Rita's value was, at this moment, purely statistical. He certainly didn't want to think what a decent person would think about fucking one girl the night after telling another girl he loved her or what that declaration had already caused the first girl to start thinking. It was probably pretty rotten what he had done, but once again, the overriding factor was New York, where men were men and women were a lot tougher than the men. In New York, you just couldn't stockpile enough women, so elusive were they to hold on to. A guy in this town had to think about women the way a baseball manager thinks about pitching: You can never have too much.

And in New York you could never have too many women. One day you could count five strong arms in the bullpen—five women who you could call and at least hypothetically get a date with—but within that proverbial New York minute, one would develop a sore arm, one would get injured, and one might just start giving up the gofer ball. There was just no security against the awful, looming specter of no women, that terrible situation of not having one woman you could call if you wanted a woman or, worst of all, if you needed a woman for some function where your friends would see you not being able to get a woman. Being woman-poor was no different than being money-poor: When you don't know where your next dollar is coming from, you tend to put a few in reserve whenever you get the chance.

So Buck felt justified about his duplicity, which is only fair after he had spent so much effort justifying it.

In the diner with Jeannie, Buck took the same booth he had used the previous morning, and the same waitress gave him a little smile. God, he thought—I'm getting to be a regular! And in point of fact, he ordered the same breakfast he'd ordered the day before, and did some of the same jokes to Jeannie he'd done to Rita, pretty funny stuff about the crummy decor, the pathetic look of the patrons, and the shotglass-size portions of orange juice.

His postcoital early-morning-diner set was starting to get tight.

So was his rap. It had worked so well the day before, he again scribbled a note for a bit on a piece of paper and told the girl he was with that she inspired him. Jeannie, however, knew what the word *inspired* meant and asked what the bit was. Buck wouldn't tell her.

"I guess I'll just have to wait till it comes out on *Mike Douglas*," she said.

Buck was flattered. He really liked Jeannie. And he would have loved to get on *Mike Douglas*.

After breakfast, Jeannie caught a cab to her pad on 12th Street and Buck bought a paper and whistled on home. He read the sports page and got into bed. He reached to unplug the phone, but called Jeannie instead.

"Listen, I just wanted to tell you again what a great time I had—even the four or five minutes we weren't eating or fucking."

Then Buck asked Jeannie a serious question: "Whaddaya think we should do about The Club?"

"Whaddaya mean?"

"Well, I mean, it's such a gossip mill. I hate to trust my personal life to the people at that place."

"Okay, let's get new jobs."

"No, come on, you know what I mean—let's just keep it our secret for a while. Give us a chance."

"Okay, fine."

"Good. What are you doing tonight?"

"Working. You?"

"Yup. Maybe we can meet after."

And so it went with Buck and Jeannie the waitress. Buck almost fell in love with her, and they were so happy for a time.

Buck and Jeannie, however, were not the only ones for whom splitting a cab earned its reputation as foreplay. On the same night, in a different part of town, Norma and Chink had de-cabbed at the same moment Buck and Jeannie had, in front of the attractive brownstone where Norma sublet a basement apartment. Chink also lived on the Upper West Side, and since he was always around at the end of the night, as was Norma on the nights she MCed, the gang at The Club had often seen her offer the boy a ride. Most decent people at The Club did what they could to help Chink, and nobody suspected she was doing anything more than letting him save some money. But the truth was, Norma was the comedienne Chink had fallen in love with, and on most nights he joined her inside her apartment at the end of the cab ride. He always offered to pay for the taxi, but his efforts were to no avail.

Neither, it seemed, was his love for her. Norma, although also very lonely, and very aware of Chink's love for her, decided early on that she would not consider allowing their friendship to become a romance. She was twice his age, and after two bad marriages and countless stupid relationships, she was not about to start up with a kid who didn't know the first thing about a woman, about what she needed or who she was. Sure, he was great to hang out with after The Club, and yes, he made her laugh, which, after being around comedians for six years, was simply a relationship sine qua non for her. But he loved her too much, and that scared Norma. In fact, everything about Chink scared her, because the qualities he possessed were the very ones she would have objectively listed as those of her perfect mate: He didn't care that she was older; he didn't care that she called the shots; and he would never leave her. He was like a dog with her, Chink was—beat me, abuse me, but just don't leave the house.

But Norma couldn't get herself to do it. It was just too— oh, too everything. She pictured the most embarrassing things happening if they were to become a couple, like meeting his mother and finding out they had gone to school together. No, he was just too young.

The proof was that he'd never made a pass at her, never even told her how he felt. There they were, so many nights, alone in her apartment, she smoking pot, he watching, she having a glass of wine, he watching, she getting into comfortable clothes, he not watching—no, he was still a boy. I know he wants to, she thought—what does he think, that he's showing how much he respects me? Who needs that much respect? God, this kid would bring along vaginal lubricant to a rape . . .

Hey, that's a good line.

And so this night started out like all the others. Just like an old married couple who take their assigned places, Chink came in and sat in the old stuffing-bursting chair he always sat in and Norma lay down on the couch. The TV was always on in the background, the bong always lit in the foreground. They were never at a loss for conversation, although from time to time they'd hush each other when a favorite scene from *Mary Tyler Moore* came on.

Tonight, though, they watched one of the two episodes that came on between 2 and 3 A.M. all the way through. It was one of their favorites, the one where Murray finally owns up to the fact that he's in love with Mary. "Fuck her, just fuck her!" Norma shouted at the screen, and Chink laughed, as he laughed at most everything Norma said.

When it was over, Chink remarked that the episode was a classic. It was such a classic, in fact, that it prompted Norma to do something she'd never done with Chink—bring their feelings out into the open.

"Because you relate to it," she said.

"What do you mean?" Chink gulped.

"You know what I mean. Hasn't there ever been somebody you were dying to get close to but you couldn't get yourself to tell them?"

Even as she said it, Norma half regretted opening so volatile a can of worms. And Chink—oh, this was just too painful for him. This was *dealing with it*, man. He wanted her so much, but dealing with it—oh, that was just so awful. So awful that it had prevented him all these months from going after what he wanted more than anything else in the world, so it must be pretty awful.

Spending time like this with Norma, it was so wonderful. Of course, if he could also wind up these nights falling asleep with his head between her breasts, that would be beyond wonderful. But was it worth risking wonderful on the chance of reaching beyond wonderful? So far, Chink had settled on the side of caution. Because if he told her—if her told her he loved her, and wanted to do everything for her, not just make her laugh, but make her dinner and make her breakfast and make her . . . *come* came to mind—but he wasn't sure he knew how to do that. He wasn't sure he knew how to make dinner either, but at least if you burned a pot roast a woman might still want to see you again.

No, it was too risky to risk . . . risking. Norma and he were like that thing in chemistry lab, the something-something bump, which meant that when you mixed two chemicals together, they either got over this bump right away and formed a new compound or they never would. The graph always showed this mountain in the beginning, and if the elements got over the mountain, the rest was blissfully downhill, the molecules easily on their way to forming a completely new compound. But if the molecules didn't do that, then you knew they never would, and Chink didn't want to maybe find that out. Yes, he wanted to form a completely new compound with Norma but, Jesus, to have to jump in the beaker with her and say so, and maybe risk having her say no—"No! No, you idiot, that's not what I meant at all! You thought I wanted you to fuck me? Gimme a break!"

"You're trying to seduce me, Mrs. Robinson . . . aren't

you?'' That was the line that made the hairs on Chink's arms stand on end: *"Aren't you?"* Oh, what an excruciating moment that would be if you read a woman wrong.

Now, on the other side of the coin, it *seemed* like she wanted him. It *seemed* like that was exactly what she was getting at—but with women, who could really be sure? If only women came with subtitles that told you exactly what they really were thinking. If only you could read a woman with confidence instead of the way you had to read her, which was like reading French, where you were kind of sure what was going on, but then again you wouldn't bet the farm that the guy in the story stole a loaf of bread. They might have said he sold a cow.

Chink looked down. There was no good answer to Norma's question that he could think of. But he had to say something.

"Yes," he finally managed.

That was still safe. He still could be referring to someone else, some other girl he loved but couldn't get himself to tell.

"Who?"

"Oh, just some girl."

Fuck, Chink thought—now I'm into a lie. And not just a yes or no lie, but a whole lie *story*! I'm going to have to invent an entire fictitious section of my life!

You'd think, he thought, for someone who lies for a living—because what are jokes but funny lies—this would be easy.

It was not easy.

"Tell me about it," Norma persisted.

When Chink could not, she came over and put her arm around him.

"Is it painful?" she asked.

God, Chink thought, she thinks I'm weepy about this other girl—what other girl? There never was an other girl. I have no point of reference! Jesus, this must be how the audience feels when I refer to something from current events that they haven't heard of.

But then she kissed him. Just like that. And then she stood up and held out her hand, signaling for him to stand too.

He did.

"I think you need some loving," Norma said, and led him away.

Where was she leading? It was like one of those stories in the tabloids about people who died for a minute and felt the sensation of walking toward a blinding white light, all the while feeling exceptionally blissful and at peace.

That was how Chink felt—except for the at peace part. Chink wasn't at peace, he was shitting in his pants. And it wasn't a blinding light, either. Okay, forget the tabloids, but it was like something totally occultish and unbelievable. "Need some loving," she had said—what was this, a pity fuck?

Well great, then, a pity fuck it is—a pity fuck, an anger fuck, a gang rape with a motorcycle club—as long as Norma was involved, Chink didn't care what it was.

What it was, was so unbelievably great, no worms could describe it. That's what Chink kept thinking: No *worms* could describe it. What did that mean? Obviously, it meant that ordinary language did not do justice to the moment.

As Norma fellated him with the greatest of skill and tenderness—not that he had anything to compare it to, but sometimes you just know, you don't need a point of reference—it seemed to Chink that the earth itself had spun off its axis and was hurtling out into deep, deep space.

Truly, no worms could describe it.

7

The Work Isn't Bad— but the Hour!

The winter of 1979–80 was so cold in New York City it felt like every other winter in New York.

Three days before Christmas, Dick took Fat to Bloomingdale's to show him the department store scam. Dick scouted the floor that had all the good-looking salesgirls behind their glass counters and settled on a gorgeous redhead. Dick's plan was to enlist the salesgirl's aid in selecting a gift for his "girlfriend"—a mythic creature he would create to demonstrate to the salesgirl what a devoted boyfriend he was. He would talk ad nauseam about this girlfriend, how he was a one-woman kind of guy, and how he wanted to give her the best gift he could afford.

But the gift—could he return it? That is, if she didn't like it, because Dick planned on coming back a few days after Christmas, fighting back tears, with the sad news that his gal had up and left him, found another guy, was going into the rodeo or radio or something, and hell, he could use a friend right about now, maybe you, little saleslady, will have a cup of coffee with me? And so there he'd be with this girl who'd already been thinking to herself, Boy, I wish I could meet a guy who had that kind of devotion in him—a guy who'd treat me like he treats his girlfriend.

Fat couldn't believe it. Not Dick's scam, because he'd seen Dick operate too many times by now, but Bloomingdale's itself.

He'd never been to the store, and he was amazed upon walking into the first-floor women's wonderland. It was a blinding spectacle of chrome and glass and hi-tech lighting and neon and chicks like on the cover of *Cosmopolitan* standing around, shopping, waiting on customers, offering to spray him.

Spray me? What are you, a cat?

"To see if you like the perfume," Dick explained.

Ohhhh.

Bloomingdale's, however, did not amaze Fat as much as what he saw a few days later at the annual Club Christmas party, when Dick walked in with the redheaded salesgirl on his arm. Fat's awe for Dick went off the meter. To not only think of a plan that diabolical, but then to have it work! To Fat, this made the raid on Entebbe seem like a game of checkers, or would have if Fat had known what the raid on Entebbe was.

Fat looked at Dick's date and drooled: She looked even better than she had in the store, which is more than you can say for a lot of the stuff at Bloomingdale's. Like Scarlett O'Hara, Fat vowed, as God was his witness, if he had to lie, cheat, or steal, he'd never be horny again! He decided right then and there, this was the kind of girl he wanted. He would work tirelessly, day and night if necessary. He would work every shit gig up and down the East Coast, and he would step on anyone in his way. But someday he would have a beautiful girl like that for his own.

All of which made it a bad time for Tammy from Wilmington to walk in.

Fat had invited Tammy to the Christmas party after several frantic phone calls from her saying she needed to see him. It was her second trip to New York to see Fat, the first coming the very next Saturday after their memorable liaison at the Executive Inn. Using Dick's pied-à-terre on 75th Street while Dick was home with his family in the Bronx, the anxious lovers had finally consummated their relationship, although with characteristic poor luck. Because while Fat had only logged a total of eighty seconds' penetration time, spread out over three different lovemaking sessions, he had somehow managed to lose his virginity and gain fatherhood all in the same night.

This was the little bit of Christmas cheer that imbued Tammy's trip to New York with such urgency.

The party was in full swing when she arrived, a little pooped after the train ride from Wilmington. She finally found Fat after spending twenty minutes at the door convincing the bouncer that she was an invited guest of Fat, who'd neglected to leave her name on the list. Finally by his side, Tammy tried to gain Fat's attention as he ogled Dick's date without pause. She begged Fat to take her somewhere where they could talk.

Outside on the sidewalk soft snow flurries fell as Tammy, fighting back tears, caused more by Fat's impatience with her hesitancy to spit it out, whatever it was, than by the problem itself, informed him of her condition. Or so she thought she had when she noted that she hadn't had her period since the night in Dick's apartment.

Fat said: "So what?"

Fully hysterical now, Tammy explained to Fat the information for which he had apparently been absent in eighth grade health class and then never gotten the notes. The blood ran from Fat's face, which was no small drainage project.

Tammy burst out in tears as it hit her what it would be like to have a man so bereft of common knowledge as the father of her child. If she retained any hopes that Fat would mature in the next five seconds, he put them to rest:

"Come on, we're missing a great party."

While Tammy was composing herself in the bathroom, Buck was also dealing with a distraught girlfriend. It seems Jeannie had leaked word of their romance to a fellow waitress, Ellen, who told her boyfriend, the house piano player, Jamie, who mentioned it to Buck, who got pissed.

"Did you tell Ellen we were going out?" he asked Jeannie, whom until then he had ignored for the entire evening.

"Yes."

"And she told Jamie?"

"She told me she wouldn't."

"They live together!"

"I'm sorry."

Buck turned away in disgust.

Jeannie said: "Look—it's been almost two months. Don't you think . . . I mean, how long were we going to keep it a secret?"

Buck said nothing.

Jeannie said: "Why don't you want anyone to know?" and started to cry.

Buck could never withstand a woman's crying, and now he felt guilty and ashamed. He took Jeannie outside to the same spot Fat had just occupied with his own lachrymose paramour and held her and comforted her. He told her she was right and he was sorry and that he'd wanted it to be a secret because he treasured what they had. Then, like Peter Marshall when someone picks the obviously wrong square, he said, "But this may work out."

When Jeannie's eyes had dried, Buck walked back in with her, holding her hand, and stood with her arm in arm at the bar while she drank several shots very quickly. She was hanging all over him, which made him self-conscious, although no one else seemed to notice or care.

Until about midnight, when Rita walked in with her friend Judy.

Suddenly, the glee that Buck had felt on that autumn morning in the diner for having scored two nights in a row was gone. This was very awkward—and what timing! Jeannie was making the kind of unmistakable physical contact that announces fucking is going on here, and Buck couldn't tell her to stop, because that's what she had just been crying about. So he had to talk to Rita like she was just a friend, which was so cold, because he knew she'd come in expecting to be his lover for the night.

In fairness to Buck, he had never said to either girl that she was the only one he was seeing; in fairness to the girls, he was a master at implying it. God, he thought, why did I say "I love you" to Rita? Why did I say it to Jeannie?

What, is there some sort of pattern here?

"Hey, Rita—what are you doin' around these parts?" Buck began, hating himself every second for taking this stupid, phony attitude with her.

"Christmas vacation."

"Oh. Well, it's a party tonight. This is our office party. Yup."

"Oh."

"Yup."

"Is there a show?" Judy asked.

"Oh no. Not tonight. No, this is for us. Yeah."

Now the silences were getting almost as awkward as the looks that hanging Jeannie and inscrutable Rita were giving each other, since Buck had yet to introduce them to each other. How does Dick handle this, Buck wondered—he's got his wife here, and I'm sure there's a hundred girls he's fucked right in this room. Indeed, Buck saw Dick talking to some girl while his eyes darted back toward his wife. And his wife was watching him—oh, it was so obvious everyone knew what was going on! And yet all the actors just played their parts. No one walked off the stage.

Buck finally made an introduction, and Jeannie and Rita both forced a smile and a hello. Then Buck said to Rita, "Sorry there's no show tonight," hoping she'd get the hint and leave, but instead she asked Buck to get drinks for her and Judy, ensuring that the awkwardness would continue for another ten minutes, during which time Rita held forth on a number of controversial topics, including arms reduction and the debt crisis—in her mind, perhaps; out loud she said her usual quota of words—none. The minutes flew by like millennia as Buck waited for the sound of ice being sucked through a straw, the international signal that a young girl has finished her drink.

Then, just before time itself ground to a halt, Rita and Judy gave each other that wanna-go? look, and without so much as slapping Buck or pitching a drink into his face, they were gone.

Next, Shit came in. He was in his Santa outfit, having just come from Macy's, where he did his turn every year listening to children's requests for toys. There would, however, be no next year for Shit at Macy's as he'd just gotten his big red ass canned on account of being too drunk to talk to children. It seems that while he was walking down to the fortress on 34th Street in full Santa regalia, more than a few seasonal revelers had stuck their heads out of bars and said, "Hey, Santa, lemme buy you a drink!"

Shit was popular enough in the bars of New York without a big red suit on, and the costume proved to be his undoing.

Buck yelled across the room to him, where he was now standing with Chink and Dick in the classic comic-riffing circle. Dick was as anxious to be free of his wife as Buck was to be free of Jeannie, so he drifted a bit toward Buck, and Buck drifted a bit toward Dick. Then Fat, anxious to be free of Tammy, appeared. So now the comics were all standing in the middle of the room, except Shit, always the gentleman, who stayed behind with Dick's wife.

"Have you seen my penis in this light?" Dick asked Buck, immediately deploying the latest we-still-haven't-run-it-into-the-ground-even-though-we've-said-it-a-million-times running gag.

"Yes, but that doesn't mean I don't want to see it again," Buck replied.

Marla, a flat-chested impressionist with a pretty face who the male comedians never stopped teasing, turned around.

"Are you boys talking about your penises again?" she asked.

"Why, yes, we are, Marla. Is there something wrong with that?" Dick asked.

"No. I just think it's kind of funny."

"And they say dykes are the hardest audience!" Buck performed, to the delight of the guys.

"Shut up," Marla feebly protested. "What is it about me that provokes this?"

"Hey, guys, Marla wants to know what it is about her that provokes this. I say it's the rumor that she'll blow anyone for a nickel and give change," Buck remarked.

Now the guys started to close in on Marla, making lascivious sounds and touching her hair and back.

"Hey, cut it out, you guys."

"Oh come on, baby, you know you love it. Come on, let's all go to my place. I'm having a party with a . . . train motif," Buck joshed.

The guys laughed and Marla didn't get it.

"What does that mean?" she asked.

"Nothing, he's just crazy," Dick said. "I've got a game. If we all put our hands all over you, it feels like rain," and the guys picked up the cue and started to selectively "rain" on Marla, making appropriate hippie sounds to go with it.

"Hey, come on, stop it," she remonstrated, but she was enjoying the attention, and she was a comic, and she knew that the guy comics wouldn't really hurt her. If anything, they were all rather protective of her.

"It's beautiful—it's not a sexual thing," Chink added as the four men pawed her in the most perverted way possible—not to cop a feel, just because it made the joke funnier.

"Stop it, I don't want to be raped tonight, okay?" Marla protested again.

"Rape?" Chink returned. "I have enough trouble getting it in when she wants it!"

"I'm getting outta here," Marla finally said after she could no longer pretend she didn't like it.

"Yeah that's right, pretend you don't like it, then you'll go home and masturbate about the whole thing," Chink said.

Chink was in rare form—i.e., he was drunk. He seldom drank, but the other comics looked forward to it when he did, because drunk, Chink was not just funny but *brutally* funny.

"Rape, gimme a break," he continued on. "I read about this rape case the other day, they were all ready to convict the guy, and then it comes out in the trial—*she* was on top!"

An unrespected comedian named Dennis came in all excited, asking if anyone had caught the final score of the Knicks game.

"Oh good entrance, come in like you're asking a question about a ball game," Chink mocked.

It was Christmas, but that didn't mean the headshredding had to stop.

"Hi, Dennis, good to see you—okay, that's enough with him," Buck said.

Buck, safely ensconced now as the third MC, was really enjoying this first Christmas party as someone who could get away with ego/power jokes like that. Chink loved it too, because it reminded him he had a friend in a high place, that his biggest supporter was now the sheriff.

Dennis tried to redeem himself with a riff about how drunk Bo looked, imitating a man leaning on another man.

"Excuse me, the visual stuff doesn't pick up on the tape,"

Buck said, producing the new microrecorder with which he'd lately been taping his sets, as well as using to capture any stray bits of brilliance that might tumble out of his mouth socially. "I'm here to gather material at your expense. I need it to be verbal, people, that's what I do—I thought we all knew that."

"Eddy, we've got a problem down here on the floor," Chink said, pretending to call up to the booth of a mythical show of which Buck was the star. "I want security. Someone is annoying number one."

Dennis could see there was no way he was going to be anything but the subject of jokes, so he moved on as well.

"I see your girl from Wilmington is here," Dick said to Fat.

"Ugh," Fat replied. "Why is God doing this to me?"

"Because God is just a real vicious character," Chink said with a little laugh.

"Whaddaya mean?" asked Fat.

"What do you think I mean?" Chink replied. "He doesn't give a shit about you. He's up there fucking Marilyn Monroe."

When Chink started in on God, everybody just cleared out and let him work.

"Why do you think she's dead? 'Cause He wanted to fuck her. God takes everybody good: 'What's Elvis Presley doing these days? I used to love that 'Hound Dog' thing he did. Get him up here.' "

"God, that's funny," Buck said to Chink when he regained his speaking powers. "I don't know how I think of stuff like that—it's like I hear a voice—and it sounds a lot like yours! Seriously, though, you should do that, it's brilliant."

"Yeah, yeah," sluffed Chink. "Just what I need, more brilliance to bomb with. Here you go, swine, another pearl . . . Seeeeeewwwweeeh! Come on, hogs, come and get it! All the pearls you can sniff at for a second and then walk away or take a shit on or something . . ."

There was more, but Chink and Buck were gone, holding each other up from laughter, unable to get the next line out. When they got like that, the rest of the world was a third wheel.

Fat was right: This was a great party.

It was a great party every year. For one night Bo Reynolds closed the doors of The Club to the public and turned it over to those who made it possible all year. And after everybody got drunk at the open bar, the comics gave themselves a show where all the tensions, all the grousing that couldn't be voiced in so many words during the year, were given vent through the miracle of satire. They performed little skits in twos and threes, lampooning the various aspects of their life at The Club—the food, the seniority system, the shared pain of not getting on, the bad crowds and, especially, the authority figures, of whom Buck was now one. The general effect was to say: We're all in it together.

And this year the show closed with something really special—a video that made many of these professional cynics a little teary. It was a film collage, made by one of the late-nighters, of all the comics who worked out at The Club during the year, over a thumping soundtrack of "She Works Hard for the Money." For a few moments while the vision of the video lingered, there was no pecking order—no A acts and B acts, no prop comics and gimmick comics being looked down upon by monologuists, no microcosmic stars and microcosmic nobodies. Seeing everybody on the same reel, all caught in the act of doing whatever they had to do to get the laugh, was a great leveler: There was Dick, bopping his head with the microphone, and Fat, puffing out his cheeks to look even fatter, and Buck, the pure monologuist, lifting his leg in a dog-and-cat routine; there was Norma, pulling her T-shirt out at the tits, and another female comic throwing out her arm for one quick moment in imitation of a Supreme singing "Stop! In the Name of Love"; and Chink, with the Chinese-people-speaking look on his face, and Shit, really making a face, a face that only a comic's mother could love.

Yeah, everybody looked pretty silly all right, while they worked hard for the money. They all had no dignity, and they all had all the dignity in the world.

The next afternoon, Buck woke up with a hangover and Jeannie. He wanted to get rid of both, but the Alka-Seltzer only worked on the headache. He wanted to get rid of Jeannie so he could call Rita, but then he'd feel guilty about Jeannie, who was in no mood to go anywhere anyway. She and Buck had just woken up from a night of bonding, what with the tears at the party and coming out of the closet and then great drunken sex when they got home. Plus, it was Christmas almost, and Buck could see Jeannie was in the mood to be in love. She wanted to frolic somewhere, or maybe build a sludgeman from the previous night's wintry blanket of soot flakes. Buck couldn't just kick her out.

Especially since he'd already insulted her enough times by doing just that, kicking her out five seconds after they'd woken up. Buck was not a morning person, even when the morning started at 2 P.M. How small that apartment was if you were newly alive and someone else was newly alive in there with you! To Buck, waking up was not something you wanted to do on the buddy system. Waking up was a private thing, what with the pissing and farting and looking bad and reorienting to the fact that, yes, that last sweet dream is over now, and yes, you do live in a small, filthy room in a big, filthy city, and no, you have no guarantee you'll ever get out. A man needed privacy for all that.

Buck finally got his privacy at six o'clock, and then he was sorry Jeannie was gone. Because now he had to make that call to Rita and that was *really* going to be torture. He had made such a big thing about getting her phone number at home, and now he was going to have to use it for the first time to beg her forgiveness. Not to mention the fact that if Rita had been so concerned about her parents getting a call from him, maybe he should be concerned about it, too. Buck had always felt embarrassed as a teenager when he had to talk to a girl's parents, but now he was five years past teenager and there was actually a reason to be embarrassed about it. Jesus, what would he say if her father answered the phone, or even, God forbid, wanted to ask him a few penetrating questions?

Hi, I'm the round-eye who's been planting your sincerely young daughter, Rita? Yes, hi . . . well, I'm very fond of her, because she's young, and pretty, and . . . did I mention young? Did she ever tell you about the time we fucked all night and through the next day? Yes, I think you were out of town at the time. Where do we go on our dates? Why, straight to bed, you silly old gook! Frankly, I wouldn't introduce Rita to an antibody—she's done to the art of conversation what panty hose did for finger-fucking. Why haven't I called before? Because I haven't figured out a way to fuck her over the phone yet!

"Dad, I got it."

"Rita?"

"Hi."

"Hey, how ya doin'?"

"Okay."

"Yeah?"

"Uh-huh."

"Okay. Well, listen, I wanted to call because I felt funny about last night . . . I didn't know you were coming in and . . . gee, I didn't know what to say."

Silence.

"I hope you don't hate me, Rita."

Silence.

"Rita—do you hate me?"

"No."

"Okay, well . . . then I'll call ya. Are you goin' anywhere over Christmas vacation?"

"No."

"Okay, well . . . maybe we can see a movie or something."

Silence.

"Okay?"

"Okay."

"Okay, Rita. I'll call you soon . . . 'bye."

Click.

She was pissed. Even her major-league inscrutability couldn't completely hide that Rita was pissed.

On the last day of the decade, Buck sat home and worshiped the red herrings of happiness. He was pleased with himself for the accomplishments of the year: acquiring power at The Club, making more money, and metamorphosing into a heartbreaker from a heartbreakee.

New Year's Eve at The Club was the predictable comedy

hell one would expect from an audience issued noisemakers and feeling an obligation to get drunk. Norma MCed, and Shit and Buck went on back to back around 2 A.M. Shit attempted to review the significant events of the decade, but the crowd was not in a mood for review. Buck, who back in Baltimore had thought Shit insane for doing topical material on a Friday night, somewhere had now stitched together enough confidence to actually think he could do better working the same side of the street, and wouldn't that be a good way to one-up his rival.

Did you see the big TV movie this year? First You Cry, *starring Mary Tyler Moore, about a woman getting breast cancer. They're doing one now with Ed Asner about a man in a similar situation—it's called* First You Cough.

And Jean Harris stood trial for the murder of a diet doctor, claiming she shot him nine times accidentally, stopping only once to reload.

Over in Iran, there was a change in government, which the New York Post *reported with the headline* SHAH HITS THE FAN.

And Nelson Rockefeller died while—well, he was a politician, let's just say "in Congress" . . . yeah, with a woman named Megan Marshack, who is now writing a book about it. It's called Rocky Died in My Arms . . . and One Other Place.

The crowd really warmed up to this material. Buck had done something real pros know to do: He had discovered the kind of material the audience wanted to hear. Unfortunately for him, and for the audience, he only had one minute of it. He was hardly startled, and thankful for the distraction, when Shit walked through the room naked.

After he got off, Buck was surprised to find Shit still in the bar.

"Don't you have some place fabulous to go tonight?"

"I'm not much on New Year's Eve," Shit said. "It's amateur night."

"Whaddaya mean?"

"You know, too many people. Everybody's doing it."

"Well, hey, there's the kind of elitist chitchat I can get behind."

"No, it's not that. It's just too crowded everywhere, everybody's drunk. You wanna go to my place?"

"Yeah. Except . . . I kinda promised Jeannie."

"Jeannie the waitress?"

"Yeah."

"Really. How long has that been going on?"

"Not that long. It's nothing serious."

"Well, bring her."

"Really? Yeah, that sounds good."

Half an hour later, the show was over and The Club had emptied out. Jeannie was still cleaning up the tables. Buck and Shit were in the bar with Norma, and they asked her to join them over at Shit's place.

Norma was happy for the invitation. The night before, she had broken it off with Chink. What she had feared would happen had happened: Chink was getting too serious too fast. He was unable to do anything halfway, and all of a sudden Norma felt completely suffocated. He was still too young. They had enjoyed a wonderful friendship, and now she was sorry she'd ruined it, not to mention what she'd done to the boy.

Chink had taken the news very hard, and with no pride. He asked if they could resume things as they'd been before, but Norma said that was impossible. He would have offered to stay on as a gardener—anything to be near her—but she knew it was best to make a clean break. Still, it was not easy, and she knew she would miss him. And on New Year's Eve she didn't want to go home to the apartment where it would be the first night in a long time without his company.

So Norma and Shit and Buck and Jeannie piled into a cab and headed over to Shit's place, landing atop the five-floor walk-up winded and exhausted from the long, difficult night and ready to let off a little steam. After a round of bongs, the boys went up to the roof that Shit considered one of the great perks of his rent-controlled building. It was a warm winter night, and Shit had a small tale to tell Buck.

"I stayed up all night with a friend of yours the other night."

"Really? Who?"

"Rita."

"What?"

Buck was taken aback. He didn't want to be aback, but he was so shocked he had no time to feign nonabackedness. Had it come to this? The thought of his best friend rubbernecking his empties was horrid and startling.

"I thought there was some kind of code among men," Buck stammered, obviously not knowing much about codes or men. "And what about your celibacy?"

"Take it easy. Nothing happened. We just talked."

"Where?"

"Right here."

"Here? On your roof? You talked with her all night on your roof?"

"Saw the sun come up."

"How could you talk with her all night? She never speaks."

"Well, she talked a blue streak the other night."

"A *blue streak*? You gotta be kidding."

"No, she's a very interesting woman. I had a real nice time with her. She's funny, too."

"She's *funny*?"

"Had me laughing."

"Intentionally?"

"There's more of a person there than you may have wanted to recognize."

"Well . . . I mean . . . how did this all come about?"

"She came into The Club looking for you. She told me to tell you she's sorry she hung up on you."

"She didn't hang up on me," Buck said defensively. "Well, she kinda did. Why didn't she just call me?"

"I don't know. Maybe she doesn't like to use the phone."

"Tell me about it."

"She really likes you, you know."

"She said that?"

"Yeah."

"What—you mean, you two were talking about me?"

"Yeah, we talked about you. We talked about a lot of things. She just needed to talk."

"Meaning what—I never let her? She could have talked all she wanted. I guess she didn't have me to complain about, then."

"That's not it at all. She was intimidated by you. She loves you, and it made her shy."

"She *loves* me?"

"Well, you told her you loved her, didn't you?"

"Oh Jesus, do I have any privacy? You know, I'm not used to a woman of my very recent acquaintance running off to impart the intimate details of our coupling to the very anxious ears of my supposed best friend. I might as well be living in Russia."

"Let's hope not. I hear they take a dim view of comedians showing their dicks to each other over there."

"I'm serious. This is lousy."

"I didn't ask her—she told me. Look, she saw me at the bar, she knew I was your friend, and she asked me if I knew where you were. Then she gave me that message for you. I made some joke about you getting hung up on all the time, and she started talking about it. I could see she was confused and upset, so I listened. I was doing it partly for you, I might add."

"Oh gee, thanks."

"I know what's happening to you right now."

"And what's that?"

"You're starting to know what it's like to be a master seducer. It's something that happens to men around your age. You discover you can get over on women easily, and you take a great joy in it. But I'm just telling you when you're through doing it, you'll feel like a schmuck."

"I already feel like a schmuck. I just wish I felt like I had the master-seducer part to show for it."

"You will in the next couple of years, and I'm just trying to warn you."

"Gee, I can't wait to regret some of the things I'm gonna do."

"That's funny, but you will regret them."

"Oh come on, how many women have I seen get hung up on you?"

"Yes, but they weren't like Rita. I wouldn't go out with

someone as young as Rita. It's very different if you're with a woman who knows the score and you're honest with her from the start.''

Buck made a big face and walked over to the edge of the roof. He flailed his arms and pounded on the parapet.

"Hey, don't jump," Shit said. "Landlord doesn't want us throwing any shit off the roof.''

"I am a piece of shit," Buck said.

"Don't be silly. It's perfectly understandable what happened. Just be aware from now on that when you're affecting someone's feelings, it's a responsibility.''

Buck chewed on that for a while, then came back over to where Shit was sitting.

"You mean you wouldn't have fucked her if you weren't celibate?''

"No. I really wouldn't. It's not worth it. And who's celibate?''

"You quit?''

Shit laughed. "It's not a heroin addiction, you know.''

"Well, how long have you been uncelibate?''

"About two months.''

"Two months? But . . . I mean, how long ago was it that you started doing it?''

"About two months. Okay, it was a short experiment. But hey, so was putting Mickey Rooney in musicals.''

"What happened?''

Shit shrugged. "Got horny.''

"Yeah, yeah." Buck sighed. "The penis. It's our bane and boon, isn't it?''

"That's what I call mine, my boonbane. Have you seen my boonbane in this light?''

Downstairs, Jeannie and Norma were digging each other's company. They were getting off on girl dishing and getting to know each other better than they had from just hanging around The Club.

"So I hear you got a thing going with one of our MCs," Norma said to Jeannie.

Jeannie bowed her head in a shy-but-proud-of-it smile: "Yup."

"Is it serious?"

"Well . . . I don't know. It's hard to tell. It's hard to tell anything with a comedian."

"Oh, honey, tell me about it."

"I know, right? It's like, he can be so sweet and thoughtful and sincere, but then he goes through these phases where everything has to be a joke, you know? I can't get him to answer any question seriously. He just goes into some character."

"He does characters?"

"Oh yeah, constantly."

Norma laughed.

Jeannie continued: "I know, it's so different from what he does onstage, right? You wouldn't believe some of the things he does with me."

"Oh tell me, tell me, what?"

"Oh, like what do you call it—you know, like the Three Stooges . . ."

"He acts like the Three Stooges?!" Norma screamed in laughter.

"Yeah, what do you call that?"

"Slapstick?"

"Yeah, slapstick."

"Oh, you have to tell me, what does he do?"

"Oh, like anything. Like . . . oh, like the other night he was putting away these plastic dishes he has in the kitchen, and he was purposefully dropping them and carrying too many and you know, like Jerry Lewis."

"Jerry Lewis! Oh God, that is too much!"

Norma was beside herself, and Jeannie was enjoying making her laugh. But she didn't quite understand it.

"Is it that funny?"

"Oh, honey," Norma said, catching her breath. "I'm not laughing at him, it's just that—the Three Stooges, Jerry Lewis—I love it! It's wonderful. It shows how much he loves you!"

"Really?" Jeannie said with a smile as wide as something really wide.

"Of course! That he would be that silly for you when he's such a snob with us? I mean, I love him, but he *is* such a snob about comedy, so when you tell me he's crashing dishes and doing pratfalls around the house—don't you see how romantic that is?"

"Well, don't tell him I told you."

"Oh no, no. No, never. But I'm gonna love him all the more now, and he'll never know why."

Soon the boys reappeared, but Buck was no longer in the mood to party. He and Jeannie left, and then Shit and Norma had the kind of sex that people of their experience know means absolutely nothing and will probably never happen again.

The new year, as all years before it, started out badly for Fat. To balance the news of Tammy's pregnancy, he had decided he should start dating other girls. Still staggered by the success of Dick's Bloomingdale's ruse, Fat was dying to try it himself, in spite of the fact that Dick had told him this particular stratagem was too advanced for him and that he should wait till next Christmas, and even then to hit a department store more in his league, like JC Penney. But Fat was like a kid with a new chemistry set, and just as knowledgeable. He could wait no longer than January 3, and on that day he marched into Woolworth's, ignoring the fact that the particular subterfuge he was about to emulate was one that worked much better the week before Christmas than the week after.

At Woolworth's, there was no football field of reflecting display cases, no models spraying perfume, no eight-foot-high pyramids of the season's trendy perfumes. There was not, of course, even a season anymore. There were only narrow aisles of sweatsocks and colanders and masking tape, and bins of $1.99 record albums that even the artists' families wouldn't buy.

And there were no salesgirls. In fact, the only woman in the store was an Indian girl at the checkout counter, but that didn't stop Fat; it started him, right toward her. She understood very little English, and obviously Fat understood very little about the English-speaking world in which he lived. All the Dravidian maiden could say to Fat was, "What you buy? What you buy?" as he tried to tell her about his girlfriend and how he was seeking help in finding a suitable gift for . . . for . . . her birthday, that's it, her birthday, because, as much as he loved her, January 3 was a little early to start shopping for a Christmas present. But as the line in back of Fat began to grow restive and as the checkoutress got more annoyed, Fat became flustered and forgot that the situation was entirely contrived. Making no effort to conceal his pique, Fat yielded his place in the checkout line and declared that he would find a gift on his own. He searched the shelves on only four aisles before realizing two things: that he had no actual girlfriend to shop for and that even a fictitious girlfriend deserved a better birthday gift than what could be found at Woolworth's.

No Set, No Hamburger

I love New York. The thing I love about it the most is, even when I'm not on the subway, I feel like I am.

Kafka, of course, wrote a book about a man who wakes up one day to find he's a cockroach—all around the world, this is a novel; in New York, it's a documentary.

The housing situation in this town is ridiculous—you can get a girl to go to bed with you if you have . . . a bed.

I have an apartment. I don't want to say this place is small, but Anne Frank looked at it and said, "I couldn't live here."

You know the kind of apartment I mean, with the paper-thin walls, where you can hear the people next door when they're screwing—which is so embarrassing—especially if you come first! I'm banging on the walls, "Hey, can you keep it up in there!"

—Buck, The Club, January 20, 1980

For a young comedian in New York, it was January that was the cruelest month. It was freezing, it was right after the holidays, and every civilian was back at work and not happy about it. There was nothing funny about January, even if anyone came out in the arctic winds to go to a nightclub, which they didn't. Combined with the two weeks before Christmas, which were also awful (during that fortnight people spent their time and money on the holiday scene, and the ones who did come to a nightclub seemed to be the hard-core victims of holiday depression), it made for the worst month of the year, comedy-wise, except for June, when the prom kids came in. In January, it seemed like you just couldn't buy a good set, and after a while that situation took its toll, since comedians are often at the emotional beck of how well their last set went. At this time of year, everyone's beck was against the wall.

For Buck, there was an additional problem: The novelty and exhilaration of MCing had begun to wear off. It was still a great job, but there were a lot of things about it that could give a guy one hell of a headache.

Like: Okay, you could hog as much stage time as you wanted, but you also had to stay up there and kill fifteen minutes after a prop comic had spewed his detritus all over the stage and the audience was still buzzing about it while the Chinese factotum mopped up the hellacious watery mess; and yes, you were the man, but you were also the man on the spot when something went wrong, like when an act went psycho and forced you to be a psychologist with the audience (as opposed to psychiatrist, who can dispense drugs, although some MCs did that too); and yes, power was fun, but with power came responsibility, and with responsibility, several more drinks. There was simply no other way to face that barroom of pathetic faces every night at 2 A.M. That was the worst part of the job— having to be the one who disappointed others.

In that, the MC was simply doomed by arithmetic. At ten o'clock, a dozen restive acts are in the bar expecting to go on in prime time; at midnight, only six have, and the other six, and six more who came in later, are staring at you with huge puppy-dog eyes every time you walk back into the bar like a coach looking down the bench to see who'll go into the game next. Each comedian knows if he doesn't get on soon, the evening will be lost, because anytime now the showroom will turn into a toilet, the crowd wrung out, picked on by every comic, tired and drunk. Not to mention that every reference has already been mentioned three times, the comedy terrain having long ago been picked over like racks of clothes on the ninth day of an eight-day sale.

And then the crowd will start to thin. Now, that's not necessarily a bad thing, because getting down with those water-tank salesmen from Paducah wasn't going to happen anyway. Also, the people from Sweden are leaving, and that's good because it's hard enough to understand the show if you're from Paducah, never mind not speaking English. And the bachelorette party has calmed down, apparently having gotten over the initial excitement of being eight stupid twats in a public place. However, the asshole table is just warming up: Any table of three or more men without the restraining influence of dates will automatically be trouble as they seek to assert that it could just as easily have been *them* on the stage, had they chosen comedy for a career instead of the nearly interchangeable carpet-remnant business. But at least they're laughing and staying, so maybe the midnight-to-one hour will be good, and three more acts will be happy, which means only six and not nine of the A and B acts will leave hating you.

Which is necessary, to make room for the hate from the late-nighters, the C acts, who are even more desperate to get on—for reasons as much nutritional as artistic: No set, no hamburger!

Finally, though, there simply is no more. None. All gone. Five pathetic faces are still looking at you, and all you can do is hold the can upside down and show them that nothing more is coming out. And licking the can will only cut their tongues.

So that's what it was like at 2 A.M. for a very tired MC with a fifty-dollar headache. Of course, that headache wouldn't be so bad if he hadn't freshened that scotch every hour (that makes five, yes?), not to mention the parts of eight joints that eight different comics offered to share.

And then it's over. The MC goes home with eight roaches, a headache, and all that guilt.

And in Buck's case, the waitress.

This January, however, for one of the few times in his life, Buck experienced the good fortune of having exactly what he needed materialize out of thin air. He needed to get away, and away made him an offer.

The gig was at the Statesmanlike Hotel in Miami Beach—not the main room, of course, but the Comedy Corner, a cute little lounge annexed to the annex of the hotel, which was across the street from the main structure. The street was really a screaming six-lane highway that scared the shit out of the poor old Jews in the annex section, who had to cross it every time they wanted to get a newspaper from the gift shop. There was no traffic light to halt the barreling, drug-motivated Miami traffic, which even young Buck found a challenge to evade. Good luck with a walker.

But the fact that even Miami Beach now had a comedy club proved just how far the comedy revolution had reached. However, if the Statesmanlike Hotel had hoped to attract a younger crowd to the land of blue hair with its new Comedy Corner, then Buck soon discovered that he was unevenly holding up his part of the load. The other two performers on the bill were Charlie Shultz, a spry, albeit bitter, sixty-three, and a fortyish ex-stripper now-comedienne named Marsha Wells, late of Hollywood, looks, and talent. Not that it mattered who was on the show, since two out of three punchlines were drowned out by the roar of a margarita-making blender from the bar at the back of the room. There were two shows a night, but since this was Miami, they would best be described as an early show and a *really* early show.

Miami had sounded great, but once again, show business had placed before one of its purveyors' eyes a shiny object that, when dredged up from the shallow water, proved only to be a worthless piece of slimy sludge fit only to be pitched back into the drink for the next sap to likewise discover.

Back in New York, a great storm was about to blow into Dick's life. Dick, of course, was used to stormy weather, and in fact thrived on the tightrope dance he did between keeping his wife never quite fed up enough to leave him and prowling for ever new and unpummeled tundra. Dick never kept a new girl around for more than a day or two, because after all, he was a man who lived in a state of—what, common-law divorce? It was a ridiculous institution, but like other ridiculous institutions, such as the mafia or the United States government, there were within it certain rules and codes that were sacrosanct: For the mob, it was *omertà*; for Dick, it was that no matter how many strange women he bedded, he never fell in love with any of them. He conquered, he fucked, he lied and cheated and used—but he did not have affairs. Janet didn't have much to cling to, but she was certain she at least had that.

But then one night, it was 3 A.M. Dick was at an after-hours bar not far from The Club, appropriately called the Tiny Bar as it was really someone's basement-level apartment and not a legal tavern. Shit, an infrequent patron, was already there when Dick entered, and it seemed that this might be the night when these two old war horses would finally break the stubborn rapport hymen that thus far had prevented colleagiality from becoming friendship.

But for Dick and Shit, it was not in the cards. Otherwise, God would never have sent in Jill, twenty-eight, beautiful, and alone.

Now, most women walking into a bar all alone, even at a decent hour, wear about them an uncomfortable air—but not Jill. She stood near Dick and Shit—she had to, the place was too small not to stand near everyone—and knew immediately they would soon be talking to her. She was right. She introduced herself and started to talk about the bar—as if anything she said after the first three seconds would have made a difference.

Shit and Dick were like two male dogs that suddenly smell the same bitch—and if this girl didn't smell like a bitch, then all other assumptions about earthly phenomena would have to be called into question. Drinks were ordered for her, competition to pay for them grew intense, policemen came in to accept bribes from the illicit establishment, and as speech patterns began to slur, the light of a new day grew nigh.

At 5 A.M., the Tiny Bar announced last call, and so came the delicate moment when the three musketeers would become two musketeers and a loser, or perhaps just three people with a crummy rapport. No one knew what was going to happen—or, more accurately, no one with a penis knew. Jill always knew exactly what was going to happen. When it came to men and sex, she was a virtual Nostradamus of late-night encounters.

As the trio stepped outside, Jill asked the two suitors where they lived, looking to Shit first, who responded truthfully, the Upper West Side. Then Dick said he lived right there in the neighborhood, and Jill said she did, too, and would he walk her, and that was the end of that. Shit muttered, "Hope to see you again" as he climbed into a cab, but the hand job was on the wall: Jill was with Dick, and Shit had wasted a night that he could have spent at home masturbating over what might have happened, instead of being slapped with the reality of what did. Not that Shit was a big masturbator, but Jill had a look that could tempt a hardened homosexual to slap the monkey. If she hadn't looked so good he would have given up long ago, because he could see that this girl was trouble.

And being trouble, she wound up with the right guy.

As Shit's cab sped away, Dick asked Jill exactly where her apartment was, and she answered with: "Can I stay at your place? I don't want to face what mine looks like," in a voice as steady and unplayful as Jane Fonda's. Of course, Dick assented, although he was nervous about it, not only because Jill was so beautiful and strong but because, even by Manhattan standards, Dick's apartment was small.

Which is why it seemed so incongruous that a woman as beautiful and sophisticated as Jill would have chosen to stay the night there, and then move in.

The minute they got in the door, Jill kissed Dick passionately, then announced she was tired and going to sleep. She ignored the size of the apartment, the state it was in, the mess on the bed—and Dick. She never said another word the whole night, not counting a grunt or two meant as stern reprimands to Dick's overtures for the sex he thought was not only in the bag but sealed with a twist-em and ready to be taken to the curb. Jill marched around this apartment she'd never before seen as if she'd been living there for years, heading first to the bathroom, then to the closet to don one of Dick's button-down shirts as a nightie, sifting through piles of mess here, opening drawers there to find what she needed, and then finally crawling into bed.

Dick watched in a daze. He didn't know what to do, and that was a feeling either entirely new to him or so old he'd forgotten it. All he could recall about women in his nonplussed state was that if there was a beautiful one in your bed, get in—which he did, but then was stuck again. Jill was curled up on one side, with her back to him, and seemingly already asleep. For the preacher of "no means yes," this sure looked like "no means no."

What it really looked like was marriage.

Dick lay beside Jill for a while, almost happy just to be looking at her, she was that gorgeous. He spent a silent minute lightly stroking her hair, which provoked no discernible reaction of either approval or disgust. He sighed loudly for her benefit, then got on his side of the bed like a good husband. He lay on his back and stared up at the ceiling.

As Dick stretched out in frustration and confusion, he gave serious thought to kicking this chick out—right here, right now: What the hell was going on anyway, and who the fuck did she think she was?

"Hey, hey, excuse me, Jill—Jill-I-don't-even-know-your-last-name: Do you think you might have the courtesy to tell me what's going on? I mean, you ask me if you can stay over, you blow in here like you own the place, stick your tongue down my throat, put on my shirt, use my toothbrush, get in my bed, and then act like I'm a hologram! This isn't a hotel, you know—if you don't want to be bothered, I suggest the Waldorf. I think your manners stink, so why don't you just take your huge purse and get out of here. And get some therapy."

It was a powerful speech, a rousing call to arms against the kind of psychotic women that roamed free on the island of Manhattan—and someday, when Dick decided in favor of saying it out loud, it surely would make him feel like a strong, virile, manly man. But on this night he went to sleep with only a faint hope that his new friend would wake up horny and turn to him for relief.

Jill woke up at two-thirty in the afternoon—not horny, apparently, but hungry, since her first words were, "I'm starving." She helped herself to the kitchen as she had the bathroom, closet, and bed, making eggs and toast for herself and Dick. As he sat down to breakfast, Dick asked Jill about the early appointment she'd spoken of the night before. She dismissed the query with the flip of a hand that was holding a piece of toast.

The evening was coming back to Dick now: Oh yeah, he was with a woman who believed her stunning beauty allowed her to get away with anything—to lie, to explain nothing, to take over a house, to lead him on. Yeah, that's what she thought. Boy, was she, well, kind of sort of exactly right.

When breakfast was over Jill got dressed and, on her way out, admitted that she'd been a bit presumptuous. In a manner for once as sweet as her physical attributes, she gave Dick her undivided attention for one minute, promising to take him for a thank-you drink that night and explain about her behavior. It was Friday, and Dick said he had three sets to do in the city, and Jill said she didn't mind a bit following him around to all of them. Dick told her where he could be found, and off she went, once again kissing him passionately at the door.

Some people need to be out in nature to feel aroused, some need the risk of public discovery; Jill, apparently, needed to be near a door which, fortunately for her, is where she spent a lot of her time.

She showed up for the last ten minutes of Dick's last set at The Club, acknowledging not in the least that she was four hours late.

"You were great," she told Dick, and hugged him. "They loved you."

Dick, who had been making speeches in his mind similar to the one he had made the night before in his bed, got no further in his quest to vent, stifled first by her compliments, then by another flip of the hand, which was accompanied by the words "I got hung up. I'm sorry. You're not mad, are you?" which Dick did not have time to answer before Jill got very close to him for the purpose of again rendering one minute of undivided attention. She kissed the side of his face and then licked the spot where she had kissed, and then said, "Let's go home, okay?" at which point Dick was an accordion and Jill was "Lady of Spain."

The lovebirds, however, were only halfway down the block before Jill asked if they could go somewhere for just one drink.

At one-thirty in the morning inside P.J.'s, Jill was sitting at a big round wooden table with five men and Dick, who wasn't feeling very much like a man. Each of the other men had taken Jill outside at some point to share some cocaine, which apparently put her in such a good mood that every so often she'd reach over and squeeze under the table the clammy hand of the glum-pussed Dick. No other displays of affection with Dick did she allow, however, leaving it very murky to all concerned with whom she had arrived and with whom she might leave.

At three forty-five, the last-call bell drew a huge groan of disappointment from everyone but Dick. The old gang lingered for another half hour until they were literally thrown out onto the street, where Jill suddenly inverted everyone's feelings. She put her arm through Dick's arm and clutched him to her and made it plain with a few smiles and a few words to the other suitors that they had wasted their time. She was with Dick.

Again stunned, Dick walked with Jill back to "their" apartment. Although this was still only their second night together, Jill made it seem like a routine as time-tested as the changing of the guard at Buckingham Palace, except without the tall hats.

For his part, Dick began showing signs of the Swedish syndrome, that phenomenon wherein a captive begins to sympathize with his captors and then embrace their preposterous philosophies. Indeed, there in Dick's closetlike apartment, the situation was taking on an eerie resemblance to the Patty Hearst case. It was only the second night, but somehow Dick knew he'd only get out of this one when *she* decided—and he didn't have a billionaire father or F. Lee Bailey waiting when she did.

And he hadn't even been laid yet! Back at the apartment, it seemed like such a pleasure might be forthcoming, since Jill had her hand on his cock. She was checking it out with her long, pretty fingers, gathering as much data as was possible through the coarse denim of Dick's well-worn Sasson jeans. Perhaps she was deciding, based on what she could feel of Dick's penis, as to how long she would stay with him.

Perhaps she wasn't. With Jill, one never knew.

9

Loyalty Is a
One-way Street

Down in Miami, Buck was busy ingratiating himself with Davey Jay, the headliner that week in the main room of the Statesmanlike Hotel. Davey was a journeyman pop singer whose heyday had been the late fifties, and as such he was a little young to be playing Miami—about fifty. However, his extremely low profile in recent years had aged him sufficiently to qualify in a town where having a record on the charts was considered abrasive and trendy.

Davey was a Jew who acted and did everything in an Italian way, like saying *marone* a lot. Davey's opening act that week in Miami was Bobby Keefer, a journeyman comic who was really Italian but always acted as Jewish as possible, liberally sprinkling his conversation with the kind of Yiddish words and phrases that show people are wont to sprinkle their conversation with. The two men had heretofore maintained a smooth working relationship by never exchanging so much as a single sincere syllable.

But then Bobby ruined everything by getting all sensitive about Davey fucking his wife—a pretty young girl named Bonnie, whom the band members met one night in Abilene, Texas.

At the time of this meeting, Davey and Bobby had been on the road together for about four years, Davey being a good, steady meal ticket for Bobby, and Bobby a good, steady pair of lips on Davey's ass. Bobby was always whining to friends

who came to see him that he had to "hang with" Davey after
the show, but he was really proud that the star requested his
company and he had nothing better to do anyway. He was very
grateful to Davey, although not quite as grateful, apparently,
as Davey thought he should be.

The trouble began when Davey's troupe came to play Abilene
in the summer of 1978. Bonnie, like the one who teamed up
with Clyde, had been looking for a ticket out of Texas ever
since graduating high school two years earlier. Although only
twenty, Bonnie had already spent enough time with older men
to have understand their musical tastes, and that, combined
with the dearth of prey in Abilene for an aspiring starfucker,
inclined her to buy a ticket for Davey's concert.

After the show, Bonnie and her friend Suzie went backstage
to the PERFORMERS ONLY door to see if there was any way
they could get back to see Davey. They were directed to the
PERFORMERS AND BIMBOS WHO WILL FUCK THEM door down the
corridor.

A mob of fan had laid the door under siege, so it took several
seconds for Bonnie and her friend to knife their way through
the completely unfettered space to where the imposing (five-
eight, one-sixty) security guard stood.

Breathlessly, but in a deliberately husky voice, Bonnie
angled with the intimidating gatekeeper.

"Hi. Um, my name is Bonnie, and I met Davey in New
York last year, and he told me to come backstage to see him
when they played here," she lied.

"Sure," said the disinterested sentry.

"He said to mention that I'm a friend."

"Go in," the man insisted as he swung wide the heavy door.

"Oh. Well . . . can my friend come?" Bonnie asked.

"Anybody," the burly Cerebus replied.

So back they went to Davey's impressive dressing room,
deep in the catacombs of Smiley Arena. They passed rooms
full of band members undressing after the show, all of whom
gave Bonnie and her friend a long look. None of them said
anything, because they knew such pulchritude was earmarked
for the boss. The girls passed a room where tray after tray of
refreshments of every kind were laid out—finger sandwiches,

potato salad . . . more finger sandwiches. Plus every brand of soft drink one could imagine.

Finally, the girls came upon the door that said DAVEY JAY on it, in solid-gold tinting.

Outside the door, Bonnie gathered her thought. Inside the room she could hear boisterous revelry, and a tingle of fear ran down her spine, into her ass, and back up a ways to her vagina, where it started a fire that Bonnie hoped she'd find a way to extinguish that night.

She felt excited, and she simply couldn't hide it. She was about to lose control.

"And I think I like it," she said to her friend, who was arranging her breasts in an attractive display. Bonnie primped a little herself in the gold tinting, then knocked on the door.

The girls could hear a laughing voice approach from the other side.

It was Dutch! Dutch, Davey's jovial road manager and man Friday, who could double on woodwinds if you really needed him to. Dutch had been with Davey longer than anybody, from way back in the neighborhood. Davey had gotten Dutch out of the neighborhood, which wasn't necessarily a good thing, since Dutch grew up in Scarsdale. He now resided in Paterson, N.J.

Dutch and Davey had had their ups and downs over the years, but on the whole Davey had been very good to Dutch, always compensating him with something nice for the times that he abused him in public or right in front of the people he cared most about in the whole world. Davey couldn't afford to give away cars like Elvis, but he did proffer generous assortments of candy and leather handbags.

Dutch greeted the girls with a friendly hello that made them feel like they'd known each other all their lives. And in a way, Dutch and Davey and the gang had known Bonnie and her friend all their lives.

Inside the spacious dressing room, a whole other tray of finger sandwiches and potato salad was laid out on the coffee table. It was covered with Saran Wrap, but no one had yet lifted it to avail themselves of the delightful snacks. The reason was obvious: Davey wasn't there yet.

Davey was still inside his walk-in closet, bathroom, and

dressing stall. He was exchanging his white-satin performing garb for some more casual lounging attire, a white-satin lounging outfit. Davey had literally a dozen different lounging outfits for after the show, when scribes for the local media often came back to say a quick hi and apologize for having to skedaddle to make a morning deadline on a late-breaking local story. But before all the craziness started, Davey liked to spend just a few moments where it was peaceful, where he could just be alone with the man he loved. It was his quiet time, the few moments every performer needs to get out of the performance bubble, let the sound of the cheers ring out of his ears, and get back into reality, to say, in Davey's case, "Hey, we're off now, and I'm just a human being like everybody else—no better and no worse. Well, no worse, anyway."

A round of applause and hearty kudos for a great show greeted Davey as he emerged into the company of his friends, men about his age who counted on his working to put bread in their mouths. Davey walked past Bonnie and her friend and headed toward the couch, where he sat down and announced his feeling that they had been a nice crowd and that the band should play here more often. On that, everyone was in easy agreement. As the guys started to settle into chairs around Davey and their spicy, guylike banter ensued, Bonnie stood in the corner, talking to Suzie and wondering if Davey had seen her at all and feeling a bit self-conscious.

Finally, when the conversation and laughter hit a momentary lull of about one hour, everyone all at once seemed to notice the presence of two newly postpubescent females smelling good on the other side of the room.

"We have visitors," Davey said in a friendly manner.

"Oh jeez, girls, I'm sorry, I forgot all about you," Dutch said as he got up to usher them over to where the party was. "You're . . ."

"Bonnie."

"Bonnie, that's right, and you're . . ."

"Susan."

"Davey, this is Bonnie and Susan."

Introductions of the band and the guys were made all around, and chairs were brought over so that the two ladies could sit down. Soon Bonnie and Susan were filling everyone in on their backgrounds—their childhood in Abilene, their jobs, career goals, hopes, and aspirations. The men were helping themselves to the refreshments and pretending they could give a fuck.

After a few minutes, Davey got up and walked over to the piano to talk to an old black man who everyone knew he really wasn't interested in talking to. Even Bonnie worried that she had bored him with her insipid chatter and suicide-inspiring stories, and she was right on both counts. Dutch knew what to do, though: He shepherded Bonnie over to sit on the couch where Davey had been and then engaged Susan in conversation in another part of the room. Bonnie sat alone on the couch for quite a while, during which time the other men in the room looked upon her like a dog does a juicy steak when it's being taught to stay no matter what temptation might be beckoning.

The band was well trained.

Finally, Davey broke off his conversation with Mr. Bojangles and made his way to the couch, where his prey awaited. He let Bonnie gush over him for a minute or two, and then, when the moment was right, leaned far back into the couch, where his request for the use of her vagina would not be audible. Obvious, but not audible.

Davey, always the sensitive one, understood that a girl of Bonnie's tender age required delicate wooing. She wasn't a brazen forty-year-old ex-stripper who'd been around and would happily walk out of a star's dressing room clutching his arm and practically announcing that she was planning to give him a blow job; she would be, but she wasn't yet. But neither did Davey want to let a girl that age out of his sight, for fear she might get cold feet and not want to go back to his hotel. So Dutch got everyone out of the dressing room and took Suzie on a tour of the cold-cut trays, and Davey fucked Bonnie right there on the couch.

After that night, the months passed, and all Bonnie's letters and attempts to make contact with Davey went unanswered. Shockingly, Bonnie was shocked. Finally in the fall, with the band booked into a week at The Sands in Las Vegas, Bonnie decided to give herself a weekend vacation in the city of long odds. Bravely, she went alone, feeling that Suzie would be a nuisance once she was reunited with Davey.

At the Sands, Bonnie again found easy access backstage to Davey's dressing room. She talked to him, but her attempts to demonstrate her hurt bored Davey, and he informed her he was now seriously involved with someone else and couldn't masturbate inside her anymore. Bobby, who was in the dressing room this time and caught the gist of what was going on, asked her to the coffee shop after Davey had exited the party. Bobby was smitten by Bonnie and felt he and she would complement each other well: She was young and beautiful and vulnerable, and he was old and not very good looking and vulnerable. But he was playing Las Vegas, and he was a celebrity, sort of, and he had enough money to show a girl a good time.

For a week.

But what a week it was! Bonnie was the most accommodating girl Bobby had ever met. She let him pay for a room of her own for all seven days and allowed him to soothe her wounded ego and consented to his showering her with attention and expensive gifts—not to mention letting him play a role in hopefully making Davey jealous enough so that he'd fuck her again. If she could just fuck Davey again, Bonnie knew he'd be more receptive to the idea of letting her be his girlfriend. Bonnie had improved her lovemaking skills in the months since they'd met and felt certain it would make a difference.

In the meantime, Bobby had completely exhausted his salary squiring Bonnie around Las Vegas. The only place they went that didn't cost Bobby money was Davey's dressing room after each show, and this was the only place where Bonnie displayed any affection for Bobby, for obvious reasons. Obvious, that is, to everyone but Bobby, who told himself he was glad Bonnie wouldn't go to bed with him because this was the girl he wanted to marry.

And so he did, on the last day in town, after Bonnie had asked Davey one last time if he had any interest and Davey replied that she blew it for all time by "screwing my opening act." This made Bonnie so mad she got married—which seemed like a doubly good idea, since she'd probably lost her job in Abilene by not showing up for work that week.

The band was on the road for another month after Vegas, and Bonnie was now a member of the traveling company. She somehow managed to sleep and be petulant in the day and still dress sexy and act flirtatious to anything with three legs at night. Bobby seemed to enjoy exercising his extreme patience, and Bonnie seemed to enjoy testing it. Yes, they were a perfect match, all right, and all seemed to go smoothly for the next couple of years. Oh, how Bobby enjoyed those wild lovemaking sessions that Bonnie allowed him once a month, whether he needed it or not. In her spare time Bonnie shopped ceaselessly, sometimes buying things for herself.

It was a shame, then, that a couple in such a groove should come to crisis.

So that was the situation—and a tense one—on the January night in Miami when Buck came backstage to meet the two stars of the main room. He was introduced by the hotel's entertainment director as one of the young comedians performing across the way in the Comedy Corner. Immediately, Buck set to work on both Davey and Bobby, his instincts telling him he was in the company of people who could help him or hurt him in the business. He couldn't have been more wrong, but Buck was young, and compared to the world he was in, these guys were big-time. So he turned on the charm.

Buck was terrific at kissing ass and leaving no print. He played the role of the bright student, eager to learn, but added enough spunk to remind the veterans of the way they liked to remember themselves at a comparable time in their careers, around the turn of the ninth century.

And he made them laugh. Buck made sure of this by combing his notebooks in the day for funny anecdotes and stories that, although not fodder for the stage, were perfect conversational apples to toss in at the many brunches to which Davey and

Bobby treated him. Even though the hotel picked up Davey's tab, Buck always remembered his manners after the meal and said, "Thanks."

Bobby, however, who in the past would have bussed the table if Davey had asked him, and did a few times, was becoming more and more sullen every day. Either it was a nagging sinus condition, or perhaps the fact that Davey had started screwing his wife. Why had Davey suddenly started doing this after two years of being around her on the road, when he must have known it could only lead to disaster and absolutely kill Bobby?

Because he felt like it, silly!

So there was Buck, stuck in the middle between these two desperate journeymen who were leading such desperate lives. He remained understanding but neutral with both, who by the middle of the week were no longer talking to each other. What a shame, Buck thought, that it had come to this—and he even flattered himself that he might be able to bring Davey and Bobby back together.

But Buck never got the chance, because on Tuesday night Bobby jumped off the roof of the hotel at exactly seven minutes after twelve, avoiding, by his death, the rebuke of hotel officials, who took a dim view of anyone using the pool area past midnight.

After hearing the tragic news in his suite adjacent to where Bobby had jumped, Davey was beside himself with anxiety: Here it was, closing night of the engagement, and no opening act! Frantic calls were made to New York in the hope that someone could fly down, but a massive storm had shut down all the airports. In desperation, Davey and the staff of the Statesmanlike looked down the bench and asked Buck to suit up and take a step into the big time.

Buck, with at least one foot still in the small time, asked who would take his place that night in the Comedy Corner, not quite realizing that the Comedy Corner was a trifling experiment that cost the hotel nothing and made it the same, and that no one cared if a stack of dirty dishes closed the show in there.

Inside Davey's suite, alone with the great man, Buck listened to some inspirational advice.

"You can bomb, but don't swear," Davey told him, instilling confidence in the newcomer. "Have you ever worked a room like this?"

Buck shook his head.

"Okay, well, it's not like playing the little shitholes you're used to playing. These are nice people in here, good people—they're my people, goddamnit, and if you offend them, they're gonna blame it on me!"

Davey was getting mad before Buck even had the chance to fuck up. Nor had Davey considered that Buck might not want to take this job. Buck had reservations.

"Say, boss," he said. "Don't you think it might be best not to have an opening act tonight, or even cancel the show—I mean, there's been police here all day, and everybody in Florida is pretty aware of what happened."

"Cancel the show?" Davey throbbed. "*Marone!* Kid, I'm not gonna get mad, because I know you don't know shit about this business yet, but lemme tell you something: You don't cancel shows. I don't give a shit who dies—you don't cancel shows."

Davey paused momentarily to consider whether he really believed this or whether he'd just been reciting show business bullshit like it for so long that it came out automatically.

Either answer was fine.

"Do you think I would let those people down? Who do you think I'm up there for? Do you think I'm up there for me? I'm not up there for me, I'm up there because people need entertainment in this country, because they work damn hard fifty weeks a year, and they bust their butts, and they come down here and they wanna forget about all their troubles for a little while. They don't give a rat's ass that my opening act threw himself off a building like the stupid ass he was—they want to have drinks and see a show, and I'll tell you something else: I'm gonna give 'em the best damn show I know how, because that's what this business is all about. You come to me, and you say you're tired, you're sick, your best friend just jumped off the roof, I say to you, Fine, okay, then only give a hundred and fifty percent! And you? You better give more than that, because you never played a room like this and you're gonna have to be the best you ever was, kid, just to pass muster. Can I count on you, kid? Can I?''

"Well, sure, Davey, you know you can, but, I don't know—I feel a little funny stepping in for a man who just died so tragically and—what's the word—*today*.''

"Hey,'' Davey objected. "First of all, he did it to himself, okay? That's number one. The Catholic Church pays no grief to them that do themselves in. And b, are you such a dumb-ass green kid from the suburbs that you don't see an opportunity when it crawls up to you and bites you on the ass? Do you know what this business is all about? Do you?''

"Opportunity,'' Buck said, mouthing the word he knew Davey wanted to hear and would enable him to get out of the room sooner.

"Opporfuckingtunity,'' Davey repeated. "Opportunities don't grow on trees, you know. You gotta be ready when they are. Now, listen to me: If you do good in there tonight, and I know it won't be easy—you're young, it's all new to you, it's not your crowd, they'll hate you for doing Bobby's job, you have no material, you're green, they're old, you're young, your clothes are wrong, you have no experience, you're nervous, you're wrong for the room, you don't know what you're doing—but if you do good in there tonight, there's practically no telling how much good could come from it. I can almost personally guarantee that Mr. Harry Gold of this hotel, who's a very close personal friend of mine, would be anxious to book you in here on a future date—and I don't mean that comedy barrel across the highway, I mean here, in the main room, where I play, where you're gonna play tonight—excuse me, where you're gonna kill 'em tonight!''

Buck winced at the unfortunate phraseology; Davey went on.

"You wanna know how you get to this crowd, kid? I know, you probably think it's all about having talent or quality or being clever, but it isn't. Do you believe me?''

Buck believed him.

"That may be the case in some hippie dive you play in Greenwich Village, but this is real show business here, and these people only care about one thing.''

Davey paused, but since he had just reduced all of show business to one element, Buck, for the first time, hoped he'd continue. To no one's surprise, he did.

"Sweat! That's what it's all about—sweat! They wanna see you sweat. They wanna see you work hard—these are working people, and they wanna see you work as hard as they do."

Buck rolled his eyes in his mind.

"And that's all there is to it. Would you like to come back here and play the big room and have a suite like this and screw some decent tail? Of course you would, but that's not why you should do the job.

"You should do it for Bobby. Because that's exactly what he would have wanted you to do. As a matter of fact, one of the last discussions I had with Bobby was about you. He told me how very much he liked you, kid. You're colleagues, for Christ's sake, cut from the same mold—comics. God, I've known a thousand of them, and they're all alike. You don't do it for the money—and neither did Bobby, and neither does Alan King or Shecky Greene or Buddy Hackett or Pat Cooper or Bob Hope—well, not Bob Hope. But you know what I'm saying, kid—Bobby would have wanted you to step in for him, to make those people laugh and get some relief. As a matter of fact, Bobby said something to me just the other day about how he'd want you to do the show if, God forbid, he fell out a window, honest to Christ."

By now it was obvious to Buck he wasn't going to get out of this no matter how hard he tried, so he kept saying yes, yes, yes, for a few minutes while Davey continued to convince him to do what he'd already agreed to do.

But Buck was scared. The audience might really hate him for taking Bobby's place, and he certainly didn't have enough old-people material to pull it off under the best of conditions. Christ, he hadn't even been doing that well in the little room.

And yet . . . it was undeniably an opportunity, a genuine shot at getting a leg up. Of course, he was using that leg to step over a corpse. But actually, that was better than stepping on someone alive, wasn't it?

Bonnie, on the other hand, secluded herself in her room all day and wouldn't talk to anyone, except long-distance. She tried to sleep, tossing and turning, and then tossing once more before finally drifting off into a deep, satisfying afternoon nap.

In show business, as in life itself, there is no draw like tragedy. On the night of Bobby's death, Davey's show did what it hadn't done in years: It turned people away. There was such a buzz around the showroom, you'd have thought that Davey was once again riding high on the charts—that is, if you really wanted to use your imagination. In addition, every newspaper and television station within a hundred miles had come in to write the story. And the first thing they'd all see was Buck.

Buck went to Bobby's dressing room an hour before the start of the show. Bobby's name was already off the door. Buck felt funny about this—not that Bobby's name was gone, but that his wasn't up.

Inside, Buck availed himself of the wet bar with generous portions of vodka and orange juice. He had worked out what he thought was his best twenty-five minutes of clean material, but he knew there were a lot of areas where the set was weak, namely the beginning, middle, and end. He had never edited so furiously in his life, knowing that the Miami audience wouldn't appreciate drug jokes or musings about what college life was like, since most of them had been out of college since the Great War, not to mention that all the dick jokes and stuff about dating had to go, as did political opinions, which they'd surely think he was too young to have . . .

God, I'm fucked, Buck thought.

But although Buck didn't know much about show business, he did know this: When they say your name, you gotta walk out there, no matter what.

Walking out there was the easy part. It was when he began to speak that the trouble started.

His first joke, which he thought couldn't miss, got nothing. Ditto jokes two through five. Buck was not a sweater, but for the first time in his young stage life, he felt a trickle on his neck. That's when he made a conscious, calculated decision: panic. If there was ever a time to panic, this was it. So two minutes into his act, he went into his closing segment, the family stuff, which he figured would be his best bet with the Miami audience.

The very strongest of it got titters. Buck felt another drop of sweat on his neck: flop sweat. He'd heard the term, but he'd always been much too cool a customer to experience it. But there it was, a bead of perspiration undeniably inspired by flop.

That's when Davey's voice rang in his head, like some bad echoing effect from an old *Superman* episode: "Sweat! They wanna see you sweat!"

Well, they were seeing it, all right. But no, that's not what Davey meant. He meant like . . . work hard?

Yes, that must be it.

With nothing to lose, Buck experienced another first. He took the microphone off the stand and started to prowl the stage. He had heretofore in his career eschewed this practice religiously, believing the focus should be on the verbal message alone. But Buck was determined this would not be another Montreal, no matter what he had to do, including taking advice from Davey. Buck began to work the room.

Since he had no material left, this consisted mainly of talking to the crowd. He started with a stock ruse of asking how many people were from out of town, and then, when many raised their hands, added, ". . . and have never had sex?"

To his amazement, this stupid, corny joke got a respectable laugh, and it led easily into asking someone in the front row where he was from. After that, he just played it like he was MCing a Tuesday night back in New York, the only difference being his concession to stage labor. Buck paced, projected his voice, and even made sweeping, overblown physical gestures. The audience didn't exactly howl, but as he well knew, a lame joke played as an ad-lib often got a big laugh, and he got a few of those.

When he got off to respectable applause, Buck felt he had at least acquitted himself in making the audience forget about Bobby. Of course, the audience had never really heard of Bobby before he killed himself, so it wasn't all that big a trick.

But it was better than bombing, which could easily have been his fate.

Buck passed Davey in the wings as he came off, but Davey was concentrating too hard to give Buck the sign of approval he was so desperately seeking. But that was understandable, because now that Davey was on, the crowd would again be thinking about Bobby. And Davey, pro that he was, knew exactly what to do about it: Open with a hit! Davey knew what the audience wanted, a combination of old music and new bathos for the recently departed "best friend I ever had." A few songs in, Davey stopped the show and milked Bobby's death shamelessly. Buck, who always prided himself on beating disillusionment to the punch, was genuinely appalled at the display.

Why don't you tell them why the poor bastard killed himself, he thought to himself, but without any fear that he actually might say it out loud. What good would it do? You have to use these people to get past them, just like at the club—don't hate people for being stupid; use their stupidity to conquer them.

Still, the atmosphere backstage was enough to turn anyone's stomach, what with all the sickly self-congratulations for getting through the horrid ordeal of another man's horrid ordeal. This, Buck thought, was the problem with human nature: Your boss fires you, and all he worries about is how bad that makes *him* feel; a guy takes his own life, and everybody feels sorry for themselves for having to put up with such an unpleasant experience. In such a world, it didn't pay to make enemies, or theoretical points, until you could do something about them.

And besides, Davey had been kinda right about the crowd.

In New York, Fat was dealing with the problem of Tammy's impending abortion in his own inimitable way. After Tammy insisted that he be with her for the ordeal, Fat got on the phone and tried to book himself in the Wilmington area sometime in the next nine months. He had done well enough at the Comedy Cave in November to be promised a return engagement as a middle act, but Dino was already booked many months in advance. He offered Fat an immediate opening as MC again, but Fat insisted on the middle spot he had been promised. Sure, Tammy was a little anxious about his child growing inside her, but sometimes in this business you just had to "hold out" for what was right.

Finally, Tammy called Fat and begged him to come down, irrespective of a gig.

"What's the rush?" Fat wanted to know.

Tammy started screaming and crying. Fat argued that if he came down now as MC, it would be even longer before he could return as a middle act. Tammy could take no more.

"Just come down here, okay? I don't care if you have a job or not. I'm pregnant for God's sake!"

Fat was hurt. "Oh great, it's nice to know you really care about my career. I'm glad I found this out about you now."

Tammy didn't know what to say. She wound up swallowing her tears and soothing his ego, telling him what a great comedian he was and cajoling him until he finally said, "Oh, all right," and bought a ticket for the following Monday.

Fat arrived at one-nineteen in the afternoon, two trains after the one he said he'd be on, while Tammy waited in the station, worrying if he'd show up.

"I though maybe you'd bring me something," Tammy said.

"Like what?" Fat wanted to know.

"Like anything. People do get presents when they go in the hospital, you know."

"Are we going to a hospital?" Fat asked.

"A clinic, yes."

"Oh, a clinic. Okay. A clinic's okay."

God knows what Fat could have been thinking.

At the abortion clinic, Fat entered a difficult situation. For any man who walked in, it was obvious what his role in the whole scheme was. Every guy there looked suspiciously like the kind of guy who would knock up the kind of girl he was with. And no one looked more like they'd done it to each other than Fat and Tammy.

Talk about dagger eyes, Fat thought.

He didn't make matters any better, however, by not realizing that the clinic, with an audience of women waiting to have children cut out of their wombs, was a bad place to argue a bill. But he did, battling for a healthy fifteen minutes over a perceived discrepancy.

"Okay, let's split the difference," the exasperated haggler finally offered. The angry lesbian who was speaking to him at her desk went backstage to find her immediate superior, an even angrier lesbian.

"Okay, sixty-forty," Fat bargained, but he didn't want to go any lower. Unless she threw something in, like a frequent user coupon or something.

Again, Tammy had to coax Fat with sweetness before he desisted. Also, she agreed to pay a little more than the half of the cost they had agreed upon (minus the train ticket, which was fifty bucks).

When he was informed that the process would take four to six hours before Tammy could be released, Fat announced that he was going over to the Marine World museum and would be back around six to pick her up.

Killing a day in Wilmington is not as easy as it sounds. After the museum, Fat ate a huge sandwich at a shop in the nearby arcade, which also housed the comedy club. Fat wandered around the shops, fighting off the temptation to go over to the club, the scene of his first out-of-town gig, a gig that had gone damn well, Fat thought—damn well! He had shown a few people something—outdoing the middle act one night and getting good laughs, and Dino had liked him and given him a return booking . . .

Yeah, it had gone pretty darn all right, all right.

It wasn't long before Fat could fight the urge no longer, so he went over to the club and stood all alone on the stage of his recent triumph and dreamed his big dreams. He saw the image of a man—a fat man, granted—at the pinnacle of show business success, with all the trappings. In fact, mostly trappings: vast wealth, a mansion, clamoring fans, autograph signings—not to mention all those people who used to treat him like shit now fawning all over him, fawning a lot and practically crying to him about how horribly they had underestimated him and what a genius he was and he, listening to them for a while but then treating them like vomit, but with bodyguards.

And girls. All sorts of girls who would do anything he wanted, and who wanted it real bad from him and who always dressed sexy for him because they knew it pleased him, so they did it, because he was the greatest lover they'd ever had, so good that they didn't care about his being fat at all. They just wanted his great cock, where obesity was an asset.

After his visit to the club, Fat got his caricature done in the arcade. If there was a person alive who didn't need to have his features exaggerated, it was Fat. But he liked the drawing anyway, and he decided it would be his gift to Tammy.

Around four o'clock, Fat decided to head into another section of town, which was an unfortunate decision because two blocks north of the club Wilmington got a bit rough—or, as Dino had charmingly put it one summer night when his club was empty: "Wait till eleven, when the niggers come out, then all the white people will want to be inside."

At five, Fat arrived at the clinic in a pool of sweat, scared out of his mind because some of the niggers had decided to come out before eleven. He sat in the lobby and waited for Tammy. When they brought her out in a wheelchair, Fat leapt up out of his seat.

"Oh my God, what happened?"

"Nothing, I'm fine," Tammy said as she stood up and put on her coat. "Just drive me home, okay?"

Fat drove Tammy's car back to Tammy's comfortable house in the suburbs, where neither of her parents had yet gotten home from work. Tammy was glad about that. She leaned on Fat to make it up the stairs to her bedroom, and there lay exhausted on the bed, surrounded by a vast menagerie of stuffed animals and the head shot Fat had sent to her, and which he had signed, in an effort to appear burdened with sending out hundreds of such photographs every day, "Best wishes," in a hurried script.

Tammy asked Fat to bring her some orange juice from downstairs, which he happily did, and then sat down on the bed facing her and tried to be tender.

Then he tried to get her to have sex.

"Please!" she said, pushing him away. "You're gross! I just had an abortion—or don't you remember why you're here?"

"I know, but how many chances do we get to be alone?" Fat asked in his insistently logical way.

At that, Tammy burst into tears and threw him out of the house. She said she wished she'd never met him and that this day would have been easier without him and that he should go straight to hell—which he almost did, because he headed back to the train station after dark.

He got back to New York at eleven-thirty, in time to do a set.

10

The Nice-Ass Act of 1980

On the first day of February, the celebration of Shit's thirtieth birthday began in earnest. Buck and Shit met in Central Park at noon and dropped some acid that Buck had bought from a cabdriver some months before. They chatted while leisurely oscillating on the swings that faced Central Park South a few hundred feet away and waited for the drugs to take effect.

"Do you feel anything yet?" Buck asked his friend.

"I don't know. I feel good. I don't know if it's the drugs."

"I think it is."

"Why?"

"Because I paid good money for them, and I'd hate to think we could be feeling good for free."

"Well, would you feel you got your money's worth if I told you that on this next swing I think I can jump over the Essex House?" Shit asked, referring to the hotel across 59th Street.

Apparently, the drugs were working. For the next fifteen minutes, every time the boys swung back toward the mammoth building with the letters spelling ESSEX HOUSE on top, they found it impossible to control their laughter.

"Hey, kid, how you doin'?" Buck asked a child on the adjacent swing as a great surge of energy pumped through his body and he struggled to make his swing realize its 360-degree potential.

The child, a New Yorker, knew better than to talk to lunatics.

He also knew that his silence would not discourage lunatics from further conversation.

"Does your mommy fool around?" Buck asked the child.

"Hey!" Shit admonished, decency-aware even on acid. "Look at us. We're like two pervert bums who go to the park in the day and abuse the facilities and corrupt youths."

"Yeah," Buck countered, "but there's one big difference between those kind of bums and us."

"What's that?" Shit giggled.

"Well, those kind of bums, they're restricted by their socioeconomic status and by a certain lack of ambition toward upward mobility, whereas we, we can jump over the Essex House!!"

And with that, they damn near did.

Okay, they didn't, but they felt they had a real shot at it. Buck put every fiber of his being into swinging, not just higher and higher, but higher than Shit, who noticed the competition.

"Are you trying to beat me?"

"Why—is one missing?" Buck responded.

Now they were nearly falling off the swings, they were laughing so hard.

"Wait," Buck said, like a little boy who's losing a race and will use any ploy to slow down his competitor. "I think I'm getting sick."

"Let's stop, then."

"Okay, but let's go off together—at the top of the swing."

"No, we'll kill each other."

"Why? We like each other."

"No, I mean we'll kill ourselves."

"Oh, well that's very different, kill ourselves. Let's do it anyway. Ready—"

"Hey, don't!—"

But it was too late. Buck had launched himself at the top of his arc, hoping to land on 58th Street, on the other side of the Essex House, but unfortunately falling short and hitting the hard pavement, which would have been harder except that the blow was softened by a mound of fresh dog shit. This bothered Buck much more than the pain of the fall.

"Ahhh!" he screamed. "I'm in shit!" and he pulled off his

pants faster than Clark Kent in a phone booth. "Is it on my shirt? Is it? Is there any on my shirt?"

"No," Shit told him as he removed his own pants in a show of support, and also because he loved to remove his pants.

"What you suffer, I suffer, pal," Shit said as he balled up his pants and threw them in the trash can after Buck's example.

After they stopped laughing, Buck said: "Have you noticed it's freezing? We should go to my apartment and put on suits so we can go someplace nice. Let's get a cab."

"We can't get a cab."

"Why?"

"Because they won't pick us up. You clean scum stains off the backseat of your car every night and see if you wanna pick up two guys without pants on."

"Good point. I knew there was some reason why you were with the firm."

So the boys went walking out on the sidewalks of New York, barely noticed, of course, for their lack of leggings. When they got to Buck's apartment, they were freezing so badly it really wasn't funny anymore. They quickly ripped the blankets off Buck's bed and wrapped them around their legs. Then they waited for the next wave of acid fever to hit them, so that once again the laughs would come in that free and easy manner rendered by drugs.

This was, after all, what they were after: free fun, which was worth paying for.

Satisfied that the next wave had indeed washed ashore inside their febrile brains, and reclad for Gotham's tonier haunts, the chums started to rummage around for suitable props to bring along. Shit settled on a candle in the shape of a human skull that Buck was too cheap to have ever lit, and Buck grabbed an oversized green pen with a jester's head on the end of it and a bell inside. They checked themselves in the mirror and somehow decided they were human.

Like badgers who accidentally find something good in a garbage can they've tipped over, the boys instinctively headed back toward where they had last had fun, the park. This brought them close enough to the Plaza Hotel to see it, and seeing it was enough to make them go inside.

The Oak Room was pretty quiet, except for a few out-of-town businessmen and a high-priced hooker or two. Shit and Buck ordered highballs, and then, for reasons known only within their electrified minds, decided that every statement they uttered was too important not to be signed into legislation, which of course involved that big green pen and a pile of cocktail napkins, a new one for every "law."

"Look at the ass on that woman," Shit said, and the Nice-Ass Act of 1980 was duly enacted by Buck, the jester's bell on the end of the pen clanging away amid the stuffy decorum of the Oak Room.

Eventually, this did attract some attention.

"Excuse me, gentlemen," an immaculately liveried hotelperson interrupted. "I wonder if you'd allow me to buy your last round of drinks and you'd consider doing your drinking somewhere else this afternoon."

"Ladies and gentlemen, you'll have to excuse my partner," Buck said, mimicking the standard apologia of ventriloquist acts the world over and laughing way too loudly for the room. "You mean that's all you have to do to get free drinks in this town—drop acid and act obnoxious in public? Where should we go tomorrow?"

"Does Sidney Eden still work here?" Shit asked the hotel official as he was about to throw the boys out.

"Yes," came the surprised response from the man. "Do you know him?"

Did Shit know him—what a silly question. Turns out, Shit not only knew him, he used to work with him, right there at the hotel.

"You were a hotel dick here?" Buck asked incredulously as a round of free drinks arrived at their table. "At the Plaza Hotel? I can't believe that. I don't believe you. How many lives have you led? How old are you?"

"Thirty—remember, this is my birthday?"

"Oh yeah. Well, here's to you, pal," Buck said, hoisting his glass. "You are really a piece of work. I get the feeling that someday I'm gonna find out that you were the long-sought fifth man in the famous MI spy ring in England. It was Philby, Maclean, Burgess, Blunt—and you."

"Don't mention it till after I'm dead," Shit requested. "I still have friends in the Kremlin."

Forgoing the invitation of a free suite at the Plaza, Buck and Shit headed back to Buck's apartment for the surprise party that Buck had planned for Shit. He had given Jeannie the keys to his place, with instructions to set up and then let everybody in at five o'clock.

"Surprise!" they all yelled when the tripping twosome came in the door. Shit absorbed the shock and then gave Buck a kiss on the cheek.

Most of Shit's comedian friends were there, including Fat, Chink, Norma, and Dick, who brought his new constant companion, Jill. Most of the waitresses from the Club were there, too.

Pretty soon it was obvious to the other guests that Buck and Shit were on something that they weren't, namely a roll.

"Are you guys doing something?" Dick wanted to know, with a gleam in his eye that said he'd like to be doing it too.

"Well, that depends on what you mean by . . . guys," Buck responded, and of course he and Shit disintegrated immediately.

"Acid," Dick stated.

"Wow," said Buck, impressed. "I think I'm losing my mind."

"You gave up a nice piece of it today," Shit reminded him.

"Do you really think so?"

"It's called acid, do you think it's good for you? But hey, what do you want, thoughts until you die? We'll have our fun now, and in about ten years we'll go down to that hospital in Dallas where they keep Kennedy's brain and play cards all day and try to remember which one of us was president."

"Hey, you wanna play a word game?" Buck asked.

"Sure, I'm word. I mean, I'm game."

"Okay, try to think of a word."

"Yeah . . ."

"That's it. That's as much as we can do."

"Okay, you go first."

"Ah . . . I pass. I'm stumped. Let's find some girls."

"You have a girl here."

"Oh yeah. I think I'm gonna break up with her, though."

"With Jeannie? Why?"

Before Buck could answer, Dick and Jill appeared with naughty smiles. Dick introduced Jill to Buck and Shit, who said to Jill: "Yes, we met the night . . . well, the night you chose Dick, quite frankly."

"Right, hi," she said, then paused for a millisecond before asking who had the drugs.

"Here you go," Buck said, producing a small square of paper wrapped in a small plastic bag. "We need something to cut it in half. Anybody have a scissors?"

"Who am I, Harpo Marx?" Dick replied. "Yeah, I've got a candle under here, and a swordfish—"

"Hey, come over here, son," Buck barked in Fat's direction, and Fat happily complied. "You got a knife or something on you?"

"Swiss Army knife?"

"Perfect."

"What are you doing?" Fat wanted to know.

"Cutting some paper in half."

"What is that paper?" Fat asked.

"Tomorrow's *Enquirer*," Dick said. "It's on a microdot for reasons of national security—in fact, to play it safe, I better eat it. Here, honey, you take the other half in case they cut me open."

Fat thought about this for a long while, then said: "No, really, what is it?" which slayed everybody.

"It's acid, you bohunk," Buck said, but Fat still was in the dark. "Acid. LSD. Whaddaya want, the chemical formula?"

"You're doing LSD?" Fat shouted.

"Who's doing LSD?" the encircling crowd now wanted to know.

"Well, everybody can do LSD if they want to," Buck announced.

But there were few takers: Norma was too old; Fat was too young; and the waitresses had to go to work. But when Jill said to Buck and Shit, "Oh come on, do some more with us," they did, thereby keeping intact her record of never having any man refuse a request of hers.

As for Chink, he already looked like he was having a bad trip, and in truth, ever since Norma had dumped him, a bad trip is exactly what his life had been. Chink had not wanted to come to this party, because he knew he'd see Norma there, and it was difficult enough having to see her at The Club. But he could not snub Shit, no matter how painful. And now Shit and Buck were pressuring him to take acid with them.

"No, I can't," Chink demurred.

"Come on," Buck pleaded.

"No, really. No."

"Come on, it's his birthday, you can't turn down a man's request on his birthday."

Chink shook his head.

"Oh come on," Shit chimed in. "When you do acid with a friend, it creates a bond that can never be broken. It's like what the Indians used to do."

"The Indians did acid?"

"Yeah, the Cleveland Indians. Why do you think they always lose?"

"Indians do peyote," Dick corrected.

"Well, I'm flattered," Chink mumbled, "but—"

"Good, then eat this," Buck said, and tried to stuff a wad into his mouth.

"I can't," Chink insisted, removing the wad from his lips.

"Why? You won't die. We know it's good 'cause we did some already," Buck lobbied.

"And now we did more," Shit added.

"I don't know," Chink whined, sounding less sure.

"Please, pal—have I ever led you astray? Do it for me, for my thirtieth-birthday present," Buck said.

"But it's not your birthday," Chink reminded him.

"Okay, well maybe not, but it will be, and then you'll have already given me a present."

Chink slunk silently.

"Plee-eese," Buck pleaded. "Plea-eee-eese."

"I'm not feeling that good these days."

"All the more reason to take it," said Shit.

"Really?"

"Of course—why do you think they call them drugs?" Shit added, not aware that he had left out several paragraphs of the argument—and a specious one at that—leading up to his conclusion.

"It makes you feel better?" Chink asked, in a tone more like a man wanting to be convinced.

"Does it make you feel better?" Buck shot back. "Hey, does one thing that's a lot like another thing . . . compare in a compelling way to . . . the first thing?"

Everyone stared at him.

"Okay, it's a little general."

"But then again so was Napoleon," Shit told Buck, "who, by the way, you've been acting a lot like lately."

By the raucous laughter, Chink could see that his friends were not lying about the drug's fun-engendering properties. Unfortunately, though, he was unaware of the drug's other properties.

"All right, just a little bit," Chink said.

"Great, I'll fix you a beginner's dose," Buck said, and gave him half a tab, same as everybody else.

In another hour, the people who were tripping were tripping and the people who weren't were leaving. And the people who were about to jump out the window, like Chink, were sitting on the ledge and looking longingly at the street below as if it were a gentle and inviting tropical pool.

"I'm worried about Jill," Dick came over to say.

"Why, is she having a bad trip?" Shit asked.

"She must be. She's acting nice. Hey, you mind if we use the bedroom?"

"You're in the bedroom," Buck told him.

"Oh. Well then, thank you in advance," Dick said.

But Jill wanted a real bedroom. They left as if the apartment were on fire.

Meanwhile, no one seemed to notice Chink. Chink, however, was noticing them—especially Norma, as she flirted and played around with the boys. Nothing unusual, but in Chink's state it was ruinous. He watched her plant a big kiss on Buck's cheek.

"Thank you for the other night," Norma told Buck.

"What?" Buck pretended not to know.

"I know you did that for me," Norma continued, "and I just want to say thank you."

"All right," Buck relented, "but don't let it get around that I'm not a prick. It'll ruin my reputation."

Indeed it might have, because what Buck had done for Norma—setting her up at his own expense—*was* pretty darn nice. And smoothly executed, to boot, because Norma had an audition at The Club for some people from a local TV magazine show who'd come in to see her about doing a segment about women in comedy or women in society or women in prison— whatever, it was women in something, and Buck knew that. So before he brought up Norma, he did ten minutes of the most tasteless male-chauvinist pig material he could remember, leaving her with all the sympathy in the room and the easy structure of rebuttal in which to do her set.

"Well, I have to go," Norma finally said.

"Oh, don't go," Buck implored.

"I have to MC."

"Oh, give it a rest for one night," said Buck.

"Yeah, rest it right over here," Shit piped up, slapping his thigh as if for the attention of a dog.

"Come on," Buck added. "His dick is thirty years old today, go sit on it for a minute."

"Well, if you put it like that." Norma chortled and sat down on Shit's lap. It was all very innocent, but across the room Chink was getting quietly suicidal.

After Norma left, Buck noticed that Chink was staring out the window like a cat.

"I think I'm having a bad trip," Chink told Buck.

"Why do you say that?"

"I can only think about death."

"Food for thought," Buck rejoined. "Okay, let's do something to cheer you up."

"The clock never moves," Chink said, indicating the digital clock-radio on Buck's nightstand. "It's always on six six six."

"Well, it's just the time, six . . . sixty-six. Yeah, it's six sixty-six."

Something about that didn't sound right to Buck, but he couldn't put his finger on what it was.

"There is no six sixty-six," Chink said softly.

"Well, that's what you get for getting your clock from a bank."

Buck went over to Shit. "Hey, we gotta get outta here. He's depressed."

"Depressed? Well give him some acid!" Shit yelled.

"No, I'm not kidding."

"Well, take him for a walk outside. The fresh air will do him good," Shit said, possibly thinking of the effect fresh air had on drunkenness.

"That's a good idea," Buck said, possibly not thinking at all.

So Buck took Chink downstairs for a walk while Shit stayed behind with the last few guests.

Outside, Chink looked bad. Buck yelled at him a little and he wasn't kidding: Chink was seriously acting like a retard. In fact, that's what clued Buck in to his next course of action.

"What are you, retarded?" he asked Chink—and then it hit him that yes, perhaps Chink *was* retarded now, retarded because he, Buck, had absolutely insisted that he swallow this illegal, toxic, and highly dangerous mind-altering drug.

Which very well might be a lot to live with.

"Okay, buddy, we're going to the hospital now," he told Chink, who was agreeable to almost anything in the way any inanimate object is if you can lift it. Chink was looking like Joey from the movie *Stalag 17*, the simpleton in camp who'd been rendered so mentally void that even the Nazis allowed him free rein.

Ignoring the party in his apartment, or perhaps forgetting there was one, Buck hailed a cab. He arrived at Roosevelt Hospital with a sack of runny kelp. He barged into the emergency room and demanded to be helped immediately.

"Excuse me, I think I have the biggest emergency," he said, pushing past a man with an ax in his head.

He stood the drooling Chink up in front of the white-coated

black staffperson and was shocked when the man quickly agreed.

"O.D.?" the man asked. Buck looked around sheepishly at all the people staring at him: It turned out his *was* the biggest emergency.

"Yes," he blurted, then looked back at the people. They had not moved. They had not blinked. They could care less. They were *all* Chinks.

But Chink was still the worst Chink of all.

"What drug did he do?" the staffer asked.

"LSD," Buck said.

"Come with me," the man said.

Buck accompanied Chink and the man to an examination room, then was told to go back and wait. He returned to the welcoming wounds of the gang who had seen his entrance. It was a fun group.

At stage left was the axman; in the corner, a guy with his foot wrapped in a bloody rag, his shirt; over by the door, another pool of blood sitting on the floor—and these were the ones who were waiting, as if this were a dermatologist's office, and their biggest worry was the outdated magazines and the fact that someone had already penciled in the answers to the "Hidden Pictures" section of *Highlights for Children*.

Oh God, Buck thought: Pleeeeeze make Chink okay! Pleeeeze!

As mortals sometimes do, even those not on acid, Buck now mortgaged all future pleasures to God if He'd just intercede on Chink's behalf. Luckily, Buck *was* on acid, so God answered.

"Talk to me," God said. "What are we really talking about here? Get specific."

"Anything," Buck pleaded. "You can have it all."

"What's all?" God asked. "You mean you'll quit comedy, give up sex, accept dead parents? I can make you an unfunny eunuch orphan if I save your friend?"

Oh God, Buck thought.

"Yes?" God said.

Damn, Buck thought—if I could only go over His head.

"I heard that," God said. "And you can just forget it. Not that I don't have a boss, but since I know what you're thinking all the time, you'll never get through. I'm your only taskmaster as far as you know."

"Then you're a middleman," Buck said.

"Never mind about that," said God, in a testy voice that betrayed his cool and indicated that Buck was hitting a little too close to home. "Just tell me what you're offering. I tell you what, you can keep one of them. You can be an unfunny eunuch or a eunuch orphan or an unfunny orphan, but you don't have to be an unfunny eunuch orphan. So what's it gonna be?"

"Fuck you," Buck said out loud, and that got a few people's attention.

"Ha, ha, ha," God mocked, not laughing but actually saying, "Ha ha ha."

"Fuck you," Buck thought, more quietly.

"Blow me," God replied.

"Eat shit," Buck shot back.

"In your ear with a nigger's spear," God said.

"Christ, you are such an asshole," Buck thought. "I can't believe I'm finally having a conversation with God, and this is what you're like."

"Takes one to know one," God said.

"Real mature," Buck thought, sarcastically.

"Oh, and I suppose you're Mr. Perfect," God rejoined.

"Well at least I don't talk like a five-year-old."

"Do too."

"Do not."

"Too."

"Not."

"Too."

"Not."

"Hmm, hmm, hmm, hmm, I can't hear you," God said, humming with his fingers in his ears.

Arright, arright, just go to hell, Buck thought.

"I can arrange that for you if you keep up this snotty attitude," God said. "My friend the devil will be happy to punish you."

"Oh, I get it," Buck replied. "You and the devil, with your good-cop, bad-cop game. The devil punishes us in the afterlife if we get bitter about the way you punish us on earth. Is that it?''

"You're very brave when you're around your friends," God snickered.

With that Buck shot up in his chair and pulled himself out of the acid-induced reverie. This was really becoming a bad trip. He couldn't let himself slip into Chinkland. He started to pester the staffer for a progress report on Chink. The man asked Buck if he'd done the drug too. Buck nodded.

"Maybe you should get yourself looked at," the man said.

"No, I'm okay," Buck said.

"Suit yourself," the man said.

Buck went back to waiting, alternating between worrying about Chink and hating himself. Each second was an excruciating instrument of torture. Then it got worse.

"He's asking for you," the intern told Buck.

"How do I find him?" Buck asked.

"Follow the yellow line till it doesn't go anymore, then take the blue line . . ."

Buck nodded as the man droned on through all the primary colors, but he knew he wasn't up to concentrating enough to memorize the instructions. Nevertheless, he started down the corridor.

Okay, he thought, follow the yellow . . . brick road? Did that guy just say that to me, or did I just dream that up because I'm on acid?

The momentary thought that he actually might be in *The Wizard of Oz* caused Buck to pause, but he continued on, and everything seemed normal: trees were hurling apples at him, munchkins danced from gurneys, the Tin Man's EKG chart showed marked improvement. Now if he could just find Toto—er, Chink. He finally stopped to ask directions from someone.

"Hi. Um, I'm looking for my friend, and I forgot the directions the man told me."

"What man?"

"You know, Roy G. Biv. The guy with all the col—"

"Oh, it's you," the man said. "You were talking to me."

Buck, it turned out, had only gone about five feet.

"Let me take you," the man said.

He led Buck down the yellow brick line, to the blue line, the IRT line, the shuttle to Times Square—it seemed to go on forever. Finally, Buck was in a huge room full of people lying down. It didn't look like *The Wizard of Oz* anymore; it looked like *Gone With the Wind*, that bad day after the battle with all the soldiers lying in the street. Buck wished the movie references would stop. Then he saw his Andalusian Dog, Chink.

"I want to see Norma," Chink drooled.

"Norma?" a confused Buck asked.

"Norma. Norma. Norma . . ."

That's all Chink could say: "Norma." So Buck called Norma at The Club.

"You gave him acid? You asshole!" she screamed. "I'll be right there."

And then Norma, who'd spent the last six years of her life making sure she was always on safe ground at The Club, abandoned her MC post and called out to the bartender that she had to leave and flew out the door.

Needless to say—well then, forget it.

The bad acid trip marked the beginning of one of those antiflow weeks for Buck when nothing came easily, except bad things. He was badly shaken by almost killing Chink; he hadn't written a new joke in weeks, so performing stand-up was in one of its periodic fallow periods; he wanted out of the Jeannie relationship; the weather sucked; and he had a big zit on his face.

The zit was the worst of it.

It really was, because it meant he hated going out, even to the corner fruit stand, where they were probably talking about it in Korean. With Jeannie, it made him constantly duck his head down lest his eyes meet hers looking at it. And he generally acted very depressed, as if the zit was the least of his problems, but it really wasn't, it was the worst of them, because a flaming blemish was bad enough during normal intercourse with people, but to go onstage in that condition was beyond the pale. What if someone heckled it? No one could live through that! So Buck said he had the flu straight through the weekend, seeing no one and venturing out only for vital supplies, like orange juice and the new *Penthouse*.

By Sunday night, Buck was depressed because he'd taken the whole week off and hadn't done a lick of work. A week all alone inside is just what I need to recharge myself, he told himself on Tuesday—I'll get a shitload of work done. But the solitary days flew by: Wednesday, Thursday—well, you get the idea. By Sunday night it was just like school: a whole week to write the paper, and you just start to think about it during *Ed Sullivan*. Buck hated himself. He'd wasted an opportunity.

Especially since a week off from having to go out every night *was* a great opportunity, because somehow the number-one priority—creating comedy material—always wound up last on each day's things-to-do list, which meant it usually never got done at all. Buck could never figure out where the time went, although his dissipation of that precious commodity was no different from that of most of the young comedians in New York:

Wake up in the afternoon, only to be greeted by an immediate need to unload some testosterone, so a little masturbation is in order—which, of course, puts you right back to sleep. An hour later you're up again, but with a headache from oversleeping. Now it's two-thirty, and there's only a half-hour before the bank closes, so you can forget about that seldom-realized goal of putting in an hour of writing immediately upon arising while the mind is clearest, like real writers do. No, you've got to get to the bank, because your sixth sense, the one that you use for financial matters in lieu of an accurate checkbook, tells you something is going to bounce. After the bank, a quick stop at Blimpie for a health breakfast seems reasonable—you know, because you're passing Blimpie anyway—but by the time you get back to the apartment, the cheese sub has sunk right to lethargy central; you're exhausted. Well then, it's a good time to read the newspaper, which, you tell yourself, is kind of like work, because in comedy, after all, you need to know what's going on in the world. Especially with the Knicks, Rangers, Yankees, and Giants.

Four-ten: Oh my golly, the afternoon installment of *Mary*

Tyler Moore—God forbid New Yorkers go twelve hours without checking in on the WJM gang—is on in twenty minutes, and watching that is also kind of like work, since it's the best sitcom ever, and memorizing every episode couldn't hurt. Unfortunately, twenty minutes isn't enough time to really start any work—but a crossword puzzle and a trip to see if the mail came yet would fit in nicely. Five o'clock: well, *Mary*'s over, I guess I'll just flick off the old boob tube—what's that? Charles Nelson Reilly is guesting on *Live at Five*? I love him!

Six o'clock?! Already? Holy cow, there's an army of phone calls to be returned. And at seven it's time to eat again and at seven-thirty to shower and at eight to get dressed . . .

So Buck invariably looked over the notes to his act while riding the bus to The Club at eight-thirty. There was a vicious cycle going on here: without any new jokes that the comedian is anxious to try out, his entire performance is suffused with ennui; and in turn, the memory of an ennui-suffused set robs the comedian of the inspiration he needs to force himself to write new jokes. Even a single new idea would suffice to break the cycle: Like a great piece of gossip you're dying to tell everybody, one new bit could invigorate an entire set, often breathing new life into old material or "making a home" for three old jokes that would now work well behind the new one. But with no new joke-blood, the entire act actually shrinks. The current-events joke isn't so current anymore, and the conceptual bit that requires extra commitment to pull off seems too risky to do, and the really old material is just so boring at this point . . .

The cure for such a period of atrophy, Buck knew, was very simple: hard work, the castor oil for creative depression. But hard work was—well, hard. It was easier to balm the ill than to cure it.

So during his week inside, Buck watched a lot of TV and read a lot of magazines and took lot of comfort and old-fashioned female soothing from Jeannie, helping himself to generous portions of affection when he was hungry for it, and seconds and thirds of solace.

And then, when he was feeling a little bit better, he dumped her.

. . .

Buck had been wanting to break it off with Jeannie for some time. Her standard three-month contract was nearing expiration, and Buck had decided to put her on waiver with the intent of gaining her outright release. Buck had gotten Jeannie to love him, so there was no further need to be charming or on the make, so what was the point?

Buck was bored. He no longer said, "I love you," only, "I love you, too." He did love Jeannie, but without any passion. He knew the second he broke up with her, he'd feel the panic of being totally alone again. But the situation had become intolerable, so the only thing to do was to be strong and tell her.

Well, maybe strong is too strong a word. Weak, on the other hand, and passive—these were easier concepts to embrace. Buck's scheme was to wait until his aloof behavior forced Jeannie to say something, and then just react. Yes, that was better.

"I can't go on having only half of you," Jeannie finally obliged late one night in his apartment.

"Jeannie, did you ever stop and think about the fact that there are some women in this city who have none of me?"

Callous ego humor—that would get her even more pissed. Now there'd be a fight.

"Well, what do you expect me to do?" she sobbed. "Why did you go out with me if you knew you were going to do this?"

"What can I say?" Buck said. "I think you're the greatest girl in the world, but I'm just not ready to get married, so it's not fair to you to keep going out. I mean, just for my own selfish purposes, I could very easily keep on seeing you, because I love you and I love spending time with you—but I don't feel right about it because I know deep in my heart that sometime it's going to end, so it's better to face that now before the involvement gets too deep."

"Well, it's already too deep for me," Jeannie said bitterly. "Is there something else you want me to do? Just tell me what you want."

"Oh, Jeannie, it's nothing like that," Buck said, trying his hand at being comforting. "I mean, we could meet at some other time and it would be perfect—that is, if you were still talking to me. But right now I'm married to my career. When I commit to someone, I really want to be able to do it whole hog, and I can't do that until I slay a couple of real major show business dragons."

Hogs, dragons—what a huge dick Buck is, Jeannie thought. She rolled herself in a ball into Buck's leather chair and sobbed while Buck paced all around her and droned on about things she didn't want to hear about.

"Jeannie, you watch comics every night of your life. Don't you see we're not a good lot to get mixed up with? Because inside every comedian, there's this fantasy time bomb waiting to go off. Everything we do, all the shit we take, is fueled by a really big, humongous dream that all of the pain will be worth it when we hit it big. You don't want to be around while that bomb is ticking away, because if I get there, I'm not going to be able to resist all the shallow rewards. And if I don't get there—well, you really don't want to be around for that. In fact, neither do I."

As Jeannie sobbed uncontrollably, Buck wondered if it was really harder on a woman to leave a comedian. He was aware of how arrogant it was to think such a thing—but then again, he couldn't convince himself it wasn't true. Sure, civilian men could be fun—but not really fun, not a-laugh-a-minute fun. Buck knew civilian men. He'd observed them in social situations, where even in the most relaxed atmosphere they tended to regard everything in life as—well, as what it actually was.

How much fun could that be?

But to be the girlfriend of a comedian was to be with this nonstop upside down machine: *Nothing* was what it was, or at least there was something to be made fun of in everything and everyone. So a girl goes out with regular nice guys all her life, and then a comedian comes along, and if they click, she's suddenly in one of those they're-falling-in-love-now montages that you see in movies that don't have time to actually show you the characters falling in love. Except in the movie montage you don't hear any of the actual dialogue causing the lovers to crack up while eating ice cream cones in the park, but with a comedian, there's plenty of dialogue, and if he's good, most of it's pretty funny.

Buck felt bad for Jeannie. Maybe he was destined to feel bad for every woman he went out with—but what was the answer? To not pursue women?

Impossible.

Especially right now, because spring was coming—green, glorious, glamorous spring. Certainly, spring was no time to be in a rusty, creaky old relationship. Spring was the time of renewal, and man on earth must be in tune with the mood of the planet.

Yes, spring was the time to dump the old and fall in love with someone new.

11

You Better Be a Winner in This Business, Because If You're Not, It's Shit

—Harry Crystal

In the spring, political stirrings were afoot in the comedy world of New York. At The Club, Luther Clippe (pronounced Clippe) had been assigned to the newly created post of creative director. This was fitting, since he had directly created more money for The Club by carving forty extra seats out of the existing tiny niche of Manhattan that was The Club, and this was how Bo Reynolds rewarded him. A carpenter by trade, Luther now found himself in the position of judging the delicate art of stand-up comedy—and what better qualifications could a man have for that than carpentry?

Luther's first move was to install a complex and unwieldy bureaucracy upon what was, in essence, a pretty simple operation. The institution of the MC meeting was founded, whereby Buck, Dick, and Norma were obligated to haul ass over to Luther's apartment on Wednesday afternoons to make up the lineup for the weekend shows, etch judgments about others on tablets of stone, forge unnecessary policies, rubber-stamp superfluous directives, and generally act like they were the triumvirate and comedy was Old Rome.

During the meetings, Luther wore many hats—berets, fedoras, derbies, bowlers: Hats were Luther's passion, and he played with them while the MCs worked. Luther wore a different hat to The Club each night, and often kept it on his head for the entire evening. But at the meeting, he just played with them. How he managed to do this while maintaining the vigil of a blank stare out the window and simultaneously picking at the seat of his pants was a wonder to the MCs, but then Luther was a wondrous man—especially the way he juggled The Club's busy schedule and his own list of unnecessary duties, which were printed on unwieldy clipboards and so not easy to catch, let alone throw up in the air.

Around the fourth week of these meetings, Luther announced the creation of a chain of command, which was urgently not needed. He formulated the post of top-dog MC and named Buck to it. This came as quite a surprise to Dick and Norma, both of whom had far more seniority than Buck.

After the meeting, Buck mentioned the precedent of Dwight D. Eisenhower, who during World War II had been promoted over 363 senior officers to head up the European Theater of Operations, a fact that, as you might imagine, immediately brought Dick and Norma around on the issue to embrace Buck's good fortune. Perhaps that was not how Norma actually felt, but since Buck was now in a position to help or hurt her, she showered gladness upon him and instinctively set out to lodge her head as far up his ass as was metaphorically possible. Dick, as usual, could give a shit if it didn't directly affect pussy.

Why had Buck been chosen? Maybe it was because Buck had always treated Luther with the respect that, in Luther's case, was a ludicrous and cynical endowment. But Buck had caught on from day one that The Club was a place that followed no logical system of punishment or reward. And although he could not claim foreseeing that the carpenter was destined for greatness, Buck remembered the example of the carpenter Jesus Christ, and also maintained a policy of keeping on the good side of anyone close to management. Propinquity is power was a lesson Buck had learned from history books: Just being in the palace and around the king had been enough to raise many a humble and unqualified chamberlain to a position he never would have attained through civil-service exams. Something told Buck that Luther just might be in that tradition.

There was, perhaps, another reason why Luther had suddenly and without cause elevated Buck above the pack. It might have been because Buck had suggested he do so the day after saving

Luther's job—or, rather, the day after he convinced Luther that he had saved his job.

History, of course, also teaches that for every humble and unqualified chamberlain who reaches the top, there's also a propinquitous but wily courtier waiting to manipulate his royal doltness.

In Luther's case, it wasn't hard. Luther, you see, was rather fond of Quaaludes, a weakness Buck immediately earmarked for exploitation. Buck had been waiting months for just the right opportunity to nail Luther, and one night he found opportunity lying downstairs at The Club, spread-eagled and saying "fuck me."

On this night, as Buck walked into The Club, he knew right away that owner Bo Reynolds was somewhere inside. It was nothing he could put his finger on, but there was an excitement in the air on nights when Bo came in. Bo was not a bright man, but he was charismatic. He was always positive, and always effusive in his physical affection. Bo hugged everybody, for any reason, or for no reason whatsoever. Where other people nodded in agreement, shook hands, momentarily clutched a knee for conversational emphasis, tipped a hat or raised a glass, slapped a back or play-punched a shoulder, for all of these social gestures Bo used the hug. And everyone loved it, including Buck. Of course, half the time Bo didn't even know who he was hugging. All the comics had seen it a thousand times: Bo hugging someone as if he were a long-lost brother while mouthing behind his back to the nearest regular, "Who is it?" then repeating the stranger's name to him.

As Chink once remarked: "Bo Reynolds built this place with his own two faces."

With an Orwellian disregard for truth, there was no one on earth more Hollywood than the always tanned, always blond, and always wavy-haired Bo yet no one who more constantly claimed to love New York and live for its famed grit and candor.

"I get my energy from the people on the street," was the simpleton's favorite Big Apple cliché.

. . . Energy from the people on the street? Buck thought— Christ, I *use* all my energy trying to get by these fucking people!

Actually, Bo got a lot of his energy from cocaine. Perhaps that was the reason he spent so much of his time at The Club down in the basement. A nearly hidden set of stairs at the back of the coatroom led down to a dank, pipe-dripping, rat-crawling catacomb where the elite of The Club—Bo, Luther, and the MCs—were allowed to escape the clamor above. Occasionally, Bo would also entertain special guests down there, men who, shall we say, eat dinner in an undershirt. Rumors had always persisted that Bo was just a front man for the real owners of The Club, the mafia, but the only evidence to support this theory was the presence in The Club every single night of the year of every gangster in New York, acting as if they owned the place and never paying for a single drink. As ridiculous as the rumor was, it was nevertheless the one subject nobody ever dared bring up in front of Bo, even as a joke.

Especially as a joke.

It was no joke.

The latest improvement to the facilities in the basement—actually, the first, since there had been no others—was a tiny office at the bottom of the stairs that Luther built as his own special sanctuary, where he could take care of the molehill of paperwork that his job entailed, and also nod out when the mood struck him. It had comfortable seating for none, a board-on-a-barrel desk, and a chair. But it had a door, which, when closed, formed a wall, and that was what interested Luther the most.

On the night of the coup, Buck, after spotting Bo upstairs, quickly and surreptitiously slipped down to the basement in the hope of finding the door of the little office closed. A closed door would mean that Luther had cloistered himself inside for a peaceable sleep-off and would be vulnerable to Operation Amazingly Stupid Fucking Idiot. Buck knocked several times on the door, and when there was no response, he was convinced that Luther was passed out inside. He grabbed a glass of water that had been sitting on the boiler since 1973 and forced open the door. He threw the water in Luther's face.

"What the—"

"Thank God," Buck said.

"What the hell are you doing?" Luther stammered.

"Jesus Christ," Buck emoted. "I've been trying to wake you for half an hour. Bo's here, and I've been stalling him from coming down, but I can't hold him off anymore. I've already taken him outside twice to talk. I can't do it again, he'll think I'm crazy. Come on, get up, sit at the desk, look like you're working."

"He's here?"

"Yes, and he's been trying to come down here for half an hour."

Luther grumbled up to a sitting position. Buck opened a spiral notebook detailing the liquor stock and placed it in front of him.

"There you go. Look like you're going over the books."

"Yeah, okay," Luther garbled.

"Don't worry about it. We gotta stick together, right? Don't fall asleep, I'll be right back."

Buck flew up the stairs and found Bo and asked him if he wanted to smoke a joint in the basement. Bo did.

When he stuck his head in Luther's office a minute later, just as Buck said he would, there was Luther doing his best Bob Cratchit impression.

"Bo!" Luther cried, or tried to, through the ton of phlegm that had gathered in his throat. Luther stood to receive his hug.

"Burning the midnight oils?" Bo ad-libbed.

"Yeah, I just wanted to get ahead on some of this liquor inventory."

"Is this guy on the ball or what?" Bo smiled and gave Luther a second, specific-reason hug.

Buck watched the two men embrace and marveled at how each could be so stupid. And he loved them for it! God, wasn't it great when people's stupidity worked in your favor for a change? And wasn't it only fair? Didn't he suffer enough from people being stupid—audiences who didn't get the jokes, girls who didn't get the jokes, club owners who didn't even get the concept?

Not to mention the folks down at the post office.

As long as he was on a roll, Buck decided he might as well push his luck. After he and Luther and Bo adjourned to the more spacious sitting area around the boiler, Buck passed around a joint and then unloaded about what had always irritated him about The Club: "Hey, as long as I got you guys together, I want to ask you something."

"Shoot," said Bo.

"Okay," Buck began, instinctively affecting a verbal tone somewhat dumber and more street than his normal voice. "It's like—okay, I'm here every night, all night, right? And I listen to the audience when they're coming out of the showroom a lot, and I gotta tell you, I think this place needs to be shaken up a little."

What Buck had in mind was bringing into The Club a half dozen acts who were currently working at some of the smaller rooms in town, a ready supply of fresh talent who wanted to work The Club, as every comic in New York did, but who could never get past the usual backlog of seniority dead wood that clogged the stage every night, the same dead wood who had clogged Buck's path and who regarded their ten-thirty spots as a birthright, like some title passed down from ancestral peers. Buck had always believed that this inertia would eventually spell doom for The Club: The audience would catch on, and then they'd move on. And now he was telling it to Bo.

"Whaddaya mean?" Bo asked, not grasping it yet.

"Well lately, I've overheard a lot of people from the audience complain about seeing the same acts they saw the last time they came," Buck fabricated. "Hell, some people even come up to me and say, 'When are you gonna get some new comedians?' I mean, it wouldn't be so bad if some of these guys were turning over material more often, but a lot of them do the same twenty minutes every night, word for word—Christ, I could do their acts for them!"

Bo nodded unknowingly.

Buck continued: "I think we need some new blood around here, or we're gonna lose our audience. Because this is known as the hippest place in New York, and we get the hippest crowd—Bo, I know you want it that way, I know that was your vision of The Club when you opened it, and it's just natural, when you get as successful as you've made this place, that you just kind of sit on the lead. But I think that's dangerous, I think you gotta be on the edge. That's how people think of The Club, and I want to keep it that way."

Bo took all this in—the good, the bad, and the preposterous compliments. Then he spoke. And when Bo spoke, he spoke slowly.

"Yeah, I hear ya. And thank you. I want you to know I appreciate your honesty. I want you to know that."

He reached out for Buck's hand and squeezed it, a squeeze that said, I'm too wasted to stand up and hug, but if I could have hugged, I would have hugged.

Buck squeezed back. Bo seemed to stop talking, but his pauses were so long, one never could tell. Buck jumped in lest Bo think of an argument during the interminable lull.

"Great. So what I want to do is ask some of the guys I know who are working the smaller clubs to come in and do sets. There's some real funny guys out there, Bo, I know you'd like them, and they're dying to get on here, but they don't even come around anymore because they know our show is such a lock."

"Fantastic," Bo said. "Let's do it."

"Great," Buck said, matching Bo's infectious positivism. "It's great to know you guys'll back me up on this, because obviously there are only so many spots a night, and some of our regulars are gonna get a little pissed if they don't go on one night—you know what babies comedians are! Christ, if anybody on the planet knows, it's you!"

Buck sold that last part as hard as he could, leaning in to Bo, working it as a joke, getting the laugh from Bo and, off Bo, Luther. And before anyone could object, he stood up and said, with his best undetectably false sincerity: "Bo—thanks. This means a lot to me. I love this club. I always want it to be the best it can be."

That was too much for Bo. He had to stand and hug. Buck hugged back, hard, then took off. He turned back to Bo at the stairs and added: "And get your ass in here more often. We miss you!"

Then he threw up.

After Buck did a set around midnight, Bo invited him to join his entourage of cronies—Luther, Andy, the ever-loyal head bartender who'd been with Bo for years, and several small-time wiseguys—for a drink down the street at P.J.'s. Buck really wanted to go home, but he felt honored that Bo would ask him and he was afraid to say no, so he went.

At the bar, Buck was the only comedian in the group, so he had to work extra hard to keep the laughs flowing in front of the boss. To Buck, it seemed like the night would never end— a prospect, he finally realized, to which these men aspired on a daily basis.

On the cab ride home at 4 A.M., Buck thought about what a political bonanza the evening had been. He thought about the bullshit he had heaped upon Bo and Luther back there in the basement, and he felt good. It was satisfying to move those two idiots around like pieces on a chessboard, first convincing Luther he had saved his job, then producing Bo in the basement to corroborate that lie, then introducing his plans for change with Luther sitting right there, knowing he owed Buck, maybe even fearing that Buck would rat him out if he opposed him, and then letting Bo agree to his plan in front of Luther, because he knew Bo always agreed to anything anybody said.

And what a nice touch to make Bo think it was all his idea— "I know that was your vision of the club"—as if this man ever had a vision; Bo was not exactly the Fatima child. And then the touching peroration: "I only want what's best for The Club."

Well, that was true. Buck did want what was best for The Club. Of course, what was best for The Club was also best for Buck, because if The Club got run into the ground the way most comedy clubs got run into the ground, then no one who could do him any good would see him there, and all his hard political work would be for naught.

And the deluge at The Club was already starting to happen; Buck hadn't lied to Bo about that. The Club was dangerously close to becoming a has-been, and for just the reasons Buck had stated: There was no danger anymore, and no surprises. As usual, revolutionaries become bureaucrats.

Chink had it right: you start out as a bird-watching society, you end up with the Nazi party.

Well, not at this club, Buck thought. Not if he could help it.

Buck opened the window of the cab and stuck his head out like a dog. The air felt so good, so incredibly good. It was that early spring air, with that slight mist, the kind of weather you only got around—

"Stop the cab!" Buck ordered.

It was St. Patrick's Day! It was four in the morning of the day that more than any other day celebrated hope and renewal. This was Buck's favorite time of year, when the lion metamorphosed into the lamb; when a fading winter still tried to bite at you but could no longer make it hurt, like the nip of a playful dog.

And when that fine mist came up, that ever so slight spray in the face that couldn't really be called rain, then you knew it was really spring week. Spring week: No accident that St. Patrick's Day was so close to the vernal equinox, or that green was the color it celebrated.

And there was the stripe! The green stripe!

Buck was walking down Fifth Avenue, and there in the middle of the great thoroughfare was a big green stripe for the parade that would begin in another few hours, when millions of New Yorkers would be thronging behind police barricades, drinking and shouting and pushing each other, and cheering and jeering at the pols and pompous fools and high school marching bands that came out to honor the Irish. But at 4 A.M., New York was a ghost town. It was dead quiet and there was not a soul or a car on the street.

For twenty-five blocks, Buck walked down the middle of Fifth Avenue all alone, watching his feet land on the green stripe and breathing in that March mist. He couldn't get over how strange that was to be all alone in a place that soon would be too jammed to get near. It was like being alone in the Sistine Chapel—and just as holy. St. Patrick's Day *was* holy, but in New York it had become just a day to get drunk or, if you were a politician, to get votes. Dumb-ass drunken brutes, they wouldn't even put it together, wouldn't even stop to think why St. Patty's Day was green—green, green, for God's sakes! Like the green returning to the earth, the green earth, the verdant earth, the vernal earth; green, verdant, *vert, verde, viriditas*!

Green! The color of fucking life, watered by that mist, giving us one more year to live again and get it right.

Yes, it was definitely time to find someone new to fall in love with and be in tune with old mother earth.

In Cleveland, spring week was still winter, and for that Dick was getting blamed.

"I thought you said it would be nice here," Jill said flatly.

"What would you like me to do about it, dear?" Dick asked. "Would you like me to try and buy the weather?"

The weather was the least of Dick's problems. In falling for Jill in a way he never had before with a woman, Dick had upset the delicate, albeit gooned-out, lifestyle that until then had passed for stability in his life. He hadn't slept at home in a month, and he was in danger of losing the wife he had divorced three years ago.

Janet thought he was having a great time. If only she could have seen him.

Dick's life had become that nightmare in which someone is chasing you and then you fall and can't get up. Dick didn't want to be with Jill—he hated her—but he couldn't get up. Jill had moved in the night they met, a mutual decision that, like all decisions concerning this couple, she made by herself. From that night on, she had explained virtually nothing about herself and wanted to hear even less about Dick, least of all about the family he had in the Bronx. She dismissed such concerns as that most bourgeois of fixations, living in the past. Jill wanted to live in the *now*.

She also wanted to live *well* in the now. To Jill, there was only one way to procure food and that was from a restaurant, preferably a "decent restaurant," which meant one where a salad cost nine dollars—not that she stopped ordering after the salad. Dick was convinced that if Jill found a bistro that listed sodden cigarette butts as the priciest entree, she would order that, although it probably wouldn't harm her, since she rarely touched what she ordered anyway and vetoed as gauche any suggestion of bringing home the untouched food. Also on the gauche list was the notion that a woman should ever carry money, as demonstrated by the time Dick asked her for a single to round out a tip. She looked at him as if he had demanded a blow job right there on the sidewalk—which he might have gotten, but the idea that a woman as attractive as herself would ever need to possess something so pedestrian as a dollar—well, it was positively insulting.

Money, however, was not the chief problem in the relationship. It was more that Jill was Satan.

"Can you get some coke? Hmm?" she asked, growing ever more despondent at the realization that Cleveland had turned out to be—surprise—cold and boring.

Jill had developed an annoying habit—no, not the cocaine— of punctuating every question with "Hmm?" because she was getting used to Dick trying to ignore her. At first she didn't know what to do when Dick ignored her but, like bacteria, she soon developed an immunity to his tactics and a new strain of behavior that was even stronger. She could not stand to be ignored, which was funny, in a completely tragic sort of way, since it was her own aloofness that forced Dick to try to ignore her. The attitude that Jill presented 90 percent of the time with Dick was that she could spend all her time with him, or she could be doing anything else at all, and it would make no difference as to how happy she was. That attitude was maddening to Dick, but it was the way she acted in the 10 percent of the time when she sensed he might really have had enough that kept him around.

"Do you give a shit about me, or are you just killing time?" Dick asked Jill in Cleveland in lieu of going out in the freezing rain and scaring up some coke.

"Stop it," she said.

"No, really. For two people who spend as much time together as we do, I think I should really know what's in your head."

"Darling, I *like* you."

Jill had also developed another annoying habit, calling Dick darling a lot, with no less sincerity than a Gabor sister.

"Yeah, you like me, but we don't act like people who just like each other."

"No? What do we act like?"

"Well, we live together, for one thing. That's fairly serious, wouldn't you say?"

"Of course it's serious."

"Well . . . do you really think you do anything to make me feel like I matter at all in your life?"

"Hello!"

Oh no—not the "Hello!" Dick hated that "Hello!" more than anything, as if *he* was the crazy person and *she* was the one who had to knock on *his* shell. There was no damn way to ever win an argument with this girl, no way to ever implicate her in any real feelings.

And that "Hello!" was the worst. It was enough to make a man go out in the cold and search for cocaine.

As the first blast of frigid air hit Dick on the street, he wondered: What exactly do I do, ask the first bad-news-looking bald black guy I see if he's got any blow?

Yeah, I'm in Cleveland, it should take about a minute.

With his collar turned up, Dick walked out of the famed Wingos Hotel and took a left on Euclid, heading into the seedy part of town, an area he would have also encountered had he turned right, gone straight, or stood where he was. Bullets of water began to pelt him, a fitting physical counterpart to his emotions.

On Euclid, Dick passed an Italian restaurant. In the window were old photographs of show business greats who'd eaten there over the years—Steve Allen, Buddy Hackett, Danny Thomas—all with their arm around the same guy, who must have been the owner, or perhaps the don of the neighborhood. And then, in a moment of sentimentality that was rare for him, Dick suddenly felt connected to the past of his chosen profession in a way he never had before. He felt history, like an awestruck schoolboy on the battlefield of Gettysburg, the feeling one gets with the realization that something happened *right here*—here, on the very spot where you're standing.

Because they were all there in the window—Hope, Benny, Burns, some comedy team from vaudeville days—all there in the pictures, evidence that they all had stood on the spot where

Dick was now standing, undoubtedly after a show, when they undoubtedly felt exactly the way Dick felt after his shows in Cleveland.

Vaudeville or the comedy clubs, 1980: a guy traveling around the country, doing the same act in different cities, living out of a suitcase, fighting with club owners and with loneliness and then with the things a guy did to fight the loneliness. And all the while driven on by something that the guy had long ago given up trying to figure out or fight.

And doing it in a place that made a day pass like a week.

That was the standard old joke about Cleveland—"I spent a week here one day"—but to Dick, it wasn't just a stock line anymore. As he stood in the freezing Erie swirl and thought about that joke, he felt connected to the men in those pictures, because one of them had *written* that joke, one of them had actually tried it out for the first time one night and felt that rush when he got laughs from a new bit. And what made Dick feel like his picture should have been right up there with the old-timers was the knowledge that *he* could have written that joke, and maybe would have if somebody hadn't beaten him to it.

But somebody did, somebody who also knew what it was like to spend time in this particular city, in this same peculiar pursuit of chasing a buck by trying to make people laugh. He said it for all of them, whoever it was who said it about spending a week in Cleveland one day. And in the years that followed, all of them, all of those comedians who were looking out at him from that window in faded photographs had felt it just the way he was feeling it now.

But none of them ever had to deal with a cunt like Jill!

Then Dick remembered why he was out on the street in the first place. He grumbled up the avenue, mumbling more soliloquies about the harpy who'd sent him into pneumonia country to get her drugs, which she hardly bothered to conceal that she needed to fuck him. He'd been aware of that particular aspect of their sex life for some time, but suddenly amid the freezing drizzle, it seemed like the last straw. He turned on his heel and headed back toward the hotel.

Dick was ready to fire when he walked in the door, but Jill

was on the phone to Geneva with an ex-husband. She was screaming into the receiver and either did not notice Dick come in or pretended not to notice. The long distance call went on for another ten minutes before Dick reminded Jill that phones weren't free. She gave him a dirty look that said, like so many of her looks: my needs!

Finally, Dick asserted himself boldly, grabbing the receiver out of her hands and telling the ex-husband that if he wanted to talk further, go fuck yourself.

"Well, you just screwed that up," Jill said coolly.

"Fuck you," Dick said.

"Umm, that's nice to hear."

"Fuck you," Dick said again.

"At least try a little variety, darling," Jill said.

"Fuck you," the unobliging Dick repeated.

"No, I don't think you will anymore," Jill declared.

"Good. Why don't you get out of here. Go back to New York and pick up somebody else and start living with him. I'm sure you'll have a place before midnight."

"Hey, look—"

"No, you look. I'm not kidding. Scram."

"And just how am I supposed to do that? Hmm? How am I supposed to get out of this place without any money?"

"Frankly, my dear, I don't give a damn," Dick said, pleased that there actually had come a moment in his life where that line fit perfectly.

"You're an asshole, you know that?" Jill said.

"Yes I do," Dick acknowledged, "but I'd like to get some peace now. You're a piece, and I've had you, but the other kind is more important to me now."

"You bastard."

"Yes, yes, I'm all those things, but you are poison, simple deadly poison that kills anything it comes in contact with. And I don't want to die."

There was a silent respite, followed by the sound of Jill actually sobbing.

"I came to this shithole for you," she finally whimpered.

Dick was incredulous: "For me?"

"Of course for you—do you really think that I'd come to

this godawful place if it wasn't for you, spending time with stupid people, going to stupid clubs—''

''Are you talking about last night? I thought you wanted to go to that place. I wanted to come back to the hotel.''

''Are you crazy? Why would I want to go to that stupid, sleazy dive with those stupid friends of yours. I was helping with your business.''

''My business? How?''

''It was the owner of the club we were with, yes? He wanted to go out with the comedian?''

''Yeah, but I don't care if he does or he doesn't—he's not paying me to go to discos with him. I thought you wanted to go for . . . the nightlife.''

''Nightlife? Please, don't make me laugh. If I wanted nightlife I'd be back in New York with my friends, who'd take me to places that are really fun. Do you really think this is fun?''

''No. I mean, yes, it can be . . . I don't know, it's my job, I don't worry about whether it's fun or not.''

''Obviously.''

''Well, why did you come then?''

''You asked me to.''

''I didn't. I mean, I said you could come if you wanted to, but it's not like I need you by my side every fucking minute.''

''From my upbringing, when a gentleman requests a lady's presence on a trip, he takes her in the best style possible and always treats her like a lady.''

''Well, you don't always act like a lady.''

''On that, you are very wrong, my friend, very wrong, and you've got your nerve.''

''Well . . . all you ever think about is yourself, *your* needs.''

''Hah! And do you think that you have the slightest idea what my needs are? You couldn't begin to fulfill my needs because you don't have so much as a clue as to who I am.''

''Oh really?''

''Yes, really.''

''Then why don't you tell me—I mean, why don't you? I want to know. I'm always trying to find out, but I can't.''

"Well, that's a shame then," Jill said evenly, and then rose and started to pack.

It had only taken her about five minutes this time to bring Dick around from anger to guilt. He'd felt this sort of frustration with her so many times before—God, how did she do it?! She was so damn lucid and irrefutable when she was arguing. She deflected his best efforts with the equivalent of that simple flip of the hand with which she had dismissed his queries on the first night they met, and she could do it without so much as looking up from whatever or whoever else she was doing.

Not that she ever really overtly came on to another man in Dick's presence or really ever got out of control, despite the awesome amount of liquor and drugs she put away. She was a bitch, a snob, a horrible, selfish monster—and yet somehow, when it came time to present evidence in support of that theory . . .

There was none.

She hadn't actually come on to other guys; she hadn't actually caused any public scenes; she hadn't actually stolen from him or blackmailed him or lied to him about anything important or humiliated him . . .

Is it all in my head?

Dick always wound up thinking that. Am I going crazy? No! I know she's a cunt! But goddamnit, there's no proof! She can prove she's a lady, but I can't prove she's a cunt! How does she do it?

Dick knew he would never know. It was like the trick you watch the opening-act magician do night after night but never come any closer to knowing how.

"Look, I'm sorry," Dick was soon pleading. "It was so nasty out there, and I walked into a bar to get you cocaine and I almost got killed and I thought, What sort of—"

"Why did you do that?"

"Go out to get coke? Because you said you wanted some."

"I didn't mean now. I didn't mean to go out in the rain."

Now there, right there, Dick thought—she did, she absolutely did want me to go out in the rain . . .

Didn't she?

She didn't actually *say* "Go right now," but I know that's what she wanted. She's lying now, saying she didn't mean that.

Isn't she?

"We can get some tonight, hmm?"

"What? Yeah, sure."

"Your friend at the club has some, yes?"

"You mean the asshole?"

"Well, what do you expect, he lives here."

Jill returned to her perch on the bed and picked up the magazine she'd been reading before the whole donnybrook broke out. She wore a slight smile, and she reached into her purse for one of the unwrapped, filthy jellybeans she constantly grazed on. Dick sank back into the chair he had occupied since they had gotten up for the day.

"So, let me get this straight," he essayed. "It doesn't really matter what we argue about—if I defend X, you defend Y, and if I attack X, then you defend X. Is that how the game works, or are we already playing a different game?"

"Hmmm?"

Jill did not bother to look up.

"Will you rub my back. My spine is a mess," she whined. "I have to see my doctor when we get back to New York."

So Dick spent the next hour and a half as masseur, till his hands were so tired he could not respond to one more plea of "Just a little more."

You can imagine how his jaw felt after sex.

12

It's Easy to Do Great, It's Hard to Be Great

In New York, Chink was only too happy to have his own jaw hurting. Norma had finally taught him the proper method of giving head, and he took to the task with relish, determined that sex would not be a problem in this, his second turn with her, as it had been in their first.

Chink and Norma had been back together since the bad acid trip. Thank God for that bad acid trip, Chink thought: Without that, and the nursing that Norma administered to him in the days that followed, they might never have grown close again. But they did, closer than ever, and with greater honesty. No more pretending, no more hiding—they were together, and Norma didn't care who knew. Of course nobody else cared, either. They just thought it was great that two lonely comedians had found each other.

When the weather started to get nice, the happy couple decided to give themselves a little vacation. Being comedians, though, it was of course a working vacation, at least for Norma. Not quite in time for the cherry blossoms, Norma and Chink arrived at Union Station in Washington, D.C., on a beautiful Friday afternoon and cabbed it over to the Shoreham Hotel, where they ordered Champagne from room service and then made love. Norma worried that the bellhop would arrive while they were still flagrante, but Chink hadn't yet come that far in his lovemaking skills. They were finished in plenty of time to straighten up, unpack, and dash off a few postcards before the bubbly arrived.

The bellhop, however, forgot to bring up the proper drinking glasses, so the lovers were forced to drink the champagne from hotel bathroom glasses that had undoubtedly previously housed someone's teeth.

They did not mind. They were in love, they were in a hotel, and one of them was working.

Chink did not even mind that he was only along for the ride. Norma had tried to get him booked as MC the way Buck and Shit had done in Baltimore, but the owner of the Washington club wouldn't go for booking a comedian he hadn't seen. But he did promise Norma that Chink could do a guest set before her on Friday night, and if he liked what he saw, a future booking would follow. So it was kind of a business trip for Chink, too.

Norma and Chink arrived at the club in plenty of time for the first show and shared a drink with the owner, Milt, who told Norma he'd been anxious to get her down there for the longest time. She responded that she'd been foolish for not going on the road sooner, but said she felt a loyalty to The Club in New York, where her MC services were in demand. Milt said he admired that and that there was too little loyalty in their business. Everyone found it easy to raise a glass to that.

Norma and Chink were impressed with Milt, with the room, which was nicely appointed, and with the crowd, who filled every seat. They agreed that here in the nation's capital it was possible that the comedy scene was more sophisticated than in some of the other provinces to which they'd traveled, a hope that had been raised by some of the other New York comedians who'd already played the Washington club.

To their surprise, Milt served as the MC and did almost half an hour. This may have been startling to Chink and Norma, but the idea of a middle-aged Jewish man who'd been a frustrated comic for so long that he bought his own nightclub was hardly new. Milt upheld the tradition well, however, exhibiting a complete non-flair for the craft of comedy and, as Chink and

Norma noted, stealing liberally from their colleagues who had already played the room.

Milt did score, however, with local Washington references, which, if anyone else in the country ever read a newspaper, would have been national references. This phenomenon was not lost on Chink, who decided to go with the flow and do all the political material that never worked in New York, as opposed to all his nonpolitical material that never worked in New York.

Chink was nervous when he got onstage. He was always nervous when he got onstage, but he was especially nervous whenever Norma was watching. Plus, Milt had given him one of those be-kind, this-guy's-real-new-and-probably-a-piece-of-shit introductions. Halfway through the first joke, he knew he'd blown the wording, so he just swallowed the punchline.

But the crowd laughed anyway!

It was an election year, and all Chink's lines about the candidates who were filling the primary season—Jimmy Carter, Ted Kennedy, Ronald Reagan, George Bush, Jerry Brown, John Anderson—went over like a decidedly lead-free balloon. Even the John Connally joke got a decent response.

At the ten-minute mark, when he was supposed to get off, Chink did not want to get off. This was a first, because Chink always wanted to get off, from the moment he went on. But for the first time in his career, Chink felt like he was on a roll, and it felt good.

So he went for broke: the Barabbas routine. Never got a laugh, and never—he had become convinced—would.

But then again, he'd never been on a roll.

It doesn't surprise me we pick such losers. I mean, what is democracy but mob rule, and when has the mob ever made a good choice? Take the case of Jesus. On the day he was crucified, the Romans gave the mob a choice to free either Jesus or Barabbas, and the crowd went: "Mmmmm, let's see, Jesus Christ, greatest man ever, or Barabbas, lowlife petty thief—I gotta go with Barabbas . . . yeah, Barabbas, he's our man. Barabbas in 33!"

People do things in mobs they'd never do alone. It's

always a lynch mob. It's never one guy out there, "Yeah,
hangin' niggers is lonely work, but I do it . . ."

And that scored, too, bringing the whole piece around to a
nice applause break. An applause break!

Another first. Chink had more often than not been lucky to
get applause when he said good night, and then perhaps only
because it meant he was leaving. But on this night he got a
genuine ovation.

"You were fantastic," Norma screamed as she hugged him.
"I'm so proud of you."

"Yeah, did you see—"

"I gotta go on," she cut him off, inching toward the aisle
as Milt asked for another round of applause for his surprise
find. Norma hoped Milt would do a little time here, for a reason
she never expected: to make the crowd forget Chink. But the
show was already way behind, so Milt brought her right up.

Norma also asked for a round of applause for Chink, which
the audience gave, but clearly with the attitude, okay, he was
good, but enough already.

It was to be the last applause break Norma would get for the
night. She worked hard for forty-five minutes and acquitted
herself as a professional, but she never came close to winning
the crowd over.

Women, am I right, over the weekend, you cannot watch
TV in the day; weekdays, that's for us: soap operas, cook-
ing shows—but Saturday and Sunday is for the guys. You
can tell by the beer commercials: "You just knocked down
a building, you sawed something in half, you fucked Cin-
cinnati—"

Okay, so they don't want to sell beer to women—at
least they could have one for GAY men: "You've been
choosing drapes since sunup—now, it's Miller time . . ."

I tell you, it's frightening for a woman in New York
City . . . I was attacked once—thank God he was
cute . . . hey, look, it was Saturday night, at least I met
a guy who was interested . . . no, he really hurt me—not
with the sex, it was just that he didn't call the next day . . .

*my fault, I shouldn't have asked for a commitment so
soon . . . a lot of guys now, they just don't want to get
involved after a first rape . . .*

*No, it is scary . . . I got one of those mugger whistles,
right? You get attacked, you blow the whistle—you know
what happened? Other muggers came . . .*

After Chink's set, she sounded hopelessly un-hip, even to
herself. Norma had foreseen a thousand problems in being
Chink's girlfriend, but not being able to follow him was never
one of them.

Chink said, "Great set," when she got off, but Norma blew
past him with a fast, "It was shit," and headed for the door.

"Where you going?" he called after her.

"Hotel," she said without breaking stride.

"But we've got another show," Chink said.

We? What do you mean we, white man, Norma thought. *I*
have another show. You did your guest spot.

"I've got an hour before I go on again," she said.

"What's the matter?" Chink asked as he caught up with her.

"I sucked, all right?"

"You didn't suck, you were great."

"Gimme a break, I know when I suck."

"Well I know it didn't," Chink said meekly.

"Just let me be by myself for a while," Norma said, still
walking at a brisk pace.

"Well lemme walk you back, at least."

"I'll be all right. Go have a drink with Milt."

Chink stopped walking. He knew Norma. He knew what she
was like when she was unhappy with herself, and he'd learned
to leave her alone. He walked back into the bar.

"Anything wrong?" Milt asked.

"Oh no. She just gets . . . you know, she's very hard on
herself. She thinks she didn't do good."

"She was fine."

"I know, I told her that. But you know, she's a perfectionist."

"Well, you're a hard act to follow," Milt told Chink.
"That's some incredible material you have there. Why didn't
I ever see you when I was looking for acts at The Club?"

"Oh, well I don't always get on there."

"What? That's insane."

"It's different there."

"Well, you can always get on here."

"Really? That's great, thanks."

"You're gonna do the second show, aren't you?"

Chink looked around. He wanted to do the second show. He wanted to do every show. He wanted to move here, get a job in Washington, bus tables, be a congressman, whatever it took.

But he said no.

"I think I'll quit while I'm ahead. I don't want to risk bombing now and blow you wanting to book me."

Milt told Chink he'd book him anyway, and Chink was sorely tempted. He wanted to do the second show so bad. But no, it wasn't worth the risk.

Not that risk. The other one.

At The Club, Buck was getting ready to throw his newly scammed weight around and start bringing in new acts. But he first wanted to make good on a promise to an old act: Shit. As usual, he thought deception was the better part of just about anything at The Club, so he plotted a way to get Shit a precedent-setting first night as MC. Appointing a new MC was still Luther's call, and Buck knew it would be tough to get him to approve Shit. So Buck waited for a night when he was scheduled to MC and Dick and Norma were both out of town. He called Shit up in the day.

"You wanna MC tonight?"

"What do you mean?"

"You know, MC—run the show, be the big cheese."

"How?"

"Well, Dick and Norma are out of town, and I'm going to be sick."

"Wait. This sounds like it should go through Luther."

"So should clean urine, but there's not gonna be time, because I'm gonna get sick right before the show."

"I don't know. This doesn't sound like the way to do it."

"Of course it's the way to do it. People don't get jobs by

waiting for their application to get lifted off the pile. Jobs go to the guy who somehow sneaks his résumé on the top."

"I don't know."

"Look, I'm knocking a hole in the line for you—do you want to run through it, or do you want to wait for the linebackers to catch on and snuff you in the backfield?"

"I don't know what that means."

"What, are you gay?"

"I don't know."

"You don't know if you're gay? Well do you feel like going down on guys, or—"

"Can't you just talk to Luther, ask him—"

"No, I told you, that won't work. He'll say no."

"How do you know?"

"Because I know. Because he doesn't like you that much."

"Why?"

"Probably because you told him to go fuck himself when he advised you on your act, instead of humoring him like every other sane person does."

"That shouldn't be a reason."

"Okay, well how about the fact that you refuse to do any late-night MCing?"

"If I MC the last hour of the show, I should get—"

"I know, I know, you should, a lot of things should. If shoulds and buts were beer and nuts, we'd have a hell of a party."

"Hmm. I don't know."

"All right, whatever," Buck said, growing weary of familiar fights. "You think about it. I'll call you at eight-thirty. If you want to do it, I'll get sick. If you don't, I'll just go in."

Not that Buck noticed, but the soft sell seemed to work on Shit, because he called back half an hour later and said yes, he'd go along with the plan. So that night Shit came in as if in a rush and announced he was taking over upon the ailing Buck's sudden request. No one argued, but when Luther came in around midnight he threw a fit. He called Buck, who, ex-pecting such a call, answered the phone as a sick person. Buck had also left a message in the same nasal voice for Luther at eight-thirty, knowing Luther would be out by then, so his bases were covered: He'd woken up late in the day sick, thought he could get through the night, but when he realized he couldn't, he tried to reach Luther but couldn't, so he had to make a decision. Shit was well qualified, had the seniority, and was available.

But none of that mattered to Luther. It all went right over his head, as most things will when your head is on the floor, which is where Luther's head was usually dangerously close to being at this time of night. And it didn't matter that Shit had done a fine job; what mattered was that there had been a breach of authority in Luther's petty fiefdom.

Luther was still plenty pissed at Buck the next day at the MC meeting. Taking Buck into the kitchen of his apartment, Luther harangued him for allowing Shit to MC and for not telling him he was feeling sick in time for Luther to make the decision, instances of miscreance he sought to fuse together as an attitude problem. Because of the tininess of Luther's apartment and the lack of a kitchen door, hushed tones could still be heard in the living room, where Norma and Dick were sitting—a fact that had no bearing on the situation at hand, since Luther was yelling at the top of his lungs.

Buck did not try to interject a defense. He knew he did not need a defense. He just stared at Luther as if he were a madman, all the while denying him the satisfaction of a hanged head or even a look of contrition.

When Luther had finally rope-a-doped himself out, Buck looked down for a moment and then came up wearing an evil smile. In look and tone that precisely echoed the reigning television star of the day, J. R. Ewing, Buck said: "Luther, if you don't want me to make decisions when you're not around—or not awake—we should have a meeting with everybody and decide how to handle the situation."

Buck watched Luther swallow: gulp! Oh, that felt good, the way J. Edgar Hoover must have felt with—well, with everybody, really. Because even Luther was not so stupid as to miss this message. Buck could have just said "I know you're a 'lude freak, and you know I know it, so let's be civilized before Bo has to know it"—but this was better, the way Hitchcock's lack of violence was scarier than a slasher film.

After that Luther was never a problem again. He and Buck practiced a tacit inversion of rank akin to the Vietnam scenario, in which incompetent lieutenants ceded authority in the field to able sergeants respected by their men.

The next day Buck was up at the crack of eleven for what had to be the most ridiculous job of his, or anyone else's, career. A nouveau entrepreneur in the low-money comedy-production business, Alan DeLaRigurge, had begun booking a series of lunchtime shows at colleges in the New Jersey stink belt. At 11:30 A.M., Buck, Dick, and Fat piled their cobwebbed faces into Alan's '69 two-tone (both rust) Cutlass and headed for East Brunswick, N.J., a town as pretty as it sounds.

The New Jersey Turnpike at noon was a six-lane emetic that was more a gauntlet for getting cancer than a highway, a nightmare for the olfactories through old factories and chemical plants. It was this stretch of road that gave the Garden State its unfair reputation as one big, stinky dumping ground. The boys had all been through it before, which was why they didn't open the windows even when Fat cut one, a Hobson's choice at which even Hobson would have blanched.

The trip, however, was a paradise compared to the gig. To begin with, no one at the school had the slightest idea that a show of some kind had been scheduled, and to say "some kind" was being kind. DeLaRigurge, who was not exactly Flo Ziegfeld, had failed to lay any groundwork for the event, and consequently blamed all the screwups on some mythical jerk-off at the school who had failed to pass out fliers or procure a stage or execute any of the other details necessary for putting on a comedy show. Thus even the comedians, who were used to impossible conditions, like doing comedy in a bar with no lighting and no mike, or doing it, as Dick once had, during a power failure by holding a candle up to his face—were surprised to learn that their stage was three adjacent milk cartons in a corridor leading to the cafeteria. There was no place for an audience, although a crowd could have gathered if they had known something was going on. But as the students passed by in the corridor, they simply looked quizzically at the men standing on the milk cartons and wondered what was going on. Was it a political rally of some kind? A sales pitch? Religion?

Buck, who as MC was the first onstage, spoke about three sentences before the preposterousness of the situation overtook him, at which point he began to giggle so much he could not speak. He began to cry—tears of laughter, but tears that choked off all words to the point where, when it came time for him to bring Fat onstage, he could not even utter his name and had to settle for pointing at the lad as he approached the milk cartons. Not that it mattered, since no one was watching, only passing by.

Fat, of course, did his act as if it were a command performance for the queen.

Dick, however, had caught Buck's case of the giggles and could go on with his own set for only five minutes, at which time he turned it back to Buck to close the show. But Dick, like Buck a few minutes earlier, was too gone to make an introduction, so he just pointed at Buck the way Buck had pointed at Fat.

DeLaRigurge had done it. He had literally set comedy back fifty thousand years, to a time before comedy was spoken.

When Buck got home from New Jersey, there was a horrifying message on his machine. It was DeLaRigurge's nauseating voice:

"I just looked at my book and you're out at Franny's tonight, so I guess I'll see you again."

Now, doing a Jersey gig on a night when you really just felt like staying in the city, which was any night you had a Jersey gig, was bad enough—but after you'd already done one in the day? It couldn't be.

But when Buck looked at his calendar, he saw DeLaRigurge was right. Somehow he had booked not one but two Jersey gigs in the same day. It was a fate worse than life. Buck was not a happy man as he waited again in the shadow of the Lincoln Tunnel for the ride across the Hudson River.

In the backseat of the Jerseymobile, Dick was not thrilled about having signed up for double Jersey duty, either, and Dick always liked to work. There was no shortage of glee in the car, however, because also on assignment this evening was Leland, a constantly grinning black comedian whom Buck always thought would have been well served by adapting the stage name Happy Blackman.

The gig this night was at a place called Franny's, located in Wayne, New Jersey, at the conflux of three roads: the Turnpike, Route 3, and the Garden State Parkway. The motif at Franny's was clowns. A lot of clowns. Paintings of clowns, clown mario-nettes, big clowns on the wall, small clowns on the menu and, to open the show: a clown. It was the practice at Franny's to hire a clown to go up for ten minutes of mime as a warm-up, with a piano tinkling in the background. And how good the clown must have felt this night when he walked onstage and was immediately greeted with the unmistakable sound of a stupid guy from New Jersey:

"Look—it's a fucking clown!"

While the clown was on, the boys were in the upstairs restaurant section ordering away from the left side of the menu, a section of the menu where they were absolutely free to order anything they wanted: a hamburger, a cheeseburger, a cheddarburger . . .

It was the side of the menu with the burgers.

During the meal, Buck was surprised by three friends of his from high school who had come to see the show. What were they doing in New Jersey he wanted to know, but not enough to listen to the answer. What mattered was they were there.

"We heard you were doin' comedy," one of them said.

"Hey, are you any good?" another asked, thinking he had made a joke.

I'll show 'em if I'm any good, Buck thought.

When the clown finished, it was Leland's turn to take the stage and get the show off to a big start or, in his case, to take it so far into the gutter so fast that no semblance of real comedy could ever follow. No one could say that Leland did not set an unmistakable tone for a show; it was just such a mistake to let him set any tone at all. But this was New Jersey and no one cared.

Except Buck, because two guys and a girl he knew in high

school and never gave a shit about and always thought were stupid had come to the show, so he wanted to do good more than he ever wanted anything in life.

Leland opened the show in his usual manner, by screaming at the crowd and then getting them to scream back at him. Then he did his impression of Ted Kennedy: a toy car dropped into a glass of water; then his Sammy Davis, Jr.: "You're just too good to be true . . . can't take my *eye* off of you"; then he brought out a huge bag of flour, which he professed was cocaine: "Let me get my spoon," which turned out to be a huge soup ladle.

> *Say owwwww! Come on, let me hear some screamin'! Owwww!*
>
> *Arright, arright, that's better—hey, I know what you're thinking, but I'm not black—this is a birthmark.*
>
> *When I was young, man, I bought myself a false I.D. once, I had to make like I was an ugly white woman.*
>
> *But guys don't understand women, man—hey, I never mind when a girl has her period—I tell her, "Good for you, bitch, now you have to give me a blow job!"*
>
> *But I'm a great lover—I know I must be, because every time I do it to my girlfriend, the cat thinks dinner is on.*
>
> *No, I am, man, I'm a great lover, 'cause I got a big one—yeah, you know what I mean. Man, my dick's so big, it's got its own knee.*
>
> *Sometimes it even tires me out, doin' the nasty—you know what I do when I'm too tired to come? I start fuckin' her from behind, then I pull out and spit on her back.*

And so on, until he closed with his closing bit, wherein he pointed to a chair onstage and asked, "How many people wannna see me fuck this chair?" That bit always got a laugh out of the other comedians because they recalled the night that Leland's protégé, another black comic named Ashley, did what he thought was a twist on this bit, inviting a girl onstage and asking the audience "How many people wanna see me fuck this girl?"

While Leland was onstage, Dick and Buck were in the parking lot outside. Buck wanted desperately to be left alone so he could go over his notes and look professional for his high school friends, but Dick, he soon found out, was a pathetic shell of a man who wanted to talk about romance.

"This is my first night away from her in . . . I really don't know how long," Dick said, referring to Jill.

"Yeah, I'm surprised she didn't come with us," Buck said.

"I told her there wasn't room in the car."

"So, what, she suggested getting a shuttle bus?"

"Yeah, right," Dick chuckled. There was a moment of silence, followed by Buck using his gift of sucking the awkwardness out of any situation by saying the exact thing the person needed to hear to have his face saved—a gift Buck used in business, when it served his self-interest, and also at those random moments when he remembered to be kind to someone for the sake of being kind.

"Well, she certainly is a looker," Buck said. He felt good about saying it, because he knew that Dick knew that he knew that this bitch was emasculating him, and it was better that he, Buck, be the one to express the thought that beauty in a woman went a long way toward justifying the kind of grotesquely pathetic thing Dick had become.

"It's not like you're some sort of grotesquely pathetic thing," Buck said. "What is she doing tonight?"

"I have no idea," Dick said. "It's unbelievable—all I want for weeks is a few hours away from her, and now I can't stop worrying about her."

"Why, what do you think she'll do?" Buck asked.

"I don't know. Blow a hockey team?"

"Oh well—then what are you worrying about? She'll blow a team, probably after the game, and then, what's that, twelve, one, she'll be home. Okay, maybe she'll blow the cabbie on the way back, one-thirty tops, you know, depending on how good she is."

"Hey, that's my bitch you're talking about," Dick said.

"I never said she was a bitch," Buck averred. "She's a full-fledged cunt."

"Hey," Dick started, feeling the obligation to muster some umbrage.

"Well, I'm sorry," Buck countermanded, "but you're too good a friend to let me stand by and watch this girl make you miserable. I mean, maybe I'm outta line and maybe you're gonna punch me right here in this parking lot, and Lord knows, 98 percent of all the punchings in the United States do take place in parking lots, but I'm sorry, I've gotten to know your Jill a little bit, and, Jesus, I know she's beautiful but, my God, she is the most obnoxious, presumptuous, pretentious . . . princess it really has ever been my displeasure to be dying to fuck."

At that the two boys laughed heartily, especially Buck, because, of course, it was his remark.

"No, you know what I'm trying to say, pal—I know what that's like to get bitten by a girl so beautiful, you're just helpless."

Actually, Buck did not know what it was like to be bitten by a girl that beautiful, and he was dying to be so helpless.

"It's like, no matter how strong you are in your own mind about it, when you get with her and she starts doing her beautiful woman thing—bang, Jell-O," Buck said, drawing on his experience—his experience of hearing other men describing that experience in words so similar they could be mistaken for exact.

As Dick began weeping openly and flagellating himself across the back with spiked chains, Buck excused himself to go off and review his notes. All the time he was talking to Dick the show was on his mind, the friends from high school, the pressure to excel. He had been absorbed in his notes for a few minutes when he heard a voice calling for him. It was Dick, sticking his head out the door of the building.

"Hey, you're on! He just introduced you!"

Buck bounded back into the bar at full throttle and ran downstairs, where no one was onstage and the room was noisy, as a room of children will be when left unattended.

"Sorry I'm late, folks," Buck said on this temperate spring night. "Damn icy roads."

It got a pinch of a laugh, but not much more. It was a subtle remark that only confused most of the patrons at Franny's.

"You guys all from Jersey?" Buck asked a youngster in the first row. "Yeah, what town you from?"

"The other guy already asked me," came the reply.

"Well, fuck me!" Buck bellowed, and wasted no time in reminding the crowd that they were stupid working-class losers from New Jersey.

Whether it was because he had already done one horrific Jersey gig that day or whether it was because he wanted to look ultra-cool in front of his friends, Buck took on an immediate sarcastic swagger that quickly turned the crowd against him. The attitude he brought with him to Franny's that night was light-years away from what he could have gotten away with. On the night when he most wanted to do well, the gods of comedy had chosen to viscerally teach him a lesson: If they don't like you, it doesn't matter how funny you are—they won't laugh.

No, I feel good tonight, because some hookers proposi-tioned me on the way over, and that always makes men feel good—right guys? Hah?

Oh yeah, right, like I'm the only one—see, these pussies won't admit it, but all men like getting propositioned, even by a hooker, because it's still a certain rock bottom validation . . . because there are men even street hookers don't ask—ever been ONE of them?

Again, fuck me, I'm the only one—I'm the only one who knows what it's like when you pass a hooker—and you can tell she's a hooker because she's black, with blond hair— Yeah, boo me, like I'm the one forcing all the hooker Negresses to go blond—I mean, what is that all about? Are we supposed to be thinking, I wonder if she dyes her hair—excuse me, is that a wig?—

But, come on, hasn't that ever happened to you, you pass a hooker and she looks at you and just . . . turns away and shakes her head. God, what is wrong with me?! Do I have a hunchback, is there a sore bleeding on me that I don't know about, is it the cum stain on my pants?

But the whores in New York have a heart—unlike you whores out here in New Jersey—no, just kidding—no, because the come-on line the whores in New York always use is, "Wanna date?"

A date—isn't that kind to call it a date? Have you ever

*had a date where the girl immediately took you to a hotel
and blew you?*

My mother used to say "Do you have a date tonight?"

*Oh, yeah . . . I got me a date, all right. Yeah, I think
we'll go to a movie, then dinner, then I'll meet her
pimp . . .*

You know, 'cause it's like I'm on a date with her?

*The jokes will be flying at about 35,000 feet above your
head, please lock your tray tables . . .*

Buck's set quickly devolved into a joke delivered badly, a
bad reaction from the crowd, and then some sort of "saver"
from Buck that indicted the crowd for not getting the joke, a
timeless comedic device that had bailed Johnny Carson out a
thousand times.

But Johnny Carson was a huge star; Johnny's audience
adored him; and Johnny didn't precede his subtle chastisement
with, "What are you, thick?"

*Oh gee, will you look at the time—I just remembered,
my flying saucer is double-parked . . .*

*But I have not had this much fun since the last time I
caught my dick in my fly . . .*

*As an audience, you have really been a group of peo-
ple—no, I mean that . . .*

*I would love to stay, but it would keep me from go-
ing . . .*

*Because this is certainly a night I will remember till I
get to my car . . .*

Thank-you, you were execrable, good night!

Alone again in the parking lot, Buck hated himself. He hated
life, and he hated the audience. He had hate to spare, but all
of it put together was not so great as the hate he had for what
was next—having to see those kids from his high school. God,
what a night to bite the big one! It was almost physical, this
pain he had for fucking up so bad.

"Hey, sorry you came all this way to see that," Buck told

his classmates in the parking lot. "It's not usually like this, but you know, if you're a comic, I don't care who you are, there's a couple of these kinda nights in every deck."

God, it was so humiliating. He had actually done so bad that these kids, who weren't ever friends and who probably never liked him in high school and were rooting for him to fail, actually felt sorry for him now. He had so surpassed whatever hopes they had for his falling on his face that they now pitied him.

But Buck wouldn't even give them the satisfaction they had voluntarily relinquished. He feigned an even, almost tranquil temperament, as if this inevitable deuce in the deck was already ancient history. He turned the conversation to what they all had in common, asking about kids from school and mocking teachers and all that sort of stuff that would have been so much fun if only he had looked like a rising star back there instead of a hopeless, pathetic dreamer.

Dick was still on when Buck's fellow alumni left, and Leland joined Buck in the parking lot.

"Hey, good set, man," Leland told Buck.

"Are you trying to be funny?"

"No, it was, it was a good set. I love it when you get on the crowd."

Great, Buck thought. He was doing things Leland loves.

"Some nice chicks in there, man."

"Yeah," Buck grunted flatly.

"Yeah, some nice ones."

"Yeah well, why don't you and the clown see if you can do some damage—ooh, Christ, there he is."

The clown was now approaching them in the parking lot. Buck wanted to be nice to him. He introduced himself and Leland.

"Tom Kelly," the clown said.

"Nice to meet you. I really enjoyed what you did up there," Buck lied.

"Yeah, that was really cool," Leland aped.

"Why do you stay in the suit?" Buck asked.

"I have to shake hands with the audience going out."

"Oh my God," Buck sympathized. "Oh, that's awful. I

don't mind playing to them—I mean, I do mind playing to them when they're like this—but to actually have to touch them individually—eecch.''

The clown and the comics sat themselves up on the hood of a big old Cadillac. Leland offered Tom a cigarette, and the clown looked funny smoking. He looked funny just talking.

''People don't understand clowns,'' Tom said as he crossed his legs, leaving his giant clown shoe to stick out into the stratosphere. ''You know, in the old days, clowns used to go insane because of the makeup. They were literally painting themselves, and slowly they'd go crazy over the years.''

''But because they were clowns, I guess no one really knew,'' Buck guessed.

''No, the people who ran the circus knew, they just didn't care,'' Tom said.

''Forerunners of the modern-day club owner,'' Buck said.

''Are all club owners that bad?'' Tom asked.

''Well, you know, Jack Ruby was a club owner, and I think most of them see him as a role model. But, you know, we're all clowns. You just have the guts to put on the uniform.''

That shut everybody up.

''How did you become a clown?'' Leland asked the clown. ''You weren't in the circus, were you?''

''Oh yeah,'' Tom said. ''Five years with Ringling Brothers.''

''Really,'' Buck said, impressed. ''What's that like? I mean, is it all the circus stuff you think it is—bearded women and freaks and frogboys and everything?''

''You mean my family?'' Tom said, and the two comedians laughed.

''But I bet they do become like a family,'' Buck continued.

''Yeah, they do.''

''Same with us, kind of,'' Buck responded.

''Yeah, exactly, same with us,'' Leland underlined. But Buck was genuinely curious, and genuinely glad to be with someone who might be more pathetic than he now felt himself to be.

''Are circus people as pure of heart as they're always portrayed in old movies—you know, always a kind word and a hot meal for Frankenstein or whatever misunderstood monster or hunted criminal is roaming the countryside?''

''Well,'' Tom said, ''they're not on any show biz ego trip, if that's what you mean.''

''Yeah, in the circus I guess you don't, like, finish a show and wait for the chicks to come backstage—although I guess that half-man half-woman can score at will.''

To which Leland erupted into gales of laughter.

Soon Buck was finished interviewing the clown, and he made sure to use his skill of telling someone exactly what he wanted to hear, complimenting the clown on his talent and courage without ever seeming patronizing or phony.

In another few minutes, the crowd started to spill out into the parking lot. Buck did not want to face them, but since there was no place to hide, he was forced to spin himself around on the spot where he stood until a hole was bored in the pavement. He remained in the hole till everyone was gone.

As the laughmobile entered the Lincoln Tunnel, the talk turned to what plans lay ahead for the three warriors. Dick, of course, would begin his futile all-night search for Jill. Leland would go to The Club because, as he explained, ''I do as many sets as I can, that's how you get good.'' Sadly, there was not enough time, given the rate of deterioration in the solar system, for Leland to achieve his plan. Nevertheless, he asked Buck to join him for the cab ride uptown.

Buck, though, had had enough of audiences for one day and felt so shitty about comedy he didn't care if he ever got good. He walked home from the drop point by the tunnel to his apartment on West 49th. Nearing home, he stopped at a deli on Ninth Avenue where Muslims offered overpriced chicken in plastic containers placed in a white bag (to keep it hot!), with a napkin and plastic utensils thrown in free of charge. Next stop: the newsstand, where *The New York Times* and the latest issue of *Nugget* comprised a balanced reading menu. At the steps to Buck's building, a bum importuned alms and Buck, like a latterday John D. Rockefeller, batted not an eye in flipping a dime to the elderly tatterdemalion.

Finally within the comforting walls of his castle, Buck selected the *Nugget* to occupy his mind while engaged in his evening toilette. Upon leafing through the issue (No. 9, Volume XII), however, he was rather disappointed with the quality of the ''models'' featured inside. Why had he chosen the *Nugget*, he wondered to himself, when a score of higher-quality stroke-books were readily available?

He knew why. It was because the women one masturbates to are directly proportional in desirability to how good one feels about oneself: If you felt strong and confident, even the babes in *Playboy* didn't seem out of reach sometime in your happy future.

But Buck didn't feel strong and confident this night. What he felt like was a beaten loser who was thankful that even the flabby skankdogs in *Nugget* would let him beat off over them.

Across town, Dick was getting worried about Jill. Actually, he wasn't worried about Jill, he was worried Jill was in fact having a wonderful time somewhere without him, so he was worried about himself, but he was calling Jill. He kept leaving messages on the machine at his apartment: ''Hi, it's me. Call me at The Club when you get in. I miss you.''

At 3 A.M. The Club locked up, and Dick went home to his empty apartment, clueless as to where to find Jill, how to deal with the anxiety her absence caused, or the larger issue of how to root the bitch from his heart. Then he remembered a piece of advice regarding women he'd once proffered to Fat: Think like the criminal. Yes, that was it—he had to think like she did.

So, Dick said to himself—if I were a totally heartless witch devoid of all goodness and purity . . . where would I be?

In the bed of one of the million or more apartments in New York City owned or rented by a man wealthier and better-looking than I am, came back the depressing, not to mention hard-to-follow-up-on, response. Consumed with grief and the inescapability of his condition, Dick felt his eyes well up with tears as he lay on his bed. He wondered why there was such a thing as crying yourself to sleep but not, even for a comedian, laughing your way there.

At noon the next day, Dick was awakened by the sound of a key in the door, which was not surprising since the door was only a few feet from the head of his bed. It was Jill, all right, but she couldn't get in because the inside locks—two chains across the top, and a sturdy metal rod propped up from the floor—prevented her access.

Jill shouted Dick's name from the hallway.

"What?" Dick called back from his fetal position on the bed.

"What do you mean, what? Open the door, please," Jill said, restraining her impulse to wax vitriolic, since she was as yet on the wrong side of the door.

Dick did not answer, but he did take the thumb out of his mouth.

"Baby, please open the door, I'm very tired," Jill moaned.

"I don't doubt it," Dick answered.

"Sweetheart, what is your problem?"

"As always, you."

"Hell-o!" Jill said.

"Goodbye!" Dick answered.

"Look, could you let me in so we could talk about it?"

"I don't want to talk."

"Great. So what is this, you're kicking me out, is that it?"

"Yeah, pretty much."

"Fine, but can I get some of my stuff?"

"Get it sometime when I'm not here. I'll give you a week before I change the locks."

"Fine, but what about today? Where am I supposed to go right now?"

"Why don't you go back to wherever you just were."

"I was with friends, and they went off to work," Jill said, invoking the mystical, and apparently uncountable, friends that she was always with when not in Dick's company.

"Ooh, darn the luck," Dick said.

"Look, I don't know what your sick mind thinks I was doing last night, but I was simply out with some pals till very late, and we wound up at Jason's flat around five, and I just ran out of steam and crashed on the couch."

Dick was tired of talking. Jill was not.

"Look, can I just please come in for one minute so I can gather a few articles of clothing and use the loo?" she asked, practicing her custom of employing, whenever possible, the British version of the English language, a habit that Dick imagined she'd picked up from sleeping with God knows how many rock stars.

Dick put his thumb back in his mouth.

"All right, fine," Jill said. "I'll just sit out here and wait for you, then, because I love you enough to do that."

Dick sat up in bed. He didn't know what was more amazing, that Jill had said she loved him or that she'd said she would wait for him, because waiting was something Jill was never up to, even when Dick just wanted to wash his hands before leaving a Chinese restaurant.

He opened the door.

"All right, you can use the bathroom," he said with toothless pride, knowing full well that once back in, Jill would again be using much more than just the loo. As she tarried inside the minuscule water closet for a good twenty minutes, Dick sat silently on the bed, relieved that she was still with him, but in another way not relieved at all, since he had just woken up and also needed to use the loo.

13

When Opportunity Knocks, All Some People Do Is Complain About the Noise

With Luther safely neutralized, the time had come for Buck to rock the boat on Second Avenue. The dead wood were in for a shock on their way to the lumberyard. In only a few days, Buck had two hours of fresh talent coming into The Club every night as word spread quickly through the loquacious comic community that there was a new sheriff in town. Of course, panic spread just as quickly through the ranks of the suddenly disenfranchised, all of whom turned to Norma as their last hope of staunching the tide of reform. Buck knew this would happen, and he didn't want the affair to turn into a battle between him and Norma. Beyond personal considerations—he liked her, he owed her, and she was Chink's girlfriend—he did not want to provoke a test of wills with someone who went back as far as she did with Bo. He knew that the sands at The Club could shift quickly and that it was dangerous to make plans around someone like Bo, who always agreed with the last thing he'd heard, from anybody.

"We can't do this to these guys," Norma told Buck in the phone call he'd been expecting for two days. "They've been loyal to us."

"But maybe if we surprise the audience a little, we'll start getting an audience in there that likes to be surprised," Buck argued. "And wouldn't that be a nice surprise."

"It takes time to build an act," Norma countered, "to build a career. Not everybody learns as fast as you. I don't know how you can do this to them."

"Do this to them? I'm not doing it to them. I'm not responsible for someone being at this little club for five, six, seven years. Don't you think that says something about their talent?"

"Speaking as one of them, I'd have to say no."

"I didn't mean you . . . I didn't mean . . ."

No, Buck never meant, but he always did. But to Norma, of all people! Norma, who'd always been so supportive, indulging that cocky side of him when she could have held it against him; Norma, who always told everybody he was gonna be the next star to come out of The Club; Norma, who went on about him so much anyone would think she was his mother, except that with your mother it was embarrassing because you knew everyone was thinking, Well, it's his mother, of course she thinks that, but from Norma it was an endowment that, especially in the early days, was even more nourishing than the free hamburger.

Buck started to cry—at least as far as Norma could tell over the phone. If they'd been in the same room together, he probably couldn't have pulled it off, but over the phone it was easy to sound too choked up to talk. Buck had learned that much from relationships.

"I'm sorry," he sobbed, "but I have to do this. Bo said he was counting on me."

"Bo asked you to do this?" Norma asked, surprise in her voice.

"Please don't tell him I told you, I'm not supposed to tell anyone," Buck sobbed. "I'm sure he would have asked you to do it, except he knows you've been with these guys a long time, so it would be too tough for you. But me—well, I guess he figured everybody hates me anyway."

Oh boo-hoo. Boo fucking hoo.

But Norma, a New York woman with as hard a bark on her as any New York woman, was still a woman. No matter that Buck had insulted her to the core only a minute ago. All was forgotten now because Buck, poor, poor Buck, was carrying this secret burden around with him, and he was afraid that everybody hated him, and he was being forced to exacerbate that very situation now in order to spare Bo's pseudopopularity.

How neatly all that fit in with what anyone who'd known Bo as long as Norma had known Bo knew about Bo—that he asked others to do his dirty work for him. Poor Buck.

"Oh yeah, he made a big deal of it," Buck poured it on. "Said we were getting away from his 'vision of The Club.' Said we had to shake the place up."

"He's right," Norma said, making the turn from comic camaraderie to self-preservation as fast as Buck had just turned insult into pity. "When you said that about his vision of The Club, it clicked in with me. I'm sorry I didn't see it before. That's why the place has always been such a success—because he's such a brilliant man, he can see exactly what it should be."

He's lucky to see the floor when he's falling, Buck thought.

"Absolutely," Buck said.

"I feel like a such a schmuck," Norma said, and then imitated herself talking like an idiot, with a finger in her nose. "Forgive me?"

"Stop it," Buck said, regaining the composure he'd never lost: "There's nothing to forgive."

On a day in May too beautiful to resist, Buck decided it was time to act on a long-standing pledge to himself—to get in shape. Getting in shape was a difficult undertaking in New York, and for that reason undertaking had always been a profitable business in the city. Joining a gym was expensive and required disciplined planning. Parks were plentiful, but most of them had long ago been set aside for drug dealing, and the parks commission took a dim view of anyone misusing them for recreation. Central Park was available for any sports played on a surface of hard shale and broken glass, but any miscalculation of time that left one there past dark meant certain death. Of course, death may have been worth risking on Central Park's one perfect expanse of verdant sod—The Great Lawn—but the Great Lawn was roped off from the public in order that it might remain a great, albeit unused, lawn.

"A New Yorker's idea of exercise is to masturbate and walk the dog," Buck had occasionally tried as a joke, without much success. Perhaps it was too close to the truth.

Nevertheless, Buck and Shit had for the longest time talked about joining forces in a health regimen, which up until this day had involved requesting fresh orange juice in their screwdrivers instead of frozen. But the beauty of this day could not be ignored: a sky of clear blue, temperature at a perfect seventy degrees, and no humidity.

After meeting on the West Side, the boys decided to warm up with a brisk walk, which would take them into Central Park. However, after a few blocks of fighting through the Calcutta-esque teeming masses, a cab ride seemed more in order, and after the stress induced by a New York cabbie, a single drink was deemed a necessary tonic.

It was not the liquor, however, but rather the fast-moving events in the comedy world that doomed the boys' health program to yet another time: There was simply too much to talk about. A day of rigorous jaw exercising began with the debate over the Big Joke-Off.

The Big Joke-Off was the brainstorm of a local promoter named Dave Schmukov, and it was a direct result of his being impressed by the new line-up of talent at The Club. Schmukov's idea was to winnow the field in New York to the top twenty young comedians, then have them vie over two nights of celebrity-judged competition at The Club for the honor of being one of five finalists. This quintet would then go head to head in an ultimate show, to be filmed for cable television, which would produce the big winner. The rewards for gaining this top honor included the TV exposure and other press coverage, the prestige of winning something in New York City, and a purse of five thousand dollars.

Naturally, Shit was against the whole thing.

"It's wrong for artists to compete," he said.

"I'm not so sure of that," said Buck, whose views on art and comedy were, as always, still evolving.

"Well, that's really sad," Shit mourned. "That's one thing I thought you were solid on."

"No, I am. I mean, it should be. I don't know. I don't feel

much like an artist when I'm telling some heckler to go stick his head in dough and make asshole cookies or when I watch Barry Badaducce juggling vomit or when Leland does his impression of Linda Lovelace with water coming out of his mouth or—''

"It's still a degradation. People should not be judging whether one comedian is better than any other.''

"Why not? That's what they're doing anyway. You don't think when people leave The Club that's exactly what they're doing, saying, 'Oh, yeah, that last guy was the best,' or, 'That first guy really sucked'?''

"And your solution is to contribute to that mentality by institutionalizing the competition.''

"No, it's not my solution, but some things in life don't have solutions. Human nature is what it is. People love competition—they loved it in the Coliseum, they loved it on *Major Bowes*, and they'll probably love it when I attempt to kick your ass in the contest.''

"You won't have to—I'm not doing it. Let them joke you off.''

"That's stupid, you have to do it.''

"No. You're exactly wrong. I don't have to dance when they play a certain tune. We should be banding together, not competing against each other.''

"Oh, here it comes.''

"Yeah, that's right, here it comes, and its gonna keep coming until I make it happen, and I will make it happen.''

"Why? If you really want to start a union so much, why don't you find a real one somewhere? Why do you give such a humongous shit about the collective welfare of fifty comedians, most of whom couldn't pay you to hang out with them and most of whom would stab you or anyone else in the back to get two feet ahead in the business? This isn't some assembly-line thing we're doing, this is an every-man-for-himself deal, except now they're gonna give some Everyman five grand for doing what we do anyway.''

"As usual, you only see what is,'' Shit replied. "I shudder to think where the world would be if everyone was like you, if everyone always threw up their hands and said, 'Okay, this is the way the world is, it'll never be better, it's a dung heap, the best you can do is to get to the top of it.' "

"The world would be right where it's always been—that's why they call it the world."

"But the world *isn't* where it's always been. You can't say the world hasn't progressed."

No matter how their arguments began, Buck and Shit always preferred bringing the world into it. If anyone could make the world's ears burn, it was Buck and Shit.

"Progressed?" Buck shot back, always ready to pooh-pooh whatever Shit had just said about the world. "The only difference between Attila the Hun and Hitler is Hitler had better technology. History is a game of inches. We beat the Nazis to the A-bomb by a matter of months, and if we had been the ones who came up an inch short instead of them, they would have won the war and we'd be having this debate in German. I didn't make the world as it is, but as it is, might makes right."

"*Your* might is for the Hitlers of the world," Shit said, "and all the others who wind up on the ash heap of infamy. But when good people hear *might*, they think of the *might* that says something *might* be something else—moldy bread *might* be medicine . . . the earth *might* not be flat . . . slavery *might* be wrong. There's all sorts of things you accept without thinking that seemed ridiculous and impossible when the first guy proposed them."

"Like alternate-side-of-the-street parking."

"No, like—well, would you say the Constitution of the United States is a great document?"

"I was thumbing through it just the other day."

"But the Constitution says Negroes are three-fifths of a human being."

"They're not?"

"The point is, the men who wrote that were not bad men. They were the most enlightened men of their day."

"They had to be, they lived in the Age of Enlightenment."

"Exactly. But when they looked at a creature that in every way was just like them except darker, they did not see another human being. They saw an animal. So somewhere between then and now, somebody had to be the first to question that.

You can't deny changes like that have taken place throughout history because somebody saw a way to make the world better.''

"I don't know, I kind of liked a flat world with slaves where you just picked the moldy parts off the bread.''

"You know I'm right.''

Buck bobbed his head in a yes-and-no sort of way. But he came up saying: "Yes. Okay, yeah, you make a good case, you're right, and I'm glad I have a friend who can scrape some of that cynicism off me. I'll never think of *might* the same way again. I'll hear it, and I'll think of Jesus and Socrates and Gandhi and Kennedy and King and Lincoln and . . . Jesus, everybody else who got murdered for their trouble! Yeah, there's your *might*—you *might* get shot!''

"Of course the world rejects radical ideas when they're first pronounced. That's your no-room-at-the-inn theory. But don't you think those ideas were worth dying for?''

Buck thought about it for a moment.

"Yes,'' he said. "Yes I do. And once again, counselor, you almost had me netted in your specious web, but if I may inject a note of reality here, what we were talking about was doing a comedy contest. That's not slavery. That's not brotherhood or independence or any other big life thing, it's show business. It's just show business.''

"But show business *is* our life.''

"Thank you, Georgie Jessel.''

"Don't you see, it's not how big the idea is, it's fighting for the right in any idea. It's every man reaching within himself, no matter what his calling, and defending a vision that is better than the one he inherited. It's the eternal struggle that every man build on the work of the good men who came before him, that he not let fall the torch of progress for those who come after him, until all trace of evil and injustice is vanished from the earth.''

Buck looked across the table at Shit and ever so slightly, and with reverence, nodded his head. Then he said:

"You wanna see a movie?

14

People: The Problem That Won't Go Away

Summer hit New York City in 1980 with all the force of one of those great weather analogies in a Dashiell Hammett detective story. On June 21, the first day of summer, Buck broke down and put the old air conditioner he had inherited from his grandmother in the other window, the one that wasn't over the fire escape. It didn't exactly make the room frosty, but when used in conjunction with a cold shower and a fan, it made it tolerable, with one great side effect: The noise from the machine blocked out the blaring, twenty-four-hour cacophony from Ninth Avenue.

If measured not strictly by the equinox but as the time of year when one felt the need to shower within one minute of walking outside into the thick air, summer in New York lasted from about mid-May until early October, at which time there'd be three lovely days before the biting cold of winter set in, which in turn would last until spring, which consisted of three more nice days before mid-May. The extremes of hot and cold dominated the city's climate, but summer in New York was perhaps the most distinctive of all the seasons: There was that never-ending grimy feeling and the soap opera of the Yankees blaring from the tabloids' back page each day and Crazy Eddie's Christmas sale, and the shot of the kids in Harlem playing in an open fire hydrant as the credits to *Live at Five* rolled on the screen.

And there were women. Lots and lots of women, all of whom must have lived with bears during the winter, because they seemed to emerge on the sidewalks from nowhere, in huge numbers and scantily clad. For Buck, who spent a portion of every day on these sidewalks, this parade of sticky, sweaty, braless women turned his libido up to frappe. It was, it made him think, the reason that people in Africa and other places with constantly soaring climates were so backward: It was always summer for them! They never covered up and so were perpetually too distracted to ever tackle anything so demanding as the Industrial Revolution. Winter, to be sure, was the key to forging an advanced civilization. People took vacations in the summer; kids, unable to think in the heat, were let out from school; and as Buck well knew, audiences were dumber—a fact that had not escaped notice in Hollywood, which released only fiery, kick-ass movies after Memorial Day.

No, summer was not a time for thinking. It was a time for drinking beer and fucking, not necessarily in that order.

Buck did not want to be reminded that the entire spring had passed without him getting planet-aligned as he had hoped. He knew the situation was desperate when I-can't-get-laid jokes started popping into his head.

But all bad things must come to an end, and on this sticky evening they did, and from a most unlikely source: audition night. It wasn't that Buck hadn't thought a million times that audition night would be a great way to meet a girl—it was just that girls who wanted to be comedians were rarely the ones you wanted to fuck. The funny girl in school was the fat one, not the cute one in the halter top. Even in real show business, there had never been a gorgeous comedienne, and those comediennes who were attractive treated it as a liability and made themselves ugly, or pronounced themselves ugly until people came to think of them as ugly. American audiences were stubborn in sticking to their comedic stereotypes: Fat was jolly; Jewish was neurotic; and funny girls were funny because they were ugly or shrewish.

But Vera was neither ugly nor shrewish. She was big-tittish and high-cheekboned, a tall, dark-haired Polish-gened statue who could look absolutely goofy dissolving into laughter one minute and like the cover of *Vogue* the next.

When Buck noticed her sitting at the bar as he flew into The Club just before show time, he never guessed that she was one of the auditioners. But then, why had she smiled at him?

Because, by God, she *was* one of the auditioners. She gathered around Buck with all the other pathetics when he called them into a circle to explain the ground rules for their five minutes in the spotlight—most important of which was that it be *only* five minutes. Audition Night had come to be the biggest migraine of all for Buck, but on this night he somehow rediscovered the bonhomie that he had once happily brought to the job. He purposefully kept his eyes off Vera during his speech, but his heart skipped a beat when she put her arm up to ask a question.

"Um, what if we don't see the light?" she asked, referring to the flashing signal that told a performer it was time to hit the road. "Are we, like, punished?"

Buck thought her use of the word *like*—which he formerly had excoriated as an unpardonable lapse of verbal facility and harbinger of the collapse of Western civilization—charming.

"You'll see it," Buck said, but then realized he'd blown a chance to get alone with her. "Do you want me to show you?"

Vera nodded, in a way that was both delightfully innocent and massively erection-producing. Buck made sure there were no other questions from the group, then led Vera into the showroom to point out where the light was.

"You don't have glaucoma or anything, do you?" he asked.

She laughed her big, goofy laugh, which, Buck noticed, shook her big tits. A tit-shaking laugh—was he dreaming?

"What's your name?" Buck asked his future ex-wife.

"Vera."

"Hi, Vera. I'm—"

"I know who you are," she said.

That was the first time anyone had ever said that to Buck. It would have sounded good coming from one of New York's many knot-haired, lice-infested bums who hadn't urinated indoors since 1968, but coming out of Vera's big, built-for-blowjobs mouth it was truly incredible. I know who you are—God, wasn't that what show business was supposed to be all about? Wasn't that the whole point of being in show business, to be well known enough that women spoke to you first, gave you a nice compliment right off the bat? Wasn't it worth all the humiliation and hard work just so that your opening line to strange women could always be: "Thank you."

Yes, it was.

"I've seen you here before," Vera went on. "You're really good."

"Thank you—thank you very much," Buck said casually, as if he had to say it a hundred times every day. "How kind of you to say that."

"It's not kind, it's true."

"Finish your thought," Buck smarmed, a line he'd used a thousand times before, but never to someone with a vagina he wanted to explore. Then he asked: "Is this your first time onstage?"

"Yeah," she said. "I'm kinda nervous."

"Don't be. Really. No one expects you to be a pro the first time up. What we're—well, I guess what *I'm*—looking for is a presence. Just be yourself. I'm sure you'll be great. You're very charming."

Throughout the evening, Buck tried desperately to look too busy to talk to Vera. It wouldn't look right if it was obvious he had a crush on one of the auditioners, and he also wanted to play the BMOClub role in front of her, deciding on this, taking care of that, bestowing kindly and brilliant insight to auditioners, and generally being a busy and indispensable bee. Not the usual party-animal demeanor for Buck tonight; he looked almost—yes, he was: presidential.

At one-fifteen, Buck put Vera onstage. Say this for Buck, he wasn't venal: This was the time slot she drew, and the fact that he wanted to impress her with his power did not prompt him to give her an earlier spot. He was determined, however, no matter how bad she might stink up the stage, to find something encouraging to say to her about her performance.

As it turned out, Vera was typical of the female novices who came in for audition night. They were no worse than the men, except that their subject list was more predictable: douche commercials are stupid; tits get in the way a lot/men unaware of same; guys just want to fuck you; tits are strange things to have; showers don't get in your pussy enough; tits have a disproportionate importance in attracting men and are in inverse proportion to the IQ of the men who covet them.

Amazing insights, all.

Naturally, Vera was way overboard self-critical when Buck came back to the bar to talk to her: I was terrible, I blew it, yada yada yada. Buck disagreed vehemently: "No you're not, no you didn't, don't be so hard on yourself—let me do it."

In fact, Buck got just a lit-tle bit angry with this young lady for being so negative and not giving herself credit when she had so much going for her. He hated to see that, by God, and his extraction from her of a promise to never let him catch her doing it again implied the future relationship that he both desired and desired to imply.

Then to ensure that she'd be around for his desires, he told her: "I can see the only way to prove to you that you weren't bad is to tell you that you passed and should start hanging out."

Vera was speechless—a quality Buck had had enough of in Rita, so he hoped it wouldn't last. It didn't. Vera was so beside herself with joy, she opened up to Buck about her love for comedy in a spume of tumbling words that only a native speaker of English could have kept up with. This audition was not some onetime dare from a friend: Vera really had the bug. She was comedy-crazy.

She was also a little regular crazy, but Buck didn't notice that, and if he had, he wouldn't have cared.

Vera showed Buck her notebook, all three rings of it, filled on both sides, every page, an illegible riot of scrawled premises, shards of observation, and funny things that had happened on the way to just about everywhere. Vera was at that highly obnoxious phase of stand-up where everything is a potential bit, and she started to tell Buck a few of the best ten thousand.

But the bar was really not the best place to bounce tits, er, ideas, off each other. Buck suggested his apartment. Vera said okay.

Now, one-thirty was certainly not too early to put up a late-night MC—except there was not a suitable candidate in sight. Chink was there, but Buck knew management did not see Chink as appropriate even for late-night MCing. But then again, with

Luther castrated and Bo lucky to even find his own club if the
cabbie didn't know where it was, Buck *was* management. Also,
Chink deserved it, and Buck wanted to get laid—three cherries
in the slot machine as far as Buck was concerned, and so Chink
it was.

Buck moved around The Club with the kind of alacrity that
had turned poor Sambo into a pile of butter, convincing Chink
to take over, leaving him last-minute instructions like a nervous
parent with a baby-sitter, and trying not to come in his pants.
Buck's presidential phase was apparently over.

For the first half hour, Chink found the job to be no problem.
He was under the impression—and a correct one—that getting
all the auditioners on before the audience left was the chief
imperative on Audition Night, and past one-thirty that was
usually quite a race, audience against auditioners, the blood-
thirsty tired against the talentless inspired.

But bad luck followed Chink like a lawyer after an ambu-
lance. He was so efficient in processing all the auditioners that
by two-fifteen, thirty people remained in the audience with no
auditioners left to aud. And it being audition night, there were
no regulars hanging around, either. After twenty-five minutes
of his act—i.e., all of it—ten more people had left. Not
enough, Chink thought. He tried his hand at a "Where you
from?" and that drove out eight more people. But there were
still two tables of people who obviously had no intention of
going anywhere. They had come to audition night to see live
pain, and finally they were getting their money's worth. Chink
was a fish flopping around on a dock. He was playing the game
onstage that he played in the bar with his friends. He was
"cleaning out his notebook":

> *I like to read children's letters to Hitler—does anybody
> do that? Most people don't know this about the Nazis, but
> they were a lot of fun in private. They used to sneak up
> behind each other and play Guess Who?—Guess who?
> Bormann? . . . Goebbels? Göring? I knew it, he gets me
> every time!*
>
> *My definition of a macho guy is the soldier who was
> interrogated by the Nazis and said he "yessed them to*

death'' . . . *I once read an interview with a Japanese kamikaze pilot who survived, and they asked him why he was a kamikaze pilot and he said, "What, you never did anything crazy? You weren't young once?"*

You'd be surprised how a lot of things in history got started—like the slave revolt that Spartacus started . . . you know, he never even thought about being revolting, but then somebody said something to him one day that just rubbed him the wrong way. They said, "Hey, I'm having a few people over tomorrow night—are you free?"

I had a relative on Columbus's ship, and he could have been famous for being the first one to sight land, but he said he "didn't think it was worth mentioning . . ."

What goes on in a comedian's mind at the moment he is completely out of material is anybody's guess, but apparently what went on in Chink's mind was a free association to similar circumstances—specifically, what happens on *The Tonight Show* when a guest doesn't show up: stump the band! Clinging to that image, Chink called the house musicians back onstage. The musicians were confused: What's he going to do, sing?

No, he didn't sing. But the results of Chink's version of stump the band were hilarious anyway. The musicians got into it, the audience got into it, and Chink, with no one there watching to make him nervous and with a shot of confidence from his Washington trip, got as loose as he'd ever been on-stage. Washington had been a triumph for him, but this was different: He'd never done anything that was just stupid and goofy. He was always the artist. But he found out on this night that there was an additional element to stand-up comedy that was really fun: fun.

Meanwhile, back in his apartment, Buck was with Vera pretending to be more interested in comedic premises than breasts.

"Okay, what do you think of this premise?" Vera would say.

Okay, what do you think of this penis? Buck wanted to say.

Great suffering Christ, how many thoughts can one person have about douching? Who gives a shit?

"Now, that's funny," he said, and hoped she wouldn't ask him to specify what.

She didn't. To Vera, this was an audience with the pope, the normal tendency of young comedians to lionize anyone higher up in the pecking order. And speaking of the pecking order, the pope was ready to get laid.

"The closest thing a man gets to knowing the pain of giving birth is taking a difficult shit," Vera read.

The pain in Buck's face from faking smiles was now catching up to the one in his crotch. After an hour of The Book, he could take no more. He got up and belly-flopped himself down on the bed.

"Oh, I'm sorry, I'm boring you," Vera said.

"Oh no, not at all," Buck said with a straight dick. "I'm just a little tired. Audition night really takes it out of me."

"Do you want me to go?"

"Oh God no. Not at all. I want you to stay."

Vera climbed on Buck's back and gave him a good, hard rubdown. He purred with pleasure and told her how good it felt.

"You're tense," she said.

Parts of me are, he thought.

She leaned over and gave him a little kiss in the ear and whispered, "Thank you for helping me so much."

He turned over to look up at her, instantly turning the innocent back rub into a sexually charged straddling of his gonads.

Vera was an aggressive woman and needed no further cue. She leaned forward to kiss him. He accepted her kiss, which was the best one he'd ever had. He did not want it to end. Ever.

Soon Buck and Vera were exploring each other like great microbe hunters on the verge of curing something, anything. Each time Buck started to take off an article of Vera's clothing, she finished the job for him, until she was completely naked and he was completely not naked.

"This is a little unfair," Vera giggled.

Buck got up and stripped off his clothes faster than Superman does for Lois in distress. But when he bent over to remove his socks, he felt a little queasy. He had drunk too much during the night, in an effort to be less shy and more confident with Vera, which was unfortunate for two reasons: because liquor robbed his member of its proper rigidity and because, due to the first reason, Buck attempted oral sex on Vera in an effort to buy time—much the way Chink had just done onstage—for his prick to harden, but instead threw up in her vagina. The combination of the drinking and Buck's general distaste for the practice itself—Buck believed that cunnilingus was an act that should be reserved for the woman you truly love, because if you truly loved her, she would truly love you and so never ask you to do it—was too much for him.

But Vera was, if anything, a good sport. She calmly went about cleaning the mess as if it were no more than a stain on the rug caused by a naughty little boy—See, all gone. Daddy will never know.

The upheaval had made Buck feel better, intestinally anyway, but he feigned great sickness now in order to garner more sympathy, and also to avoid owning up to the fact that he'd just tossed his cookies in a date's womb. In fifteen minutes, however, he was bored with pretending to be sick, so he went to the bathroom in order to emerge in a different state: well. While in the bathroom he also tested his penis and, to his surprise, found that he could now cadge an erection out of himself after all. Buck desperately wanted to impress Vera with his studly prowess, but he knew it would not be easy—genital vomiting is not considered good foreplay in most cultures, but then again one never knew about the Slavic nations. Plus, he and Vera were already naked and in bed and, in a sense, feeling closer due to the bonding that shared tragedy engenders. Hoping that Vera had done a thorough cleaning job—fucking in the wet spot is one thing, but atop a puked-up Spaghetti-O would be quite another—Buck brushed his teeth and made his way back to bed.

"Feel better?" Vera asked, sitting up beneath the covers.

"Yeah, yeah, I think so," Buck muttered, climbing under the covers as if he'd just had a little gas. "I shouldn't drink sake with clams."

"You had sake with clams tonight?"

"Yeah," Buck lied. "I ate downtown just before I came to The Club."

"What kind of place serves sake with clams?"

"Well, you know, Chinatown is spreading over Little Italy now, so sometimes you get kind of a mix."

Vera didn't argue. It sounded worldly to her, and she didn't want to appear stupid, not that she could have appeared any stupider than a man claiming to have eaten sake with clams. She listened as Buck used the occasion of his tremendous vulnerability to show Vera a side of him he usually waited much longer with a woman to fake: humble, sheepish, apologetic, needy. It was as if Buck were saying, Hey, when a man ralphs at the altar, it's kind of pointless to keep up the bravado.

"Vera, I don't know what will happen to us," Buck began. "We may get married—and boy, won't we have a good story to tell on *The Newlywed Game* about our first time in bed together—or we may never see each other again, but whatever it is, I want you to know that for my whole life, I will always remember how kind you were to me tonight."

"Gee," Vera said. "I feel like I should say, 'Don't worry, it can happen to any man,' " which was so genuinely funny that Buck felt less guilty about passing her at The Club. Maybe she could be funny, if she threw away that copy of *Silas Marner* she called a notebook.

The lovers laughed and hugged, ending in a tender kiss, which led to a passionate kiss, which led to sex. Buck didn't have what he called his good fastball, but he had recently learned how to get batters out with finesse and location and off-speed stuff, as any cagey pitcher does. There would be no seconds this night, but when Vera fell asleep in his arms, he was satisfied that she was satisfied.

And she had gotten a bit out of it. Somewhere in the middle of fornication, a premise, not surprisingly, came into Vera's head, at which point she asked Buck if they could pause for a moment while she jotted it down on the notepad he kept on the nightstand. Buck objected not a bit, as there was something he also wanted to record, and did so on the back of a fortuitously nearby Con Ed bill. By stretching in opposite directions but never uncoupling their uglies, the two comedians recorded their ideas, ideas that would perhaps grow into whole routines that one day would delight or even enlighten audiences all over the country.

Then they returned to rutting like pigs.

Six days after their memorable first night together, Vera had still not left Buck's apartment. The falling in love that Buck had hoped would come with spring arrived late, but it finally had arrived. Like Dick and Jill, except without the horrifying turpitude, Buck and Vera parlayed their one-night stand into inseparability. They walked through the park a lot and ate in a lot of diners and did a lot of people watching—or, more accurately, people-making-fun-of: No one in New York was safe from their ridicule. They were in love and they were comedians and nothing makes comedians feel more in love than debasing everyone else on earth.

On their seventh day together, Buck asked if the cat at Vera's apartment might not now be dead. But he found out there was no cat. In fact, there was no apartment. Vera did not have one. She had been in an illegal sublet but got tossed out, her stuff was at a friend's . . .

Vera started to cry. She had avoided telling Buck about her situation, but a little thing like not having a home is bound to come up in conversation. She swore through tears that she really loved Buck, that it wasn't like that—not that if it was like that it would have made her unique in New York, where the housing crunch and romance were known to be a powerful interacting force: How much someone wanted to live with someone else in this city was often imbued with considerations about floor space and water pressure.

But in Vera's case, there was no need for tears. All Buck said was: "I don't care why you're here, I'm just glad you are."

It was not a lie. He meant it.

Buck was no sooner celebrating the glory of cohabitation, however, than Vera announced she had to leave New York for a while to make a long-delayed pilgrimage back home to Scranton, to visit her mother and retrieve the rest of her belongings. Buck was a little disappointed, but the timing was actually good, since it was now the week of the Big Joke-Off and he wanted space to concentrate—not as one of the entrants, because Buck was smart enough to know that his own act would not yet win any prizes, but as the MC. This was the role in which he felt most comfortable, and even though no official honors would accrue from it, MCing the shows would give him a stature above the rank-and-file saps pitted against each other. Buck couldn't admit it to Shit that day—because then what would there have been to argue about—but Shit did have a point about the contest: It *was* gauche to make comedians compete so nakedly. But MCing was a way to be a part of it without being a part of it—and wasn't that the best way to be part of anything?

By the sudden preponderance of sportscoated and necktied young comedians at The Club on the first Monday in July, it was obvious that something big was going on. The Big Joke-Off had been well publicized, and there was an excitement at The Club not seen in a long time. As promised, promoter Dave Schmukov had delivered a panel of celebrity judges, one of whom, Catskill and television veteran Marty Breen, opened the show with a number of his timeless routines—timeless in the sense that one felt certain while listening to them that they had indeed been recited over the entire span of time.

Then Marty got serious.

"I think it's great what's going on with the kids today," he said. "When I started, we never had a place like this where you could be bad," and then, perhaps to make up for lost time, Marty was very bad for another twenty minutes.

He did, however, absolutely kill.

Along with Marty at the judges' table was Sid Allen who, like Marty, Buck remembered well from his umpteen appearances on *The Ed Sullivan show*. Sid also hadn't been on television much in the last ten years, but he was still well remembered if the crowd's wild ovation for him was any indication.

How different was the response when the audience knew who it was they were cheering for, Buck thought. Not that this phenomenon hadn't been amply demonstrated before at The Club, on those nights when a name comedian stopped in and a dead crowd suddenly sprang to life. The instantaneous mood change at such a moment was almost frightening; it made Hitler's success with crowds easier to understand. Whereas only a second before they were sitting with a palpable show-me attitude, now it was the exact opposite: They were humble; they were honored to be in the presence of greatness; and they were suddenly eager to be the ones doing the showing. Among the show business laws Buck had often heard was that in comedy, no matter how famous you were, you still had to be funny to get laughs—but like so many hoary chestnuts of the profession, the reality told a different story. Not that a big name couldn't bomb: That chestnut, the one about anyone can always bomb—*was* true. But it was also true that people were starfuckers, and for a star they seemed a lot less picky about what deserved a laugh. And at The Club, which greatly publicized the fact that big names often dropped in to try out new material, the audience was always a little disappointed on any night when no luminaries appeared. They could laugh their heads off, but if they hadn't seen a star, they would leave saying, "We came on a bad night."

Well, tonight they came on a good night. There was Marty, there was Sid, and there was Reggie Drapper, a British comedian whose old sketch shows from England were now running on American, or at least local New York, TV every night at eleven. Reggie, too, was fawned over by the audience as he mugged shamelessly during his introduction.

Comedy: timing, material, recognition. That was also in the show business handbook, but recognition was so seldom encountered by the young comedians, it was easy for them to forget about it. But not on this night. This night made Buck think of antediluvian legends like Bob Hope and Danny Thomas, who hadn't said anything funny for twenty years and yet were still adored by the public. Or Buddy Hackett, who, the story went, told a sluggish crowd one night in Las Vegas: "I'm sold out. *You're* on trial." Yes, it seemed that if you were well known enough for something you used to do, you didn't have to actually do it anymore. There was a ritualistic aspect to show business, same as there was with any other time-tested institution, like Catholicism or married sex. Was Bob Hope still funny, or was he just remembered as funny, like that tomato at the Blue Spoon that only triggered the memory of a tomato?

Out in the bar, Buck got a drink and joined a coterie of his colleagues, many of whom were not in the contest but had come because this was an *event* in their little world and it had to be seen. Leland was among those who'd been shut out, but this, like everything he encountered, did not crimp his happy-go-lucky demeanor or deprive the world of his constant, blinding, thousand-tooth grin, which flashed across the bar, setting off small fires in places where its beam lingered. Leland was currently leading a discussion, or perhaps following a discussion—in any case, he was happy to be in a discussion—of the three judges, and the tone was somewhat less reverential than that of the audience. Big laughs from the group were forthcoming at the rapid-fire jibes aimed at the older comics' antiquated style, their Vegasy attire, and their failure to have reached the zenith of their profession.

Buck listened for a minute and then put a quick halt to the mockery. Leland immediately agreed with him, not even pausing, as the others did, to be shocked: Buck not joining in on some routine intercomic libel?

But here was Buck sticking up for the old farts. Maybe they hadn't been setting the comic world on fire lately, he said, but they deserved respect because they came from a generation that appreciated wit and intelligence and subtlety. And how did Buck know that? Because they were laughing at *his* material!

Do you know what the Guinness world record is for most children by a mother? Twenty-nine. A woman in Mexico had twenty-nine children. She said she would have had thirty, but she wanted a career, too.

Did you read where Alex Haley is being sued for plagiarism—this is the guy who wrote Roots—*it turns out he was adopted . . . he's not even black, he's Swedish—*

Swedish people have the most guttural sounding names, don't they? Sven! Gunter! I found out why: Swedish moth-

ers, Nordic, very hearty women, actually give the name
of the child AS they're giving birth: Olaf! Bjornborg! . . .
sometimes it's an easy birth—Ooskadoo!

People confuse the Swedes with the Swiss—the Swiss
are the ones who have never been in a war—people think
it's because they're so peaceful and evolved, but the reason they've never been in a war is because of Swiss
banks—even the vilest dictators in history all agreed,
there has to be one place where the money is safe—they'll
bomb orphanages, monasteries, refugee columns—savings and loans, no way! It was a stroke of genius . . .

Genius—you know I read Einstein's biography, and it
said that he was such a genius, that he used to leave the
house without his pants on—no, true story, because from
the moment he woke up, he was thinking all the time,
formulas, theories, and he would just walk out of the house
with no pants on, which . . . well, it must have been tough
dating . . . I can see him walking up to a girl's house,
and the father is looking out the window thinking, Boy,
this guy must be a genius!

Have you noticed that you never see an intellectual on
The Newlywed Game? It's never, like, Mrs. Sartre, where
is the last place your husband saw the howling nothingness
of human existence? She says, "Deep within his own
soul." He says, "Deep within his own soul"—you're our
grand-prize winners!!

The three judges, in fact, laughed at all the right things, from
Buck and from the other comics as well. And when they did,
it got the audience laughing too. This recognition factor was
strong stuff, Buck thought—so strong that it could even be
transferred from the celebrity, by his approving laughter, to
another comedian onstage. Buck had seen Johnny Carson do it
a thousand times, seen some comic on The Tonight Show do a
joke that was about to be pronounced dead on arrival, only to
be saved by Johnny's late-arriving "hack hack hack" from
over there at the desk. And when that happened—when Johnny
thought something was funny—his flock made a second effort
to appreciate the joke.

Flock indeed, Buck thought: God, what starfucking sheep people are—and how many times *I* could have used a legend hacking away at a desk behind *me*. Modern audiences were no better than medieval courtiers who laughed at the jester when the king laughed, and hailed a beheading when he didn't.

But then Buck remembered what he'd learned from Luther and Bo and Davey Jay: Don't hate people for being stupid, *use* their stupidity to achieve victory. Buck was pleased this rubric had returned to the fold, but as sometimes happened these days with rubrics, he couldn't help but hear stupid old Shit's voice in his head, arguing with him about it. This was a phenomenon Buck had noticed before—that if you spent a whole day with someone, the next day you'd hear his voice, even though the person wasn't actually there anymore. And since Buck and Shit had lately been having more marathon arguments than ever, Shit's voice was beginning to fill the nooks and crannies of Buck's skull.

And naturally, it was appalled. Shit did not want to use people's shortcomings, he wanted to eradicate them. But geez, was there really time for that? It was already after one; plus, as Buck had just argued with Shit—the real Shit, not just the voice—wasn't there something to be said for cynical manipulation in the cause of good? Wouldn't all those just crusades that he, Shit, so revered, have been doomed to failure if not prosecuted by hard-bitten, bare-knuckled ballbusters, like Lyndon Johnson with civil rights to give just one example? In a world that was nothing if not fraught with paradox and contradiction, wasn't the use of evil in the cause of good a fitting, if not inevitable, approach?

Sure, why not. Especially since on this night, in the situation in which Buck now found himself, all the elements were in place to give this theory a whirl: There was the starfucker audience; there were the stars, Marty, Sid, and Reggie, spewing forth their loud, attention-demanding, I-know-funny-and-if-I-say-this-is-funny-it's-funny guffaws; and there was the good cause.

The good cause, as always, was Chink.

"You're next," Buck told Chink in the bar, as routinely as he did at the same hour on nights that were actually routine.

"Is the contest over?" Chink asked.

"Well, sort of," Buck said. "I'll introduce you as the last contestant."

"But I'm not in the contest."

"You are if the judges see you and vote on you."

"But—"

"Just do what you usually do when I say your name," Buck commanded as he headed for the stage, and soon after, said Chink's name.

The audience was tired by this time, but they applauded, as did Sid, Marty, and Reggie, who were not tired at all, and Bo, who seemed a little confused but was used to that.

Chink was also confused, but in his case that was a good thing. The performance he now began was so unexpected that he had not had time to get nervous or worry or picture the failure that picturing failure usually engenders. He barreled, to the extent Chink could barrel, right into his act, and in no time at all had the judges howling. Yes, Sid and Marty and Reggie were doing their part, all right, just as Buck had predicted. The audience was sure to follow.

People say great things about Jesus, but is He really the best one for the job?

Why not give the devil a shot at running the universe— how much more screwed up could it be?

But God doesn't even run the whole universe—He's some sort of middleman, I think—even in the Bible, it says God created heaven and earth . . . Heaven and earth? In the whole universe, that's like Baltic and Mediterranean in Monopoly.

And Jesus, you forget how He got his job—nepotism. Of course, God kind of set the kid up . . . but Jesus had to die. Where would the world be today if Jesus had gotten off with two to ten? . . . then he'd get old like the rest of us, so Jesus would be seventy and kind of crotchety: "Yeah, turn the other cheek—but don't let them walk all over you, either!"

Did you know that Judas was the first person in history

to use the phrase, cash or no deal*? They tried to give him a check—thirty pieces of silver, and <u>NO</u> CENTS—but he said forget it.*

But you can tell Jesus had a lot of charisma, because when they crucified Him, there were two other guys who got crucified right next to Him at the same time—but who gets all the ink?

And Mary, they make out to be such a saint—a virgin when she gave birth—okay, maybe, but they don't tell you what she did after *He was born—she'd fuck anything!*

They always say Jesus will return to earth to "redeem us." Redeem us? What are we, a pawn shop? Thanks a lot, Jesus, maybe you can pick up a transistor radio for two bucks while you're here!

Surely, the audience would follow. That the audience would follow was sure. What could be more sure than that they, the audience, would follow.

Come on, you bastards, follow! Buck screamed in his head. Come on, laugh! Laugh! Laugh! You've been doing it all night—they laugh and then you laugh! Don't stop now!

But they did stop. The audience did not laugh at Chink, no matter how much he convulsed the judges, and he convulsed them a lot. For the first few minutes, the crowd chuckled over the sight of the three celebrities cracking up, Sammy Davis–style, even though it seemed to be for absolutely no reason. But after a couple of minutes even the laughter at the laughter subsided, and then it was just three comics laughing at Chink bombing, same as any other night at The Club.

Buck was ashen. He was blood-drained. He was pants-shitted. He'd really done it this time—believed his own publicity about making his own rules and getting away with it. Except this time he hadn't gotten away with it. He'd spoiled a perfect evening for everybody by making it end with a bomb, a big, ugly, unscheduled, crowd-chilling, all-his-fault bomb. He'd tried to handicap the audience but got trumped by a more powerful principle: In show business, especially as regards the audience, nothing is ever completely predictable. It was almost as if the audience had heard Buck plotting about them and decided to teach him a lesson. And the lesson was: We're the boss.

A lot of ex-heads of TV networks and movie studios could testify to that.

When Buck went onstage to cadge a pity applause for Chink and close the show, he was so distraught that he forgot the reason for the whole evening. But Marty reminded him, and passed up to the stage a piece of paper with the names of the night's three finalists. The first name was Chink's.

At that moment Buck really should have felt gladness for Chink, but he was too consumed with relief from his own plight. Relief, and actual humility, for he had been saved by the guts of three old hacks who chose to watch the comedian and not the audience.

"Thank you, thank you," a humbled Buck gushed at the magi as they tarried to sign autographs for a throng of well-wishers.

"You're funny, kid," Marty told Buck. "We kept saying we wished we could vote for you."

Buck hung his head for one more moment of genuine humility. Then he picked his head up.

"Finish your thought, Marty," he rejoined, relieved that his true personality had returned.

15

I Dreamed I Went to See Mort Sahl, and He Was Doing Dog-and-Cat Material

As a result of Chink's placing in the finals of the Big Joke-Off, he and Norma were struggling through a certain species of domestic problem that had plagued many a show business couple before them. Celebrity spouses from Ethel Merman and Ernest Borgnine on down—not that there's much below that example—had seen their relationships destroyed by the entertainment industry's peculiar version of professional rivalry—and now it had even reached that garden of love on the Upper West Side. In fact, if *A Star Is Born* hadn't been remade for the third time just a few years earlier, Chink and Norma would have been the perfect choice to star in a new version, except for the fact that they were not stars or actors or people who had ever been remotely considered for film work.

Nevertheless, the plot was the same: Chink's triumph in Washington, coupled with his sudden ascendancy in the contest, had the effect of turning his relationship with Norma upside down. Suddenly, he was the comedy star in the family, and she was furious—not, she claimed, at Chink, but at Buck: Why, she wanted to know, if he was going to take the law into his own hands, hadn't he put *her* on for the judges?

Chink did not have an answer for that. He thought he had an answer—"Because you weren't there?"—but it apparently was not a good answer.

"I don't want our careers to get in the way of our relationship,'' Chink told Norma after finally catching on to what the real problem was. "You're more important to me than anything.''

Norma agreed. She agreed so much, in fact, that it was soon decided there was room enough for only one comedian in the family, and that's when Chink's brief career in comedy came to a close.

"Quit? You can't quit!'' Buck hollered at Chink that night.

But Chink could quit, and he did, without any regrets. He had never possessed a fire in his belly for the profession, and he was actually pleased that in the last few months he'd reached a level he never thought attainable, as lowly as that level still was. And now, he would use whatever he had learned in his time as a stand-up comedian in a new capacity.

Chink was going to be Norma's manager.

At the same time that Chink was quitting comedy for a woman, a woman was quitting Dick for comedy—or, rather, because she'd apparently had enough of comedy. Jill's timing was unfortunate, because Dick was also one of the finalists in the Big Joke-Off, and here it was the night before the finals and Dick's mind was not on comedy. He hadn't seen Jill in two days, and even though that had happened before, a sixth sense told Dick to worry even more than the normal allotment of worry he allowed himself in this situation.

Buck, on the other hand, was getting pretty sick of Dick's worrying. Especially on weekends, when, after a long night of MCing, he was the only one still around when Dick was looking for comfort at the end of the bar. Some nights Buck could listen to Dick for a while, and some nights he just had to blow him off and go home, and feel like the callous prick everybody thought he was anyway.

On this Friday night, however, Buck was actually happy to listen to Dick, because hearing about a romantic problem worse than his own was just the pick-me-up he needed.

Not that what I have is really a problem, Buck kept telling himself: Vera's just staying on in Pennsylvania a little longer

than she said, and she's too busy with family stuff to talk about
it. But she'll be back.

Won't she?

Poor Buck. No wonder he never wanted to let a girl out of
his apartment.

But whatever the story was with Vera, it still couldn't be
worse than Dick's story with Jill and that was good enough for
Buck, who was not so much a proponent of misery loves company as he was a proponent of misery loves the company of
even *worse* misery. And when it came to Dick's case of worse
misery, a guy could skip right past the Hey-what's-the-matter?
preliminaries:

"What'd she do now?" Buck asked the dejected cuckold as
he settled onto a barstool.

Dick's look told Buck that Jill simply hadn't shown up again
and still was not in the one place that made him feel secure:
within eyesight.

"You wanna get some food?" Buck asked.

"No, I'm gonna go home," Dick said. "A lot of times she
just falls asleep there and doesn't hear the phone. She doesn't
sleep for days, and then she passes out so hard it's scary. You
wanna come with me?"

The two comedians walked the few blocks to Dick's building
and then the Empire State Building stairs up to his apartment.
Jill was not there, but in her place on the bed where she could
normally be found sleeping off God knows what was a letter.
Scrawled on one of the attractively embossed Club stationery
pads that found their way into the home of every comedian, it
read:

WHILE YOU WERE OUT

I decided I must leave you forever. By the time you
read this, I will already be married, so please do
not try to contact me, as my husband will not
tolerate it. I guess you know by now, although
we never discussed it, that I am pregnant. I feel a
responsibility to provide my child with the very

best care, and father, available. I enjoyed our
time together, and good luck in your career.

Gotta run—Love, Jill

Dick picked up the note and read it. Then, without comment
or expression, he passed it to Buck. Buck, having never lived
with Jill, was a good deal more stunned than Dick, who went
about examining the rest of his mail, as if the note were just
one part of that pesky stack of bad-news bills and notices that
always piled up at month's end.

"I don't know what to say," Buck stammered. "This chick
really takes the cake."

"Did she take that, too?" Dick asked, opening the refrigerator. "Don't say anything, okay? I mean to the other—"

"Oh God, of course not," Buck assured him. "Are you
okay? Do you want me to stay with you?"

"Why, so you can dump me too?"

Buck was still too dismayed to laugh. "Are you going to be
okay for tomorrow?" he asked.

"I don't know. I guess we'll find out tomorrow. That bitch
really has timing, doesn't she?"

"Well, if you need anything . . ."

"Thanks. I'll be okay. Hey, I'll get a bit out of it anyway."

Buck thought about that on his way down the interminable
staircase. It was preposterous, but it wasn't any different from
what he or any comic in any tragic situation would think: I'll
get a bit out it. It sounded cruel, but maybe artists were just
those people smart enough to always get a receipt for their pain.

The big finale was held at the Bottom Line in Greenwich
Village, a bigger room than any of the contestants had ever
played to, with press and security people and TV cameras and,
most impressive of all, free food backstage. Buck was sure
Dick wasn't going to show up when he hadn't arrived by show
time, but then he did, just in time for his set. He didn't exactly
have a bit about his recent romantic debacle, but throughout
the show he referred to it occasionally in an offhand way, like
"That's okay, my girl dumped me last night and I was in love
with her, and I don't even know you people," after a joke had
died.

Uncharacteristically, Dick vented some real pain on this night; characteristically, he did so with a smile, and the audience loved him all the more for it. They undoubtedly thought it was just part of the routine.

The fact that it wasn't may have been what won the contest for Dick. Not that those half dozen ad-libs about Jill dominated his show or were even among the biggest laughs he got—but when there is something in a comedian's act outside his normal script and it tumbles forth as a surprise to both himself and the audience, it raises his show to a higher dimension. Maybe Dick would have won the contest anyway, but in a business where so much of what contributes to the highest level of success is beyond analysis, it didn't hurt that Dick was hurting.

Dick thought about that later, and he could just imagine what Jill would have said: "I knew if I left you you'd win, darling—that's why I did it."

He was glad he no longer had to argue with her.

Winning the big contest did not, in the end, change Dick's life much, except for hipping him sooner than most of his colleagues to the fact that in his profession, it took a lot of events that seemed sure to change your life before one actually did.

For the people who made the real money from comedy, however, the contest turned out to be a bonanza. The publicity from it put The Club in the enviable position of turning away business almost every night for the next month, and on weekends anyone traveling down Second Avenue could not help but notice long lines of people around the block. This phenomenon did not escape the attention of a few entrepreneurs in New York who reasoned that a city that once supported three baseball teams could certainly support another comedy club.

The first of these comedy carpetbaggers to open shop was an insane businesswoman named Calvina Fryberg. Calvina was the bitter ex-wife of a William Morris agent, and her goal in life was to drive her former husband to suicide by achieving some show business–related success so enormous that the man would be literally unable to live with the thought of it. For a decade, Calvina had tried to make her dream come true by staging Off Broadway, Off-Off Broadway, and Way-Off Broadway (*Oh, Mitosis!* opened in Finland) productions, but they had all been such failures that she was almost ready to give up on the suicide plan and just go over there and shoot the guy, à la her hero, Jean Harris. But then Calvina heard about the Big Joke-Off, and she saw the long lines. She knew nothing about stand-up comedy, but she did know a bandwagon when it rolled over her foot.

And so Apple of My Eye opened in the shell of a former jazz club on Bleecker Street, in Greenwich Village, in the late summer of 1980. It remained a sawdust-on-the-floor dive with all the charm of a Mexican railroad station, but when you got below 8th Street, that was a selling point; certainly, the comedians didn't mind. The young comedians of the early eighties knew well their comic history, and so they knew that Greenwich Village was where titan predecessors like Pryor and Carlin and Woody had reinvented stand-up in the early sixties— and now they imagined a second renaissance of their own making.

But no, it was still the middle ages when the Apple opened on a humid Saturday night in August. The comics expected intellectuals, but they got tourists—and not tourists from any place real far away like Paris or London or even Ohio, but mostly from New Jersey. Greenwich Village, you see, was just too easy to get to from New Jersey, what with the tube right there funneling into lower Manhattan. By 1980, the Village on Saturday night had become a kind of Six Flags over Bohemia, an open-air amusement park where suburbanites could go see all the crazy people, the artists, the homosexuals, and the weirdos of every stripe, not to mention the shops and restaurants, which stayed open well past the hour when the malls of New Jersey had closed their doors.

Nevertheless, the appearance of another comedy club in New York was propitious for one comedian in particular: Shit. This was because Shit, right after getting his foot in the MC door at The Club, earned himself a lifetime ban from that same establishment for distributing leaflets to all the comedians urging them to boycott the Big Joke-Off and join a union. Luther had gotten hold of one of the leaflets—it wasn't hard, Shit handed them out right there in the bar—and, spoiling for a way to get back at Shit and Buck for what he deemed their earlier machinations against his authority, brought it to Bo. Since The Club had a big stake in the contest, staging the semifinals and profiting from the publicity, Bo was incensed at Shit's treachery and ingratitude—or at least, Luther said Bo was incensed at Shit's treachery and ingratitude: Buck could not be sure which it was. But since Bo had every right to be so incensed at Shit's treachery and ingratitude and since Luther had thrown the issue in Buck's face with such confidence and relish, Buck decided to let the whole thing cool down for a while and recede into the very short memories of his adversaries.

This, of course, made Shit incensed at Buck's treachery and ingratitude.

Buck didn't see it as treachery. He saw it as smart to wait for an auspicious moment to plead Shit's cause to Bo, but apparently he didn't wait long enough. Bo didn't raise his voice, but maybe that was just because he didn't want to risk passing out. But he was firm, which in itself was a side of Bo that Buck had never seen. Bo formed no complete sentence in his reaction to the issue and he articulated no string of words that could be reasonably called a phrase. But even dogs can make clear what they're feeling, and it was clear to Buck that Bo was indeed aware of what Shit had done and was indeed pissed about it.

"Yeah, I hear you," Buck said, despite the fact that he had not actually heard anything.

"It's just . . ."

"Right, right," Buck sympathized.

"The whole thing is . . ."

"Absolutely," Buck agreed.

Truer words were never unspoken.

"Look, it was a stupid thing to do, I know," Buck assured his boss. "Believe me, I know. I'm just telling you, he's sorry and he feels awful about it, and he loves you and he loves this place."

"Yeah, yeah," Bo answered, "but . . ."

Buck waited for Bo to finish his "but," but Bo was a man of few words, none of them coherent.

"You don't have to say any more," Buck assured him, staunching what surely would have been a torrent of marble prose. "The guy made his bed, and now he's got to lie in it."

Bo hugged him, a hug that said, I wish you were always around to say what I would say, if saying was a thing I could do after eleven o'clock.

The next words Buck heard, outside of a cabbie ten minutes later grumbling over a bad tip, were Shit's. He woke Buck up the next day to say thanks for selling him down the river.

Buck quickly got dressed and met Shit at an outdoor table at an upscale beanery on the West Side. Apparently, someone had overheard Buck's conversation with Bo the previous night and relayed it to Shit, who was not in a giving-the-benefit-of-the-doubt mood.

"Look, the man was not of a mind to change his mind," Buck pleaded. "The best thing to do was to stay on his good side and wait till he gets over it."

"Look, I don't care if you don't want to stick your neck out for me, but don't go around telling anyone I'm sorry when you know I'm not."

"Don't want to stick my neck out?" Buck exploded, not realizing that quite a few places on his neck *were* sticking out. "I've stuck my neck out for you plenty!"

"That's different. That was out of friendship. I appreciate that, but this is not about friendship, it's a larger issue."

"Well, I don't think there is a larger issue, or I wouldn't have done it for you, because it may have been for friendship, my friend, but it certainly could have had consequences for my career, very dire consequences indeed."

Shit gave him a look and buried his head in his soup, which Buck interpreted as skepticism.

"What, you don't think that's true?" Buck asked, his ire rising with Shit's continued silence. It rose until he could hold it no more, at which point Buck launched into a tirade that lasted almost one full page.

"Let me tell you something about my neck, my friend, and where it's been on this long road with you. My neck has been stuck out until it was about to be chopped off, and I'm sorry if you're disappointed that I won't stick it out any farther, but

that's where I stop, because it would do no good for both of us
to be out. Maybe you think that would have been noble, but I
call it stupid. You'd love to have us go down together, wouldn't
you? We could be the Loser Brothers, going nowhere, but, oh,
we could tell each other, instead of you just telling yourself,
that what we have is better, that we're on the moral high ground,
but you're not saving the Church of England by boycotting a
stupid contest or refusing to work Washington because the pay
is so exploitative. You hate me because I know how to eat as
little shit as possible while I'm on the bottom, but some shit I
will eat, because that's what being on the bottom is all about,
and you're not going to change that by not working on their
terms. What is it you want, to leave a perfect system for future
comics? Let them get through it like we did—do you miss the
sixties that much, the protest, the evil establishment? It's not
like that anymore—the protesters *are* the establishment now!
Why do you think comedy sucks, why do you think Ronald
Reagan is running for president? Honestly, man, I would stand
with you if I thought there was something to stand for, but there
isn't.''

"There's always something to stand for. And there *is* going
to be a union."

"Oh Jesus, why?"

"Because we can win now. Isn't that your big thing—life
is unfair, so win? There's two clubs now. There's some competition. We have some leverage, it's not a monopoly anymore.
We don't have to keep being exploited."

"*Who* is being exploited?" Buck screamed in such a tone
that even the diners who looked up knew it was something he'd
said a thousand times before.

"*Three* dollars," Shit yelled back. "That's what we get to
perform on a weeknight—three dollars. That's not even cab
fare. You don't call that exploitation?"

"No, I call it mutual using. They're using me to make money
and I'm using them to learn my craft."

"But what you're doing is irrelevant if people are still paying
money to see it and someone else is getting the money. They
could be paying to see you jerk off, and if they are, you should
get the money."

Buck sat there and stewed, then stopped eating his stew.

"You're just like them," he finally said. "You're just like the Hoffas and the Meanys, who scream for shorter hours and higher pay while the Japs laugh at us and keep beating our brains out, until the whole plant closes down and then nobody has a fucking job. Yeah, you're the friend of the working man, all right—you'll close the clubs and then no comics will work. People will get hurt, and for what? I'm telling you it's a waste and that nothing is going to change. Nothing. And after five or six years of bad blood, when it's practical for some fascist producer to hire some communist writer to save his ass because his movie's in trouble, he'll do it. They'll both do it. They'll make movies, they'll have dinner, they'll play tennis, they'll make passes at each other's wives, and what in the hell did anybody ever go to jail for? People are what's important. You and me. Not causes. Not principles."

"Huh?" Shit asked.

"It's from *The Way We Were*," Buck said. "I thought it fit."

"Oh."

"Your line, by the way is: 'Hubbell, people *are* their principles.' "

"Exactly. The difference between you and me is—"

"The difference between you and me is, I know when I'm lying and you don't."

Buck looked down at his stew, pleased with the ring of his last riposte.

But where was the rebuttal? The battle over there on Shit's front seemed awfully quiet. Too quiet, perhaps. Was Shit really mad this time?

It seemed that he was, judging by the color he was turning, a red to which even beets might fear comparison.

Shit rose from the table and told Buck after an excruciating pause: "Never talk to me again. Don't get in my way. You think you know it all, but you're about to get caught in your own web."

"Hey, I'm sorry. Sit down, will ya?" Buck said as Shit gathered his belongings. "Come on . . ."

But Shit was already on his way.

"No, no, I'll get this," Buck shouted after him, the unpaid check in his hand as Shit stormed away, annoyed that he was already on the sidewalk and denied the pleasure of slamming a door.

If Buck had made Shit feel like shit that day, Shit knew where to go to feel like he was not shit, or rather, to feel like he was very hot shit: the Apple. Shit may have been exiled from The Club, but from the day the Apple opened, he had been an exile in a new land, and in the new land he was king. Calvina had fallen completely and immediately in love with Shit and his old world, old New York charm, which was exactly what she, with her lifelong life in the theater, thought a comedian should personify. It didn't matter a whit to her that old-world charm was not exactly what the Fort Lee crowd responded to; Shit was more the undisputed star at the Apple than any comic had ever been at The Club, and not only onstage. He advised Calvina on every aspect of running a comedy club, from finance to publicity to suggesting which performers she should favor, and then, when he had a minute, did a bang-up job revising the menu, spearheading the movement toward the lighter fare that would sweep the nation in the coming decade.

Then he formed his union and called a strike and drove the place out of business.

The union meeting that Shit finally got the comics to attend took place in Central Park on a Saturday afternoon, where The Club softball team was playing in the Broadway show league. The turnout was impressive. In addition to the twelve members of the team, two dozen other comedians showed up, which, compared to previous attempts to organize comedians for anything, was phenomenal. It wasn't that the comics had previously been hostile to the idea of a union, it was just that, well . . . they were comics. And comics aren't very political, especially during the day. They would agree to show up but then call and say they forgot they had to do something or were out of town or just got sick or were about to get sick or knew someone who was sick. Most of them agreed to go along with whatever the majority did, which turned out to be not show up or be out of town or get sick.

But Shit impressed them this time with the fact that he was willing to sacrifice his mondo-enviable deal down at the Apple. If he was willing to jeopardize that, they figured, okay, he's a moron, but at least he deserves a listen. So out there in Central Park, sitting on the rotted wood of the stands by the ball field after the game was over, the comedians listened. Shit did not waste the opportunity.

He gave his "I have a dream today" speech, and his dream was lofty: that one day all comics, black comics and white comics, prop comics and monologuists, comedy teams and improv groups—even magicians, the kind that make jokes during their tricks, tricks that they bought in a little shop on Broadway, and who got people up onstage to help out, usually a good-looking girl, and then asked that the audience give them a hand for being good sports—someday all of them, even the magicians, would get a piece of the door, he had a dream today. Shit had a dream that one day all comics would be judged not by the quality of their act but because they showed up every night and wanted to make it just as bad as the next guy and even endured pissing off their parents, who wished they'd get a job and thought thirty-two was too old to still be living at home, except the Jewish mothers, who were glad about it because this way at least they knew their sons were eating right, he had a dream today. Shit had a dream.

And apparently, Fat had a dream as well, because halfway through Shit's speech, he was moved to pipe up with his own oration. He seemed impassioned about the main issue before the group, although no one in the group could tell to which side he was throwing his considerable weight. Fat spoke of the value of working on the road and how well he was doing at that and—well, mostly he just spoke about how well he was doing. He told his colleagues how good a living he was making on the road, quoting his salary in a number of different cities, and how the road had polished his act and how the road is where a comic really gets his chance to stretch out and develop a style and new material and even how single women were more friendly in that environment.

Then he sat down. No one challenged or corroborated his points. All accepted that, like many passages in the Bible, his words could be used to support either side of the argument at hand.

As puzzled looks dissolved into who-knows? shakes of the head, Shit resumed his sermon in the stands. As a comedian, Shit had always been a little too speechy, but that trait served him well in the role of polemicist/rabble-rouser. He painted a picture of two comedy worlds—the one his listeners now endured, and the one they could be enjoying. The latter, it seemed, could never be born within the current system—"it's the system, I tell ya"—the club system, and the establishment villains who ran it, the fat cats who exploited the comedians and lived high on the hog off their toil, all twenty minutes a night of it. The fault, dear comics, lies not within the stars but within those who refuse to treat us like stars, Shit seemed to say.

When Shit finished speaking, everyone was impressed, including Buck. Buck was not speaking to Shit these days, and he had no intention of joining the union, but he was still playing third base, so he was in the park that day anyway. Which was a good thing, because he would have looked stupid pretending that he'd just happened by a meeting that he had every intention of invalidating.

From the bench, Buck asked the chair for the floor, but the chair asked him to table it. Buck, however, was not about to be treated like a piece of furniture. He persisted, and the chair folded.

Buck sought to couch his arguments in the language of reality, however, and for that, as any politician would know, he paid a dear price. Buck, in fact, turned out to be the best weapon Shit had, and gave Shit his best day since the surprise birthday party on acid.

The reason was this: At this stage of his life, Buck was much better at maneuvering the people above him than below him. With the Bos and the Davey Jays, Buck's guiding virtue was tact; with his peers, however, it seemed to be honesty. On a day that called for him to speak to a lot of people who were doing less well than he, comics who were already jealous of him for getting to be the MC or hated him for not putting them on enough, he did nothing to increase his popularity, what there was of it, and everything to seal his reputation as an arrogant prick. It was ironic that Shit, who played the room like the slickest of old pols, stood now as the Mr. Smith of the comedy world, and Buck, oily old Buck, got hung out to dry for telling everybody exactly what he really thought, just as he had rehearsed so many times in those discussions with Shit: that getting paid in showcase clubs would stifle experimentation and the motivation to graduate, that show business was a meritocracy and rightly so, and that even if a strike were called, it wouldn't work because comics were selfish bastards who could never stick together.

On the last point especially, he was, of course, right. But so are politicians who tell the voters taxes have to be raised, and those are the politicians who don't get reelected. Buck was twisting in the wind when Shit moved in to finish him off:

"He wants to stop us so he can go back to Bo Reynolds and tell him he saved his club from a strike and be a hero to management."

"That is not true!" Buck shouted.

"I'm not finished," Shit cut him off, and then continued nailing him to the cross.

"It's not. It's not true," Buck said more quietly, but by then nobody was listening, including Buck, who was thinking:

Wait—it is true. I *would* be a hero to management. But by God, that's not why I said what I said. I said what I said because I believe what I said. Still, it would be a good thing to be a hero. But that part of it never entered my mind until right now. How did I miss it? Because I never thought it would actually come to this. Well, it has come to this, and good, I can be a hero with complete integrity, because I believe what I believed all along, so I guess I get to have my cake and eat it too on this one.

Except for one thing: He hadn't stopped the strike. He probably started it by sealing Shit's case for him, and he'd made everyone hate him even more, and he'd probably lost his best friend forever.

Okay, three things.

MCing at The Club that Saturday night, Buck expected a chilly reception from the other comedians on the show, but he was pleasantly appalled at their total lack of consistency. In the park just hours before, he had felt like the devil himself, but now, back in the routine of putting on a weekend show, his colleagues made him feel like Barry Goldwater: "In your heart, you know he's right." It was as if the strike had already happened and finally everybody was back to work and anxious to forget their differences and resume life as they'd once known it.

But around midnight word spread fast that a meeting with management—Bo and Calvina—was scheduled for the next day at noon, when the comedians' demands would be presented and, if not accepted, the strike would be on. The mood thereafter was rather dour, as the stand-ups realized that the good feeling they had in the day for voting to stand up would now have to be followed by actually standing up.

Soon after, someone who no longer needed to give a fuck about all this walked in.

"Hey, pal, great to see you!" Buck shouted at Chink, and then embraced him. "Wanna put the old spikes back on?"

But no, Chink was not having any second thoughts about retiring.

"Where's Norma working tonight?" Buck asked, knowing that she must be out of town for Chink to be out *in* town.

"Columbus, Ohio," Chink said, inviting himself to explain to comics who had overheard from as far away as the Bronx that Columbus, Ohio, now had a club, and would he find out who they should call, etc.

When the business of the night was over, Buck and Chink were ready to go home and Dick was ready to talk them out of it. Nursing the double disappointments of losing Jill and not skyrocketing to stardom from the Big Joke-Off contest, Dick had been drinking steadily since nine o'clock—nine o'clock

Tuesday of the previous week, that is. Concerned friends had tried to warn him of the dangers of this form of absorption, but Dick maintained that since he drank free at The Club, "at these prices, I can't afford *not* to be an alcoholic."

As persuasive at 3 A.M. in the bar as Shit had been at 3 P.M. in the park, Dick managed to corral Buck and Chink into one— just one, he promised—nightcap over at the Tiny Bar, the after-hours place where he had met Jill. Once there, Dick bought a round for his pals, and then for a few people he ran into that he'd known for minutes.

"There's nothing that feels as good as buying the affection of drunk strangers," he remarked.

"Who you calling strangers?" Buck teased

"Who you calling drunk?" added Chink as the second round came without anyone admitting he'd noticed.

"I wonder if there's anyone in this bar drunk enough to fuck me," Dick mused.

"I doubt it," counseled Buck.

"Good, then let's get a whore."

"Oh Jesus, are you serious?"

"Yeah. We'll get a whore and we'll all fuck her. My treat."

"Is this what you're doing with the contest money? Liquor and whores?"

"Partly," Dick admitted. "Some of it I'm just pissing away."

Buck pondered Dick's proposition for a while. Buck had never had a whore, and it crossed his mind that twenty-four was getting to be a little old for never having had a whore. It wasn't exactly like still being a virgin, but as excuses go for doing stupid things, it would do.

"And where are we going to get this whore?" Buck asked, his speech starting to slur.

"Call girls. You call up, they deliver," Dick answered.

"What if she's ugly?"

"Then you can go first."

"No, really, she could be ugly. And it's gonna be light soon. This whore thing, it's twenty-four hours?"

"Seven days a week."

"Christmas?"

"Especially Christmas."

"You're a sick fuck."

"Well, that's what a whore is—a sick fuck."

"They must have diseases that Columbus brought over."

"Rubbers."

"You've got an answer for everything," Buck said, and looked to Chink.

"Don't look at me," Chink said. "I'm not doing it."

"Why?" Buck asked.

"I went out with a whore once. Then I found out—she was fucking, like, twenty other guys!"

Dick and Buck laughed, and then Buck said: "I can't believe you're quitting comedy."

But he knew why Chink was quitting, and he knew it was the same reason why Chink wouldn't fuck a whore.

It made Buck a little jealous. It made him think of Vera and wish that he could say there was someone in his life, too, someone important enough to make whoring unthinkable. But Vera wasn't in his life, he remembered; she had given him a week of pure bliss and then disappeared. It was enough to make a man throw down another drink and be persuaded by another man who was throwing down another drink.

Back at Dick's apartment, Buck and Chink watched in amazement as Dick actually ordered pussy over the phone, as casually as if it were a pizza and with considerably less respect.

"Original Cunts?" Dick said into the phone. "We'd like a medium whore, half plain, half pepperoni."

Was there really someone on the other end of the line?

Apparently there was, because a half hour later, Buck and Chink were sitting outside on the steps of Dick's brownstone, waiting for Dick to complete his turn. Even though Chink was not participating, Buck had pleaded with him to stay around and offer immoral support. Out on the steps, Chink was making Buck nervous just the way Buck had made him nervous on that train ride to Baltimore.

"Make sure you put your fingers in first, make sure it's clean," he told Buck. "You don't know what might be up there—razor blades, a blender, a garbage disposal."

"Maybe I should just lob in a grenade." Buck gulped.

"No, too much noise. At least she's good-looking."

"Really? We're pretty drunk."

"No, she was nice. Big tits."

"Yeah, they probably hit the floor when she takes her bra off, from ten million guys sucking on them," Buck whimpered. "Jesus, what am I doing? Can you imagine what this chick has had lying on top of her before this? What breed of desperate, slobbering losers sank low enough to give her a call?"

"Like you?"

"Don't be funny."

"She didn't look all that shopworn to me. She's very young."

"Yeah, but she probably started when she was twelve. Her father screwed her or something, so she ran away and became a whore."

"Maybe not."

"No, she went to Smith and next year she's going to graduate school, but she wanted to take a year off first and suck every guy's dick in New York. Jesus, the rubber's gonna break and in five years I'll be stark staring mad, like Al Capone or Hitler."

"Hitler had V.D.?"

"Every fucking evil guy gets V.D. How should I know? But yeah, I think I read that somewhere."

"Where?"

"Probably in *The New York Times Book Review*, since every book in there is either about Jews or Hitler."

The chums' banter was interrupted by Dick's devilish laughter from the window above: "Who's got number ninety-one? Number ninety-one, please step to the counter."

"Good luck," Chink said to Buck.

Once alone with the whore, Buck immediately excused himself to use the bathroom. He urinated, then sat and worried that his drunken dick would never get off the ground. But the whore, of course, was trained in the very art of making nervous, drunk guys come and had no trouble imposing her will on Buck. She touched him in a place that, Buck was certain, only whores knew about, like that seemingly simple hold that only wrestlers know that could paralyze an opponent in seconds. In the same way, whores—and only whores, never your girlfriend or your wife—knew of a certain spot on a man's body. It wasn't really your asshole and it wasn't really your balls, it was the secret spot that God created just for whores so they could make a living. And also as a test: If you were a woman and you found that spot, then your destiny was to become a whore—which, of course, you'd want to do anyway, because you knew the spot.

The grievance meeting, as Shit called it, took place as scheduled, the next day at noon, in the showroom of The Club. It gave everyone an odd feeling to be meeting on the very spot where the audience's laughter, and the comedians' hopes and dreams, played out nightly, and maybe that's just what Bo had in mind. Maybe, but not probably, since Bo was not that crafty. In fact, if Shit was playing Huey "Every comic a king" Long in this drama, then Bo was more in step with the times, because Bo was nothing if not a doppelgänger for the man who soon would be elected president and put his unmistakable stamp on an entire decade of American history. Like Ronald Reagan, Bo was dim, and like Reagan, he made it work for him. Both men were lazy, charismatic figures who were constantly being underestimated. Both disliked confrontation, and so delegated that chore to others. The standoff at hand would be no exception.

Bo opened the meeting by jumping onto the stage and sitting on the tall stool that was always up there, which put everyone at ease: There's just something about sitting on a tall stool that projects relaxation and intimacy. It was the kind of winning gesture Bo did without thinking, and he was lucky indeed that not thinking usually served his needs so well. Waiting for the noisy room to come to order, he smiled and small-talked with some of the comics who were sitting below him in the audience. Ever the gentleman, he asked Calvina if she wanted to speak first, but Calvina was frightened of public speaking and intimidated by her surroundings. So Bo said a few words.

Now, unlike Reagan, no one would ever accuse Bo of being a great communicator. But he was every bit that rare human being you just couldn't hate, a trait that went a long way toward lulling adversaries into a specious comity. He thanked all the comics for coming and said he was willing to listen to anything they had to say and knew an accord could be reached, and maybe they should have this kind of rap session on a regular basis because communication was so important, and boy, who could argue with that? Then Bo waxed ineloquent during a rambling, personal paean to The Club, the joy it had given him and so many others, the good times, the saintliness of giving laughter to the world, yadayadablahblah.

When the comedians woke up, they discovered that cars could fly now, and also that Shit had finally been invited to make his case.

Standing in the back of the room, Shit forthrightly and impressively cited calculations about the kind of money management was raking in and, more important, not sharing with labor. In response, Bo mumbled something about how no one who never ran a bar or restaurant could imagine all the costs involved, then invited Calvina to agree with him. She did, enthusiastically.

But if Bo was hoping that Calvina would jump into the void left by his own Reaganesque anti-grasp of specifics, he was disappointed. Or maybe not, because now that the real confrontational part of the festivities had begun, he didn't want either himself or Calvina to do the talking, and in lieu of their further participation, he brought up a guy named Lou.

Lou knew the specifics.

Lou also looked like he knew how to break a guy's legs at the kneecap so that the guy might never walk again. Bo claimed Lou was The Club's accountant, but, gee, everybody thought, even in New York, accountants don't *pack*, do they? Given the rumors about gangsters really owning The Club, the comics didn't know which was the more frightening thought: that Lou actually *was* one of these gangsters or that these gangsters were so tough even their accountants scared the shit out of you.

Whatever he was, Lou did not seem pleased about having to take time out from either accounting or murder-extortion-numbers rackets to talk to a bunch of comedians.

In a thick New York accent, he read, as if from a statement at the onset of a press conference: "I've listened to all the speakers, and this is what I'm authorized to grant the comedians: cab money for any comedian who performs during the week will go up to five dollars, ten on the weekends. The fee for MCing will go up ten dollars for all nights.''

Oh great, Buck thought, now everybody will really hate me. They'll think I had something to do with that; they'll think that's my thirty pieces of silver.

It was true, Buck did not have good luck at looking good.

''As for the method of running the club,'' Lou continued, ''it is impossible for any changes to be made in that regard.''

Then he put aside the paper from which he'd been reading and stared down at his audience.

''Now, I'm gonna tell you something else, and please understand this is the gospel. This is not a threat, it's just the bottom line. This nightclub is here for fun, because we enjoy entertainment and entertainers. But as far as this nightclub goes, it does not make us a lot of money. I don't care what you think you know—you don't know. You don't run restaurants, you don't run bars, you don't know what it costs. No one's getting rich from this place, believe me, and if it becomes a headache, it's gone. Period. We can put any business in here and make money and not have headaches, and this is a headache. That's all. That's all there is to it. I hope you accept the offer, and I hope you understand the consequences if you don't. Thank you and have a nice day.''

Well—so much for specifics. The scary man hied out of the club and into a waiting Lincoln Town Car, the preferred transportation of CPAs. Bo announced that he'd entertain Calvina down in the catacombs while the comics discussed things amongst themselves, and off they went.

Shit took the stage and immediately condemned what had just transpired as a scare tactic. Apparently it was a successful one, however, because the first suggestion from the gallery was that the voting on management's proposal be executed by secret ballot, and said motion was quickly endorsed by acclamation. Shit could see the writing on the wall, but when the cocktail napkins were counted, the tally was humiliating for him: 35 to 11 against a strike. He walked out with the same brisk pace as Lou, but with no Town Car waiting.

Everyone else felt kind of bad. But so the day would not be a total loss, funnyman Phil Keeler stood up to suggest that as long as everyone was gathered together, it might be a good time to plan the Club picnic as the summer was not getting any younger. This issue proved far less divisive than the strike as most of the comics agreed that: a) a picnic was indeed a good thing to plan; and b) that the people best suited to shoulder the lion's share of responsibilities involved in staging such a large outing were the waitresses. A heated debate then raged over the busing issue, but finally it was agreed that two buses would be adequate if everyone limited themselves to one guest.

All that was left was to deliver the good news to Bo. Many rude conjectures about what he was doing with Calvina in the basement brought back to the showroom the kind of big laughs that it was, after all, there for. That everyone almost assumed without asking that Buck was the most appropriate delegate to the dungeon did not make Buck feel any better.

But Buck wanted to be the messenger, because he felt there should be one more item on the agenda, although not one he wanted the craven comedians to vote on. After he poked his head into the cellar, Buck told Bo and Calvina that the comics had agreed to management's terms under one condition—that no comic would thereafter be punished in any way for his participation in the strike, including Shit above all, as he was the most likely target of retribution.

Calvina went into a rage. Not a staged rage, but a very sincere and very personal one. She swore Shit up and down and made it plain that no one could ever force her to let him near the Apple, and if they tried, it was a deal-breaker. As it turned out, the resolution of this issue didn't matter in the end, or even in a week, because Calvina, despite the ridiculously inconsequential raise for the comedians, decided that the comedy business was already too much of a headache. Apple of My Eye closed the next day.

At the moment she was fuming, however, Buck knew only this: Calvina could never be turned around regarding Shit, so that's when he started to go to work on Bo, who made a living turning around so fast on so many things it was a wonder he didn't throw up more than he already did. Bo's argument against reinstating Shit was that Shit's dismissal preceded the strike, so it did not pertain here. Buck argued that Shit had been tossed out for distributing leaflets that led to the strike, so it really was the same issue—and anyway, he wasn't a bad guy except maybe he could become a bad guy if he didn't have any place to work out, because then he'd have nothing to lose by further agitating and plenty of spare time to do it.

Bo held out for Buck to lay down a little phony-bologna show biz there's-a-lot-of-love-in-this-room bullshit, but soon the hugs were coming fast and bearlike. Shit was out at the Apple, but back in at The Club.

Buck took the deal. He knew that Shit would hate him for compromising, hate him for getting half a loaf even though some friends in the middle of not speaking to each other wouldn't have tried to get any loaf at all. But he figured it would always be that way with Shit, that Shit would always hate him a lot of the time anyway for whatever he did, but that at the end of the day—even though the day might take a month sometimes—they'd still be friends.

16

When You Can't Light the Joint, You're Stoned Enough

Half a loaf or no, Buck could barely wait to call Shit the next day and brag about what he'd done for him. His good deed had not been seen by anyone, but Buck was not much for being an anonymous benefactor, which was a good trait if you were in a Dickens story, but Buck wanted a little credit from the guy he benefacted.

Shit was not answering his phone, however, and that went on for a week, a horrible, maddening week in which Vera was still not answering her phone either, or at least never seemed available to come to the phone in the house of her mother. Take a hint, Buck finally told himself: It's over, she's gone; she blew into your life and blew out just as fast, and now she doesn't even have the guts to tell you why.

Buck wondered: Did comedians attract flaky chicks, or did chicks go flaky after being with comedians for a while? Whoever knew the answer to that knew the answer to the corollary: Does show business attract assholes, or do people become assholes from being in show business?

On the women question, at least, Shit had provided something of an answer.

"You get the women you deserve," Buck recalled him saying, on more than one occasion—and what a scary thought *that* was! Buck always wondered how women just *knew* Shit was a great guy before they even met him, to which Shit would say:

"It reads." So what were they reading about me, Buck wanted to know?

Buck knew Shit could give him an honest answer to that question, but luckily for Buck, Shit still wasn't home. He had, in fact, been away since the night of the strike meeting, estivating in the resort town of Myrtle Beach, South Carolina, where he had taken up an offer to visit made to him some months ago by a group of people he typically met one night in a Manhattan bar. Naturally, they fell in love with him, and had been just about begging him to come down ever since. Disgusted at what had just gone down in New York, and with nothing to keep him there (like being able to work at either of the clubs, as far as he knew), Shit decided he needed a vacation from comedy, perhaps a permanent one.

But Shit was not destined to leave comedy behind just yet. The folks he was staying with in Myrtle Beach were fun-loving social creatures like him, and it only took a couple of days and nights before Shit intimately knew a thousand people there and was something of a celebrity. Considering how he had conquered a city the size of New York, this was not all that surprising.

However, talking a local restaurateur into putting in a comedy club and paying him fifteen hundred dollars to headline the first week—that *was* surprising, even for Shit. This restaurateur, James Newberg, was out with Shit one night and just about had to go to the hospital for a busted gut. Then Shit got serious and told him all about the explosion that was going on in comedy, and he told Shit all about the unused downstairs section of his restaurant. The only thing left to decide was where to hang the mandatory poster of Groucho.

By the size of the salary Shit negotiated for himself, it should be evident that James Newberg, along with the entire town of Myrtle Beach, was a veritable tabula rasa regarding the new comedy scene—or, for that matter, the old comedy scene or anything else pertaining to show business. The only thing these incredibly happy, friendly Southern people did feel they knew about show business was this: They didn't have nearly enough of it. Myrtle Beach was a resort, for heaven's sake, and it was about time it caught up to Las Vegas.

James Newberg wanted to be the first, and he wanted to catch up in a hurry. There was no leisurely Southern pace as sound equipment was purchased, waitresses hired, advertisements placed, and a stage built. Shit had not been in town a fortnight when he opened the Comedy Cellar of Myrtle Beach on a Saturday night, to a packed house.

And what a house it was! Friendly, Southern, and starved for entertainment, the audience was impressed before the show even began. Newberg had been talking up Shit all over town as if he was the next huge star to come out of those "comedy stores in New York," and no one doubted it. Nor were they disappointed when this surefire celebrity-to-be opened his mouth: "Good evening, ladies and gentlemen" got a laugh on the observation. Every old joke was new to these people, and when it came to hip, new jokes that they didn't get, they laughed anyway, not wanting to offend the visitor and figuring he must know better, being, after all, a professional comedian from New York. Steeped in Southern gentility and honored by the presence of so extraordinary a visitor, the Myrtle Beach citizenry had no idea that there were a hundred boneheads in New York calling themselves professional comedians, with ever more on the way.

But Shit was not about to tell them. What he was experiencing was akin to what the settlers of America must have felt as they found paradise somewhere farther west than anyone had gone before. Myrtle Beach was virgin territory for a comedian, unspoiled and unexploited. Every comedian in 1980 should have been so lucky as to have found a Myrtle Beach, because like the American West, the frontier was soon to close. Comedy spread quickly throughout the land and, dagnamit, before long townsfolk everywhere got used to slick, perfumed varmints from the East ridin' into town and tellin' their stories and preyin' on their serving wenches, poor gals who didn't know any better.

I can tell I'm in the South now, because I smell shit on somebody's shoes . . .
No, I love the South. I used to go out with a girl from

*the South . . . rich girl—she had two cars jacked up on
her front lawn.*

*I stayed with her folks when I was down here the last
time—there was almost a tragedy—yeah, there was a fire
that started in the bathroom . . .*

Luckily, it did not spread to the house . . .

*No, I love Southerners, even if they think that wrestling
is real . . . and the moon landing was a fake.*

But here in Myrtle Beach it was still 1872, and back in the
waitress station, the six pretty girls hired to bring drinks to
Shit's adoring public were more than a little starstruck by this
varmint who made possible their exciting new job. Unlike cities
where a comedy club had been in operation for some time, and
thus where the waitresses had seen comedians come and go and
heard all their come-on lines and fallen for a few before they
got wise, here in Myrtle Beach no one was mad at anyone yet.
Shit had stumbled into a Shangri-la of unsullied reputations, a
veritable Eden before the Fall. It was an embarrassment of
riches, and boy was his face red.

When Shit finally exited the stage after doing nearly twice
as long a set as he'd ever done to a crowd that just did not want
him to stop, he was every bit the conquering hero that his build-
up had promised. Newberg insisted that he stand at the egress
and personally greet everyone in the audience on their way out,
which made Shit feel like the minister after a particularly good
service or, worse, like those shameless comedians, such as
Dick, who did this of their own accord. But hey, Dick wasn't
here, and neither was anybody else from New York, so Shit
allowed a few more logs to be thrown on the ego fire, up close
and personal.

Shit's attention, however, was not entirely focused on the
praise from his departing flock. Looking into the room, he
could not keep his eye off one waitress in particular, a straw-
berry blonde named Rhonda Baines, as she went about her task
of clearing the detritus of Shit's admirers.

To understand just how smitten Shit was by this girl, understand that among the many perks Shit had negotiated for himself

for this gig was unlimited free food from Newberg's fine restaurant—not some greasy hamburger from the left side of the menu, but anything he wanted—and before he went onstage, he had ordered up the best steak that his money was not needed to buy. So for a man who had always been downright psychotic about grubby treatment from club owners, to give up the free prime rib that he had dreamed about for so long . . .

Well, it must have been love.

After hurrying through the last score of handshakes, Shit walked up to Rhonda, who was wiping a table with a wet sponge.

"Listen, I've got a steak coming—" he started.

"I know," she cut him off in her distinctive speech, Southern in pronunciation yet New York in pace. "It's gettin' cold back there."

"Well, that's okay." Shit smiled, a glint in his eye that said Come on to any woman who also had an eye. "Your boss told me it was the best steak in town, but I'm willing to give it up for you. How 'bout joining me for a bite somewhere?"

Shit did not mean to sound haughty about giving up the steak, and in New York, the tongue-in-cheek nature of the line would probably have seemed charming. But this was not New York, and Rhonda was not some antebellum bimbo. Her polite but unequivocal remonstration toward Shit's presumption prompted him to marshal every ounce of his Northern charm in an effort to kindle the spark he had so clumsily extinguished, and thus gave their fledgling romance the illusion of pursuit.

Begging Rhonda's pardon, Shit summoned a humility not seen since the Emperor Henry IV kneeled ill-clad for three days in the snows of Canossa. That done, he asked again about dinner.

"Well, there's not many places to go around here at eleven o'clock," she responded.

"I don't care," Shit said. "I'll go anywhere if you'll come with me."

"Well, I don't know if I wanna go to a bar."

"Anywhere."

And so Shit wound up watching Rhonda eat a hamburger at Denny's, where he picked at a bad plate of spaghetti à la Denny, as he had a few times before on the road when he hadn't left behind a twenty-dollar steak.

"You want some of this?" Rhonda asked, referring to her hamburger, as if they were sitting in a nice Chinese restaurant with a variety of delicious entrees to pool.

"No, thanks," Shit said.

"You don't look like you like yours."

Shit offered up a sheepdog look, which brought out the first instance of Rhonda's other side.

"Oh, poor thing," she said, breaking into a smile that was half sympathy and half satisfaction that this was compensation for Shit's earlier gaffe. "You had a delicious steak back at the restaurant, and now you're eating at stupid old Denny's instead."

"Don't worry about it," Shit said.

"Oh, I'm not," Rhonda replied with a teasing smile, followed by one of the most sexy bites into a hamburger Shit had ever seen.

"I'd have eaten garbage to be with you," Shit said. "Unfortunately, this is a little worse."

Rhonda laughed at that, and for the first time since he got himself expelled from her Eden of good graces, Shit shared with Rhonda a warm smile. This, however, was not enough for him—he wanted to share her entire mouth, and began helping himself to generous portions of it out in the parking lot after the meal was over.

"Excuse me," Rhonda said after holding the clinch just long enough to belie the sincerity of her next tirade. "Maybe girls in New York City are used to being attacked in restaurant parking lots, but where I'm from it's not considered good manners. Now, if you want a ride, get in the car. It's already pretty late."

"I'm sorry. Rhonda, please, wait," Shit pleaded at her back once again. "I'm sorry. I just wanted to kiss you."

Rhonda wheeled around: "Do people from New York always do just whatever they want?"

"Of course. That's why we fought the Civil War."

"Oh brother."

"No, I'm just kidding, please—"

"Well, I don't find any of it any too funny, Mr. Comedian."

"I know, I'm acting like a buffoon. It's because I like you."

"Am I supposed to be flattered by that? Is this your way of telling me I'm special, because you're not rude and insulting to a string of women who mean nothing to you?"

"No, that's not what I meant at all," Shit stammered as he felt himself losing her, and boy, wasn't that exciting. "Hey, can we start all over again?"

"Not tonight."

"Please, I'll do anything for one more hour with you."

"Hon, I ain't some jukebox you can hire for three more of your favorite songs. I'm going home. Do you want a ride?"

At eleven-thirty Shit found himself back at the hotel. He was too riled up to go back to his room and watch TV, so he walked the few blocks over to the restaurant/comedy club where he had just performed. In the showroom, there were three people still lingering, along with the pungent aroma of marijuana.

"Oh wow, it's the comedian," exclaimed the woman of the group, a semiattractive cocktail-dressed Southern flirt. She introduced herself to Shit, then introduced him to the two men competing for her, who welcomed the presence of a third suitor like an inoperable rectal complication. Still, they were Southern and hospitable, and Shit was a celebrity. They virtually begged him to smoke their grass, with the cliché certitude that hinterlanders often have that offering local drugs to visiting show people is the expected, even proper, thing to do, like burping after dinner in Peking. They even forced him to accept as a gift what pot was left in their little plastic bag, which he did. But Shit declined to smoke any of it; he didn't really want to be there, and yet, as long as he was, he found himself drawn into the situation and, by force of habit, the competition.

The floozy inspiring the competition sat on a stool facing out from the bar, and the three men stood around her jockeying for position like basketball players anticipating an important rebound. In the best tradition of Scarlett O'Hara, she kept each sap guessing which one she preferred, maintaining physical contact with both hands and one foot, and keeping all three heads in play with a dexterity not seen since the plate-spinning guy on the old Sullivan show. She enjoyed her own flirting banter and coquettish confessions so much that she invariably followed them with a great raucous laugh, which either struck one as wonderfully vivacious or cause to thrust a broken beer bottle into her throat. She also laughed equally at anything any of the men said, which is what quickly caused Shit's abrupt departure: He could amuse himself with a bimbo as much as the next guy, but to be regarded as equal in wit with these country-ass rednecks was too much.

Before he departed, however, Shit had a what-the-hell change of heart about the pot and power-dragged a couple of long ones off the joint that was already rolled. He hadn't smoked pot in a while and, he soon discovered, had never smoked pot as strong as this stuff. Clearly, it affected his thinking for the rest of the night.

Out in the parking lot, Shit was beside himself, which was a bad place for anyone to stand, as he was now kicking at objects littered on the ground. He was unaware of this, however, as he was of everything his body was doing, because he was so totally and royally ripped, blotto, impaired, polluted—the kind of stoned that makes people say, "God, I was *tripping* on that pot!" After finding a car antenna in his hand that he had no recollection of breaking off, Shit sat himself down on the curb by the highway, unsure whether to walk into traffic or view the whole evening as a turning point in his life. Since this was midnight in South Carolina and there was no traffic, Shit became consumed with the latter option. Lost inside the kind of drug takeover in which everything that crosses your mind seems like the most momentous, important thought you or anyone in the world ever had, Shit decided that this was like one of those days depicted in classical dramas or sitcom pilots, when all the issues and conflicts of an entire lifetime come to a head and then get resolved in the space of a twenty-four-hour period. But wait: Tennessee Williams had also used the classical unity— Tennessee Williams, the archetypal Southern writer, and here he was in the land of cotton, where old times were not . . .

Shit could not remember how the rest of that went.

But it didn't matter, because everything was making sense now, coming together in some strange anagogical way.

And wasn't it significant that all of this was taking place in such an unpredictable setting? Wasn't that always the way it happened in prophecies and sagas and other assigned reading, like long poems that are really books and can only be understood in conjunction with—although never as merely a substitute for—the Cliff's Notes? Destiny had led him here, he thought, as surely as the magi had followed a light in the sky two thousand years ago.

Shit looked up at the sky. The stars were brilliant, shining in a way he'd never seen in New York, which probably had more to do with pollution than portents, but Shit was not thinking in such pedestrian terms. He stared at the sky for what seemed like an hour, although it was only a second. Then he asked himself a question: How the hell do you follow a star, anyway? Wherever you go, it's never gonna be like you're standing right under it . . . without a compass or a gyroscope or something, maybe the three wise men got it all wrong. Maybe some guy in Europe, or even on another planet, is the son of God.

Shit broke out in a cold sweat as a lifetime of Catholic indoctrination suddenly seemed meaningless, the Bible perhaps just a cruel joke that started out as a game of Mad-Libs. He looked down in despair, but when he opened his eyes, his faith was restored: the car antenna that he did not remember procuring was leaning against the curb, forming a perfect cross. No traveler on the road to Damascus could have been shown a clearer sign: the horizontal line of the curb, the vertical line of the antenna . . .

To Shit, everything seemed imbued with an urgent destiny now, which was bad news for Rhonda's parents, who were trying to sleep. Taking a page from the Benjamin Braddock handbook, Shit ran the mile or so down the highway back to Denny's. He remembered that Rhonda had talked to one of the waitresses there, not the one who served them, but one who seemed to be a friend. She would know where Rhonda lived.

Sweating like a racehorse, Shit barged into the diner and

frantically scanned the room for the waitress who knew Rhonda. She was balancing three plates of waffles and placing a fourth on her forearm when Shit grabbed hold and demanded her immediate attention.

"Watch out!" she said. "Could you wait a minute? Anyone can see I'm busy."

Anyone but Shit.

"Do you know where Rhonda lives?" he asked.

"Rhonda? Yeah, I know where she lives," the girl said a little suspiciously, then took her orders over to the table.

"Yes, we were here a little while ago, I ate dinner with her," Shit continued, following her to the table.

"Oh yeah, okay, I remember. Why do you want to know?"

"I'm her cousin. I'm staying there tonight. I lost her address, so I need to find out."

Rhonda's house was not really in walking distance, the waitress told Shit, but that didn't matter to him because he was planning to run the whole way anyway. He sprinted out of Denny's and down the first suburban side street, hoping desperately that he'd gotten the directions right and clutching in his mind the name of the street and the number of the house. Shit was not in shape for marathon running, but like tiny moms who somehow find the strength to lift a car under which their baby is pinned, Shit ignored the stabbing pain in his side and ran like—well, like a guy who had some grounded-in-reality reason for running, like criminals pursuing him or freedom on the other side of a wall or something, not like a guy who just had some totally gooned out motivation concocted during a nervous breakdown in a parking lot.

Shit arrived on the doorstep of Rhonda's *Leave It to Beaver* house at midnight precisely, and Ward came to the door in his robe. Ward was pissed. Luckily, Rhonda was still up, though, and more out of embarrassment than anything else, she told her father that she did know this gentleman and would talk to him out back in the gazebo for a few minutes and then he'd go, accent on the *go*. Shit frantically agreed, and off they went to the gazebo, Rhonda screaming under her breath what an asshole he was, Shit just trying to get some breath.

Rhonda was still fuming when Shit got his breath back, but

she was also a romantic, and in that Southern night under those bright stars, the comedian's gift for charming an audience, for relaxing their tension in a hurry and for winning them back after losing them, was never put to better use. Shit babbled on in his drug-induced trance, which did not seem to Rhonda like a drug-induced trance. Rhonda only heard a guy who was a thousand times more intense than any guy she'd ever listened to before.

Who else but Shit could get a woman he'd just met, a woman who only hours before had disliked him intensely, to make love to him in her own backyard right under the bedroom where her concerned father was probably too pissed off to sleep?

No one else, because if Shit couldn't do it, it couldn't be done, and Shit couldn't do it. Not until the next day, anyway, after they watched a beautiful sunset from the balcony of his hotel room, hot on the heels of one of those movie-montage days that comedians are so adept at serving up to romance-yearning young women.

It had been a long time since Shit had fallen so hard so fast for a woman, and yet the intoxication induced by Rhonda seemed even more powerful than that of the acid-pot of the previous evening—although the role of the drug in casting the relationship in epiphanous terms was considerable. Whatever it was, when the sex turned out to be absolutely cock-ariffic as well, it seemed to Shit that the case was closed. As he again struggled for breath after a climax worthy of the name, Shit was ready to have his mail forwarded to cloud nine.

And that's where the trouble started again, because there had been a little misunderstanding about just where the post office was sending Shit's mail these days. It was ironic that Shit, who never lied to women, a fact which made him the only comedian in the world who never lied to women, now had to convince the one woman he really wanted that he hadn't lied to her.

The problem arose from a show person's tendency to forget how little civilians know about show business and from Rhonda's being a civilian. As Shit went on about how much he loved his new gig in Myrtle Beach, Rhonda assumed *gig* meant *job*, and a job wasn't for just one week. A new business had opened and positions were filled: a bartender, six waitresses, and a comedian. Shit got the comedian job, she thought, and like some lounge trio at the Holiday Inn, he was there to do it pretty much on a permanent basis.

So when, right in the middle of the postcoital glow, Shit told Rhonda he absolutely did not want it to end with her after he went back to New York in five days, the postcoital glow ended abruptly. Rhonda felt duped, like when a guy waits till after he's gotten laid to tell the girl he's married.

When Shit and Rhonda arrived at the club that night, Shit was still explaining himself, and continued right up to the moment when Rhonda had to stop him so she could start doing her job.

But then Fat walked in. It was Fat! Shit was glad to see him, and Fat was glad Shit had gotten him a job on the road, as the middle act that, as Shit had explained to his new employer, was de rigueur for any real comedy club. With such little notice, Fat hadn't been able to make the opening show Saturday night—of course, he was booked on a Saturday!—but here he was the next night, ready as always and, as always, stupid and pathetic and annoying.

But funny. Fat hadn't been kidding about the glory of the road; he had really gotten a lot better. Not better in the sense of quality, because his act was exactly the same, but better at perfecting the rhythms of the kind of hack that he was—and boy, if that wasn't just the kind of comedian the people of Myrtle Beach had been waiting for! The audience the previous night had loved the idea of having Shit there—possibly more than anything Shit actually did—but when Fat launched into his tight set to start the show on this second night of the Comedy Cellar, the crowd was genuinely amused.

Shit, not so much. First of all, Fat went over his allotted time. Way over. Like Shit the night before, Fat had found comedy nirvana in this room and was not about to give it up until he shared with the audience every bit, every premise, every stray nothing he had ever scrawled in a notebook. As Shit watched from the back, half worrying about this, half about Rhonda, he realized that in the space of one day he was going to go from the hero of Myrtle Beach, with a monopoly on everybody's attention, to the second funniest comic in a town that had only seen two.

And then there was another problem. Because when Shit took the stage to the kind of ovation a performer only gets when the crowd already knows his work, he soon discovered there was a reason for that, which was that most of the crowd *did* already know his work, because most of them had been there the night before. What they didn't know was that comedians do not write a different hour of material for every show they do.

And still they laughed! Not big laughs like the night before, but Shit attributed that to his following Fat. It wasn't until he started recognizing a lot of the answers whilst doing "Where-you-from? What-do-you-do?" with the crowd that Shit got an inkling of what was going on, because now he *and* the audience were doing the same show twice.

But Shit was not a panicker. He took a long, dramatic pause, and then asked: "How many of you folks were here last night?"

A lot of hands went up. Shit just laughed, then the audience laughed.

"Okay, well," he continued, "I guess a lot of you folks don't think I'm quite the genius I was twenty-four hours ago."

The crowd laughed again. They didn't know about show business, but they weren't dumb, and they caught on and accepted the fact that comedians tell the same jokes the way singers sing the same songs, except that songs get better with familiarity and jokes get worse. Even so, they would have accepted Shit going right back into the rest of the material they'd already heard, but Shit wouldn't do that to them. He knew a thousand old jokes, real joke-jokes, and to the audience's delight, he told the best 985 of them.

It was not the way Shit had wanted the show to go, but the fact that it did go that way convinced him even more that his life was now being guided by a powerful destiny. Because it was precisely this second example of Myrtle Beach not quite understanding everything about show business that gave credence, in Rhonda's eyes, to Shit's explanation regarding their own show business-related misunderstanding. All of which meant that the lovers now had a lot of talking to do about working out their future together.

But it would have to wait, because a much more powerful force in the universe was nigh: Fat was hungry.

"They just gave you a big dinner," Shit reminded him.

"It didn't fill me up," Fat explained, and then begged Shit for his company through another meal, much the way Shit had begged Rhonda the night before.

At Denny's once again, the waitress was more than a little nervous about having to break some bad news to Fat.

"We're out of the chocolate chip pancakes," she quivered.

"Damn, always out of what I want," Fat lamented as Shit and Rhonda nuzzled each other across from him. The lovers could not keep from gazing into each other's eyes, they could not keep their hands above the table, and they could not even consider eating another meal at Denny's. They wanted to be alone, but they were so happy just to be together that even watching Fat eat was kind of fun, in a Felliniesque sort of way. Whatever it was, they were in it together. They were a team. They were falling in love.

They were making Fat sick.

"You two wanna get a cot, or do I have to turn the hose on you?" he asked, spewing some of the lasagna in his mouth across the table.

"Whoa, incoming!" Shit said, and the lovers laughed, took cover under the table, and generally celebrated the concept of errant pasta with a series of deep kisses on the floor.

"Do you have a sister or something?" a frustrated Fat finally asked, causing more laughter.

"So, ah . . . lasagna, huh?" Shit asked. "That *is* a natural second choice when you really want pancakes. Some people might say waffles, French toast . . ."

Rhonda and Shit did not sleep together that night. They did not need to. Rhonda dropped the boys off at the hotel, where an effusive Shit would not leave Fat's room.

"Okay, she's a great girl, I get it. Can I go to sleep now?" Fat asked from his bed, where he was already tucked in.

"Not just great, my friend. This is the one—this is the

woman I've been waiting for. The one who will forever live for me in the amber light of godliness.''

"Hmmm,'' Fat grunted. "Dja fuck her?''

Shit smiled at his young friend and then headed for the door.

"Get the light,'' said Fat, and then, when it was dark: "Hey, what about me?''

"What about you?''

"I need a girl if you're gonna be with her all week.''

"Well, there's plenty of 'em here, and they seem to love comedians.''

"Yeah, but I need a sure thing.''

"Well, stick a roll of quarters in your pants.''

"What?''

"You know, so it looks like you have a big schlong,'' Shit explained with a chuckle. "Good night, pal.''

Lying awake in the darkness, Fat's mind raced: Sticking things in your pants—what a concept! I bet a lot of guys do it, he thought, turning on his back to begin the kind of restful sleep that only comes after downing two consecutive heavy main-course dinners.

The next day, Fat, always looking to build a better mousetrap, was badgering the teller at the First Carolina Savings and Loan for a roll of—even better than quarters—*half dollars*! But the teller was stubbornly uncooperative.

"Why don't they make rolls for half dollars?'' Fat wanted to know.

"I don't know, they just don't,'' the teller said.

"Well, what do people do when they have a lot of them?''

"I don't know. I don't think people usually have a lot of half dollars. How many do you have?''

"None.''

"Then why do you want a roll?''

"That's personal.''

"Well, we don't have any.''

"Okay, give me a quarter roll. Here's ten dollars.''

"I can't do that, either.''

"What? Why?''

"We don't give coin rolls, we take them.''

"Oh come on, I know you have some in there.''

"Yes, but I can't give them out."

"Come on!"

"I'm sorry, that's bank policy."

"Come on, who's gonna know?"

"Sir, I just can't."

"Okay, I'll give you eleven dollars for a ten-dollar quarter roll."

"Sir, I can't."

"Okay, twelve dollars . . . fifteen dollars—come on, you gotta take fifteen dollars!"

After he was escorted from the bank by armed guards, Fat struck upon the idea of making the same offer at a liquor store, where the clerk happily took his fifteen dollars for ten dollars' worth of quarters, plus the roll. Happy with himself, Fat rushed back to his hotel room to check himself out in the mirror, the way normal people do with a new clothing purchase. None of his pants were tight enough to hold his minted dildo in place, so he procured a safety pin from the gift shop and pinched the slack from his crotch.

"Perfect," he announced to himself, and then became so excited at the thought of what sexual rewards his stratagem might produce that, ironically, he sprouted an impressive erection. He marveled at the sight in the mirror, for now he seemed to possess two penises.

Boy, wouldn't that be something!

From the back of the showroom that night, Fat scanned the crowd for any pretty belles who just might be interested in a guy who, although a tad overweight, obviously had a cock like . . . well, like a roll of quarters.

Then he went into the bathroom and locked himself in a stall. He felt like Peter Graves receiving an impossible mission: Good morning, Mr. Phelps—your mission, should you decide to accept it, is to look to all the world like you've got yourself a really big dick.

Fat took a deep breath. He checked the safety pin, positioned his penis—the real one—and then, with the glee of a crooked fight manager sneaking brass knuckles inside his boxer's glove, slipped the copper-sandwiched hard-on into place. He had thought of everything.

Well, not quite everything. What Fat should have reminded himself to do—or, rather, not to do—was a certain bit that had become a staple of his act, a wonderfully insightful and enlightening impression of his constipated father struggling to achieve the results that such a sufferer desires. During the impression, which involved being in a prolonged crouching position ("He looks like a Sumo wrestler!"), the safety pin on the inside of Fat's pants came undone, which put the slack back in his crotch, which caused the quarter roll to fall down his pants leg and onto the stage, where the impact broke open the paper bonding and sent forty quarters bouncing and clanging into the audience.

Now, in his time, Shit had saved a lot of people. Passing a burning building in his neighborhood one day before the fire trucks came, he ran in and pulled out two people who otherwise would surely have perished. And every comic knew the story of the time he foiled a bank robbery, only to have his credit card from the very same bank canceled on the very same day. Shit was a Renaissance man, and apparently saving asses was a big thing back then.

But saving Fat's ass on this night may have been his greatest feat, because if he hadn't, Fat would surely have died of embarrassment. Luckily, Shit was in the room when the quarters dropped, and seeing the look on Fat's face, he could tell Fat was not up to doing the one thing that would get him out of it: Play it like a joke! Make like you meant it to happen! After all, that was one of the great bonuses in being a comedian: Any embarrassing situation, and certainly almost anything that happened onstage, could be sold off as a purposeful stunt from one of those crazy people in life who'd do anything for a laugh.

But apparently the road hadn't taught Fat everything just yet. So from where he was standing at the bar in the back, Shit grabbed the nearest thing that would fit in his own pants, which in this case—not that it happened a lot—was a handful of popcorn. He shoved it down his front, then ran on stage and put his arm around Fat.

"I told him not to use quarters, but you know kids today,"

Shit told the crowd as he unzipped his fly and let loose a cascade of the buttery confection.

"Popcorn, that's what you gotta put in there, popcorn! It's easier on the gonads, and it gives your crotch that full, bulging look!"

The crowd went nuts. It was like one of those magical nights replayed on *The Tonight Show* anniversary program, with Burt Reynolds and Dom DeLuise pelting Johnny with eggs and shaving cream. Fat half nodded, a glazed look in his eye, but he was still too shell-shocked to catch on, so Shit asked the crowd for a big round of applause for him in the familiar, showcase tone that Fat would recognize as an MC taking a comic offstage. And with a little push from Shit, Fat finally did get off the stage, leaving the crowd to think that the old sundries-in-your-pants routine was a little skit the boys always did or all pairs of comedians did, or whatever. The important thing was, thanks to Shit, they didn't think Fat was really trying to get away with what he was trying to get away with.

Still, for the rest of his life, it would be hard to imagine Fat thinking of anything else when asked the oft-posed show business question: "What was your most embarrassing moment onstage?"

17

The Power of Negative Thinking

When Shit got back to New York, he was full of love. Each night he would spend many late hours on the phone with Rhonda, agreeing to resign the conversation only when she pleaded utter fatigue. But the Irish say goodbye very slowly, and half the time Rhonda was snoring into the phone before Shit concluded his rambling valedictory, which made for an all-night phone bill, and then an all-day phone bill when she woke up to find *he* was now snoring into the line. All in all, it was a good time for the phone company.

Rhonda's parents, as one might guess, had grave doubts about this gentleman caller who, overnight, was *just there*, like some awful blemish that makes one gasp in the morning upon seeing it in the mirror for the first time. Even though Shit was thirty and Rhonda twenty-three, everything about the affair had the flavor of adolescence: their initial antipathy, its sudden reversal, the desperation, the drama, the endless phone calls. It all seemed so teenage, they thought, which is exactly what it was and why it was so great.

"What sort of man thirty years old acts fifteen—and isn't even ashamed of it?" Rhonda's father wanted to know.

"A comedian, I guess," said his wife, with perhaps more insight than she knew.

But the situation was also driving Shit nuts. He urged Rhonda nightly to settle up her affairs in Myrtle Beach and come to live with him in New York. Shit told Rhonda that being without her seemed like an "infinity plus one second"—the one second being necessary because the laws of physics, their own bad selves, knew that she was so special that even their immutable ways had to be slightly altered. Yes, Shit was in a bad way, in a good kind of way. He had so much love to give, but alas, the person he wanted to give it to wasn't there. But that was good for Buck, because, as brimming with love as Shit was, he didn't want to be mad at anybody.

Buck was pouring Ragú over spaghetti and some almost defrosted meatballs he'd made during the Ford administration when Shit rang him up. Buck never doubted that he and Shit would talk again, but still, hearing Shit's voice on the line made him nearly delirious; it was just the tonic he needed to rouse him from the Vera-inspired moping he'd been indulging himself in for the last few weeks. Of course, because of that moping, Shit's gushing report about finding the perfect woman was not exactly the ideal topic for two highly competitive friends trying to rediscover the magic.

And yet, how wonderful to be promenading again with an old pal, on a day when Fifth Avenue was gloriously alive with flowers and tourists and tits, not to mention sudden stenches that made you nearly ralph if you didn't immediately hold your nose very tightly and cross the street, never mind the traffic.

In addition, Shit had a present for Buck. It was the little bag of acid-pot that Shit had accepted as a gift on that portentous Saturday night in South Carolina, when he had met Rhonda. Buck was ecstatic at the prospect of getting stoned with his best friend, but then Shit announced that he did not do drugs anymore, of any kind.

Buck was crushed—and suspicious: first celibacy, now drugs—what's he gonna give up next, TV and rock 'n' roll?

But okay, Shit was weird. He'd get over this like he always got over all his other stupid ideas.

Still, even for him, Shit was acting strange.

But Buck knew there was one thing that would wake Shit up, the thing he'd been dying to tell him for weeks: that he'd saved his ass right after the strike meeting, and that the two of them could look forward to hanging out together at The Club again. It was good news, just the kind that was sure to make Shit angry.

But Shit was not angry. He was calm and polite and appreciative that Buck had stuck up for him at The Club.

What? Buck thought—you're not mad at me for not getting you the Apple *too*? The Apple, it's not even there anymore, what a perfect irrational point to go nuts over!

But no, Shit was not angry. He didn't seem to care very much about The Club or the Apple. He only wanted to talk about Rhonda, going on and on about love, which apparently was grand. The more Shit protested-too-much about love, the more Buck wanted to say, "Yeah, right, love, love, love, just one more cop-out to make comedy seem less important, because love is what really matters, and anyone who'd argue with that would have to be some kind of shallow, ruthlessly ambitious cur of a human being."

In days past, of course, taking the ruthless-cur position was not a problem for Buck, even if he didn't feel like a cur that day, because at least it would keep the argument going with Shit, and what was more enjoyable than that?

But on this day, Buck did not challenge Shit. He sensed that Shit didn't want any damn mirrors being held up anymore, that he wanted tongues to be held, like a man at a dinner party that means a lot to his wife.

Buck felt a profound sadness about that. For God's sake, he thought—hate me, hit me, slam a door in my face—anything but *this*! Don't go polite on me!

And shut the fuck up about this bitch in South Carolina!

But Shit would not shut up about her, and that's when Buck, on the pretext that he had not been officially dumped by Vera— that is, Vera had not, after all, actually come on any phone line and *said* it was over—told Shit that he, too, was in love.

Not that something as sublime as love could ever become, no matter how highly competitive two old friends might be, fodder for one-upmanship.

So Buck went first.

"Vera exceeds my fantasies," he said. "I never thought that would happen. I'm writing everything down about her in my journal, because I want to remember every detail."

"Rhonda has given me the best thing love can give to you,"
Shit topped, then let it rest until Buck, curiosity winning over
pride, demanded to know just what that thing was.

"Perspective. That's when you know it's real—when it puts
everything in your life in perspective."

Well yeah, sure, Buck thought, perspective, exactly—I've
got perspective up the ass from my chick! I'm chokin' on the
stuff, for Christ's sake, I can't give it away fast enough!

"The things I jerk off about aren't as good as the things she
does to me," Buck anted, and then, right away, was sorry he'd
said it. Because dammit, it was true—true, but now vanished.
How much crueler it was to have tasted that phenomenon for
one week and now know it existed than to have never tasted it
at all. Goddamn that Vera, why did she have to be so beautiful
and so sexy and so hot.

And so adoring.

Maybe that was the problem: when you start out a relationship as idol and worshiper, there's nowhere for the idol to go
but down. When Buck met Vera, he was a god to her, but gods
live on Mount Olympus, not walk-ups on the West Side, and
gods don't struggle with bad crowds at one in the morning. It
was the catch-22 of celebrityhood: When you reach down and
embrace a breathless commoner, you are no longer, by that
very act, ungettable, unapproachable, so your very celebrity is
diminished by your availing yourself of its rewards.

Buck wanted desperately to tell all this to Shit, to cry on his
shoulder about Vera and tell him how hurt and confused he was
about her disappearance, and then find out what to do about it.

But he couldn't. And when that happened, he knew that a
much more important relationship than the one with Vera had
ended.

18

The Sweet Stench of Success

On a Tuesday night at The Club, in the midst of one of his routine too-many-free-drinks, too-many-acts-up-my-ass MC headaches, Buck was called to the phone. He answered with the same gag greeting of which he never tired: "Hello, The Club, can you help me?"

From somewhere in New Jersey a man wanted a comedian. Buck had trouble hearing most of what the man said above the din of the bar, but he had no trouble hearing the words *one hundred and fifty dollars*.

Buck was a comedian, and one hundred and fifty dollars was good; there was no need to involve anyone else.

What the caller, a Mr. Mark Donohoe, of Livingston, N.J., had on his mind was for one of the unrecognizables at The Club, an up-and-coming funnyman fast on his feet, to come out to his house in New Jersey and perform at a private party he was throwing.

This was not an altogether unusual request. From time to time citizens of the land, after having visited The Club for their Saturday night entertainment, would call The Club the next day wondering if they could get takeout. The money for such a gig was usually pretty good, because the Joe Blows of the world didn't know how desperate the young comedians of the world were or how cheaply they could be bought. Of course, a hefty paycheck was also justified because private-party gigs were usually not easy. At least at The Club, comedians got the minimal respect that came from being on their own turf, and in a public place and in a place that had actually forged stardom for prior alumni. But in somebody's home you were on your own. You were a clown at a kid's birthday party, but the kids were big and often had a decidedly snooty attitude.

What Mr. Donohoe had in mind for this comedian—who, it was settled now, would be Buck—was something special. It seems he wanted Buck to pose as an old college buddy that none of his other friends had ever met. Special orders don't upset us, Buck told him, but for this, an additional fifty dollars would have to be coughed up.

"Okay, okay," said this New Jersey lawyer, who made fifty dollars every five minutes somebody didn't know what a tort was.

The next day, he called Buck at home and fed him a lot of quasi-personal and wholly embarrassing tidbits about the other guests who would attend the party, and informed Buck that it would be his job to accidentally-on-purpose start dropping these tidbits during dinner, leading the guests to think that Mark had been blabbing about them in a none-too-discreet manner all these years, which, he hoped would lead to big laughs, or perhaps a suburban shooting. Okay, fine, yeah, yeah, whatever, Buck thought: God, civilians must be so bored all the time!

But two hundred dollars was two hundred dollars, and he could probably get back to the city early enough to do a real set.

So on Saturday night Buck hauled ass over to the Port Authority and climbed on the bus to Livingston. Once out of the stultifying smog of the bus platform and the Lincoln Tunnel, the cool, clean suburban air was like—well, like a breath of fresh air, not that anyone on the bus would know, since the windows were sealed and it still stank like a bus and would have carried the stench of its own horrible busness into outer space.

Livingston was a bedroom community in central New Jersey, and at seven-thirty Buck got off in the middle of nowhere. He wasn't sure if it was the right stop, so before the bus pulled out, he ran in front to check out the electronic crawl on the front of the vehicle. Sure enough, it said THE MIDDLE OF NOWHERE.

Buck had been informed by Mr. Donohoe that the house of his destination was only a few blocks from the bus stop, and he set out on foot according to directions he'd scrawled on the back of the note on which he'd taken down the infamy that this man wanted leveled at his close personal friends.

As it began to seem more than a few blocks, Buck started to get a little pissed: What am I, the Abe Lincoln of comedy, walking miles to do a gig, but always returning the jokes?

But then there it was, Ayer Street, just as this asshole-suburban-thinks-he's-funny twit had said.

Buck paused before turning up the street, which was well lit with forty-watt bulbs on every other front porch. He had debated with himself on the bus whether to get stoned for this gig, but now, with the house in view and God knows what inside, it wasn't a debate anymore. This was definitely a marijuana-friendly situation, and besides, that stuff from South Carolina that Shit had given him had been burning a hole in his pocket for two whole days.

Buck stood under a big oak tree on someone's front lawn and produced a joint from the lint riot at the bottom of his velveteen jacket pocket. He lit it and took a drag.

Mmmmmm, that is tasty, he thought. Boy, that is really some sweet-smelling, sweet tasting—ahhhkkkk—hackhackhack. Hack hack hack.

Buck was having a coughing fit on someone's front lawn in The Middle Of Nowhere, New Jersey, and he was glad to be having it. He knew that when one hit induced a painful wrenching of the lungs, the seed was potent and soon would be dispersing its million mirth microbes throughout his system, or whatever pot did that made it work.

Marijuana, which, it is no big news, affects the thought process, often had the effect on Buck of making him *picture* the thought process, especially the humorous thought process, which he imagined in terms of movement. As Buck saw it, the brain was just a collection of millions of individual random concepts—not even concepts, really, just orts, crumbs of perception: a stop sign, a coffee pot, sibling rivalry, andirons, magazines, Yom Kippur, a couch—just an endless list of all the things in the world that a person comes to have knowledge of, and which, by themselves, are useless, certainly useless in terms of entertainment value. But the *combining* of orts—well, now we're talking, because that is what held out the possibility of producing humor, which was nothing more than two orts put together in a surprising new way. A barbarian isn't funny, and Jewish isn't funny but a *Jewish barbarian*!

Okay, that isn't funny, either, but you get the idea, and the idea was to have a lot of orts swimming around in your head at a brisk clip, the better to have them bump into one another and thereby produce out of two nothings one something that was good. And that's where drugs were helpful: They made all those orts swimming inside the brain swim a lot faster.

Before Buck reached the door to the house, the orts were definitely swimming fast. They were winning the backstroke competition, the breaststroke race, the Australian crawl, funny dives off the low board—this was Olympian-quality pot. Jesus Milhouse Christ, Buck thought—maybe I'm *too* stoned!

But hey, if a guy can remember how to ring a doorbell, he's probably okay, right?

Buck rang the bell.

Mark Donohoe came to the door with a shit-eating grin and ushered in his—wink, wink—"college buddy"—to the well-appointed dining room. Four other couples, completely unspectacular white people, age forty-two regular, were already seated for supper around a large dining table, the kind that was supposed to look like something the pioneers ate off of but actually cost three grand at Lord & Taylor. Buck was introduced as his character, Bill—yeah, right—and sat down.

For the first few minutes, Buck assumed an extreme diffidence, the better to size up the situation, and also because he was so fucked up, he wasn't completely sure that he *wasn't* Bill.

But then Buck got his bearings, and was confident that the situation was sufficiently sized. Mark's friends were all like him: They appreciated their own company. Well, here goes, then—hope they can take a joke.

"Barnes is a stockbroker," Mark told Buck to get things rolling.

Oh good, Buck thought, an easy one: I remember what I was supposed to know about this guy.

"Barnes!" he exclaimed, perhaps too loudly for the suburbs. "Mark has told me so much about you. And you, Helen," Buck continued, looking across the table at Helen, who Buck knew was not Barnes's wife and whom he was now about to gleefully embarrass—in fact, get paid to embarrass. "Didn't you two have a thing before you married—I forget their names—these two other people who married you?"

There was a brief moment of tense silence, but luckily for Buck, the people at the table were even more pretentious than the table itself. They treasured nothing more than the myth that they were hip—and what was more hip than to be casual about things that, in truth, one did not feel casual about?

Barnes was very casual.

"Helen and I did have a thing," he said with a twinkle. "But I was too much for her in bed."

Oh touché, Barnes, touché! That was just too, too, *too* fucking ché! Yes, everybody got a good, hearty Jesus-Christ-we-really-*are*-hip laugh out of that.

Which just made Buck want to bury the motherfucker.

"What, you kept the reading light on after she wanted to go to sleep?" he asked.

That got a laugh, too, but it was one of those laughs with an oooooh-what-he-just-said undercurrent. These people may have been upscale, bourgeois, kissy-kissy, truth-draining, nouveau riche social climbers—not that that's bad—but they didn't get there by being dumb, and it didn't take many more barbs from Buck before they began to smell a rat. Apparently, this was not the first time Mark had played some kind of practical joke on his friends, and once they knew they were being had, they didn't like it. The problem for them, of course, was that they couldn't admit they didn't like it, because they were too hip! And because Buck, who really was hip—at least to this bull-shit—knew they were too hip to admit they didn't like it, he made his comments even more outrageous and more slanderous, which actually was appropriate tacking now that everyone was in on the gag, and it pleased his employer immensely.

For everybody else, though, enough soon became—really, no kidding—enough. Fun is fun and hip is hip, but this guy, whoever he is, should, really, just, not to be rude, but he should, to be perfectly frank, really, just shut the fuck up about our personal lives right now, all kidding aside.

From the subtle inferences of long acquaintanceship, Mark knew just how much his friends could take, so after he dislodged the carving knife from his scrotum, he gave Buck the old finger-across-the-throat sign, savvy as he was with the mimeology of show business. The cut sign was fine with Buck, because the orts were now swimming so fast that Buck was happy to see the original plan for the evening wither away, allowing him to evolve into simply the fastest, funniest, liveliest dinner guest these people had ever sat with around a table they wanted you to think Indians carved turkey on. As long as the orts kept up their frenetic pace, it was almost too easy for Buck to find apropos moments in which to sprinkle in bits from his act—to say nothing of the ad-libs! Ad-libs were one thing, but these ad-libs all seemed to be clean, perfectly formed whole routines that in the future would work anywhere! Christ, Buck thought, I'm practically writing a whole new act!

And forgetting it just as fast!

Buck cursed himself that this brilliant performance was being wasted in somebody's living room for eight goddamn people. He was in the zone of perfection, and nothing could touch him.

Well, almost nothing. On several occasions, one of the seeking-to-demonstrate-hipness men at the table made a remark on the order of "I think he's doing his act for us now," which amused Buck, or perhaps didn't amuse him so much as made him wish for the man's incineration by the heat of a thousand suns.

But that was a small matter amid a much larger, worth-way-more-than-two-hundred-dollars-sterling performance. For a solid hour after the dinner was over, no one got up from the table because they were all howling at Buck too hard to think about moving.

And then, quite suddenly, the howling stopped; Buck, it seemed, was no longer amusing. He was still funny, but he was no longer amusing. In literally a matter of seconds, awkwardness had taken the baton from hilarity, and when it did, as if on cue, the women got up and cleared the table and the men farted their way toward the living room. Neither party invited Buck to join them.

Buck sat at the table all alone for a few minutes, feeling like the new girl at a Sinatra party. Then he got up and walked over to where the men were sitting together, talking shop and neighborhood and trying to laugh as hard at each other as they had just been laughing at Buck. Buck tried to join the conversation, but no one would talk to him or even acknowledge what he said.

Jesus, he thought—what dicks! It was so high school—no, not even high school!

Then Mark, in what Buck thought was going to be a gesture of sensitivity, got up and went over to him—to throw him out! Not to say, "How 'bout some coffee," or "Why don't you just relax now and join us on a more casual level?"—no, he was throwing him out! The show was over and it was time for the performing seal to squint his way back to the bus stop, so here's your check, don't let the door hit you in the ass.

Mark somehow found a way to put aside his concern that Buck was not getting the opportunity to bid adieu to his hostess or the other women in the kitchen. As for the men in the living room, they gave a hearty shrug and seemed resigned to not getting Buck's home number. Buck waved and yelled goodbye, but they, it seemed, were too busy making their own jokes now to say goodbye to the real comedian.

And that was that. In a flash, Buck was standing in the deep darkness of—who the fuck's house is this?—front lawn. *Where* am I? *What* just happened? Dazed, Buck held the paper on which he'd written the directions up to the light of a firefly, and with the help of a passing blind man retraced his steps back to the patch of dirt by a road where he hoped a bus would come.

In due time, Buck found the correct patch of dirt and began to wait for the bus. The quiet was deafening. Buck did not see a soul, or even movement of any kind, for half an hour. Was there really a bus that came to this patch of dirt in the middle of nowhere? At ten o'clock on a Saturday night?

Buck soon grew tired of waiting, but given the situation, he had to admit, the time had passed quickly. It had passed quickly because his mind was chewing on something that wouldn't go down: *What had happened in there?*

As usual with Buck's epiphanies, the revelation seemed too obvious to have been missed for all the previous times in his life it had indeed been missed. But somehow he had missed this one, too. Somehow, Buck had not realized thus far in his comedic journey that he had only been thinking of himself. Just himself, and never about the audience. The audience was just there. They weren't people, they were just—the audience: a black, amorphous sound monitor and nothing more. Just something he liked when the sound came back full and strong and something he hated when it didn't.

But never people. Never did Buck see them as people.

Until now. Until he was forced to. Because the audience he'd just left back there at the house had not been strangers in the dark, and now he couldn't help but see them as people. And by the force of his hatred for them—"consciousness through suffering," the Greeks used to say—he could *still* see them. He could not help but see them as he waited for the bus on the hard ground in the quiet night. They were there, in the picture of his mind, those awful men talking and laughing on the sofa, laughing at each other and ignoring him as the door slammed shut in his face.

The bastards, he thought—too busy making their own jokes now.

Thank God the bus was late, because Buck bitched about that ten times before anger turned into insight: too busy making their own jokes . . . too busy making their own jokes . . . too busy making their own jokes . . .

Too busy making their own jokes!

That was it! That was why they wanted him out of there so fast! Because he was fucking up their Saturday night! Because this was *their* night to be comedians, to sit around with friends and feel great when everybody laughed at something *they* said. It was so easy when you did comedy for a living to forget why you had wanted to do it in the first place—but wasn't that it? Because it made you feel great when everybody laughed at something you said? Okay, maybe when it came to hearing laughs, comics were like alcoholics—they had to get their fix every day—but that didn't mean there weren't millions of other *social* drinkers, too, and Donohoe and his pals were the social drinkers of comedy. On Saturday night they wanted to get a little high on being funny, too, and they didn't want some professional hogging the keg.

At least for once in my life I know *why* someone hated me, Buck thought.

It was the depth of their hostility toward him, though, that made Buck ultimately understand the dirty little secret of show business: As much as an audience may love you for entertaining them, some of them also envy you for being the recipient of that love. People acted like they loved their celebrity idols, but ultimately wasn't it the divorces, addictions, accidents, and other assorted tragedies of those idols that their loyal fans seemed most interested in hearing and reading about?

Buck thought about that. He knew there was a lot of truth to it, and yet it did not depress or alarm him. Rather, it made him feel lucky. Because it meant that God gave a lot of people the desire but very few the talent. And for some reason, God had seen fit to give him both. That was lucky.

Buck let out a long breath and raised his head toward the sky. A drizzle had commenced, and Buck let it spray his face. He liked it. It was almost that St. Patty's Day mist he loved so much. It was cleansing; it was good. He felt cleansed, and good. He felt thankful, and he was amazed at how good it made him feel to feel thankful. He felt humble; he felt lucky. God had taken him out here, like . . . oh, whatshisface, whoever it was there on the road to Damascus, or the road to Jerusalem, or the Turnpike—whatever, some damn road where some damn guy saw the light and saw for the first time how lucky he was.

I'm lucky, Buck thought to himself—and I ought to remember that more. Buck pledged that from this day on, he would be a different person, a different comedian. He pledged that he would be a better practitioner of both.

Buck paused, and looked down. Then he looked out into the distance, into the good black night that still had so many secrets for him to uncover.

And then, as he looked out as far as he could see, he thought: So where the fuck is the bus?

Epilogue: The Future Isn't What It Used to Be

A year later, Fat was doing okay. He was just starting to get work as a headliner, and he reveled in the perks, shitty as they might be, of that status. In addition, in 1981 he met a girl—and not a fat or ugly girl—and almost had a girlfriend. She was no classic beauty, but Nina was a short, sexy girl with big brown eyes and bangs and olive skin—exactly the girl Fat had been masturbating about sixty-one times a day for the last eight years. She showed interest, and he pursued her for months but never got her into bed. Then she told him she'd start fucking him if he lost enough weight that she could describe him to friends as normal.

Thus, Fat was faced with a dilemma that only a fat comedian could face: your lover or your act. Because if Fat wasn't fat, then his act would disappear—none of the jokes would make sense. Even so, Fat could not let Nina go, so much was she the holy tail for him. So after a night of tears, he promised he'd eat only salads until he was normal, a pledge he maintained until dinner that day, thereby setting a personal record of diet longevity—two meals, or on Fat's daily scale, five meals. But whether it was his love of his comedy or simple hunger, Fat's instincts served him well, because the thing Fat always had going for him was defiance—defiance for all those who wished him to be something he was not. So true to that code, and with a mouth full of food, Fat told Nina to shove it. Luckily for him, it turned her on, and she fucked him that night.

Yes, Fat was doing okay, all right.

All through 1981, Chink watched in amazement as his legend grew, the tale of a brave comedy frontiersman who fought the good battle but in the end was gunned down in his prime—actually, well before his prime. In show business the best possible career move is death, but short of that, retirement can be good too, and for Chink it was very good. Of course, not having gone very far, his fame would not spread very wide, but for now it was fashionable at The Club for the acts to proclaim Chink's greatness, to quote from his act—which also served to keep the comics honest when they became tempted to start picking at the now unused corpus of jokes that used to be Chink's act. Even Bo, who saw Chink perform once and didn't like it, picked up on the fact that it was hip to dig Chink, and for a while brought him up in every interview he gave.

In practical terms, all this postmortem buzz was good for Chink in that it produced two offers for writing jobs—one, a pilot for a comedy news program, the other, a sitcom.

But Chink, of course, could take neither job, because, after he and Norma discussed it, they agreed that the demands of managing her career—up to one twenty-minute period of desultory effort every day, literally six or seven phone calls to return each and every week—were too great to allow Chink the diversion of a writing job.

So Chink turned down the offers, claiming he was working on a novel. And then, so pleased was he that all the comics immediately attributed integrity to his decision and applauded him for not "selling out" to TV, he actually started writing it. And he found that he liked it. Almost as much as he liked staying inside, in the same room, with Norma, all day.

A year later, Dick's life had changed drastically. Not his act or the professional rewards from it—those, unfortunately, were completely static—but his social life. The reason was fifteen pounds. Dick experienced what all men experience somewhere in their thirties: that with the same amount of exercise (in Dick's case, none) and food intake (as much as he wanted, whenever he wanted), your body weight increases by fifteen pounds.

For Dick this was disastrous, since he was not the type either to eat less or exercise more, and his little potbelly suddenly turned him, in the eyes of most young women, into a dirty old man. All of a sudden the gray in his hair wasn't sexy on a young guy, it was the appropriate hair color for a spreading middle-aged man. All of a sudden it wasn't so much, "Oooh, that older guy wants me," it was, "Ewwww! That older guy wants me!" Dick was still charming and sexy, but he had to fast get used to many more nights alone than at any time since he had started doing comedy. It was the kind of blow to a person's ego that often inspires him to make radical changes, like maybe concentrating on his career or straightening out his personal baggage.

But this was Dick, so he just settled for what pussy he could get, which, at a certain point, was pretty much his wife. And that's how Dick came to tell Janet one day how he had finally come to his senses and realized that true love with one woman was the most important thing, and then proposed they marry again, which they did on New Year's Eve, 1981, in Las Vegas, where Dick lost the honeymoon money on his wedding night and ended up sleeping in the bathtub of their hotel room at Caesars Palace.

A year after Buck's revelation in New Jersey, our hero still had not managed to get an act. He had more jokes, which made it easier to get out of the tight spots that he continued to get himself into onstage, but the jokes still had not been strung together enough to be what you'd call an act. As in the rest of his life, Buck had all the ingredients and none of the answers.

Buck had spent the last year headlining at clubs on the East Coast—sometimes doing good, sometimes bad, always glad when a new club opened that hadn't yet seen firsthand his inconsistent performances and bruising personality. Not that he wasn't invited back, because even people who didn't like him, and they were many—even Harvey, after a year had gone by—invited him back, because he was funny and smart and interesting—if not always onstage, certainly it was worth it to bring the little prick down from New York just to hear what he had to say in the bar for two nights. Club owners wanted to make money, but they generally got into the business because they loved comedy and wanted to be around comedy, and this little shit Buck, well, he had that going for him anyway—he was a real comedian, a born comedian, and even though he could be godawful up there sometimes, nobody thought Buck wouldn't get it together someday and go places. Of course, after he went to those places, they all figured he'd never give them the time of day again, so they enjoyed him while they could, and took no small measure of delight in the frustrations Buck still endured in being the comedian he was instead of the one he wanted to be.

In the weeks following his final meeting with Buck, Shit campaigned hard for the election of Ronald Reagan, and took great satisfaction in the victory, which he admitted others had had a hand in as well. Rhonda used the occasion of Shit's victory party in November to move to New York and marry Shit before the month was out. Buck was not invited to the wedding and was terribly hurt.

But this was a new era dawning, the Reagan era, and Shit was right: Give boot to the old that no longer fits in. Included in that were making the rounds at the comedy clubs—no longer appropriate behavior for a family man. Luckily for Shit, soon after the new year started, he found a niche that suited him well—convention gag speaker. Corporations all over America, every night of the year, hold dinners for themselves in hotel ballrooms and hire everyone from Bob Hope and Andy Williams on down to entertain them. Somewhere near the bottom was Shit, who'd go around to various functions and speak as some expert on a subject close to the hearts of the corporate types to whom he was speaking, with the audience catching on to the gag about halfway through, and in Shit's capable hands, rendering delight at the personalized element involved in the entertainment. Shit was good at this, and in no time was getting booked almost as many nights a month as he cared to fly out of New York, first-class (on the company), and do it.

Of course, appearing exclusively at conventions is as surefire a way as there is to never get noticed by anyone who could do you any good in real show business. But it did pay well, at least by working men's standards, and Shit for once in his life enjoyed a steady, respectable income. In addition, Rhonda had landed an excellent, high-paying job with the Xerox Corporation, and she worked at it right through the eighth month of her pregnancy. Shit's son was the spitting image of him—he had bright eyes, and he was always screaming about something.

Next came the house, a darling two-bedroom in Great Neck. And there, on a Sunday afternoon in the late fall of 1981, you could see Shit raking the leaves on his front lawn, always keeping one ear open for any sound that might indicate his wife or baby needed him. This family man, Shit, this man of Middle America, Shit, finally had found himself in step with the times: he was the first yuppie. Shit, in fact, extolled the virtues of family so unendingly, one could only wonder how he had not struck upon this avenue to happiness previously, what with it being as oft written about as it is, and quite well known.

But how can anyone ever know what lieth in another man's soul? Perhaps Shit was just playing the part of a happy family man, but if so—if a man plays a part so well, so committedly, that he himself gets sucked in by the performance—does it matter?

To that hypothetical question Shit would have said yes: Yes, it matters—it matters plenty.

Buck, on the other hand, would have said no.

Acknowledgments

I would like to thank my editor, David Rosenthal, for "getting" this book, and my managers, Marc Gurvitz and Bernie Brillstein, for getting it to Mr. Rosenthal. In addition, my deepest appreciation goes to Stacie Otto for helping to make the text presentable.

About the Author

BILL MAHER is the host and creator of *Politically Incorrect*, Comedy Central's weekly talk show. A successful stand-up comic for the last fifteen years, he has appeared regularly on *The Tonight Show* and *Late Night with David Letterman* and has starred in two HBO specials. Maher also has had leading roles in such films as *D.C. Cab* and *Pizza Man* and TV shows including *Sara* and *Hard Knocks*. He lives in Bel Air, California.

About the type

This book was set in Times Roman, designed by Stanley Morison specifically for *The Times* of London. The type-face was introduced in the newspaper in 1932. Times Roman has had its greatest success in the United States as a book and commercial typeface, rather than one used in newspapers.